PRAISE FOR THE
GRIGORI LEGACY NOVELS

"A dark urban fantasy novel like you haven't read before. It is electric, thrilling and extremely intelligent. Linda Poitevin's world building is rich and layered and her writing is excellent. A fantastic new series which will appeal to urban fantasy, paranormal romance and thriller fans!"
—*Ex Libris*

"Poitevin's series is a passionate and emotionally powerful written story combined with a gritty urban fantasy detective mystery."
—*I Smell Sheep*

"Ms. Poitevin ripped my heart out, left me for dead and then stitched everything back together"
—*Romancing the Dark Side*

"An epic battle story of good and evil with so many scrumptious twists and turns . . . Using scintillating character development and fast-paced action, Linda Poitevin has crafted an amazing series in the Grigori Legacy."
—*Fresh Fiction*

"The Grigori Legacy series has become the benchmark that other Urban Fantasies are compared to for me."
—*Book Mood Reviews*

"Urban Fantasy deeply infused with a richly developed mythology, excellent world building, characters you'll love, and villains yo

"It's got sexual ten What more can a that keeps on movi and go to sleep. De

—*Heroes and Heartbreakers*

Books by Linda Poitevin

THE GRIGORI LEGACY SERIES
SINS OF THE ANGELS
SINS OF THE SON
SINS OF THE LOST
SINS OF THE WARRIOR

THE EVER AFTER SERIES
GWYNNETH EVER AFTER
FOREVER GRACE

JZ

CI

SINS OF THE
WARRIOR

THE GRIGORI LEGACY

LINDA POITEVIN

DISCARDED

STAUNTON PUBLIC LIBRARY

MICHEM PUBLISHING

MICHEM PUBLISHING
Published by Michem Publishing
Canada

This is a work of fiction. Names, characters, places, and incidents either
are the sole product of the author's imagination or are used fictitiously, and
any resemblance to actual persons, living or dead, business establishments,
events, or locales is entirely coincidental.
SINS OF THE WARRIOR

September 2015

Copyright © 2015 by Linda Poitevin

Cover design by Designs by Lynsey
Interior design by Book Ninjas

All rights reserved.
No part of this book may be reproduced, scanned, or distributed in any
printed or electronic form without permission.
Purchase only authorized editions. For information or to obtain permission to excerpt portions of the text, please contact the author at info@
lindapoitevin.com.

ISBN: 978-0-9919958-6-8

MICHEM PUBLISHING

If you purchased this book without a cover, you should be aware that
this book is stolen property. It was reported as "unsold and destroyed" to
the publisher, and consequently, the author received no payment for this
"stripped book."

For Pat...always

ACKNOWLEDGMENTS

This book marks the final chapter in the Grigori Legacy series. It's been a long road getting it to publication, fraught with construction detours, monstrous potholes, and countless other hazards, and frankly, I couldn't have managed it without the unflagging support and navigation skills of the many people who never stopped believing in me.

Marie Bilodeau, my wacky and wonderful partner in brainstorming both writing and business solutions—thank you for listening to me whine and moan, for sharing in my successes, and for refusing to accept my excuses when I wanted to give up. You set a shining example for me, and I can never thank you enough.

Laura Paquet, my incredibly patient copy editor who accepted multiple schedule changes at my end and then pulled out all the stops at her end to give me the turnaround time I needed.

Lynsey from Designs by Lynsey, my cover artist who continues to amaze me with her sheer brilliance at giving me exactly what I want even when I don't know what that is.

My long-suffering husband and daughter, who surely must get tired of boxed pizza when I'm on deadline, but they never complain (and even make that themselves).

My beta readers: Shawna, Karen, Lori, Amy, Reanna, Stephanie, Sharon, and Ceri. Thank you so much for working around my timeline, and for your insight and feedback. Your comments made the story so much stronger.

And finally, you, my readers. Thank you for your patience in waiting for this book, and for your gentle reminders that you were still waiting. Your nudges spurred me to finish Alex's story and to give you the closure we all needed. I hope you enjoy!

PROLOGUE

Five thousand years ago

Emmanuelle stared at the Archangel steps away from her. Massive black wings rose above his head, half-extended against the riotous pink backdrop of the rose garden, their rigidity the only sign her words had had any impact on him. She sure as Hell couldn't tell from the granite of his face.

"That's your decision, then," Mika'el said, his voice as flat as the emerald eyes watching her. "You're running away."

Her chin shot up. "I'm choosing not to be a part of my parents' game anymore," she corrected. "We've been at war with my father for almost a thousand years now, and a piece of parchment isn't going to stop that. Neither will making my brother into a pawn. As long as the One and Lucifer remain unchanged, their very nature makes peace impossible. My father won't back down, and the One won't do what's necessary to stop him. Theirs is a struggle without end."

"And so we should all stop trying?" His voice went

cold. "Give up? Pretend we're not part of it?"

She laughed at that. Harshly. "You really don't get it, do you? I'm *not* part of it, Mika'el. From the day I was born and it turned out I wasn't enough of a gift for my father after all, I haven't *been* part of it. A handful of obscure Virtues raised me, and my mother pays more attention to this damned rose garden than she ever did to me. I'm not part of anything here, and I don't want be."

"You think she doesn't love you, but she does. All of Heaven does."

"Including you?"

Hands in his pockets, Mika'el paced the perimeter of the little rose garden with long strides, his wings brushing the blooms. Pink petals drifted to the ground in his wake. His jaw grew harder with every step. When he stopped to face her, the width of the garden stood between them.

"You are my soulmate, Emmanuelle," he said heavily. "What you and I share has always been a gift. But it's not a calling."

Ice speared a corner of her heart and slowly spread to fill it. She swallowed against the universe of hurt waiting for her. A universe she would endure alone.

"That's your decision, then?" She echoed his words, but as a question she wanted—needed—him to refute. "You're staying?"

"You couldn't seriously have imagined otherwise."

"I had hoped you would choose..." She trailed off, unable to finish.

His lips tightened. "You hoped I would choose you?"

She flinched from the accusation in his voice. From the idea that he thought her selfish. "No, Mika'el. Us. I hoped you'd choose us."

For a moment, he hesitated.

For a moment, she hoped.

And then the great black wings sagged, trailing against the gravel path.

"I am her warrior, Emmanuelle. She needs me."

Anger surged in her. Helpless. Impotent. Agonizing. She wrapped her arms over her belly, anchoring them there, holding herself together. Oh, how she ached to go to him. To bury her head against his chest and feel his arms go around her. To be one with him again.

Mika'el sighed. "She needs you, too. More than you know. More than she knows. If you leave—"

"Whether I leave or stay makes no difference. Unless my mother grows a spine, my parents will continue gouging out bits of one another until they destroy themselves. And they'll take all of Heaven with them, Mika'el. They'll take *you* with them. I won't stay to watch that happen."

Fierce emerald eyes fastened on hers, their pain reaching inside her to wrap around her lungs, her heart.

"Choices have consequences, Emmanuelle," Mika'el said. "Are you sure this one is how you wish to define yourself?"

"I've made my decision."

For a long, silent moment, he stared over her head, the flint of his face edging its way into his eyes. Then his gaze returned to hers.

"So be it," he said, and turning from her, he lifted from the rose garden on his great black wings.

ONE

Alexandra Jarvis jammed her hands into the pockets of her coat and leaned against the rough brick wall, hunching her shoulders against the bite of wind-driven snow. Steps away, a jumble of train tracks crisscrossed, stretching east and west under the thin glow of lights lining the narrow rail yard that ran through Toronto's heart. A mesh of metal designed to carry things into and out of the city.

Things, maybe, like her niece, who had only six days to live.

"You holding up okay?"

Alex started at the voice. Damn, she was getting sloppy. She hadn't heard a sound as Raymond Joly approached. She shrugged.

"As well as I can," she replied. "Anything yet?"

The other homicide detective shook his head.

He turned his gaze toward the railway tracks. Together they watched the massive black German shepherd casting about for a scent halfway across the steel network. Its chances of finding one diminished with every passing minute, every snowflake that fell, every bitter gust of wind.

Alex burrowed more deeply into her scarf.

Joly squeezed her shoulder. "Hey. We'll find her."

"You don't believe that and neither do I." She looked sideways at her colleague, who had miniature icicles clinging to his handlebar mustache. "I'm running out of time, Ray. We've been chasing sightings all over the city for almost two weeks. This is the only place the dogs have caught a scent. If she managed to get onto one of the trains—"

The dog's handler gave a shout and Alex's head snapped around. Nose a few inches above the ground, the dog headed diagonally across the tracks toward the west, moving with new purpose. Alex straightened up from the wall. Everything in her screamed with the need to follow, but she made herself stay. Terrain like this didn't hold a scent well to begin with, especially in this weather. Another person walking around out there would only confuse things.

She blinked snow from her lashes. The police dog stopped, lifted its head, tested the air with its nose, and swung left. In the concrete wall lining the yard, almost straight across from Alex and barely visible through the snow, stood the door to a utility access. It was mostly closed. But not entirely. The dog's ruff stood up along its neck and shoulders, and a warning, deep, low, and guttural, rumbled from its throat. Alex's heart smashed into her ribs.

Nina?

The dog gave a sudden yip and bolted—not toward the door it had indicated, but away, further down the snow-covered tracks, until it hit the end of the lead still held firm by its handler. Then it cowered, tail between its legs and the whites of its eyes visible in the beam of the flashlight Joly shone toward it.

"What the hell?" Joly muttered.

The dog handler barked a command, but the dog only sank lower. The hairs on the back of Alex's neck prickled. No police-trained dog ever backed down from a threat. Ever. She'd seen them go up against people with knives, guns, baseball bats...

Oh, fuck.

"It's one of them," she said harshly. "Call everyone off. Get them out of here."

Joly looked blank. "What? One of who?"

"*Them*, Ray." She had to make herself meet his gaze. To force the words past lips that were frozen but not from the cold. "The Fallen."

Joly's hand went to the gun at his side. Alex tugged her own hand from her pocket and grabbed his.

"Guns won't—"

On the other side of the tracks, the utility door crashed open, slamming into the concrete wall beside it. The snow fell faster and thicker now, muffling the thud. A hulking figure emerged. It ducked under the door header and stepped into a pool of light.

Huge. Male. Winged.

And carrying a very pregnant Nina in his arms.

Alex inhaled sharply. Beneath her hand, Joly's fingers closed over the handgrip of his weapon.

"Don't," she croaked. "You can't."

"Listen to her, mortal." The Fallen One's rumble rivaled the earlier one of the dog. His gaze swept their small assembly: the dog handler on his right, backing slowly away to join his cowering animal; the handful of uniformed officers down the track to his left, standing in an uncertain half circle, guns drawn but still at their sides; Joly and Alex across from him. His focus settled on Alex. Narrowed. His head tipped to the side.

Alex stood rigid beneath his scrutiny. Did he know? Could he tell what Seth had done to her, what he'd made her?

Would it matter?

"I have no bone to pick with any of your companions," he said. "But you...you are persistent. Three times I've had to move the Naphil because of your efforts."

They'd come close that many times? Alex shook off the agony in the thought. Tried not to stare at the fragile, unconscious bundle in the Fallen One's arms or to see the pallor of Nina's face.

Tried, desperately, to be a cop and not an aunt.

"She's my niece," she replied. Sheer determination kept her voice from reflecting the quiver in her gut. "I want her back."

"She is the bearer of Lucifer's unborn child," he corrected, "and no longer your concern. Moving weakens her. You will stop seeking her."

Joly's fingers went rigid under hers. Her own gun hand itched to close over her weapon. Maybe if they shot enough lead into him...

She shook her head. "I can't do that."

"Then you invite death."

Her chin lifted. She didn't know how far Seth's little gift would go in a confrontation with a Fallen One, but she wouldn't back down from finding out. And she wouldn't let Lucifer's henchman take Nina again. She stepped away from Joly. "I'm not like the others. I'm—"

"Not you. Them."

Without warning, the Fallen One swiveled to his left. His wings unfurled, spread wide, and swept forward in a mighty surge. Snow, gravel, and rail ties all lifted from the ground, driven by a gust of wind more powerful than a hurricane, and hurtled toward the cluster of uniforms. Men and projectiles alike slammed into the wall. Gravel and ties remained, embedded in the concrete. The cops dropped to the ground, silent, still. Four bright crimson splashes marked their places of impact, garish, hideous, undeniably fatal.

It was over in less than a second.

Beside Alex, Joly's mouth opened and closed, but no sound emerged. The Fallen One's implacable gaze met Alex's across the interlace of tracks.

"You will stop seeking her," he repeated. And then he lifted into the air and disappeared into the night above the lights, taking Nina with him.

From a long way off, Alex heard Joly's frantic voice barking orders to the dispatcher he'd reached on his cell phone. The dog handler's shouts for help as he ran to the fallen uniforms. The distant whistle of an approaching train that would now be delayed for hours. Joly shoved past her, bellowing her name and wrenching back the part of her that hovered on the brink of disappearing forever.

Breath returned, its shattered edges shredding her lungs. She responded to a second bellow from Joly with a nod, and then, stripping off her gloves, followed him toward the downed officers. But where he ran, she walked, knowing there was no rush. Knowing none of them survived.

She tucked the gloves into her pocket, listening

for the wail of sirens. Others would be here within minutes, and then there would be much to do and many questions to answer—all except the one that had already been answered.

The Fallen One had known about her, all right.

And others had paid the price.

TWO

Samael strolled into what had once been Lucifer's office, his gaze taking in the changes to the room. The Light-bearer's thousand-plus journals and their shelves were gone; the ever-present bowl of peppermints no longer sat on the desk; the rug stained with the blood of Raziel had been removed.

"I see you've made yourself at home," he said. "Much better."

Seth stood at the window behind his departed father's desk, his back to the room, his grunt the only indication he'd heard. Samael's eyes narrowed. It had been nearly a week since the Appointed had regained consciousness, and still he showed no signs of taking up the reins of Hell or interest in doing so. Unless one counted minor redecorating.

Which Samael didn't.

He cleared his throat. "I thought you might like to go over our current status now that—"

"You thought wrong."

Samael snapped his teeth shut. His jaw flexed. He chose his next words carefully. "I understand you're disappointed that the Naphil—"

Seth moved so fast that Samael had no time for more than a single step back before the Appointed's fingers closed over his throat. A glittering black gaze bored into his with a ferocity that bordered on viciousness.

"You understand nothing," Seth spat. "*Nothing*. All your urgings, all your promises—I did everything you told me to, and I lost her. I lost the one thing in the universe that I wanted more than life itself. That I *needed*." His grip tightened. "I should kill you now."

The tremble in Seth's fingers told Samael he could likely break the Appointed's grasp—Seth was nowhere near recovered from the injury inflicted on him by the Archangel's sword—but he clamped down on the urge to twist away. Instead, he studied the dark, hate-filled eyes only inches from his own. Had he miscalculated? Made a mistake in recruiting the Light-bearer's son to take Lucifer's place as Hell's leader? Perhaps Seth was *too* like his father. Perhaps it would be best if—

No. Even if he managed to kill Seth—and it was a big *if*, even in the other's weakened state—it would only leave him with a greater problem. A rudderless Hell didn't stand a chance against Heaven. Whether he liked it or not, the Fallen needed Seth to lead them. And it was up to Samael to get him to do so.

"You may have lost the battle for her, Appointed," he rasped past the vise-like pressure on his larynx, "but not the war."

Seth scowled. "Explain."

Samael tugged at his hand. After a moment's hesitation, Seth's fingers loosened until he could draw air. But only just.

"Aramael is gone," Samael said, "and Mika'el and the others are preoccupied with the war. The Naphil will be alone. Unguarded. If she really means that much to you—"

Seth's hand tightened again. "And more."

"Then let me get her for you," Samael croaked.

"And why would I need you to do that?" Seth growled. "Or trust you?"

"Because I can do this"—Samael reached up and prised the fingers from his throat—"and you're wise enough to know you're in no shape to move between the worlds right now, Appointed. And I'm wise enough to know Hell needs a leader, and it's not me. Each of us has what the other wants—or we can get it. It makes sense that we would help one another."

Seth's hand balled into a fist and dropped to his side. His expression turned stony but for the fire seething in the black depths of his gaze. Samael coaxed himself to patience. The urgency that had driven his actions when Lucifer still lived no longer existed. Seth might not be the powerful leader Hell needed just yet, but with the right encouragement, he could grow into the role.

Damaged though he might be, he was still more of a leader than Heaven had anymore.

Seth wheeled away and returned to his place by the window. "Talk."

Samael strolled forward to drop into the chair facing the desk. "Without the One's will driving them, Heaven's forces are scattered. Weak. They outnumber us, but their casualties are greater, and we don't even have all the Fallen engaged in battle yet. Better than ten thousand remain with the Nephilim children."

"Why?"

"The children are young. They need care and training."

"I meant why do I care about the Nephilim at all?"

Samael swallowed his retort. Bloody Heaven. First Lucifer had been wholly focused on the creation of his Nephilim army, and now Seth saw no point to it? Was Hell to be forever burdened with leaders who couldn't see past their own selfish desires? Was he to spend his entire existence drawing maps for them?

"Two things came between you and the Naphil woman," he reminded Seth. "Aramael, and the Naphil's concern for the human race. The former might no longer be a concern, but as long as humanity exists, the entire race will stand between you and the Naphil as it did between your father and the One. It was why Lucifer created the Nephilim in the first place."

"I know why he created them." Seth brushed off his words with an impatient wave of one hand. "But they're only just born. It will take months for them to grow up; years before they're able destroy humanity. We could wipe out every mortal on the planet in a fraction of the time."

Really? Samael rubbed fingertips over one temple and the headache forming there. He'd heard this argument from Lucifer so many times that he'd lost count, and now Seth, too? Bloody, bloody Heaven. He unclenched his teeth.

"Actually, we couldn't," he said. "Heaven—"

"Heaven would come after us," Seth interrupted. "And then we'd be fighting the war on Earth, where human casualties would be catastrophic. Isn't that the whole point?"

"Yes, and no. With all due respect, Appointed, your

approach has three flaws. First, not all mortals would be killed. Some would survive, and now that you've made her immortal, your Naphil will never stop fighting to save them. Second"—Samael ticked off another finger—"we might have the advantage over Heaven right now, but if we take the fight to Earth, I guarantee we'll lose that edge. Nothing will unite and motivate the angelic forces like a direct assault on the One's mortal children, Seth. Nothing. If that happens, humanity's destruction becomes the least of our worries, because we'll be fighting for our own survival."

The Appointed's jaw flexed. Relaxed. Flexed again. Thunder gathered on his brow. "You make it sound like you expect me to wait for her."

"I think it might be best."

"And for exactly how long would you suggest I do that?"

"As long as it takes. You made the Naphil immortal, remember. That means you have eternity on your side."

Seth glowered, but didn't argue.

"You said three flaws. What's the third?"

"If the woman sees you strike directly at humanity, a thousand eternities won't be enough to win her back."

Back and shoulders rigid, Seth turned away. Samael gave him a few moments to process his words, then, satisfied he'd made his point, levered himself up from the chair.

"I have maps and strategies posted in war council chambers," he said, crossing to the door. "If you'd like to have a—"

"No."

Samael stopped mid-stride. He looked back at Seth, who still faced the window. "No, what?"

"I won't wait."

"You can't be serious!" Samael didn't bother trying to hide the scowl this time. "Have you not heard a word I've said?"

"I heard." Seth swung to face him. "And I don't care. You want a leader for Hell? Then I want Alex. Now."

THREE

Seth stayed on his feet until the door thudded shut behind Samael. Then, legs buckling, he dropped to his hands and knees before sprawling full length on the cold, hard flagstone, fire consuming him from ribcage to hip. Blackness encroached on his vision. He fought it off, gasping for air, gagging against the gorge that rose in his throat.

Fucking *Heaven*, that hurt. More now than it had yesterday, twice as much as the day before that. His attack on Samael had made it worse. Had the other sensed his weakness? Known how incapacitated he really was? Seth grunted, his fingers tingling at the memory of being prised from Samael's throat. Who was he kidding? Of course the Archangel knew. With a dozen former Virtues dancing attendance on Seth, at least half the realm would know.

He curled his fingers against the stones, drawing his focus inward. He was the Appointed, son of Lucifer and the One. He could not—would not—be caught lying prone on the floor, should someone come in. Taking a slow, careful breath, he hardened his muscles and, in one swift motion, pushed grimly, fiercely to his knees, grabbed the desk, and pulled himself upright. Nausea washed over him. Through him. Became him. He swallowed, retched, and, only through sheer force of will, stopped from spewing his earlier meal across the polished mahogany desktop. Lights sparked behind his eyelids. Sweat beaded his forehead and his upper lip.

When he could draw breath again, he stretched out a hand and tugged the bell rope to summon those tasked with his healing. Then he stumbled to the sofa and collapsed onto it, waiting for the fresh assault on his stomach to subside. It would be at least five minutes before one of the Virtues made his/her way to his side, if not more. The wait grew longer every time he called for help, as did a subtle but pervasive air of insolence.

He scowled. He may not have wanted to admit it to Samael, but the Archangel was right. Already Hell grew restless without an undisputed leader in place. Even in his weakened state, Seth could sense the shifts in energy outside the confines of the building, the rumblings of discontent. If he didn't take up the reins soon, things would get ugly.

He rested his head against the cushions. So. Was that what he wanted to do? Step into his father's shoes and take up the fight against Heaven? He snorted at the thought and immediately regretted even that slight movement of his diaphragm. Another moment of white-hot fire slid by.

His vision clearing again, he stared into the cold, grimy fireplace. Now that Aramael was gone, he didn't give a damn about Heaven. Couldn't care less if the Fallen reclaimed a place there or not. Humanity, however, he did care about, for the exact reason Samael had voiced. The One's mortal children would always stand between Seth and Alex. She'd proved that when she sent him away. Again, when she'd called on Aramael to protect her from Seth's gift of immortality. And a third time, irrevocably, when she herself had taken up Aramael's sword and inflicted this injury that refused to heal.

Eyes closed, Seth focused on the throb that radiated from his side. A mortal of Nephilim bloodlines, twice brought back from the very edge of death, made immortal by his own hand, wielding a sword given to her by the Archangel who was her soulmate. There was no doubt that the will of Heaven itself had somehow been behind that blow. The question wasn't why the wound had been so severe, but how he had survived it at all. And the only answer he could come up with was—

A knock sounded at the door, signaling the arrival of a Virtue. Seth barked a command to enter. The door opened and footsteps padded across the stone floor.

The answer was that Alex had hesitated. She'd held back. She hadn't, despite everything, wanted to kill him. Somewhere inside her, she had still cared, and she would learn to care again. Perhaps not as soon as she was brought to him, but certainly once mortals no longer interfered.

And for that to happen, Seth needed the Fallen. He needed Samael. And he needed to heal so he could take his place on his father's throne.

Efficient fingers lifted Seth's shirt and began peeling back the bandage. The putrid scent of rot wafted upward. Seth gritted his teeth and braced for what followed. Scissors snipped, biting into flesh, cutting away the gangrene, slicing into nerves made raw by infection. He gagged, digging his fingers into the soft leather of the sofa. His last thought gathered strength. Settled into his soul. Became, in its truth, more powerful than the agony being inflicted on him.

He needed to heal.

For the first time since he had given Alex her immortality, he gathered the full force of his will to him. He focused on the fire that began in his injury and wrapped around the very essence of his being, held its tangle in his mind, stilled its violence. He saw how the loss of Alex had become inextricably ensnared with the physical pain, until he couldn't tell where one began and the other left off. So much pain. So many threads.

Doubt slithered through him, gnawing with tiny, sharp teeth at the edges of his will. He shoved it away and studied the morass. One of the threads glowed brighter than the others. He took it up, disengaged it, and followed it to the wound in his side, to where the Virtue's hands continued their work, snipping, cleansing, their every movement tugging at the thread he held. This, then, was the physical pain. He laid it aside and returned his attention to the tangle. Another thread, this one dark, fragile. He lifted it, extricated it from the rest, and followed it down, ever deeper, to the ache in his very core. The place where Alex's loss resided—unending, all-consuming, threatening to swallow him in his entirety. He inhaled sharply, and the Virtue hesitated.

"Continue," he ground out between his teeth.

He flinched from the cooling sting of antiseptic and

forced his focus back to the tangle, continuing his own work, sifting, sorting, separating one pain from the other. Physical from emotional. Body from soul. While the Virtue taped a fresh bandage into place, he stared into his emptiness, facing the betrayal, trying to come to terms with it, hating the weakness it exposed within him. Then, as the other's hands withdrew, the solution surfaced, whisper-soft. The one thing that would allow him to let go of what had passed.

Forgiveness.

The very thought brought a surge of peace. A wave of magnanimousness. Seth squeezed his eyes shut against the relief. Of course. Alex hadn't meant to hurt him. She hadn't known the depth of his love for her, or how to adjust to the enormity of the gift he had given her. She hadn't understood, hadn't been capable of understanding. But she would be. Once he explained, once she realized the depths of his connection to her, everything would change. *She* would change. Everything would be better.

It would be the way it was supposed to be.

Just like that, the tangle within him eased. He took a deep breath, the first he'd managed since regaining consciousness a week ago. His lungs filled, expanded, pressed against his ribs, and...nothing. The bandage tugged against tender flesh and blood throbbed through inflamed tissue, but the soul-deep agony that had plagued him was gone. His fingers probed the wound beneath its covering, but nothing more than the slightest sensitivity remained, entirely tolerable. His lips tugged into a smile. He'd done it. He'd begun healing. Finally. He seized the Virtue's wrist, then opened his eyes.

"How long?" he asked.

The Fallen One shrugged narrow shoulders, her indifferent gaze sliding past his. "I've told you I can't predict—"

Seth's grip tightened, and surprise flitted across her expression.

"Assuming I've turned a corner," he said, "how long?"

The Virtue placed her free hand over the bandage. One eyebrow rose, then dipped again to meet its mate. "You're right. It seems better."

"I asked you a question."

"If you can maintain this? A week until you're fully healed. Two at the most."

"What about until I'm able to cross the realms?"

"You should—"

His hand left her wrist and fastened around her throat. "I *said*, how long until I'm able?"

Pale, blue-green eyes widened, and the Virtue swallowed, a ripple of skin and muscle against his hold.

"A few days. Four, maybe five. But—"

He shoved her away, and she stumbled against the fireplace, extending her wings for balance. He tugged his shirt into place.

"Get out," he said. "And next time, send someone who knows better than to have an opinion."

FOUR

"**D**id you hear me, Detective?"

Alex jolted back to the present. She turned from the window to face her supervisor, Staff Inspector Roberts. "Sorry. I was..."

She didn't finish. There didn't seem much point in telling Doug Roberts that her mind was still in the rail yard, that she couldn't get the image of the four murdered cops out of her brain and would never scrub their deaths from her conscience. He already knew. He just didn't know how long *never* meant for her.

Her gaze returned to Toronto's frigid mid-afternoon.

Roberts sighed. "You really should go home, Alex. Have a stiff drink or two, and call Henderson or Dr. Riley or someone. Talk it out."

It was good advice. Required advice, under the circumstances, except maybe for the drinking part. For a moment, Alex considered the idea. Riley was out of the question, of course. While the Vancouver psychiatrist knew enough about what was going on that she no longer wanted to have Alex committed, she was too astute by far, and Alex couldn't handle going the feelings route today. Not after last night's events.

And talking to Hugh Henderson wouldn't be much better. As the only other person on the planet who knew every impossible, messy detail of humanity's current plight, the Vancouver detective had been an anchor for Alex on more than one occasion, but she wasn't ready to reach out to him on this. Not yet. Hugh would have too many questions, want too many details. The whole scenario was still too fresh for Alex. Too sharp. She shook her head.

"I'm good," she said. "Really. You need me here."

Her supervisor scowled. "I need you in one piece, too. I can't afford for you to have a breakdown."

Alex snorted. "If I haven't gone off the deep end by now, Staff, I'm not going to."

Even though a part of her wished she could take exactly that escape route.

"Besides," she added, "I need to keep looking for Nina."

"No."

"Pardon?"

"The search has been called off, Alex. That's what I was trying to tell you."

Numbness crept over her, from the top of her head to her toenails. "I don't understand."

"I think you do." Mouth tight and hands on hips, her supervisor met her gaze, his brown eyes sympathetic, sad, and unyielding. "Four cops died tonight, Alex, and one of our best tracking dogs is a quivering mass of jelly. Now that we know this—thing—has Nina, we can't keep pursuing it. I can't send more cops up against it. Not knowing what it's capable of."

He waved a hand at the window overlooking Homicide's cramped, temporary quarters, where desks butted up against one another in haphazard disorganization, a stark reminder of the battle between angels and Fallen that had destroyed the top two floors of the building.

The battle between Seth and Aramael.

Her breath hitched.

Roberts didn't seem to notice.

"We have no weapons against it, no way to stop it, and no way to take Nina from it, even if we do find her," he continued. "I can't risk more lives. I *won't* risk them. Not when Nina is—"

His words dropped into silence. Where he'd stared her down a moment ago, now he wouldn't meet her gaze. A muscle twitched along his jaw, an indicator of how much his words cost him. She didn't care. Devastation licked through her, churned with denial, became white-hot fury.

"When Nina is going to die anyway?" she finished harshly.

Roberts paled.

"Damn it, Alex—" He broke off and took a deep breath, making a visible effort at control. "Look, I'm sorry about Nina. You *know* that. But what the fuck am I supposed to do here? I have an entire city coming apart at the seams. Have you *seen* the boards out there?"

He jabbed a thumb at the window between his office and the rest of Homicide, where dry-erase boards flanked the office perimeter. Fifteen of them. She'd counted them on her way in to write her statement at four this morning. Then, as now, she'd cringed from the murders they catalogued, the chaos they represented—and from the burden she'd realized her colleagues had carried while she'd single-mindedly pursued her niece.

Roberts pushed up from his chair. "I'm sorry," he said again. "Really I am. But the decision is made."

"So now what?" She threw her hands wide. "I'm supposed to give up? Stop looking and leave Nina to die out there on her own? She's *seventeen*, Staff. She's just a kid!"

Roberts snatched up the phone and hurled it across the room. It shattered against the wall, scattering fragments of plastic and wired components across the carpeted floor. "Goddamn it, Alex, do you think I don't know that? Do you think this is *easy*?"

The office door opened and Tim Abrams, another detective, poked his head in. His gaze swept over Alex and their staff inspector, settled on the destroyed phone, and flicked back to Alex. Without a word, he withdrew again.

Alex stood frozen in place. She sensed Roberts wasn't finished yet, and she waited for his words even as her every muscle, her every cell, screamed denial. He had more to say, but she didn't want to hear it. Didn't want him speaking the unspeakable things that had been slowly building in him—in all of them—over the last two weeks. Even in herself.

Especially in herself.

She closed her eyes.

"Nina is *gone*," he said, his voice raw. "Even if you could find her again, even if you could get her away from whatever she's with, even if you survived trying, you can't save her."

Alex's head jerked from side to side, pulled by the invisible strings of repudiation. *You're wrong,* she wanted to say. *There's a way. There has to be a way.*

"She's my *niece,*" she whispered instead. *She's Jennifer's little girl, and she's all I've got.*

"I know."

Hands settled onto her shoulders and squeezed. Gently, compassionately.

"I know," her supervisor repeated. "And if she were mine, I've no idea what I'd do. But you have no choice, Alex. I can't give you a choice, because we need you. Here. With your head in the game. Because you're the only one who has any fucking idea what's going on in the world right now. You're all we've got."

Alex bit down on the inside of her bottom lip, using the pain to distract herself. To keep from letting in the quiet panic that underscored Roberts's words, or from giving in to the tears burning behind her eyes or the gathering rawness in her throat. He was wrong, of course. Not about her being needed, but about her not having a choice. She'd been making choices for weeks now, always for the greater good. Making them, living with them, suffering their consequences.

No, there was always a choice.

The question was whether she was strong enough to make this one.

"Call Henderson," Roberts said wearily. "Talk to him. Please."

Alex pulled away and walked out.

FIVE

Resting his elbows on the desk, Mittron pressed fingertips to his temples and massaged the ache forming there. On the far side of the office, Samael paced the length of the peeling, graffitied wall, muttering under his breath. The near-ceaseless din of thousands of children screaming for attention floated in through the broken panes of the room's only window.

What a Hellhole. The noise, the stench of decay, the complete lack of any creature comforts. Conditions were nothing short of abominable, and beyond unsuitable for Heaven's former executive administrator.

Mittron pressed harder against the thumping in his skull. *Dear One in—*

Right. He sighed. The One wasn't *in* Heaven anymore. She wasn't anywhere. Both she and Lucifer were gone, leaving him to deal with eighty thousand Nephilim brats and a handful of idiots who thought they could run the universe. Not to mention a crazed Principality that was, without doubt, stalking him even as he sat here. His heart gave an uncomfortable thud at the thought.

He'd been expecting Bethiel on his doorstep every moment of every day for the last two weeks. Ever since he'd told Samael how to open the gates of Limbo, knowing the Principality he'd unjustly imprisoned there was among the Fallen loosed upon the universe...

Mittron shuddered, his brain caught in the incessant loop that had him jumping at shadows, imagining the rustle of wings behind him, anticipating the bite of a sword through his flesh at every turn. Bethiel, free to come after him. Free to carry out the roared threat that had reached Mittron's ears over and above the clang of Heavenly metal intended to imprison the Principality forever.

"By all that is holy and righteous, Seraph, I swear I will find you if it takes me all of eternity!"

Mahogany-dark hands slammed, open-palmed, onto the desktop before him. Mittron jolted in his chair, swallowing—just barely—an involuntary and undignified shriek of terror. He stared past his fingers at Samael, looming over him.

"Are you even listening to me?" the Archangel demanded.

Mittron linked his hands together and lowered them to the desk. He took a long, deep breath, gluing together his nerves. "Of course I'm listening. Seth refuses to take up the reins and now you want to dump him."

Samael glared at him, his gaze narrowing. Seeming to decide Mittron wasn't being entirely flippant, he stood tall and stalked the room's perimeter again.

"Well, he's of no bloody use to me if he's going to moon over the Naphil the way his father did over the One. Hell needs a ruler, not a spineless, weak-kneed—" Samael shoved a chair out of his way. It hit a wall and splintered.

Mittron winced. He wished the Archangel had cooled off after his meeting with Seth before coming here. Too little existed in the way of usable furniture in this godforsaken place to begin with. He couldn't afford to lose any of it to tantrums. Samael kicked aside a chair leg and rung.

"Bloody Heaven," he snarled, whirling to face Mittron. His outstretched wings smashed a new hole in the rotted ceiling. "It's not like I'm asking him to actually fight in the war. I'm not even asking him to take over the strategy. All he has to do—"

"All he has to do," Mittron interrupted, "is play by your rules."

Glittering golden eyes pinned him.

"You would do well to remember who controls the drugs keeping your demons at bay, Seraph."

The veiled threat took away Mittron's breath, and he waited for a new surge of panic to abate. For the memory of Judgment to release its grip on his throat.

"*I find you guilty of treason, Seraph...I therefore sentence you to witness the consequences of your actions. You will live among the mortals you have failed and feel the agony of each and every soul lost to the Fallen Ones as if that agony were your own.*"

The words were branded forever on his soul. A sentence imposed on him by the One that meant the voices of millions of souls followed him everywhere. Had become a part of him. Cried out to him in their misery and unrelenting sorrow, until their suffering had driven him to the verge of insanity and beyond. Until Samael had plucked him from the human jail cell and provided him with the drugs that all but silenced them.

Mittron would do anything to prevent their return. He and Samael both knew that. But Mittron also knew his mind was clearer now, almost as clear as it had been when he still held the revered position of Highest Seraph, Heaven's executive administrator.

It was also sharp enough to see how Samael's problem might cancel out his own. He lowered his hands to his lap and surreptitiously wiped sweat-slicked palms against his robe.

"I intended no offense, Samael," he said, careful to keep his tone neutral, "but I don't think you came here looking to have me soothe your wounded ego, either."

The former Archangel's scowl deepened. "I presume you have a plan of some kind to back up your lack of diplomacy?"

"I do. I think you should send someone to find the woman."

"I don't need you to tell me that. Seth made it patently clear I have no choice."

"But not to bring her back."

One of Samael's eyebrows ascended. "The drugs have addled your brain, Seraph. Sending someone to kill the Naphil would be akin to signing my own death warrant. Or is that your intent?"

"My intent is to give you a ruler who isn't distracted by things that have no place in your Hell. Without the Naphil—"

"Without the Naphil," Samael growled, "Seth would become so immersed in misery he'd be even *more* useless than he already is."

"Not if he thought one of Heaven had killed her. Revenge is a powerful motivator." Mittron suppressed a shudder at the truth of his own words—and the accompanying image of the Principality he'd condemned in order to save himself.

Samael's expression stilled. Frustration slowly turned to thoughtfulness, narrowed to speculation, and then, in a blink, shifted back again. He shook his head. "It won't work. I'd never find a Fallen One I could trust not to run to Seth with the plan, and if I go after her myself, the entire war effort will disintegrate. Seth is in no shape to take control yet. I'm the only thing standing between him and utter chaos."

Mittron took a deep breath. There. That was it. The invitation, the opportunity. The chance to put things right.

"There is one who might be trusted," he said slowly. Carefully. "One with no connection to Hell."

"You want me to ask one of *Heaven?*"

"He's not of Heaven, either. At least, not anymore." Mittron pushed back from the desk and began his own tour of the office, his steps measured. Controlled. Even if the tremble in the hands he locked behind his back was not.

"His name is Bethiel, of the Principalities. He uncovered evidence of my plan to trigger the Apocalypse, and I arranged his exile to Limbo. The evidence has since been destroyed, so he has no way to prove his innocence or return to Heaven, but he'll want no part of Hell, either."

"Then why would he help me?"

"He doesn't know the evidence has been destroyed. Or that it's not in your possession."

"And when he finds out?"

Mittron met his gaze calmly. Samael tipped his head to one side and crossed his arms.

"I see. Bethiel solves my problem, and I solve yours, is that it?"

"Yes."

Samael leaned a shoulder against the frame of the window overlooking the square below. He jerked his chin toward the commotion. "Noisy, aren't they?"

Mittron's head throbbed agreement. "You have no idea."

Samael unfolded his arms and passed a hand in front of a broken pane, healing the glass. The din from the children below became half. He stared out for another few seconds, then he chuckled.

"Do you know, I think your plan might actually work, Seraph. I'm beginning to see the value of having saved your ass. I'll have a chat with your Bethiel and see what he says."

Beginning to see the value? Mittron pressed his lips together as Samael strolled toward the door. *Patience. You're not quite done with him yet. Not if you're to get what you deserve.*

He cleared his throat. "Of course, there's still the matter of the war itself to consider."

Hand on the doorknob, Samael looked back at him. Irritation flashed across his features. "The war is my concern, Seraph, not yours."

"Then you've already taken measures with regard to finding her? Excellent," Mittron said.

"Finding whom? The Naphil? We just had this conversation."

"Not the Naphil. Emmanuelle."

Shocked seconds slid by, punctuated by muffled shouts from beyond the window. Samael closed the door again. He leaned against it, wings sagging behind his back.

"Fuck it all to Heaven and back," he said slowly. "I haven't heard that name in so long, I'd forgotten her."

"I suspect that was her intention."

"She's still alive?"

"I have no reason to think otherwise."

"And you think they'll go looking for her?"

"They have no choice. Without the One to hold them together or free will of their own to drive them, the angels will fracture. They cannot win a war on their own."

"They still have Mika'el."

"Mika'el knows as well as anyone he isn't enough. Not to lead all of Heaven."

Samael rubbed both hands over his face. "Wonderful," he muttered. "Just fucking wonderful. I still have ten thousand troops tied up here on babysitting duty. What am I supposed to do, pull them out and let the Nephilim die? What if something goes wrong and we still need them?"

"What if I can give you all but a handful of your Fallen back?"

"You plan to look after eighty thousand infants on your own? I know you think you're good, Mittron, but not even you can pull that off."

"Not the Fallen. Mortals."

The Archangel gaped at him. "You want to use *mortals* to care for the Nephilim?"

"All I need is a computer and access to the human Internet."

"You're serious."

"Quite."

"And in exchange?"

"I want a place in the new order. Something suitable."

More seconds. From outside came the roar of an angry Fallen One, pushed beyond the limits of patience, t he high-pitched wails of dozens of children. Mittron offered silent thanks to Samael for repairing the window, but he didn't interrupt the other's thoughts.

"The combined realms of Heaven and Hell will need an executive administrator," Samael said finally. "Someone to oversee things, make sure everyone follows the new rules. The position is yours if you want it."

Mittron inclined his head. He wanted—and deserved—a great deal more, but it was a start. "I am in your debt."

"I'm aware of that." Samael's smile held no warmth. "I'll see that you get the human technology this afternoon. How long do you need?"

"Two days."

"You have one."

SIX

Seventeen dead.

Mika'el slammed the door shut with a force that jarred his teeth and vibrated through the entire building, right down to its stone foundation. He rested his black gauntlet-covered hand against the dark oak. Curled it into a metal fist. Stared at the dark crimson glistening in its joints, the still-wet blood of the Fallen One he had cut down on the field, too late to save the Principality quivering on the end of the other's sword. Too late to save so many.

Seventeen.

Seventeen more to add to those they had already lost.

How many did that total? Eighty? Ninety? Were they even keeping count anymore?

Should they bother?

Mika'el spun away from the door and strode across the war chamber, stripping off the gauntlets and throwing them into the center of the table. The clatter of metal on wood echoed from the vaulted ceiling. Other pieces of armor followed. Pauldrons, couters, vambraces and rerebraces. He unbuckled the hardened leather scabbard from his waist and laid it beside the growing pile, then hoisted the molded breast and backplate over his head. The door opened behind him.

"Not now," he growled. He lifted the armor clear and set it on the table with a thud.

"If not now, then when?" a tart female voice responded. "After we've lost another eighty-six angels? Or would you rather it be a hundred and eighty-six?"

Verchiel. With the answer to his question about whether they were keeping count.

Bloody Hell.

He lifted one foot onto a chair so he could remove the armor protecting his knee. "Samael is a skilled strategist," he said. "I've underestimated him until now, but I—"

"We're losing, Mika'el."

His fingers stilled. Denial rose in his throat, but it refused to be spoken. Heaven, losing to Hell? The very thought should be impossible. Angels outnumbered Fallen by at least three to one. Victory should have been messy but certain, yet Verchiel was right. Even with half the Fallen still missing, presumably guarding the Nephilim army Lucifer had created, Heaven was losing. And it wasn't because of Samael's military strategy.

Verchiel's obstinacy pressed against his back, insistent, unyielding. Mika'el let his head drop until his chin rested against his chest. His heart, still unhealed from the loss of their Creator, seeped fresh blood into his soul.

"You're doing your best," the Highest Seraph said at last, her voice gentling, "but you cannot take her place."

He rested a forearm across his armored thigh and bowed his head. "I'm not trying to take her place."

"Fine. Then you cannot be Heaven's will, and the angels cannot fight without one."

He rubbed a hand over the back of his neck, knowing what she wanted from him. Resisting it with every fiber of his soul.

"We don't know that Emmanuelle can be their will, either," he retorted. "Even if we find her, there's no guarantee she'll listen. Or that she'll agree to help if she *does* listen."

"I know that. But she's our only chance. We have to try."

His mouth twisted. "I'm sure you *have* tried. To find her, at least."

Heaven's executive administrator didn't bother to deny it. She shifted her stance in a whisper of robes against flagstone. Sighed.

"It's as if she's disappeared from the universe," she murmured. "But if something had happened to her, we would know, wouldn't we? The One would have felt it, or..."

Her voice trailed off. She didn't need to finish. They both knew how her sentence would have ended. *Or you would have felt it.*

He would have felt it because he had been Emmanuelle's soulmate. Had been, was, always would be. And would, without doubt, know if his connection to her had been severed by death. Even if he hadn't set eyes on her for nearly five thousand years and wasn't at all sure if he wanted to again.

Not after the way she had betrayed all of Heaven.

Mika'el stripped the quisse from his thigh, shoving away the memories and the ache that accompanied them. "The Guardians haven't heard or seen anything?"

"Nothing, and they've been actively seeking her for almost two weeks. If she's still on Earth, she's not using any of her powers, and she's not among humans who have Guardians."

Mika'el's lips thinned. The only mortals who didn't have Guardians were those who had turned their backs on them, who had chosen be influenced by the Fallen Ones that tried to corrupt humankind, to continue what the Grigori had started six millennia before. If the One's missing daughter had made her life among such mortals, it didn't bode well for Heaven's search. Or for her willingness to return to her realm.

"Well, then? What do you suggest we do?" he asked. "I'm assuming you're here because you have an idea."

"We ask for help."

Mika'el tossed the black steel quisse onto the table and reached for the greave protecting his shin. "From whom? If Heaven can't find her—" He stopped. "The humans? How in all of Creation can they help?"

"Not just any human. The Naphil woman."

"*Alex?*" Mika'el added the greave to the pile of armor.

"I don't understand. How could she possibly find what we cannot?"

"As a police officer, she has a potential network that spans the globe. Her connections will be invaluable in detecting one who has disappeared into the unguarded."

"Assuming Emmanuelle has any kind of human

record."

"In humanity's current digital age, it would be almost impossible for her not to have. Not without using her powers to avoid it."

"And we would notice if she did."

"Exactly."

Mika'el rolled the argument over in his mind. Then he shook his head. "Even so, it's virtually impossible that Alex will be able to find her."

"Virtually. Not completely."

"There are seven billion souls on that planet, Verchiel. There is no way—"

"There has to be a way."

It wasn't the interruption that stopped him. It was the quiet desperation underlying the Highest's voice. The thread of despair.

The utter desolation.

In silence, he stripped the remaining armor from his other leg. Verchiel's pain hung between them, heavy in the air, heavier yet across his shoulders. Damn it to Hell and back. Damn Lucifer, damn Samael, damn the Nephilim, damn the—

Mika'el whirled and pitched the quisse he held at the door. It burst through the four-inch-thick oak and clattered against the stone wall of the corridor beyond. The building shuddered beneath the violence. Verchiel flinched, but didn't move from her place. No one came to investigate. In all likelihood, no one had been near enough to hear, because they were all assigned to the front, fighting to save their realm, themselves, the seven billion souls the One had left to their stewardship.

He closed his eyes. Tipped back his head. Sighed.

"Fine," he growled. "Locate Alex. I'll speak with

her."

GROCERY BAG IN HAND, Emmanuelle paused on the wooden steps of the beach house, staring at the nearly leafless climbing rose bush beside the door with its single pink blossom waving in the breeze. She scowled at it. Three times she'd dug that damned bush out of the ground over the last ten years, and three times it had come back—and now it had started blooming in the middle of November?

If she didn't know better, she'd think she'd conjured the thing up, given how much of her thoughts had been preoccupied with past events lately. Ever since—

She broke the thought off with another scowl.

She'd promised herself she wasn't going there again today, and she knew damned well she hadn't caused the rose to bloom. She'd made it such a habit over the last five millennia not to conjure anything, she sometimes wondered whether she'd even remember how.

But if it hadn't been her—

She sent the pink bloom a last baleful look. If the damned thing wasn't so close to the house, she'd pour gasoline on it and set fire to it.

She wrenched open the door and stomped inside.

"I thought I heard you," said a bleached platinum blond, coming into the kitchen. "Good ride?"

"Cold," Emmanuelle said. "But yes, it was still good."

She shrugged out of her leather jacket and hung it on a hook by the door as Jezebel took the groceries from the bag. Coffee, bacon, eggs, salted caramel ice cream, and two bottles of Jack Daniels. Jezebel shot her a look.

"Interesting selection."

"I forgot to take a list with me."

"So you thought you'd just pick up the staples?"

Emmanuelle sent the groceries a dour look. Then she sighed. "They were all I could think of while I was in town."

Lips pursed, Jezebel put the ice cream in the freezer, then leaned against the counter.

"Manny, what's going on? You haven't been yourself in weeks. Even Spider has noticed, and you know how observant he is."

Emmanuelle opened her mouth to deliver an outright denial, but she couldn't quite utter it. Neither could she tell the truth, however, and so she settled for shaking her head.

"I'm just feeling restless, I guess. Must be the time of year. You know how I get in winter, when I can't get out onto the road as much."

Jezebel crossed her arms. "Actually, I don't know, because in the ten years we've been here, I've never seen you like this."

Emmanuelle sighed. Creation save her from too-perceptive friends. "It's nothing, Jez, really. Family stuff. Old memories. I'll get over it."

"Would it help to talk?"

She shook her head. She'd made it five thousand years without having a shoulder to unload on. She didn't need to start now. "Thank you, but I'm fine."

Jezebel watched her for another few seconds, then shrugged. "Well, I'm here if you change your mind. In the meantime, how about breakfast, seeing as how we have all the necessary ingredients now?"

"That would be great, thanks," Emmanuelle agreed.

"I'll change and then come give you a hand."

She pushed through the swinging door that led to the rest of the house. Breakfast first, then she'd find the shovel and take care of that damned rosebush once and for all, even if she had to dig up half the house's foundation.

SEVEN

Alex glanced at the clock over the main door. Twenty past eight. An entire day and most of the evening gone. Those most likely to notice one small, pregnant girl on the streets of Toronto wouldn't be out there much longer in this cold. If she didn't leave soon, she'd miss the chance to talk to them, to ask the questions that might lead her to Nina again.

And yet, she hesitated.

As much as she ached to continue the search, the looks of utter relief on her colleagues' faces when she'd sat down at her desk had been hard to mistake. They'd never been stretched this thin before, and it was only going to get worse. Especially if she bailed on them again. So. Stay and help her colleagues, her city? Or go, because Nina had only six days left, and even if she couldn't survive, she shouldn't have to die alone?

Choices.

"Is the going rate still a penny?"

Alex jolted in her seat and blinked at Tim Abrams,

who had somehow managed to cross the office and settle onto the desk beside her without her noticing. "What?"

"For your thoughts. You know, a penny for them?"

She gave a snort. "Hell, I'd pay you to take them, if I could."

"I don't doubt it," he said. "That was a hell of a thing you and Joly had last night. You holding up okay?"

She tipped her head toward the boards lining the office. "About as well as all of us, I suspect."

"You should be at home."

Alex slanted a suspicious look in the direction of Roberts's office. It was empty, and she remembered that their staff inspector had left a couple of hours ago. But Abrams's next words confirmed her suspicion that Roberts had called and asked him to talk to her.

"He's worried about you. We're all worried about you. When's the last time you even slept?"

"What are you, my nanny?" Before he could retort— or worse, press for an answer—she waved at the case boards. "One of you should have called me. Told me what was going on."

"And what, you would have waved your magic wand and solved them for us?" Abrams shook his head. "You had stuff of your own to worry about. We're coping."

"Fifteen open cases in the last two weeks? That's not coping, Abrams, that's failing to notice you're going under for the third time. You should have called me."

"Because you're so good at keeping your head above water right now?" He rested a hand on her shoulder and repeated, "You had stuff."

It was his second use of the past tense. *Had*, not *have*. Alex scooped back the hair from her forehead and settled an elbow on the desk beside Abrams. She stared at the boards. Thought of Nina.

Choices.

"Hey." Abrams's voice was gruff. "Just because the brass shut down the search doesn't mean we stop looking for her."

The memory of four dead officers swamped a surge of gratitude. Alex shuddered, swallowed hard, shook her head.

"No. Don't. If anything happens to—"

"We won't do anything stupid," Abrams promised. "Not after yesterday. We're just keeping eyes open and ears to the ground. Any one of us hears something, we'll let you know. You have my word. Besides, we've already decided, so there's no point in arguing. She's your niece, and we look out for our own. You'd do the same for us."

He stood. "Now, I'm heading home, and you should, too. You're not invincible, my friend, and you won't do anyone any good if you drop from exhaustion."

She didn't bother correcting him as he gave her shoulder a final squeeze, lifted his coat from the back of a chair, and waved as he headed out the door. His words remained hanging in the silence he left behind: *We look out for our own. You'd do the same.*

Except she hadn't, had she? Not lately. Hadn't given any of her colleagues more than a passing thought for two solid weeks, never mind had their backs. Alex's gaze traveled the white boards lining the room's perimeter once more.

Choices.

She rose and, coffee in hand, wove her way through the clutter of desks. Greg Bastien, the sole remaining occupant in the room besides her, raised his head as she approached. Her steps slowed. She should ask about his wife, whose first pregnancy had been confirmed a scant few weeks before, just as the chaos of the Nephilim births had begun to consume the world. Should ask, but wasn't sure she could.

Bastien's cell phone rang, and he reached to pick it up. Alex breathed a sigh of relief and walked past.

She stopped in front of the board nearest Roberts's office. She'd read the details a dozen times today, but not a single one had stuck. This time needed to be different. This time she needed to make a decision: stay on the job, or go after Nina? Her grip tightened on her cup. Reaching deep, she found the fragments of a focus that had once been second nature to her and turned her eyes to the case before her.

Janine Todd, age 23, 12 weeks pregnant, knifed in the subway on her way to work, suspect still at large. Board number two: Amala Prakash, age 28, 26 weeks pregnant, burned in her bed. Suspect, her brother, in custody. Board three: a list of seven names, all women, all pregnant, killed in the church basement bombing of a prenatal class a week before. Suspect, one of the husbands, dead by suicide.

Continuing her tour of the room, Alex skimmed the remaining boards. Of fifteen cases, two involved men. The remainder were women. Pregnant women.

The birth of Lucifer's Nephilim army hadn't changed a thing. People hadn't even noticed that the bizarre pregnancies had ended. They were still terrified, and still reacting to that terror by lashing out at mothers-to-be. And the fear was spreading, because if all of this was happening here, in Toronto, it meant that things were much, much worse in other parts of the world.

Which meant whatever message governments were putting out wasn't working. Roberts was right. The world needed her. It needed every rational head it could get.

Choices.

With careful deliberation, Alex set her coffee on a nearby desk and crossed her arms over the aching emptiness of her belly. From behind her came the murmur of Bastien's voice, pitched low. A personal call, most likely. She closed out the sound and conjured an image of Nina, pale and limp in the Fallen One's arms. Jen, silent and unresponsive in her hospital room. Both damaged not by human hands, but by the Fallen.

Closing her eyes, Alex breathed in the unending pain of utter powerlessness. Tentacles of grief wrapped around her core, squeezing out the last of the denial that had driven her for the past two weeks, leaving behind the despair of an admission she could no longer deny.

She couldn't fix them.

She couldn't make them better.

Nina would die giving birth to Lucifer's child; Jen would remain inaccessible, her mind shattered by what had happened to her daughter; and Alex would live forever, unable to repair the damage inflicted by beings she could never hope to stop.

She opened her eyes again to the boards and the victims outlined there, the families they had almost certainly left behind. She couldn't help them, either, but maybe she could help others. Maybe.

Choices.

Leaving her coffee where it was and files strewn across desk, she picked up her jacket, returned Bastien's farewell wave, and headed out of the office. Fuck it. She couldn't think straight anymore. She

needed to get away from those damned boards and
the hideous cases that accompanied them and the
impossible responsibility that pressed in on her. She
needed to see her sister. She needed sleep.

And she definitely needed that drink or two Roberts
had mentioned.

EIGHT

"Let me get this straight," the not-quite fallen Principality stared at Samael, his blue gaze flat and assessing. "I kill this Naphil woman for you, and you hand me my ticket back to Heaven."

Samael uncorked the bottle of port he'd rescued from Seth's cleanse of Lucifer's office. The Appointed might not share his father's taste in wines, but Samael was happy to be the recipient of the cast-offs. He poured a generous measure of the ruby liquid into a glass, then raised the bottle in Bethiel's direction. The Principality shook his head, continuing his back-and-forth prowl, tattered gray wings folding and unfolding. He hadn't stopped moving since he'd walked in, and his restless energy set Samael's teeth on edge.

"That's exactly my proposal," he agreed, recorking the bottle.

Bethiel swiveled and retraced his steps yet again. "Why?"

"Why what?"

"Why do you care if I get back to Heaven?"

Samael chuckled. "You misunderstand me, Principality. I don't give a good goddamn whether you get back to Heaven or not. That's what *you* want. *I* want the Naphil."

"Dead."

"Yes." He sipped the port, swirling it around his mouth, letting the rich, oak-y flavor settle over his palate. Lucifer may have had a lot of flaws, but his taste in wines had been impeccable.

Bethiel slid his hands into the pockets of the loose-fitting pants he wore beneath his tunic. "And what has this Naphil woman done to you to deserve such negative attention?"

Samael masked the tightening of his lips with another sip of wine. "The price I'm willing to pay you doesn't include answering questions."

"But the one you exact in return is about as steep as it gets. Murder, Samael?" Bethiel shook his head. "Proof of my former innocence might get me into Heaven, but I would never be allowed to remain if I killed a human, Naphil or otherwise. I would never pass Judgment."

"You forget there is no Judgment anymore. The One is gone, Bethiel. No one need know of our bargain unless you choose to tell them. Show your proof at the gate, and they will have no choice but to admit you. You'll be home."

Bethiel regarded him, his expression neutral. "Tell me again how you came to be in possession of the evidence proving my innocence?"

"I didn't tell you in the first place. And that's another question."

More pacing. Samael rolled his eyes and drained

the glass of port, resisting the temptation to throw the glass at the Principality's head. Bloody Heaven. What if Mittron was wrong, and Bethiel turned down the proposition? Samael couldn't risk him going to Seth with—

"Is *he* still there?"

The hungry glint in the Principality's eye belied the casual tone. Of course. Samael should have realized Mittron would be the carrot he needed to hold out. The Seraph himself had pointed out that nothing motivated quite like revenge. Samael damped down a surge of triumph. He needed to tread carefully here. Bethiel's mind might be dulled by his years in Limbo, but Samael had no doubt the other would put the puzzle pieces together if he knew the so-called evidence had come from Mittron. Nor did Samael doubt what would happen if Bethiel knew Mittron was on Earth.

He pretended disinterest. "Is who still where?"

"Mittron. Is he still in Heaven?"

"I don't know who remains." Samael shrugged. "And frankly, I don't care. Do we have a deal or not?"

Bethiel made two more circuits of the room, his steps jolting and uneven, fists inside his pockets tapping against his legs. His expression alternated between clear refusal of the idea and a kind of agonized longing that made Samael want to roll his eyes. He waited for the decision he knew to be inevitable. Sometimes others made it almost too easy for him.

Bethiel stopped. He turned to face Samael. Then he took a deep breath and handed over his soul on the proverbial silver platter.

"Where do I find her?" he asked.

STANDING ON the heavily salted sidewalk, fresh snowflakes drifting down around her, Alex stared up at the hospital windows glowing in the night. Was Jen sitting at hers now, looking down on her and wondering why she wasn't coming inside to see her? Would any part of her be aware enough to care, or to even notice Alex's presence?

Her cell phone trilled. She tugged it from her coat pocket, glanced at the name *Elizabeth Riley* on the display, and sighed. She'd been avoiding calls from Henderson all day. It just figured that he'd sic Riley on her instead. She hesitated. While she still didn't want to talk to anyone, the calls wouldn't stop until she did, and the Vancouver psychiatrist seemed the lesser of two evils at the moment. At least she could count on Riley's acerbic manner to shore up her defenses, whereas she suspected she'd fold up on the spot if she heard Hugh's gruff concern.

She thumbed the answer icon. "Jarvis," she said.

Riley's voice reached across two thousand miles, cool, brisk, professional. "We heard what happened last night. Hugh said you haven't returned any of his calls. Are you all right?"

"I'm fine," she said. "I'm on my way home and just stopped by to see Jen first."

A second of silence slipped by. Alex pictured Riley's piercing blue eyes behind her wire-framed glasses, the furrow between the graying brows, the compression of the psychiatrist's lips against the urge to probe further.

Riley cleared her throat. "How is she? Any change?"

Alex's gaze flicked back up to the rows of blank windows. Did she confess she hadn't made it inside? That she'd been standing on the sidewalk long enough for her toes to go numb?

"I just got here," she lied. "I haven't made it inside yet. But there's been nothing so far."

"And Nina?"

An image of her unconscious niece flared to life in Alex's brain: matted dark hair hanging over the Fallen One's arm; too-thin arms dangling limply from within the folds of a blanket; face pale and pinched. She tightened her grip on the cell phone and realized her fingers had gone as numb as her toes.

"He had her," she said, her voice hoarse but steady. "The Fallen One we found. He had her."

She listened to the hiss of Riley's breath. Felt the sound slip between her ribs like the blade of a knife. Clamped her lips together.

"And is she...?"

The knife blade in Alex's ribs twisted. "Yes."

Riley's voice lost its professional edge. "I'm so sorry. I'd hoped..."

The psychiatrist trailed off a second time, and Alex locked her knees, remaining upright through sheer force of will. She knew what Riley had hoped. She'd hoped it herself, though she never allowed the thought to fully form until now. Until this moment.

She'd hoped they'd been wrong, that Lucifer hadn't gotten to her niece after all, that Nina wouldn't die in less than a week. She'd hoped that recovering Nina would bring Jen back from wherever she had gone, so Alex could once more have a family. She'd hoped...

A snowflake landed on her cheek, ice against ice.

God, how she'd hoped.

"What now?" Riley asked.

Alex stamped frozen feet. "I don't know. They've called off the search. They had no choice. Not after what happened."

The silence stretched so long this time that she glanced at the display to make sure she hadn't lost the connection. An ambulance pulled into the emergency bay, lights splashing red through the falling snow. At last Riley cleared her throat.

"And you? Are you calling it off, too?"

Alex tried to curl her fingers into a fist, but they were too stiff to comply. That was the million-dollar question, wasn't it? The one that had kept her standing in the cold for more than ten minutes, unable to make her feet carry her into the hospital. She still didn't have an answer.

Choices.

"Alex? Are you going to keep looking?"

"I don't know," she croaked. She shoved her free hand into her pocket. "I don't know, Liz. Christ, even if I find her, she's with a Fallen One. He's not going to just hand her over to me, and I have no way to take her from him. But I don't know how I can give up, either."

"Oh, honey..."

Alex blinked furiously at the tears that threatened. Shit. Now Riley was going to turn all caring and sweet? Maybe taking one of Henderson's calls would have been better after all. Holding back a telltale sniffle, she swiped a hand under her nose.

"I should go. I haven't slept since night before last and I'm beat."

"All right. But you'll call if you need to talk? And you know I can come—"

"God, no." Alex winced at the speed and harshness of her response. "I mean, thank you, but I'm fine. Really."

She heard a muffled snort from the other end of the

line. "I know what you meant, Alex. I'm not offended, and the offer stands. I'm here if you need me. Hugh and I both are."

"Of course. Thank you. Speaking of Hugh—"

"He's been up to his ass, according to him. I don't know if you've seen the news, but things aren't good out here. They aren't good anywhere right now. He said to tell you that's why he's been so lenient about you not returning his calls, but I'm supposed to report back to him after I speak with you. I'll tell him you're coping, shall I? That should buy you a little time until you hear from him."

"Yeah. That'd be great. Thanks, Liz, and—" Alex's voice caught. "Just thanks."

Ending the call, she looked up again at the hospital where her beautiful, broken sister sat. Grief, ever present beneath her surface, tightened the talons embedded in her throat. She trudged toward the main entrance.

NINE

Palms slick with sweat, Alex stepped into her sister's room. She'd visited Jennifer every day for two weeks, and she'd swear the walk down that corridor got longer each time. Knowing Jen had descended into the same blackness that had claimed so many other minds trapped in the ward, the same blackness that had claimed their mother...

God*damn* it, this was just so wrong.

Pausing inside the door, Alex let her gaze travel the familiar utilitarian space: the wheeled bed, neatly made and unoccupied; the functional washroom to the left; the gleaming linoleum floors and pale green walls. And Jen, sitting in the same chair she always did, staring out the same window, her gaze as empty and unfocused as it had been since the night Lucifer took Nina.

Alex closed her eyes and braced herself for their one-sided visit. Two weeks and no change. Not a single word, not a flicker of recognition, nothing. If

Jen stayed like this, if her mind didn't come back from wherever it had retreated...

If I have to continue alone...

Guilt churned through Alex's gut, mixing with self-loathing. Christ almighty. Her sister's mind had broken, and all she could think about was herself? Would it really be any better if Jen *did* come back? Did Alex *want* her sister to return to a reality where Lucifer himself had raped and impregnated her daughter, sentencing the seventeen-year-old girl to death through childbirth? Just so she—Alex—didn't have to face it alone?

She pushed away from the doorframe.

Face it, Jarvis, you are alone. And you'd better get used to that, too.

Her booted heels thudded hollowly against the gleaming linoleum as she crossed the room. She rested a hand on her sister's shoulder, gave a gentle squeeze, and brushed a kiss across the pale, cold cheek.

Jen didn't react.

Thrusting her fists into her coat pockets, Alex perched on the empty chair facing Jen. She swallowed on a throat made of sandpaper.

"Hey, sis. I'm sorry I'm late today. The streets are awful with all this snow. And we had some trouble at work last night."

Nothing.

"Some of our guys—" Alex's voice cracked. She swallowed again. "Some of our guys were killed last night. Four of them."

Not so much as the flicker of an eyelash.

Alex's fists tightened. Her jaw ached. *Goddamn it, Jen, respond. Do something—anything—to let me know you're still in there. I can't do this alone, damn it. I can't keep looking for Nina by myself, not when I know how it's going to end.*

Blinking back the blur of tears, she stared out the window.

"I saw her," she said, and cringed from her own words. She'd promised herself she wouldn't mention Nina. The doctors had warned her that doing so might drive her sister even further away.

But what if they're wrong? What if Nina's name is what Jen needs to hear? What she needs to bring her back?

Alex wavered. Exhaustion and the events of the night piled in on her, fogging her thoughts. She didn't know what was right anymore. Didn't know who to trust or what to do. She just knew she needed her sister. Needed to try. She steeled herself.

"Did you hear me, Jen? I said I saw Nina. She's alive."

For long seconds, she held her every fiber still, studying her sister's face, the lines of her body, waiting...and then she slumped back in the chair. Raw agony shot through her every fiber, cramping her muscles, filling her lungs with shards of glass, turning her tears to fire. *God damn.*

Hysteria bubbled in her throat at the whisper of thought. *God* damn? Who the hell was she kidding? God *couldn't* damn. Hell, God couldn't do anything anymore, because she no longer even existed. She'd left. Abandoned Heaven, the angels, her so-called beloved mortal children, the entire fucking universe. Up and left it all. And now Nina was out there somewhere, held by a Fallen One, sentenced to a death no one could stop; and Jen was here, like this; and humanity was on its own, facing potential decimation, if not at the hands of the Nephilim army created by

Lucifer, then through its own shortcomings. Its own sad, crippling arrogance.

And she—Alex herself—would get to stand by and watch it all. Every disaster. Every war. Every death. Every loss of every person she had ever known or cared for, because thanks to the being she had tried to love, tried to save, she herself could no longer die.

Fuck.

She took her hands from her pockets and viciously scrubbed away the tears that had spilled over. Then she shoved herself upright, out of the chair. She couldn't deal with this. Not tonight. She had to get out of here. Now, while she was still capable of driving herself home. Leaning down, she put her arms around Jen, wincing at the frailty of her sister's too-thin shoulders. Just how much weight had Jen lost since—

She stiffened as fragile arms crept beneath her jacket and around her waist. Her breath jammed in her throat. Holy hell.

"Jen?" she croaked. She closed her eyes against fresh tears and buried her face in her sister's hair. Astonishment unfurled in her belly, became a swelling of hope. "You heard me? You heard what I said about Nina?"

"Let her go," Jen whispered, the first words out of her mouth since she'd been found unconscious in her house, the front door demolished, Nina gone.

"I don't understand."

"She's dead, Alex. Let her go."

"But she's not dead." Alex drew back far enough to stare into the familiar doe-skin brown eyes and the clarity in their depths, the first she'd seen there in more than two weeks. Clarity and—Alex's heart jolted at the defeat there as well.

She shook her head with a ferocity that made her brain hurt. "No. No! She's alive, Jen. Didn't you hear me? I saw her. And I'll find her for you again, I swear."

"Let her go," Jen repeated. "Let us both go."

Alex hugged her again. Tightly. Fiercely. "I can't do that, Jennifer Abbott. I *won't* do that. We can get through this. You and me, together. You just need to stay with me. Promise me, Jen. Promise you'll stay. *Please.*"

Jen's arms tightened for the space of a frantic breath—long enough for Alex's fledgling hope to surge—and then they began a slow withdrawal. Alex's hug turned desperate, clinging. Her sister's hand snagged on the sidearm at Alex's waist and, from a long, long way off, Alex felt a snap give. Felt the tug of her pistol leaving its holster.

She reared back, hand instinctively going to cover the weapon, to protect it, but it was too late. Her own shout filled her ears. Jen's gaze met hers.

The world exploded in a crimson wash of blood.

TEN

Mika'el straightened up from the map spread across the round war table. Three breaks in their front line in the last twenty-four hours. Their defense was weakening faster than any of them had predicted. His gaze traveled along the lines of grim-faced Archangels flanking him. Azrael, Uriel, and Zachariel to his left; Raphael and Gabriel to his right. Five Archangels—six including him—to patrol the infinitely long border between Heaven and Hell. To inspire the others to hold fast.

"We can't keep this up, Mika'el." Azrael, voicing what every one of them thought. "There just aren't enough of us."

"Are you suggesting we give up?" Gabriel snapped.

Azrael's expression darkened. "I'm *suggesting* the truth. If the other choirs don't get their act together, we're going to lose. There are only six of us, Gabriel. We can't win this war on our own."

"Enough." Mika'el shot a fierce look around the table. "We can't win at all if we start fighting amongst ourselves. No one denies the challenges we face, Azrael; the question is, what do we do about them?"

Azrael shifted his feet and said nothing. Uriel, Zachariel, and Raphael stared down at the map. Gabriel cleared her throat.

"We fight smarter."

Mika'el raised an eyebrow at her. "You have an idea?"

The female Archangel tossed her flaming red hair over one shoulder and leaned across the table. "The breaches have been here, here, and here"—she jabbed a finger at three spots on the map—"all positions that are the most easily defended from a geographical perspective."

"And?"

She straightened. "And yet we've had difficulty defending them because the majority of our forces are elsewhere. Guarding the *least* defensible positions."

They all studied the map for a moment, then Zachariel grunted. "You're saying we've inadvertently created new weaknesses for ourselves."

"We put angels at the weaker geographical points for a reason," Azrael pointed out. "Any breaches there would be more difficult to contain if they occurred."

Mika'el held up a hand to ward off further debate. "Let Gabriel finish."

"Azrael is right. It makes sense to protect our more vulnerable positions, and yes, if we redistribute the angels more evenly, we put those positions at a higher risk. But there are only five of those places, and there are six of us."

"You're suggesting we tie five of us to fixed locations?" Uriel shook his head. "What if none of the Fallen ever attack those places? We'd be no more than glorified sentries."

Four heads nodded assent. Mika'el scowled at the map. They were right. But so was Gabriel.

"What would you have us do?" he asked.

"The sheer length of the border is what's killing us," she said. "Six of us cannot police it effectively. Not when the others are—"

"Fucking useless?" Azrael muttered.

"That will do," Mika'el growled. "I'll not blame Heaven's forces for something that is beyond their control, and neither will you. Understood?" Taking the other Archangel's agreement for granted, he gave Gabriel a curt nod. "Go on."

"I think it makes more sense to redistribute our forces over the longer stretches, keeping a bare minimum at the danger points. Then, as Uriel said, five of us remain at those points as well. Glorified sentries or not, we'd be more effective there than doing what we're doing now."

Assuming the increased forces along the rest of the border could summon the collective will to hold back the enemy. It was a big assumption. Mika'el rested his hands against the table and drummed his fingers in a restless rhythm. "And the remaining Archangel?"

"Would remain near the center of the front line. As a last resort."

"It would be a tremendous distance to travel in either direction if anything happened."

"Yes."

Mika'el frowned at the map. He sensed the dissent in the others and didn't blame them. The idea was counterintuitive, going against basic military strategy. On the other hand, that could be the very reason for trying it. At the least, it might put the Fallen off their stride for a bit and buy Heaven some time—buy *him* some time—to find Emmanuelle.

As if conjured by his thoughts, a knock sounded at the war chamber door. He looked around as it swung inward for Verchiel. Something electric sparked in the pale blue gaze that met his. He caught his breath, and the Highest Seraph nodded. They'd found Alex.

"Right." He turned back to the others. "It's worth a try. Gabriel will oversee the planning and execution in my absence. Raphael will be her second."

"Hold on." Azrael put an arm out to stop him as he stepped away from the table. "What absence? Where are you going?"

Mika'el met each of the Archangels' gazes in turn. He'd said nothing of his doubts to any of them so far, talked to no one but Verchiel of his fears. Sooner or later, however, they would have to know. They deserved to know. He took a deep breath, but a touch on his hand stopped him. Verchiel, pressing a slip of paper into his palm.

"Go," she said. "I'll deal with this."

"I should be the one—"

"You'll be the one to save us. Go."

With a last glance at the gathered Archangels, he nodded. "Tell them everything."

"Even...?"

"Even that." Curling his hand over the paper Verchiel had given him, Mika'el strode from the chamber. The Highest's voice followed him across the threshold and into the empty stone hallway.

"We need Emmanuelle to come home," she said calmly, "because we're losing."

Mika'el closed the great oaken door on the utter silence that followed her words.

ELEVEN

Alex huddled in the corner of the room, unmoving, unblinking. The blanket someone had placed around her slipped further off her shoulders with every breath, every treacherous beat of her heart in her ears. She did nothing to retrieve it. Could do nothing.

A photographer's flash surprised her eyes into closing, but only once. She was prepared for the next and forced her lids to remain open. Forced herself to continue staring at the spray of red and the flecks of gray matter spread across the wall behind her sister's slumped body.

Behind Jen.

A third flash. The police photographer muttered an apology and retreated awkwardly from recording the gore that had dried on her face and neck. The lanky frame of her staff inspector filled her field of vision as Roberts squatted before her. His hand covered hers, its heat near scalding. She flinched.

"They're going to move her now," he said.

His voice was gruff. Exhausted. A part of Alex wanted to apologize to him for what had happened, for adding to his burden. A larger, colder part of her recognized the ludicrousness of the idea. Her sister had died because of her. There were no words of apology big enough. She met his concern. Nodded her understanding.

"I know it's late, but you'll have to come back to the office. We need a statement."

Another nod.

Roberts stared at her for a long moment, his Adam's apple bobbing in his throat. Then his lips went tight.

"What the hell, Alex." The words were raw, seemingly ripped from him against his will. "You brought your *gun* into a *psych* ward?"

She looked past him, over his shoulder. Excuses— lame, pitiful, meaningless excuses—piled up in her mind. *There was no one at the nurse's station when I went by. I didn't think. I was tired. I wanted to go home, but I had to come here for Jen first. I had to tell her I'd seen Nina.*

I didn't think.

A forensics member wheeled a gurney into the room. Someone unzipped a body bag, and the *zzzzzzt* grated through the room.

I didn't think.

Invisible steel clamped around Alex's throat. That was all that mattered. She hadn't thought. And now Jen was dead. Holy mother of—

A god that didn't exist.

She choked on a bubble of hysteria. Clamped her teeth together. Watched Jen's lifeless body lifted onto the gurney, tucked into the bag, zipped away from sight. The coroner met her gaze, hesitated, and then wordlessly followed her sister from the room. Alex folded her arms over her belly.

Roberts's hand tightened on her arm. "You okay?"

She nodded. Shook her head. Then shook, period. Tremors engulfed her, slamming her teeth together, rattling through her entire body. Muscles went so rigid that they screamed in agony. She heard Roberts say her name, his voice insistent, but she couldn't make herself answer him because her jaw had locked shut. Roberts put his arms around her and called to Abrams to find a doctor. Footsteps thudded out the door.

Faint alarm sounded in the back of Alex's mind. Could a person actually shake to death? Then fresh hysteria bubbled. Maybe. But it didn't matter, because *she* couldn't. No, *she* was going to get to live with this—with what she'd done to Jennifer—for thousands upon thousands of years. Millions of years.

Eternity.

Jennifer's head exploded across her vision again, and Alex jerked back in her seat.

Ohgodohgodohgod...

"Alexandra."

The deep, imperious voice shot through her agony like a hot bullet through—

Fuck. She gasped, seized her sanity in both hands, and held on with every atom of her being as she stared into the glittering emerald eyes of the Archangel Michael.

"I need your help," he said.

IF SHE'D STILL had her gun, Alex had no doubt she would have shot him. Twice.

She stood before Michael, fists clenched, trembling from head to toe. Her head swam from her violent lunge to her feet. Roberts had risen with her, and he reached for her arm. She shook him off and stepped forward, toe to toe with the Archangel who dared invade her grief. With every fiber of her being, she wished for the feel of her pistol nestled into her hand. Wished it wasn't zipped away into an evidence bag. Wished she could fire the instrument that had taken her sister's life at the being she held most responsible.

It didn't matter that no bullet could hurt Michael. Or that he might not even let one near him. It mattered only that he would have known the level of her fury. Her contempt. Her utter lack of regard for who and what he was.

Because then, maybe, he wouldn't be standing before her in a hospital room while her sister's body was wheeled away, asking for—

"*My* help?" Alex snarled. "On what fucking planet do you live that you would think—for even a nanosecond—that I would help you? Oh, wait. I forgot. You're from Heaven, where you *don't* think. At least not about anything other than yourselves."

Roberts seized her wrist. She pulled free.

"Get out," she told Michael.

"You don't know—"

"I don't *care*. Just as *you* don't care."

"I never said I—"

"Fuck you," she said. "*Fuck you*, Michael. And fuck all the others like you, and fuck Heaven and Hell, and fuck the one who—"

"Stop." His voice cracked out, as sharp as the retort of a rifle, and wings that had been hidden made a sudden, shocking appearance, half unfurled behind him. Those who still moved about the room froze in mid-stride, mid-sentence, mid-breath.

Alex looked into the fury that glittered in the emerald depths of Michael's eyes, eclipsing her own a thousand times over. Reminding her of the awful power she challenged. For a moment, she quailed, taking a step back, holding up a hand in apology. Conciliation. And then she remembered what she had become, the losses she would endure for eternity. She dropped her hand to her side. Fingernails bit into her palm.

"Or what?" she asked, her voice soft. Flat. "You'll kill me? Be my guest. We both know you'd be doing me a favor."

For the third time, Roberts's fingers clamped over her arm. This time his grip was unbreakable. He leaned in and hissed, "What the hell is going on, Alex? Who *is* this?"

Alex met the challenge in Michael's gaze, his steel-jawed, silent command. She waited for the familiar surge of defiance but felt nothing. Felt empty, hollow. Finished. She shook her head. "It's nothing, Staff. He's leaving."

Michael opened his mouth to speak.

"Now," she said.

"We're not done, Naph—Alex."

She laughed at that. A short bark that held no humor and made Michael's eyes narrow dangerously.

"We've been done for longer than you know," she said. "Now get the hell out."

TWELVE

"In!" Seth's voice barked through the door.

Samael pressed his lips together and inhaled a slow breath through flared nostrils. Then, pasting as pleasant a look as he could muster on his face, he pushed into the Appointed's office. A shirtless Seth stood by the fireplace, scowling at the ministrations of the Fallen One changing his bandage.

Samael glanced at the exposed wound. It was still red and inflamed, but the green ooze had finally dried up. He nodded approval.

"That looks better."

"I didn't ask you here for a medical opinion. Have you found her?"

"It's been less than a day. You can hardly expect—"

"I expect you to do as I've asked. Without making excuses."

Samael set his teeth against the desired retort. "Of course. No, we haven't found her yet. But I have found someone we can trust to look for her."

"Everyone should be looking for her. Including you."

The Fallen One unrolled a fresh length of gauze, his gaze flicking between them.

"Leave that." Samael jerked his head toward the door. "Come back later."

Curiosity turned to speculation, but the former Virtue nodded. Leaving his supplies on the low table before the fireplace, he retreated from the room in silence. Samael waited for the click of the door. Then he turned to Seth.

"I don't think you fully appreciate how tenuous our situation is at the moment," he said. "Your position here is hardly cemented, Seth. If the Fallen sense weakness—"

Seth vaulted the couch and backhanded him before Samael registered movement. From his new position on the floor against the opposite wall, he put the back of his hand to a split lip and stared up into cold, black eyes. Bloody Heaven, the Appointed became more unhinged by the day. Bloody, *bloody* Heaven.

Settling his back against the wall, Samael rested an arm across one upright knee, keeping a watchful eye out for any more sudden moves. "May I ask what that was for?"

"I'm sick of your lies and half truths, Archangel. I took back my power for you because you said I would have Alex, and now you try to excuse your failure to give her to me."

"That's not how the conversation went. I said you could have her, yes, but I never once said I would deliver—"

"Semantics!" Seth spat. "You wanted a ruler? You have one. You want me to lead your war? You give me

Alexandra Jarvis. You have three days. After that, if I'm still unable to cross the threshold between the realms myself, I will pull every single Fallen One out of battle and send them after her. Do I make myself clear?"

Out of the father's madness and into the son's. Bloody, *fucking* Heaven. Lucifer would have laughed himself sick at the mess Samael had landed himself in. The sooner the Naphil died and they redirected Seth's attention to where it belonged, the better.

"Perfectly clear, Appointed," he said. "You'll have her in three days."

Her body, at least.

SETH STARED at the door Samael had closed behind him, clenching and unclenching his fists, swallowing against a bellow of fury and pain and bewilderment. A tentative knock sounded—the Virtue attempting to return and finish nurse duty, no doubt, and he snarled at him to fuck off. Footsteps scurried away. Silence descended.

Fear slithered into his chest, wrapped around his throat, tried to become panic. He was alone again. Alone with the ghost of his father and his own memories, feeling himself bleed to death in his very core. Seth gripped the hair on either side of his head and pressed fists against his skull. *Damn* it, what was happening? This slow unraveling of his very sanity, this relentless ache within him. Even as his physical wounds healed, even as he heard and on some level agreed with Samael's lectures on becoming a leader, Seth felt himself coming apart. Felt the hollow in his core growing.

He couldn't lead. Not like this.

Alex.

It all came down to Alex. To the driving, all-consuming need to find her. To hold her and know her and *be* with her.

And if Samael didn't get that, then Seth would find someone who did.

THIRTEEN

Roberts's hand appeared in front of Alex's face, a steaming mug of coffee in its grasp. She blinked, then extended an arm from within the folds of the blanket someone had given her.

"Thank you."

Her supervisor grunted. He walked around the plain metal table and lowered himself into the chair opposite. "Joanne's almost done typing your statement. It should only be another few minutes."

Alex nodded and returned to staring out the window beside her. Seconds ticked by, measured by the rhythmic drumming of Roberts's fingers on the tabletop.

Eyes burning, her gaze flicked to the wall of white boards lining Homicide. She should have stayed. Should have kept working on the files. If she hadn't gone to the hospital tonight, hadn't told Jen about seeing Nina—

The echo of a gunshot reverberated through her

skull, making her jump. Hot coffee sloshed onto her hand. Across the table, Roberts made to rise, but she shook her head at him and used a corner of the blanket to swipe at the spill. Then she made herself sip the coffee, gagging at its sickly sweetness.

"You're in shock," Roberts said. "You need the sugar. Drink."

Funny how he said that as if she cared. As if she should, too. She thought about putting the mug down, but fighting with Roberts about it would require too much energy. She sat back and took another mouthful. Swallowed. Her gaze trailed back to the boards again.

So many dead. So many hurting.

Roberts cleared his throat. "So. You ready to talk about the...other stuff?"

"Can we do this tomorrow?" Her throat ached from unshed tears. Unspoken grief. Bottomless, infinite despair.

"He had wings, Alex."

She squeezed her eyes shut. "I know."

"And he asked for your help."

More like demanded it, but whatever.

"Who was he?" Roberts's voice gentled, but it didn't lose its edge of insistence. He wasn't going to let this go.

"Michael," she whispered. "He was the Archangel Michael."

Silence. The audible sound of Roberts opening and closing his mouth. Clearing his throat.

"I thought it might be," he said at last.

Alex didn't think for an instant he was as calm as his tone tried to suggest. The interview room door opened and heels, the sturdy, sensible ones preferred by Roberts's assistant, clacked into the room.

"Your statement, Staff Inspector."

"Thank you, Joanne."

Papers shuffled in an exchange of hands.

Joanne's gentle touch descended on Alex's shoulder. "You okay, sweetheart?"

Looking up into the warm, motherly compassion of a woman who normally epitomized brusque professionalism, Alex nearly came undone on the spot. She gripped the mug, holding fast to the remnants of a toughness she wished she could abandon, but didn't dare. First, because it had become such a habit that she didn't know how to let it go anymore; and second, because she suspected it might be all that held her together. All that prevented her from following her sister's descent into the madness she herself had once wished for. A madness that turned out not to be the escape she'd imagined after all.

Unable to summon a smile, she instead unlocked one hand from its hold on the coffee cup and gave Joanne's capable fingers a reassuring squeeze.

"I'll be fine," she said. "I'm just going to sign this, and then I'm going home to sleep. Thank you for coming in tonight to do this."

"Pfft." Joanne waved away her words. "It was nothing. We're a team here. We look out for one another. Which is why I'm sure the staff inspector will make sure someone drives you home when you're ready."

Roberts's mouth twitched at the thinly veiled command. "Of course."

Sturdy heels clacked away. The interview room door closed again, shutting out the ringing of a phone and the mumble of voices belonging to people Alex couldn't see. People who had given up sleep and returned to work because of her sloppiness. Her stupidity.

Abrams, she thought. And maybe Bastien. Joly would still be at home. Had anyone called to tell him about this latest incident? Not that it mattered. He would find out soon enough.

Her supervisor slid the statement across the table to her. Alex uncurled from the chair and leaned forward to set the mug on the table. With cramped fingers, she accepted the pen and put its tip to the signature line.

"You should read it over," Roberts said.

Her fingers tightened. Relive again, in black and white this time, the part she had played in Jen's suicide? She scrawled her name, set the pen across the paper, and sat back, tucking the tremble of her hands into the blanket folds. "That's it? I can go now?"

"We haven't—"

She stood, letting the blanket fall to the floor. "Tomorrow. I promise."

Roberts stared at her, conflict in his brown eyes. Then he sighed. "I'll get Abrams to run you home."

FOURTEEN

I t was three a.m. when Alex locked the apartment door and leaned her forehead against its cold, unyielding metal. Silence loomed behind her. Not the comforting silence of coming home, but the kind that pressed in, squeezing the air from her lungs, making her smaller, trying to push her into the floor. She sagged beneath its weight.

Tick. Tick. Tick.

The wall clock in the living room marked the passage of seconds. The bundle of keys in her hand bit into her palm.

Tick. Tick. Tick.

Through the windows overlooking the street came the wail of a siren and the strident klaxon of a fire truck's horn.

Tick, tick, tick.

The keys dropped from Alex's hand. She pressed her palms over her ears, but the everyday noises continued to intrude. The clatter and whirr of the refrigerator motor in the kitchen; a truck rumbling by on the street. Overwhelmingly familiar sounds incurred by a life she was no longer sure she wanted to live...

And one she couldn't escape.

Nostrils flaring, she turned from the thought to face the emptiness. The light from the ceiling fixture above her gave up halfway into the living room, leaving the corners in deep, impenetrable shadow. A liquid chill slid down her spine.

Anyone could be in one of those corners.

Stop it. Seth is gone. He's not coming back.

No one is coming back.

She stooped to snatch up the keys she'd dropped.

Tick, tick, tick.

BANG.

The crack of a gunshot dropped her to the floor. She scrabbled for her gun, instinctively, automatically. Fingers connected with an empty holster. Her heart stopped. Then she remembered. Her eyes closed.

Fuck.

There was no gun, just as there was no one hiding in the apartment. She was alone, and the shot hadn't been real. It had been the sound of Jennifer dying all over again, imprinted on Alex's brain, on her every fiber, for eternity.

Beautiful, clever, funny, gentle Jen.

Dead.

Alex lurched upright and bolted for the toilet.

A few minutes later, she lifted her head from the sink and stared her reflection's hollow eyes in the mirror. Water dripped from her chin and trickled down her neck, wetting the t-shirt someone had given her to replace the blouse covered in blood and bits of Jen's brains. Beside her, the toilet gurgled as it emptied, then refilled. She turned off the tap, swiped a hand towel over her face, and dropped it onto the counter. Then she headed for the Scotch.

Bottle and glass in hand, she shoved aside the jumble of blankets on the couch where she'd taken to sleeping since Seth's departure, poured a generous three fingers of amber liquid into the glass, and tossed it back in a single swallow. The liquor burned its way down her throat and into her belly. She waited a moment to make sure it wouldn't go the way of Roberts's oversweetened coffee, then sloshed more into the glass and set the bottle on the table. She leaned back.

A hard lump dug into her tailbone, and she probed the cushions behind her. Her hand closed over the barrel of her spare pistol. She'd forgotten to lock it away before leaving the apartment. Damn, but she was getting sloppy.

She pulled out the gun and stared at it. Then she tossed it onto the table beside the bottle, snorting at her naiveté. She could sleep with an entire arsenal, and it wouldn't do her one iota of good if Seth decided to come for her.

Her gaze rested on the pistol. Cold curiosity whispered through her. Tilting the glass, she turned her wrist outward and traced a fingertip over the forearm that had been laid open in the fight for Aramael's life and her freedom.

No trace of injury marred the skin, but what did that prove? The room had been filled with the energy of angels. Maybe that's what had healed her. Maybe Michael had been wrong and Seth had failed. Maybe she could still—

"Trust me," a deep male voice drawled, "it won't

work."

Alex froze. In an instant, her every cop instinct leaped to life. She tuned into the presence looming behind her, gauging his distance from her. Her own distance from the weapon she'd just set on the table.

Her chances of reaching it before her visitor did.

"I said it won't work," the voice repeated, punctuated by the rustle of feathers.

Alex's hope died.

An angel. Or a Fallen One. Either way, she didn't stand a chance of moving fast enough, and even if she did, the gun would be useless against him. Her fingers tightened on her glass. With her free hand, she reached to switch on the lamp at her side. Then she looked over her shoulder to the figure beside the window. Tall and brooding, with tattered gray wings rising above him, their dishevelment marking him as Fallen.

Alex could think of only one reason for him to be here.

She waited for the fear to kick in. The terror at having her worst nightmare come true. This was it. Seth had found her. He'd sent someone to bring her back to him. He intended to claim her as he'd promised.

But as the wall clock behind the Fallen One ticked off the seconds, only a flat, cold calm settled over her. This might be it, but damned if she couldn't summon so much as a whisper of hysteria. Too much had happened in the last day. The uniforms, Nina, Jen. She had nothing left. No reaction. No energy to care.

She studied her uninvited guest, meeting his gaze with an assessing one of her own. Well. If she couldn't escape him, and she wasn't going to fold in on herself, only one option remained. She raised her glass.

"Drink?" she inquired.

The Fallen One crossed his arms and rested a shoulder against the window frame. He surveyed her with a mix of annoyance and interest. "That's it? An angel appears to you, and all you do is offer him a drink?"

She moved the glass in a half-hearted wave of dismissal. "Sorry if my lack of shrieking offends you. It's been a week from Hell, and I seem to be fresh out of hysterics."

Her visitor scowled, and she swallowed a snort. Had she really just apologized to a Fallen One? And referred to her week as one from Hell? *Maybe you're losing it after all, Jarvis. Christ, maybe you've already lost it.*

She pinched the bridge of her nose. Too bad immortality couldn't make her immune to headaches.

"Do you not want to know why I'm here?" Irritation threaded the Fallen's voice.

"I'm pretty sure I already do." She downed her drink and reached for the bottle. She looked askance at her guest.

"No," he said. "Thank you."

She sloshed more liquid into her glass, then slipped the boots from her feet and leaned back again. Time to get down to it. She closed her eyes, inhaled, exhaled.

"So," she said. "I was right to think he'd come after me."

"You *knew* Samael would send for you?"

Samael? Alex cracked open one eye, a ripple of interest disturbing her calm. "Who the Hell is Samael?"

"He *was* Lucifer's right hand." The angel shrugged. "Presumably he's now Seth's."

That made her open the other eye. She studied him, noting again the air of neglect. The shabbiness. "You don't know?"

"I'm not from Hell."

"Well, you're certainly not from Heaven."

Disheveled wings gave an irritated shake. "And you're an expert on angels and Fallen, are you?"

She ran fingers through her hair. They snagged on a dried bit of something, and with a shudder, she dropped her hand to her lap. Damn, she needed a shower. She scowled at the Fallen One. "Wherever you're from and whoever sent you doesn't matter, does it? You're still here to take me to Seth."

Genuine surprise flickered in the zircon-blue eyes. "What in all of Creation would Seth want with a Naph—"

He broke off. Stared. Then he rubbed the back of one hand along his jaw. Slowly. Thoughtfully. "I'll be damned. You're *that* Naphil? The one who struck down the Appointed with an Archangel's sword?"

He hadn't known? Then why was he here? Why had this Samael sent him?

"I asked you a question." The Fallen's gaze took on a dangerous glint.

Alex's muscles tensed. Regardless of who'd sent him, if he had connections to Hell, he might not react well to knowing she'd tried to kill their precious Appointed. An insidious whisper filtered into her mind: *Maybe if you tell him, he'll kill you instead of taking you back there. Maybe you won't have to live for an etern—*

Cruel fingers sank into her shoulders and yarded her to her feet. The Fallen One shook her with a force that snapped her head back. Pain streaked through her skull, and the glass of Scotch flew from her grasp.

"Answer me, Naphil!"

Fear flared, driving a response past her lips.

"Yes! Yes, I'm the one with the sword."

"How? No human can wield the sword of an Archangel."

"I don't know. He—Aramael gave it to me. He was dying. I had no choice but to use it."

Another shake, another jolt of pain. "You're lying. Aramael was a Power, not an Archangel."

"He was promoted. After Heaven found out Caim's murder wasn't really his fault, that Mittron planned the whole—"

This shake made her teeth slam together.

"*Mittron*?" His breath scorched her cheek and spittle sprayed her lips. He shook her again. "You know about Mittron? Where is he?"

Alex twisted against his hold, but he paid no attention. "I don't know. He disappeared from his cell after he attacked me and—"

"What cell?"

Shake. Alex's head swam. An unexpected and very human instinct for survival struggled to the surface, surprising her with its strength. She shoved against the Fallen's chest.

"Stop it! I can't think when you're shaking me, and I won't be able to talk at all if I pass out."

The Fallen's hold tightened for a second, then he thrust her away, watching as she toppled to the floor and sprawled at his feet.

"Everything," he said though clenched teeth, towering over her. "I want to know everything you know about him."

FIFTEEN

"It didn't go well," Verchiel said. A statement, not a question.

Mika'el dropped into the wingback chair in front of the Highest Seraph's desk. Bracing an elbow on the padded arm, he rubbed his hand over his temple and along his jaw, then rested his cheek against his fist. Creation help him if he didn't feel more tired after a three-minute encounter with Alexandra Jarvis than he did after a full day of battle with the Fallen.

"No," he growled. "It didn't."

"She refused?"

"She didn't give me the chance to ask." He shook his head, knuckles digging into his cheekbone. "She's beyond reach, Verchiel, and well beyond any inclination to help us. Seth may have made her immortal, but she still has the fragile mind of a human, and too much has happened to her at the hands of the divine."

Verchiel's lips tightened. "More than you know,"

she said, sliding a sheet of parchment across the desk. "Our timing may have been somewhat poor."

Mika'el stared at the buff-colored sheet for a second before he took it. He scanned the spidery scrawl of a Principality's incident report, destined for the Archives. His blood turned cold. "Her *sister?*"

"Half an hour before you got there."

"Bloody *Hell*, Seraph—you couldn't have found this out *before* I barged into that hospital room? No wonder she reacted as she did. How did we not know this?"

"Internal communications aren't what they used to be. We're doing our best, but with so many at the front..." Verchiel shrugged. "Some things are bound to fall through the cracks."

Mika'el resisted the urge to crumple the sheep of paper and hurl it across the room. Or to burn it right in his grasp. He dropped it onto the desk instead, then raked his fingers through his hair. He wanted to rail against the Highest for allowing such an error, but in all good conscience, he could not. Not when he knew she spoke the truth. And not when internal communications wasn't the only branch to show signs of slipping. Gardens went untended and hallways unswept; books in the library had remained unshelved for more than two weeks. With all but a handful of angels on the front line, the entire realm wore an air of neglect.

It was one more irritation that sat like a grain of sand in his shoe.

He leaned his head back against the chair and closed his eyes.

Verchiel cleared her throat. "What do we do next?"

"Honestly?" he asked wearily. "I have no idea."

He sensed her startlement and waited for the objection he knew hovered on her lips. The building's emptiness closed in on him.

The Highest Seraph rose from behind her desk with a rustle of robes. He listened to her cross the office and heard the quiet click of the door closing. For a moment, he thought she'd left. A part of him wouldn't have blamed her. But the swish of fabric heralded her return to the desk.

"I don't think I can keep this up, Mika'el. Not without someone to lead us. Not without hope."

The weight across Mika'el's shoulders bore down another notch.

"Well, you'll have to, Verchiel, because I sure as Hell can't do it alone."

Hands slammed onto the desktop with a crack of sound that made his eyes snap open. He found the Highest Seraph scowling—actually *scowling*—at him, her pale blue eyes crackling with fire. She leaned forward.

"When," she demanded, "will you get it through your obstinate head that we cannot do this together, either? We've tried, Mika'el. Damn it, we've tried everything, and still the realm crumbles around us. Without a god to rule it, Heaven is lost. *We* are lost."

Mika'el pushed out of the chair. Fingers locked behind his aching head, he paced the open floor between Verchiel's desk and the bookcases lining one side of the room. The idea he'd been wrestling with since he'd looked into Alexandra Jarvis's torment crept back into his mind, dark and forbidden.

Ice brushed against his soul. What he thought... what he considered...

He flexed his tightly folded wings and spun to face

the Highest.

"I'll talk to Alex again."

Verchiel frowned. "You said she's beyond reach."

"She is. In her current state."

The Highest's slow blink devolved into a gape as she registered his intent. "You would interfere with a mortal? You can't be serious."

"Alexandra Jarvis isn't mortal anymore."

"That's semantics, and you know it. Regardless of what Seth did to her, she is still human, and the Cardinal Rule—"

"The Cardinal Rule isn't going to find Emmanuelle."

"Think about what you're suggesting, Mika'el. The One—"

"The One is *gone*, Verchiel." The words came out harsher than they needed to. Harsher than he'd intended. Mika'el swung away from the startled disbelief in the Highest's gaze, the accusation. He slammed a hand against the window frame, splintering the wood, struggling to contain the fear-laced fury coursing through him.

He knew the risks. Knew that Heaven itself might deny his return if he broke the most sacred of the One's laws. He sure as Hell didn't need a Seraph lecturing him about it—any more than any of them needed to be faced with this decision in the first place. Flexing wings that ached with the need to unfurl, he turned back to Verchiel.

"The One is gone," he repeated. "And you're right. You've been right all along. We cannot do this on our own. We need Emmanuelle, and so I will do whatever it takes to get her."

"Within the *laws*, Mika'el."

"No, Highest. Not within the laws. If we're going

to save Heaven, save the world, I cannot be bound by laws."

Silence sat like a great chasm between them, a chasm between him and the rest of his kind. Between him and the Heaven that might not be able to welcome him back.

But at a least Heaven that would still exist.

He hoped.

SIXTEEN

Alex squeezed her eyes closed, gathering the thoughts scattered about her brain after the violent shaking, trying to make sense of the Fallen's appearance in her living room and his intense interest in the angel responsible for her involvement in the affairs of Heaven. Still seated on the floor, she scooped back the tumble of her hair and peered up at her attacker.

"You knew Mittron?"

Cold fire glowed in the blue eyes. "I'm asking the questions, not you."

"And I'm trying to figure out what I know that might be important."

"All of it," he snarled. "It's all important."

"Maybe. But it will make more sense if I can put it into context. It's what I do."

The Fallen frowned. Alex struggled to her feet and sagged onto the arm of the sofa. She ignored the shakiness of her limbs, the quiver in her belly.

"I'm a police officer," she explained. "An investigator. I might be able to help you put the pieces together, but only if I know what those pieces are."

Her attacker's frown became a glower, and she steeled herself against a flinch as his hands curled into fists by his sides. He didn't move against her, however, and so she waited—and watched—while he considered her words. At last he gave a grunt and a short, sharp nod of tacit agreement.

"I am Bethiel," he said. "Of the Principalities, keepers of the records of Heaven and Earth. A long time ago, I discovered evidence that someone plotted against Heaven. I suspected it was Mittron, but I wasn't sure until I confronted him. He forced me—"

Bethiel looked away and swallowed hard, convulsively. A half-dozen emotions flitted across his face: hatred, fury, contempt.

And a hollow, haunted fear that sent a chill down Alex's spine.

"He forced me into Limbo," he finished, his voice harsh.

"When?"

"Three thousand years ago."

"So you knew about Aramael and me."

"If you were the soulmate Mittron arranged, yes."

"Am." Alex's voice was husky. "I *am* the soulmate. Apparently it's not something that goes away. Not even when one of you dies."

If Bethiel felt any sympathy, he didn't show it.

"Mittron," he repeated. "Tell me about his imprisonment."

"He attacked me in an alley. He was trying to provoke Aramael into killing him, but it didn't work. He was taken into custody—"

"*Human* custody? Impossible."

She shook her head. "He didn't have his powers—or his wings. And he was completely baked."

"Baked?"

"Stoned. On drugs." She grimaced. "If it makes you feel any better, I don't think he has a good life."

"It doesn't," he growled. He paced the living room, wings twitching irritably. "If he is without powers, how did he escape?"

"We don't know." Alex took a deep breath. "But a black feather was found in the cell."

Her would-be attacker spun on one heel to face her. "An Archangel took him?"

"Not one of Heaven."

Bethiel's eyes narrowed.

"Samael." Part hiss, part snarl.

He resumed his pacing. Alex stood and edged away until the length of the sofa stood between them. A lamp parted company with an end table in the wake of his wings, landing with a resounding crash and scattering chunks of ceramic across the parquet floor. Alex flinched. Bethiel kicked aside the lampshade.

"Why?" he muttered. "What need could Samael have of him? Where would he take him?"

He didn't ask the questions of Alex, but her mind turned them over anyway. Sluggishly, reluctantly. She didn't want to get involved in Heaven's mess again. She'd turned away Michael himself to avoid it. But her visitor raised questions that, as traumatized as it might be after the day's events, her cop brain just couldn't shut out. Why *had* Hell wanted Mittron? What could he do for them?

"Wait," she said. "You said you were in Limbo?"

"For three millennia. Behind gates that could

only be opened by the One or Heaven's—" He went still, and something dark and ugly shadowed his expression. "*Mittron*."

Alex's brain worked furiously now. Samael, Hell, Mittron, Limbo. If Hell had wanted to beef up its ranks, what better way than to reclaim those of their kin who had been imprisoned? She shivered.

Did Michael know? Is that why—?

No. It couldn't have been that, because she could no more influence the war between the angels and the Fallen than she could sprout her own wings. And it didn't matter anyway, because her job was—

Her brain shied violently sideways.

Choices.

She looked over at Bethiel. "Could Samael have taken him to Hell? Could Mittron survive there without his powers?"

Will I?

"Survive, yes," Bethiel responded, "but it's unlikely he's there. There would be talk."

"Then he's still on Earth."

Bethiel narrowed his eyes. "You know something."

"No, but I might be able to help find him."

"How can a human help find an angel?"

"When we arrested Mittron, he was entered into the system."

Bethiel looked uncomprehending.

"Computers."

"I've been absent from the universe for three millennia," he reminded her.

She waved an impatient hand. "Machines that communicate with one another and store all our records."

"Your archives?"

That would have to do.

"Kind of, yes. The important thing is, it means he's on record. I can put out an international alert for him, and if he's spotted anywhere we have an extradition agreement with, he'll be taken into custody and held for me. There are no guarantees, but it gives us a chance."

"And why would you want to help me?"

She gave a bitter laugh. "Why wouldn't I? My soulmate is dead, my sister witnessed Lucifer's rape of her daughter, my niece will die giving birth to the child of that rape, humanity is on the verge of Armageddon, and Mittron—" Alex lifted her chin and met the feral gleam in Bethiel's gaze. "Mittron is responsible for all of it."

Bethiel made another slow tour of the room's perimeter.

"How long will it take you to find him?" he asked.

"I don't know. Weeks, months...maybe never. All I can do is try. If..."

"If?"

She took a deep breath. Maybe, just maybe, she could avoid the only fate worse than spending eternity alone. "If you don't take me to Seth."

"You misunderstand, Naphil." Bethiel regarded her with detachment and—amusement? "I'm not here to retrieve you."

"You're not?"

"Samael wants you dead."

She blinked. "I...what? Why?"

"He didn't say."

He looked like an angel holding something back. Alex frowned.

"But?" she prompted.

"But there are rumors about the Appointed refusing to take his father's place unless the Naphil who injured him is returned to his side. They say he's even more obsessed with you than Lucifer was with the One, and there's talk of revolt if Hell doesn't have a leader soon," Bethiel said. "I think Samael views you as a distraction best removed."

Dead. Her life over. An eternity of memories and loss, an eternity spent in Hell, at Seth's side—gone. Fierce hope soared in Alex's breast, tangled with unexpected sadness, and became a jumbled mess of feelings she couldn't identify. Didn't want to identify. She struggled to rise above the conflict, to find again the objectivity that was fast becoming her anchor.

"How many?" she asked. "How many of you did he send?"

"Only me. But if I don't deliver, he'll send someone else. And if you're right about Seth wanting you retrieved..."

He trailed off, but Alex didn't need him to finish. She could more than fill in the blanks for herself. Others would be coming for her, some sent by Samael, some by Seth. None stopping until they found her.

"You'll need protection," Bethiel said.

"Against Seth and Samael and an army of Fallen. You're kidding, right?" She would have laughed, but something in Bethiel's expression stopped her. "Wait...you?"

"Unless you have another angel at your beck and call."

In a heartbeat, she was back in the wreckage of her old office, holding her dying soulmate in her arms, calling for the Archangel Michael's help, achieving the impossible. But Michael had responded for Aramael's sake, not hers, and he would certainly never respond again after the scene at the hospital. Alex tightened her hold on herself and shook her head in response to Bethiel's sarcasm.

"Then I will conceal you from the Fallen for as long as I'm able," he announced. "In exchange, you will find Mittron. Agreed?"

"On two conditions." She lifted her chin. "I need your help finding someone, too."

"You are hardly in a position to demand conditions, but I've heard about your niece. I assume she's the one you wish to locate?"

Alex nodded, blinking back the prickle of hope behind her eyes.

"What is the second condition?" Bethiel asked.

"If we find Mittron before Seth finds me..." Alex closed her eyes and stared into the hollowness she had become, seeking...what? A way out? Something to change her mind? But there was nothing. Nothing except that single word perpetually reverberating in her core.

Choices.

Without flinching, she met the zircon gaze and voiced the thought whispering through her.

"I want you finish what Samael sent you to do."

SEVENTEEN

Bethiel gaped at her. "You *want* me to kill you?"

Alex walked—no, jittered—to the coffee table where she'd left the bottle of Scotch. She picked her glass up from the floor where it had rolled, poured yet another drink, and balefully eyed the two-thirds empty bottle as she set it on the table again. The adrenaline rush of Bethiel's visit had erased the alcohol's effects, putting her right back to square one. Drinking herself to sleep became more expensive by the day.

She looked up to meet the not-quite-Fallen One's zircon gaze. "Yes," she said.

The exiled angel's brow furrowed. "You're serious. You want to die."

Alex gave a short, humorless bark of laughter. "I don't *want* any of this. But if I have to choose between death and whatever Hell Seth has sentenced me to, then yes." She took a deep breath. "I want to die."

"You cared for him once."

A small, hard ache formed beneath her ribs. She turned away from it.

"I cared for what he was," she said. "What he could have been. Not what he's become."

Bethiel held her gaze for a long, silent moment, and then he looked out the window beside him, his expression flat. Unreadable.

"You ask a great deal of me," he said finally. "I never intended to carry out Samael's instructions."

"But you came here—"

"To find out what he was up to. Why he had it in for a mortal. But not to kill. Three thousand years in Limbo may have had its impact on me, Naphil, but my loyalty to the One has never wavered. Not once. I will not murder."

The despair she'd expected earlier gripped her at last, snuffing out the tiny spark of hope that had sprung up in her heart. She fought back the desire to curl into a fetal position in a corner somewhere. Made herself breathe in, out, in.

This. This was why she hadn't let herself think about Seth, or what he'd done to her, or how she would never escape. Goddamn it to *Hell*, there had to be some way to convince Bethiel.

She drained the glass and blinked back tears not entirely caused by the burn of alcohol. "What about Mittron?"

"Mittron deserves no such loyalty."

"So you'll kill him."

"I will."

"Isn't that still murder?"

Bethiel didn't respond. Alex closed her eyes, willing him to agree. To see that this would be the compassionate thing to do, that it would be her one chance to be free of Seth, free of an eternity of loss and anguish and—

"Very well."

Her eyes shot open. She had to swallow twice before she found enough voice to whisper, "You'll do it? You'll..."

Kill me? Despite the desire, the words still stuck in her throat. But Bethiel nodded anyway.

"I will end your life," he agreed.

"Like fucking *Hell* you will," a new voice snarled.

In the space of Alex's single, startled inhale, massive black wings unfurled between her and Bethiel with a thunderous crack, overturning the coffee table and smashing through the drywall between the living room and hallway. The bottle of Scotch flew across the room to shatter a framed picture of Jen and Nina before dropping to the floor in a shower of glass and liquid.

And a sword left its sheath with the unmistakable hiss of metal against hardened leather.

"Michael, no!" Alex launched herself at the Archangel, catching his sword-arm in mid air. The force of his swing hurled her over the couch and into the wall. She landed with a grunt and the audible snap of at least one rib. A streak of pain lanced through her, but she fought past it and scrambled to her feet. As the Archangel recovered from her interference and swung again, she threw herself in front of Bethiel.

The sword's blade stopped against the side of her neck.

Shocked silence filled the room. No one moved. A trickle of warmth made its way down Alex's neck and over her collarbone. Slowly, not daring to even breathe, she raised her eyes to Michael's. The stunned emerald gaze impaled her. She cowered from the gathering fury there but held her ground. At last, his face a hardened mask of control, Michael moved the blade from her skin and lowered it. He didn't, however, return it to its sheath.

"Talk," he growled. His gaze flicked past her shoulder to the angel radiating heat at her back. "Not you. Her."

Alex held up a hand for time. She took a deep breath for the sake of her oxygen-starved brain. Her ribs screamed instant disapproval, and she grunted at the error. Holy hell, she hoped broken bones healed as quickly as sliced skin. Speaking of which—she pressed her free hand to the side of her neck to stanch the trickle that had become a flow when Michael withdrew the sword. Blood seeped between shaking fingers. Michael's jaw flexed.

Alex spoke before he decided to take another swing at Bethiel. "He came to help."

"By threatening to end your life?" Savage eyes narrowed on the other angel. "Not helpful."

"Samael sent him."

Michael's gaze snapped back to her. "Samael! Why?"

"Because Seth—" Alex looked away and swallowed. She focused on the shattered picture hanging askew on the wall, splinters of glass disfiguring her sister's face. "Seth wants me back. With him. In Hell."

The clock on the wall ticked into Michael's lack of response. Bethiel's wings rustled as he shifted. From the corner of her eye, Alex saw Michael's sword-tip drop to the ground.

"Explain," he ordered. This time he spoke to Bethiel. "And I suggest you start with who you are."

EIGHTEEN

In the silence following Bethiel's departure, Mika'el joined Alex in the tiny kitchen, flexing wings that ached to be unfurled, to launch him away from there, away from what he had come to do. What no angel should ever do.

"You sent him away." Accusation rang in Alex's voice. She didn't turn around.

Mika'el studied her back, rigid and unyielding, screaming defensiveness and hurt and fear...and a thousand other emotions he couldn't begin to untangle. Knowledge of her pain sat cold and heavy in his own heart. He might have lived among humans for the better part of six millennia, but he doubted that twice that time could have prepared him to take on the chaos churning inside this woman. So much was broken in her, so much more than he'd thought, he didn't know where to begin.

He cleared his throat.

"He can't protect you," he said. "Not from Seth."

Alex's entire body flinched, folding in on itself for a moment before she stood tall again. She sent a look of pure dislike over her shoulder. She wasn't going to make this easy.

"Well, he sure as Hell can't now." She slammed a mug onto the counter and reached for the pot of coffee.

"I needed to speak with you. Alone."

"And you don't trust him."

There was no point to disagreeing.

"No," he said simply. "Bethiel may have been loyal to the One at one time, and I'm sure he would like to think he still is, but Limbo isn't a pleasant place. It does things to an angel's mind, and he spent three thousand years there."

"Well, I do trust him. And I want him back."

Belligerence underlined her words, defiance her tone. They both knew why she wanted to continue her association with the exiled Bethiel, and under the circumstances, Mika'el didn't blame her for seeing death as her most attractive option. But neither could he let it happen. Not when his purpose was to protect life.

Precious seconds ticked by. Mika'el strived again to find the words he needed. The words Alex needed. As long as there remained the barest thread of chance he might elicit her voluntary compliance, he had to try. For both their sakes. He sighed.

"Bethiel can't protect you," he said, his voice flat, "but I can."

"Your protection in exchange for my help? Times must be tougher than I thought if Heaven has resorted to blackmail."

Filled mug in hand, Alex turned to face him. The wound on her throat from his sword had already healed, but her free hand went to the ribs he knew she had broken. He sensed their ache, along with that of the heart they sheltered.

Mika'el slid his hands into his pockets and leaned a shoulder against the doorframe. He saw no point in wasting time. "Heaven is losing."

Mug halfway to her lips, Alex stared at him. She blinked.

"Losing," she echoed. "As in...?"

"As in Hell is winning, and if I don't find a way to change that, the entire universe, your realm and mine, angels and humanity alike, will fall to Seth."

Coffee sloshed dangerously near the rim of the cup she held. Haggard, haunted eyes met his. "I can't...I don't..."

Mika'el's heart twisted.

So broken.

She clamped her lips together and inhaled deeply through her nose. Exhaled. Inhaled again. Then, "How?" she asked.

"You know that one-third of the angel host fell with Lucifer."

"Ara—" She bit down on her soulmate's name, grief contorting her mouth. "Yes. I know that much."

"Their choices pitted them against those who remained loyal to the One. Their own kin. Husband against wife, mother against son, brother against sister. The pain of having to fight those we loved..." Mika'el paused, remembering the agony that had filled Heaven in that dark time, feeling again the One's own despair. He shook off the memory of his parting from her and returned to his story. "The One offered the angels a Cleanse. An erasure of the memories of soulmates and families, a lifting of their free will.

Her intention was that they would no longer need to choose between her and the ones they loved. No more regrets, no more pain."

Alex's gaze flickered. "But?"

"With no will of their own, they became dependent on hers, and now that she's gone, they have nothing driving them anymore. Nothing to fight for. They're lost, and they're losing, and I can't help them. Heaven needs a leader, Alex, and I'm not it."

The coffee cup dropped to the floor, shattering in a spray of liquid and ceramic shards that shot across the room. The color drained from Alex's face, leaving lake-blue eyes adrift against skin the color of paper. Bloodless lips parted but made no sound. And what little had been left of the broken woman began to crumble away.

In an instant, Mika'el realized his error. He lunged across the room and seized her shoulders. Shook her. "Damn it, Alex, no. That's not what I meant. Not Seth. Did you hear me? *Not Seth.*"

Shock-glazed eyes slid past his, unfocused. Unable to focus. Bloody *fucking* Hell. He thrust her onto a chair and knelt before her, taking limp hands in his. The cold of her touch knifed to his core. He was losing her.

"Did you hear me? I'm not asking you to find Seth. This isn't about him, it's about his sister. Emmanuelle." He shook her, not as gently as he might have done, desperate to stop her disintegration before she was beyond even an Archangel's reach. He gathered himself, reaching inward, preparing to chance his connection to Heaven itself. Hoping against hope itself that the Cardinal Rule would not apply where a Naphil was concerned. That if it did, the risk would at least be worth it.

He took a deep breath.

Concentrated his entire being on the woman seated before him.

"Seth has a sister?" Alex croaked.

BETHIEL STOOD on the sidewalk below the Naphil's apartment, staring up at the single square of light in the otherwise dark building. The Archangel Mika'el had lost none of his highhandedness over the course of the millennia. None of his autocracy. Arriving the way he had, in the middle of what had been a private negotiation, taking over as if Bethiel's wants and needs were of no consequence. The Archangel had simply assumed Bethiel would agree and fall in with his wishes, that he would comply without argument.

As he would have done at one time. Before Limbo twisted him up inside so that he barely recognized himself anymore. Bethiel passed a shaking hand across his brow. Three thousand years of plotting Mittron's downfall warred with an almost, but not quite, lost loyalty to Heaven. To the One who was no more. To the warrior who fought on in her name.

Mika'el was right that events had grown beyond simple revenge. On a higher level of himself, Bethiel knew that. He even wanted to be a part of it: to do as the Archangel asked, and help in the search for Emmanuelle, the fight against the Fallen, the fight to save humanity. He wanted it badly.

But not entirely.

Because one way or another, the orchestrator of this whole fucking mess still had to pay.

And Bethiel still intended to make him.

NINETEEN

"Let me make sure I have this straight," Alex said. "In five thousand years, all of Heaven hasn't been able to find Emmanuelle, but you think I can. How?"

They sat at the dining room table, she and Michael, the stench of spilled Scotch wafting between them. Michael leaned forward in his chair, elbows resting on knees, fingers clasped.

"Verchiel—Heaven's executive administrator— has pointed out to me that you have connections we don't," he said. "Humanity's technology can take a search global, and you're our fastest way to access that capacity."

Heaven had an executive administrator? Why did that not surprise her? No wonder human bureaucracy was so entrenched.

"But you have a whole network of Guardians. Surely they'd be more effective than our technology."

"Normally, yes."

Alex raised an eyebrow at his reticence. "But not in this instance?"

"Not if she isn't in the company of humans who have Guardians, no."

*Not in the company of...*the breath whooshed from Alex. "But the only humans who don't have Guardians are the descendants of the Nephilim," she said slowly. "Like me. Either that or they've—"

"Turned their backs on their Guardians," Michael finished. "Yes."

Alex's back stiffened, and she narrowed her eyes. "Criminals turn their backs on their Guardians, Michael. People who have made really, really bad decisions in their lives. Repeatedly."

"Yes."

The wall clock ticked into the long silence that followed. Just past four a.m. A mere eight hours since Jen had died. An hour since Bethiel's appearance in Alex's apartment. A half hour since Michael nearly sliced off her head. Balefully, she eyed the remains of the Scotch bottle littering the living room floor.

"You're serious," she said, determined to focus on one crisis at a time. "You really mean to put her in charge."

"I can't *put* her anywhere," Michael replied, "any more than I can force Seth to stay where he is right now. All I can do is ask her, and hope she agrees."

"And if she does? How can you possibly think this will go well? She's hanging out with mortals who have turned their backs on anything to do with Heaven, Michael. On morality itself. Does that not tell you anything?"

A muscle flickered at the side of Michael's jaw. "It tells me she doesn't want to be found."

Alex threw her arms wide. "And *that* should tell you something, too."

"It does." Emerald eyes scowled at her. "It tells me I need your help to find her."

She stared at him for a moment, then shoved back her chair and stood. Hands on hips, she paced the floor, everything cop in her bristling with warning. Was Heaven that desperate? Had it really come down to pitting brother in Hell against sister who might very well belong in the same place? She glanced over her shoulder at the whiteness of Michael's knuckles, the rigidity of the wings at his back.

"You're certain about this."

"I'm certain we have no choice but to try."

She stopped at the living room window. Outside, snow fell heavily into the city night, shrouding the cars parked below, muting the street lights. Heaven losing to Hell, a Nephilim army poised on the fringes of humanity, Seth waiting to reclaim her. She blew out a long, slow breath. What more could go wrong... right? She swung to face Michael, still at the table.

"And you're sure she's here? There's no chance she might be—?"

"Dead? No. That we would have known."

The flat note in his voice piqued her curiosity, but he didn't give her a chance to pursue it.

"Well?" he asked. "Is Verchiel right? Can you help us find her?"

His earlier words hung in the air between them, both a promise and a threat. *"Bethiel can't protect you, but I can."*

She thought about refusing. Thought about telling him what he could do with his offer. Then she thought about Jen's daughter, still somewhere out there on the winter streets.

"*Let her go*," Jen's voice whispered in her ear.

Never, Alex responded. She straightened her shoulders.

"Right. What do we have to go on?" she asked. "It's not likely she'll be using her own name."

"She will," Michael said. "It's her only connection to our realm, and she'll have had no reason to change it."

"Apart from not wanting to be found."

"Only humans have the means to track her through a name, and she'll have had no reason to expect us to work with you."

"No reason to expect such interference, you mean?" Alex inquired tartly.

Michael regarded her without answer. She sighed.

"Fine. We have a name and a description. It's not much, but it's a start. I'll get my coat."

"What about sleep?"

Standing up from the table, she pointed at the smashed bottle in the living room.

"Can't," she said, attempting to convey humor with a twist of her mouth. Suspecting she failed. "I've run out of sleeping potion."

Emerald eyes narrowed. Glittered. "That's how you've been getting to sleep? For how long?"

Heat crept into her cheeks, and she turned away. "None of your—"

"How long, Alex?" Michael's hand closed over her arm, his hold as gentle as it was unbreakable.

Alex stared down at his fingers, then raised her gaze to his. "Since that night," she said.

"Dreams?"

"You have no idea."

"That"—he pointed at the broken remnants of the

Scotch bottle—"isn't the answer."

"Why? Because it isn't healthy?" She gave a hard laugh and pulled away. "The way I understand it, that's no longer a problem."

"I can help," said Michael.

She started down the hallway to the closet. "Can you undo what's happened?"

"No, but—"

"Can you take away the memories?"

Silence.

"No," he said at last. "I'm sorry, but too much has happened."

"Then no, you can't help."

"I can—"

"Let it go, Michael." Taking her coat from its hanger, she turned to face him. "If you want my help finding Emmanuelle, then you need to let me do it my way, because I'm only just barely holding it together anymore, and I'm not sure how much longer I can keep doing so."

He regarded her, the impact of his gaze traveling all the way into the depths of her soul. Then he nodded. "All right. Your way. Except for one thing. We need to work from somewhere other than Toronto."

"No."

"You're too much of a targ—"

"I said *no*."

"If it's because of your niece—"

"It's not just about Nina. I have colleagues here. Friends. They need everybody they can get on the job. I won't leave them."

"You're just one person, Alex. Your presence here won't make a difference."

"I'm not leaving."

His mouth drawn tight, Michael shook his head. "You are hands down the most stubborn human I've ever met," he growled. "And that's not a compliment."

Before she could think of a response, he held out his right hand to her, and a familiar sword materialized in his grasp. Alex recoiled, shaking her head.

"I told you—"

"I know what you told me. And now I'm telling you. You're the one who insists on staying where you're most at risk. If more than one Fallen One comes for you, if anything happens and I can't be at your side every second of every day—"

"No." Alex waited for the knife in her chest to stop twisting. She closed her eyes again, but the image of Aramael's sword had burned itself into her brain. The memory of its feel into her palm. The sword of an Archangel. She'd held the weapon once before. Used it to stop Seth from killing her soulmate, but she'd been too late. Aramael had died anyway. There on the floor of the destroyed washroom, his blood mingling with Seth's in the water flooding across the tiles...

Michael took her hand in one of his. His thumb prised open her fist. He laid the sword in her palm, curled her fingers around its scabbard, held them there. "We need your help, Alex. And for that, we need you here, on Earth. Take the sword. Keep it with you. Please."

The sword tingled in her grasp, and faint electricity arced through her arm. Of their own accord, her fingers tightened, holding on with all their strength to the remnants of the connection she'd once had with her soulmate.

Aramael, her heart whispered. And then it wept.

TWENTY

Alex's cell phone vibrated at her waist as she and Michael stepped into the elevator in the parking garage below the building housing Homicide's office. She answered it without looking to see who called. She didn't care, because talking to anyone was better than the continued interminable silence between her and her self-appointed bodyguard.

"Jarvis," she said. She jabbed the button for the ninth floor.

"I heard about Jen." Hugh Henderson's gruff voice held bottomless compassion.

Alex waited a second for the vibration it set off in her to go away. It stayed. She sighed.

"I was going to call you this morning," she said. "When I got to the office."

Startled silence. The door slid closed.

"You're going to work? Is that wise?"

She flicked a look at Michael, his wings folded awkwardly to fit into the elevator. "Necessary."

"Alex, you just lost your—"

"Are you sitting down?"

A pause, and then the squeak of a chair came over the connection. "I am now."

"Michael is here." Green eyes sparked fire at her. She turned her back on them. "And so is someone named Bethiel."

"Um…"

"Seth wants me back, Hugh."

Silence—so long Alex thought the call had been dropped.

"Hugh?"

"Here," her Vancouver colleague said. "I'm here. And I'm coming out there. Today."

Yes, please.

"No." Alex closed her eyes against the wave of wanting to be held. Needing a friend. "Thank you, but no. There's nothing you can do for me, and I already have protection."

"This Bethiel character, or Michael?"

"Michael."

"Shit. I was afraid of that. Why? He doesn't do anything unless there's something in it for him. What does he want?"

The elevator chimed their arrival on the ninth floor, and the doors slid open. Two uniforms stood waiting to get on. Alex sidestepped them and started down the hallway.

"I just got into the office," she told Henderson. "I'll call you later and fill you in, but in the meantime, I'll be sending two BOLOs out to Interpol this morning. Keep an eye out for them and make sure they get circulated?"

The chances that either Mittron or Emmanuelle

might turn up in Vancouver were astronomically small at best, but it never hurt to ask.

"Of course," Hugh said. "Anything else? You sure you don't want me out there?"

Alex paused beside the door to Homicide. She examined the compartmentalization that had taken place in her brain, a trick she'd learned when she was nine and had come home from school to find her father dead on the kitchen floor and her mother dying in the hallway outside the dining room where their family had once shared their meals.

Jen was there now, too. In the same compartment as their parents. The same place as the rest of Alex's pain.

Alex's fingers tightened on the cell phone. She breathed in. Closed her mental door. Breathed out.

"I'm sure," she told Henderson. She ended the call and pointed at the coffee room across the hall. "Wait there," she told Michael.

When Michael looked like he might argue, she added, "Some of the people from the hosp—from last night might be here. They'll recognize you."

"I'll make sure they don't." He reached past her for the doorknob to Homicide.

Alex put her hand out, but drew back before it touched his. She'd had enough of touching angels in her lifetime.

"I'd still have to explain you," she said, "and I'd rather not. It's easier if you wait here."

"And I'd rather remain near you."

"Damn it, Michael—"

An unintelligible growl rumbled from his chest. "Fine. You have the picture of Emmanuelle I gave you? And the sword?"

She shifted against the chafe of the harness he'd

crafted for her. Aramael's sword nestled between her shoulder blades along the length of her spine. Michael had assured her it wasn't visible beneath her coat, but she wasn't convinced. Not when it made her walk like she had a stick up her—

"Yes to the first question, and you saw me put it on at the car to the second," she reminded him. "Though I still don't know what good it will do, because I have no idea how to use it in a fight."

"If you weren't so stubborn about remaining on the job here, I could teach you."

She opened her mouth, came up dry, and contented herself with a malevolent glare over her shoulder as she pushed into the office and closed the door in his face.

Greg Bastion looked up and sideways at her as she sidled past his desk to her own. He frowned. "You're not supposed to be here."

She reached to remove her coat, remembered the sword, and thought better of it. She perched on the edge of her chair, ramrod straight. The sword's hilt pressed between her shoulder blades. "Why not? Am I suspended?"

"No, but you should still be at home."

"I have paperwork." She switched on her computer.

Bastion stared at her as if she'd sprouted a second head. "Please tell me that's shock talking."

"I'm fine, Greg."

"Balls." Bastion lowered his voice. "You just lost your sister, for chrissakes, Alex. You're not *fine* and you sure as hell shouldn't be here doing *paperwork*. Go home. Call someone. Go get hammered."

She bit back an invitation for her colleague to mind his own business, reminding herself he meant well.

"It's seven o'clock in the morning," she pointed out instead, rummaging in her drawer for a pen.

"So add coffee," Bastion retorted. "Just go."

Taking a deep breath, Alex prepared to deliver a reassurance about her mental state. Then she noticed the surreptitious slide of Bastion's gaze toward Roberts's closed door. The blinds were down.

"He's in already?"

"Umm…"

Roberts was never in this early, and he only closed the blinds when he wanted something kept private. Alex looked askance at her colleague.

Bastion slumped in his chair. "We hoped you'd stay away," he muttered. "Roberts was trying to get rid of them for you. At least for a day or two."

Her gaze flicked back to her supervisor's office.

"Get rid of who—" The question died on her lips as the blinds opened and she met a familiar bespectacled gaze through the window. Stephane Boileau, aide to Canada's minister of public security, looked out, surveyed the office, and zeroed in on her. He stared, then lifted a hand, pointed at her, and beckoned. The headache she'd been fighting throbbed anew.

"Oh, hell," she muttered. "You have got to be kidding me."

"If you want to make a run for it, I can trip them," Bastion muttered.

Alex didn't think he was entirely joking. Everyone in the office knew of Boileau and his campaign to recruit her to his extraterrestrial cause in Ottawa. He'd called every day since the explosion on Parliament Hill, threatening, cajoling, promising, deaf to her increasingly irritated refusals—and to all suggestions that his E.T. theories were wrong. She'd stopped answering his calls three days ago, letting them go through to voice mail instead. But wait. Bastion had said…

She glanced at him. "Them?"

"He brought reinforcements."

Roberts's door opened, and their grim-faced staff inspector emerged. He caught Alex's eye and jerked his head in a come hither this instant gesture. Boileau stood in the center of the office behind him, a dark-suited man seated at his side, back turned to Alex.

Shit.

Maybe she should have let Michael come in with her after all. She might need him to hold her back from saying something stupid. Or doing something stupider.

She scowled.

"You think they came down here to escort you personally?" Bastion asked.

"I wouldn't doubt it."

"Will you go?"

"Not a chance."

Bastion grunted something that sounded vaguely approving. Then he reached over to squeeze her arm.

"Abrams was right, you know. We won't stop looking for her."

Across the office, Roberts cleared his throat. Alex stood up from her chair. She looked down into Bastion's compassionate eyes, but words of thanks, entirely inadequate, jammed in her throat. Pressing her lips together, she shook her head and clapped him on the shoulder instead. He gave her fingers a quick press in return.

"Go." He jerked his head toward their supervisor. "Take care of whatever that is, and then for chrissakes, go home."

"I will," she promised.

"What was that about?" Roberts asked as she approached.

"Nina." She saw no reason to hide the truth—at least, not that part of it.

"Ah." Her supervisor looked as if he might question further, but settled for, "You okay?"

She met his gaze squarely. "Honestly? No. But I'm still upright, so I figure that counts for something." She scooped back her hair and fished an elastic from her pocket. Her gaze went past him to the door he'd pulled closed. "Can't say I'm thrilled to see Boileau, however."

"I wasn't expecting you in."

"I have something I need to do."

Her staff inspector raised an eyebrow, but she didn't elaborate. She continued twisting her hair into a ponytail. Roberts sighed.

"Well, maybe it's best that you *are* here," he muttered. "You should probably see this for yourself."

See? Not hear?

Alex shot Roberts a quick, sidelong look, but he only stood aside and pushed open the door. After an instant's hesitation, she stepped into the office.

Stephane Boileau had taken a seat at Roberts's desk. His fingers paused in their dance across the computer keyboard as she entered, and his wire-framed gaze lifted from the monitor to stare at her. Roberts nudged her forward.

"Detective Jarvis, I believe you know Mr. Boileau from the minister of public security's office, and this is Mitchell Lang, deputy minister of national defense."

Lang, a heavier set man than Boileau, stood up from

his chair, his hand outstretched. "Detective Jarvis. A pleasure."

"You'll forgive me if I don't return the sentiment." Alex ignored his hand, crossing her arms and flicking a cold look at Boileau. "It's been a long day. Let's make this as short as possible, shall we? I'll start us off. I'm not going to Ottawa."

Boileau pushed back from Roberts's desk. "You don't even know what's happened yet."

"I don't care. It won't change anything. I'm not leaving Toronto, and I'm not chasing down your half-baked alien—"

"Alex." Roberts's voice stopped her.

She clamped an imaginary lid on the boil-over of impatience. Reminded herself she still wanted to work in this office. Made it as far as three in her count to ten.

"My apologies," she growled. "But I have work to do, so whatever it is you have to show me, let's get it over with."

Roberts cleared his throat behind her.

"Please," she added, rolling her eyes at him over her shoulder.

A somberness in her supervisor's expression pulled her up short and sent a trickle of ice water through her belly. She glanced back at the monitor on the desk. Foreboding crawled over her skin. Suddenly, she didn't think she wanted to see whatever Boileau had to show her. Roberts's hand settled onto her shoulder, urging her forward.

Behind the desk, Boileau stepped to one side, making room for her in silent invitation.

TWENTY-ONE

As Alex took up a position beside Stephane Boileau, the minister's aide leaned forward to draw the computer mouse nearer to him. He clicked on an icon in the bottom taskbar and a video image sprang up on the monitor, frozen on a dark, grainy image of trees.

"How familiar are you with the city of Pripyat?" he asked.

"I've never been, if that's what you mean. But I know it's the Ukrainian city that had to be evacuated when Chernobyl blew."

Boileau looked surprised. "Very good."

"I didn't realize there'd be a test," she retorted. "Shall I go study, or can we get to the point?"

Deputy Minister Lang moved to stand on her other side, hands in his pockets. He nodded at the screen. "About a week ago, satellite images showed unauthorized activity, but—"

"Define activity."

He frowned, obviously not a man used to being interrupted.

"People," he said. "A lot of them. The Ukraine government had been allowing tours into the area for the past few years on a small scale, but those were discontinued recently when radiation levels spiked."

"Spiked? Why?"

Lang and Boileau exchanged glances.

"We don't know," said Lang. "But, for the moment, no one is allowed within five kilometers of the city."

"Go on."

Boileau took over. "There were two satellites sending images of the area. We lost contact with both of them before we could take a closer look, so the Ukrainians sent in a drone."

Alex didn't think she liked the direction this seemed to be taking.

"The photos came back black," said Boileau. "No images whatsoever. Not even ghosts. Then the Ukrainian government sent in two fighter jets, but those had to turn around when their onboard computers went haywire. They didn't get close enough to see anything, either."

She definitely didn't like the direction this was taking. She stared at the frozen image on the screen and waited.

Beside her, Lang rocked back onto his heels. Forward onto the balls of his feet. Back again.

"Yesterday, the Ukrainians sent in a ground force to do reconnaissance," he said quietly. "An elite force. They shared this video with other governments this morning at four a.m. eastern time."

Roughly three hours ago. They would have had to haul the prime minister out of bed for that. The president of the U.S., too, no doubt. She herself had still been awake, of course, dealing with not one but two angels in her living room, instead of getting drunk as she'd planned. Or grieving the loss of her sister, as any normal human being would have done.

She flapped a hand at Boileau, and he clicked on the video's play arrow. The image on the computer screen began moving.

At first, Alex saw only trees, seemingly shot with a night-vision camera that was most likely attached to a helmet. Then a shape rose from the ground a few feet ahead of the soldier with the camera, green and ghostly, automatic weapon in hand, face concealed behind a full bio-hazard mask. A smattering of words was exchanged, low and rapid, unintelligible in their foreignness. Another masked green man joined the first. The image turned wobbly as the camera-wearing soldier began to move.

Tree trunks passed by on either side, branches slapping against the lens.

Hushed voices clipped short their words. Twigs snapped underfoot. An owl hooted.

A few hundred feet on, a short, sharp warning came, its tone of delivery recognizable in any language. More words. Shouted this time. Aggressive, challenging. The camera-wearing soldier lunged sideways, and the monitor darkened as a tree blocked the view.

Warning prickled across the back of Alex's neck.

Then another figure appeared: small, unmoving, devoid of the protective clothing worn by the soldiers... and glowing blue instead of green. Alex blinked. She'd worn night-vision gear on takedowns. She knew how the devices worked, knew that the phosphors glowed green and only green. So what the—

A second blue figure appeared behind the first, this one tall, brighter than the other—and winged. Alex inhaled sharply. The sound of automatic gunfire erupted from the computer speaker, and the monitor turned gray with static.

Then came the first scream...and the next...and the one after that. Screams that went on and on and on, ripped from the throats of some of the world's most highly trained men, until finally, blessedly, silence descended.

Alex tried to swallow. Her throat refused to cooperate. The screams of the men in the video clip reverberated in her brain.. Boileau reached out and pulled a USB key free of its computer port.

"How many?" Her voice was hoarse.

"Five teams of five men," said the deputy minister. "Given the outcome, the Ukrainians have requested international support."

"And you're telling me this because...?"

"There's more," Boileau said. He clicked on the Internet search tab and then began typing. "We've seen an unusual rise in travel to Ukraine over the last two days. Upwards of three hundred people have landed at the Boryspil and Gomel airports. On open-return tickets."

"How does that tie into the video?"

"Fifteen of those people have been detained trying to cross the perimeter into Pripyat. Three of them were Canadians. When we questioned them, they said they were responding to this."

Another click of the computer mouse. A website popped up on screen: a black background with a bold red header and small yellow print below. Not what one would call a professional design.

Alex scanned the header. "The end is here? There are dozens of sites claiming that right now."

"Hundreds," he agreed. "But only this one originates with the New Children of God."

"New—" Her gaze went back to the screen. New Children of God? She read the header again, then the yellow print beneath it. *Armageddon has begun, but there is hope! A new world order will rise from the ashes, led by the New Children of God, and a chosen few can still be saved. Are you one of them? Can you still find salvation? Eternal life? Email today for details and*—Alex stopped reading.

The travelers to Ukraine.

She closed her eyes against the roll of her stomach. Holy hell. The Fallen were advertising on the Internet for help—and humanity had responded. In all of the eternity she had to look forward to, she would never have seen that one coming.

"We've accessed the email records of the fifteen detainees," Lang said. "They were all in touch with whoever is running the site."

"And the IP address? Have you been able to track it?"

"We're still trying. It keeps changing."

"What exactly do you want from me?"

"The New Children of God," he said. "Can you confirm they're the missing children? The ones that disappeared after those bizarre pregnancies?"

"Confirm absolutely? No. But I can add my suspicions to yours." Strong suspicions. Given the Nephilim children's superhuman abilities, the abandoned city's ongoing radioactivity would likely have little to no effect on them. It would be the perfect holding place for Lucifer's army.

"And the winged alien we saw would be one of their protectors?"

Alien. Alex bit her lip against comment. She nodded. "Yes."

"Then we need you to help us get to the children."

She shot a look at Boileau.

"Deputy Minister Lang has read your file," the minister's aide said. "He knows your involvement."

The government had a file on her?

Of course the government had a file on her.

Crossing her arms, she leaned against the window ledge behind her. "And did you include in your file that I've already told you everything I know?"

Lang slid his hands into his pockets again. "Detective Jarvis, these aliens possess technology we're unfamiliar with—technology that's capable of knocking out our own. Satellites, cameras, computers. You've had the most contact with them. Seen their resources. If you can just describe to us—"

"Mr. Lang, you've either misread my file or been misinformed," Alex interrupted. "The only Fallen I've had any contact with were trying to kill me. Even if they did have the kind of resources you're talking about, I wouldn't have had time to notice. But they don't, because they don't need technology, because they're not aliens, they're—"

"Oh, for the love of God!" Boileau snapped. "Do you not realize we have a fucking nightmare in the making here?"

Her mouth still open to speak, Alex stared at him. Fury glared at her from behind the wire-framed glasses.

"Don't you get it, Detective? The entire world is on the brink of utter panic. If we're to have a hope in hell of maintaining control, we need people focused on a common goal, not some goddamned fairy tale."

Common...

Her head snapped around to Lang. "What common goal? You can't mean to try and attack the Fallen!"

The deputy minister shrugged. "Historically speaking, war is the single most powerful unifying event we can tap into. People still want to believe their governments. They *will* believe us if we stay smart and ask them to work together against the aliens."

"But you can't win against them. You saw what happened on that video! They'll wipe out anything— and *anyone*—you send after them." Alex looked to Staff Inspector Roberts for help, but he stood gray-faced and mute.

"In case it has escaped your notice, Detective"— Boileau waved a hand at the window—"half the bloody world is already at war. You've seen the news reports. There have been four military coups in the last week alone. Fatwas have been issued across the Middle East against Christian women of child-bearing age; pregnant women have been rounded up and detained in Saudi Arabia, Kazakhstan, Somalia, North Korea, and a dozen other countries you've probably never heard of. China is under martial law. Radical nationalism is at its highest point in Europe since the Nazis were in power. How much more *at war* do you need us to be?"

Alex swallowed. She hadn't known. Hadn't watched a news report since Nina had gone missing. Had been so focused—

But that was no excuse, because she should have expected it. Had known it was coming. She and Henderson had discussed this very scenario, the one where humanity would be the author of its own destruction.

She just hadn't thought it would happen this soon.

Let me at least find Nina first, she thought. *Let me bury Jen.*

"The world needs someone to take charge of this situation before it rips itself apart," Lang spoke again, "and before those children in Pripyat reach maturity. Have you seen the records of the ones we had a chance to study? Do you know what they're capable of? Babies that can control their caregivers' minds, break out of any locked room...if they're turned against us, if they're weaponized—" He broke off and shook his head. "God knows what they'll be capable of once they're grown."

She struggled to recover. To find the words to convince him. To stop what would only hasten the deaths of who knew how many.

"Please," she said. "Whatever you're planning, don't. You'll never get to those children. The Fallen can't be killed. Not by us."

"Everything can be killed," Boileau said. "You just need the right weapon."

She could do nothing more than gape at the sheer arrogance. Across from her, Lang's lips drew into a thin, tight line. He shook his head.

"Boileau tried to tell me about you," he said. Contempt laced his voice. "I didn't want to believe him, but you really are going to refuse to help, aren't you?"

Alex's headache throbbed behind her eyes. She didn't have the energy to argue anymore.

"Whatever," she said. She looked to her supervisor again. "Am I done here?"

Roberts tipped his head in the direction of the door, and she started toward it. Christ, she couldn't get out of here fast enou—

"I can have you detained, Detective," Boileau called. "I can *make* you help us."

She stopped. She swiveled, regarded him for a moment, and then, without speaking, calmly elevated the middle finger on each hand. Boileau's face turned the most interesting shade of scarlet she'd ever seen on a human. Lang scowled. Roberts pinched the bridge of his nose between thumb and forefinger, closed his eyes, and hung his head.

Alex stalked out and slammed the door.

TWENTY-TWO

Boileau and Lang left shortly after her own exit from Roberts's office. From behind a curtain of hair, Alex watched them wend their way between desks. She didn't lift her head to meet Boileau's malevolent glare. She'd already made her point. She did, however, exhale in relief when they reached the door.

The appearance of a black-winged man in their path turned the exhale into a choke.

She came up out of her chair, poised to—what, intervene? She subsided again. Maybe an up-close-and-personal encounter with one of their *aliens* was just what Lang and Boileau needed. Maybe—

Michael stepped aside, and the two men stalked past him, oblivious to the wings he kept hidden from the rest of the world. From everyone but lucky, lucky her.

The emerald gaze met hers. An imperious eyebrow lifted. *Are we done yet?* it asked. Her supervisor's voice cut her off mid head-shake.

"Jarvis!"

Alex sighed and raised a hand to Michael, flashing thumb and fingers at him twice. *Ten minutes.*

Michael regarded her without expression, then, ignoring her signal to wait outside, stepped into the Homicide office, closed the door, and leaned against the wall. At the desk beside Alex, Abrams frowned, glancing between them. Alex's jaw went tight.

Stubborn damned Archangel. If she ended up having to field a bunch of questions about who he was and what he was doing here—

"Jarvis!"

"Coming." Alex collected the papers she needed her supervisor to sign and turned her back on Michael. Roberts closed his office door behind her.

"I'm—" she began.

He cut her off with the lift of a hand. Pushing back his jacket to rest hands on hips, he walked to the window and stared out. Alex swallowed her apology and waited.

"Twenty-four hours," he said. "That's how long they've given you to look after your sister's details before you're expected in Ottawa."

Her mouth flapped twice before she found her voice. "You can't be serious."

"I'm deadly serious. And so are they." Roberts turned, his face haggard, his eyes weary.

Damn her quick temper to Hell. She should have kept her hand signals to herself.

Roberts shook his head. "They would have done the same thing even if you hadn't given them the finger," he said, reading her mind. "They're trying to do their jobs the same way we are."

She snorted. "I'm pretty sure Armageddon wasn't part of our job description when we signed on."

Her supervisor said nothing.

"Fine. We're all just doing our jobs," Alex growled. She dropped into one of the chairs before his desk. The sword's scabbard dug into her spine. "But attacking the Fallen isn't the answer, Staff, and neither is dragging me off to Ottawa."

"You saw the video, Alex. You know what they're capable of. We can't just sit back and—"

"Doug." She kept her voice deliberately gentle. She didn't need to be harsh. Didn't need to yell. The use of her supervisor's first name at work, within his office, was enough to stop him in his tracks.

Roberts's skin grayed. In silence, he pulled his chair out from the desk and lowered himself into it. Then he leaned as far back as it would permit.

"They're really..." His voice trailed off.

"That invincible?" she finished. "Yes. There's nothing we can do to get at those children. We're going to have to wait for them to come to us."

"And then what?"

I don't know.

She shrugged. "Whatever we can, I suppose. There are only eighty thousand of them, so as long as we—"

She broke off, clamping her lips together. *Only.* Did that word even apply when it referred to half-human, half-angel creatures with unknown superpowers and the potential to wipe out the planet?

"We can't panic," she finished lamely.

Roberts rested an elbow on the arm of his chair, fist against his mouth, clearly weighing whether he wanted to press for details. Just as clearly deciding he did not.

"I agree with the not panicking," he said at last. "That's why I think Lang and Boileau are right about not making it public knowledge."

"It's a little late for that, don't you think? There are hundreds of videos posted on the Internet of Seth's attack here. Half a dozen Archangels were caught in full flight, their wings as clear as day. How do we hide that?"

"We don't." He scrubbed a hand over his hair. "But we don't have to come straight out and admit we're up against honest-to-god angels, either. The extremists are already crawling out of the woodwork, Alex. Imagine what will happen if we provide official fuel for their fire."

"Are you saying you think Boileau and Lang are right? We should pretend they're aliens and start a war against them?"

"Go along with the alien thing, yes. Start another war, no." Roberts grimaced. "But I don't think we can prevent it from happening, either. There are too many Langs and Boileaus in the world. You can't stop them all."

A chill slithered down Alex's spine. War was so much bigger than she wanted to wrap her head around right now. She had enough to deal with. Nina, Jen, Bethiel, Michael, Mittron, Emmanuelle…

War was also what Lucifer had wanted humanity to do. What he'd predicted it *would* do. She hunched her shoulders. The sword shifted against her back.

"Whoever they send in against the Fallen will die, Staff. You know that."

A door slammed. A murmur of voices passed by Robert's office. Quiet fell. Alex's gaze strayed to the clock on the wall. It was just past eight. Twenty-seven hours since she'd found—and lost—Nina again, and already so much had happened. Changed.

Irrevocably altered.

"We can't save everyone."

Her gaze swiveled back to her staff inspector. "What?"

Bleak brown eyes met hers. "I said, we can't save everyone. If things are going to get as bad as we think, there will be casualties."

I know, she wanted to say, but the words stuck in her throat. She did know. She'd always known. But saying it aloud felt akin to giving up. Admitting defeat. Admitting this was real.

We can't save everyone. There will be casualties.

Alex clamped her hands together in her lap. Roberts was right. People were going to die. A lot of people, and they could do nothing to stop it. *She* could do nothing to stop it. The world had moved beyond mere conflict into something greater. Darker.

Armageddon wasn't just looming anymore. It was here. Now.

She looked up at her supervisor.

"What do you want to do?" she asked.

"What we've always done," her staff inspector said. "Solve murders, hold people who break the law accountable for their actions. Peacekeeping isn't going to start with Lang or Boileau; it's going to start with us. We're the front line in this, Alex, and our front line is here, in this city. You, on the other hand, are a whole other issue."

Her hand clenched over the papers she held. "I'm not going to Ottawa."

"And I won't tell you to. But Boileau was serious about the twenty-four hours. If you're still here at this time tomorrow, he'll have you detained."

"You're kicking me out?"

Roberts gave an impatient huff. "I'm telling you—for your own good and against every job imperative I have, I might add—to stay away from the office. Go to ground, at least for a few weeks. Boileau's bound to lose interest sooner or later, especially if they go ahead with whatever they have planned."

A few weeks. Did the world have that long?

"Staff—"

"Goddamn it, Jarvis, can you just once do what you're told without arguing? Go home. Bury your sister. Do whatever you have to do for Nina. But stay the hell away from the job."

Alex glared at her supervisor. He glared back, lines of worry carved around his eyes. She tried to care that he cared, but after seeing that video, an odd emptiness had formed at her center. A hardness. As if the caring had been drained right out of her. Not where Roberts and her colleagues were concerned—or the rest of the world, for that matter. She still cared a great deal about the survival of humanity. But when it came to herself?

She paused her thoughts, turned them inward, and took a long, hard look at her reality. Her cold, eternal,   no-matter-how-she-looked-at-it-she-was-screwed reality. So what if Boileau caught up to her? Chances were that Michael would just remove her from his custody anyway, because he wanted her to find Emmanuelle.

Or Bethiel would, because he wanted Mittron.

Or Seth would, because he wanted her.

What was the point of caring when her life didn't even belong to her anymore?

She stood and slid the papers across the desk toward Roberts. "I need these signed," she said.

Roberts studied the international intelligence alerts she would send out to Interpol, one for Mittron, no last name, and one for Emmanuelle, last name Batya. Daughter of God, Michael had said it meant when Alex asked. But she didn't think Roberts needed to know that.

Her supervisor took a pen from the cup on his desk and scrawled his signature across the bottom of each form. Then he put his hand over the documents.

"I'll enter them into the system myself," he said. "Go home."

Alex reached over and tugged the papers from his hold. She met his gaze calmly. "I will," she said. "In twenty-four hours."

She'd made it as far as opening the door when his voice stopped her, but not with the reprimand for insubordination she expected.

"Hold on," he said instead. "What the hell is that under your coat?"

Shit.

She looked over her shoulder. Her supervisor had one elbow on the desk, and his fingertips supported his right temple. Curiosity and wariness warred for top billing in his expression. Wariness won when she didn't reply.

He motioned for her to close the door again.

She held up the papers. "I really need to—"

"Detective Jarvis, do you still work here or not?"

Alex closed the door. She returned to stand before the desk, feeling remarkably like she'd been called before the principal.

"Well?"

She heaved a sigh and braced for the storm.

"It's a sword," she said.

"It's a *what*?"

Alex flinched from Roberts's raised voice. Her gaze flicked toward the windows, ensuring the blinds were fully closed. She shrugged out of her coat and turned so Roberts could see the scabbard at her back.

"A sword," she repeated. She let Roberts stare at it for a few seconds, then she reached over her shoulder and grasped the hilt. The blade left its hardened leather home with a slow, deadly hiss of sound. She laid it across her supervisor's desk.

Roberts's brown gaze lifted to hers. She watched disbelief struggle with outright shock. She held up a hand to ward off the questions gathering.

"Seth is coming after me again," she said.

More staring. More silence. Then a barely-there mutter. "Christ."

Alex slumped into a chair. God, it felt good not to sit up straight.

"You're sure?" Roberts asked.

She nodded, wondering how much she should tell him and how much she should hold back. She decided she didn't have much more to lose. Leaning forward, she set the papers he'd signed on the desk between them.

"These are in exchange for me remaining here for the moment. As long as I'm looking for them"—she tapped the papers—"I'll have protection. This"—she nodded at the sword—"is for backup."

"Fuck, Alex..." Her supervisor's voice trailed off. He looked away. "Fuck," he said again. "Does nothing in this goddamn world make sense anymore? Every time I think I'm getting my brain wrapped around what's happening, something else comes up. How the hell are you coping, never mind staying sane?"

She laughed. There was no amusement behind the sound. "I think the sane thing might be questionable right now."

"You know what I mean."

"I've had weeks more than you to take it all in, Staff. I've been living with this since Ara—Jacob Trent came on the scene, remember?"

Would she ever be able to say Aramael's name again? Or her sister's? Eternity was a long time, but would it be long enough to take away the pain?

Roberts rubbed a hand over his head. Leaning back in his chair, he stared again at the weapon atop his desk.

"May I?"

Alex lifted a shoulder, let it drop. Roberts reached for the sword's hilt but drew back with a yelp when blue light arced between it and his skin. "Jesus! Is it supposed to do that?"

"I had no idea it did."

He grunted, rubbing his hand. "Well, at least there's no danger of anyone taking it away from you in a fight. But how in hell are you going to defend yourself with it against one of...them? You don't even know how to use it."

"I've been offered lessons," she said.

"By whoever—whatever—is protecting you?" Roberts paled and swallowed. Hard. "Hell. He's here, isn't he? Where?"

"Out there." Alex jerked a thumb over her shoulder at the door.

Roberts stared past her, a thousand other questions jostling behind his expression. He voiced none of them. Just groaned, folded his hands on top of his head, and leaned back in his chair.

"All right," he said wearily. "If anyone asks about him, he's your new partner. Call him whatever you want. And you can carry the sword, but for God's sake, keep it out of sight."

She nodded and stood, then slid the sword back into its scabbard. Aramael's sword. But she wasn't thinking about that anymore. Just like she wasn't thinking about Jen.

Again she made it to the door. Again his voice stopped her.

"Jarvis."

She looked back.

"You're going to ignore the twenty-four hour thing, aren't you?"

"Most likely," she agreed. "But I'll stay clear of the office so no one here has to do the arresting. We'll call it a compromise."

He sighed. "We've been asked to provide backup for a demonstration at Queen's Park this morning," he said. "If you're going to be here anyway, you might as well make yourself useful. Briefing's at ten."

MIKA'EL CAUGHT HOLD of Alex's wrist as she walked past him. "Are you done?"

"Roberts signed the forms. Now I need to have them entered into the system."

"Let someone else do that."

Alex gazed pointedly at his hand, and he released his grip on her.

"Fine," he growled. "But we leave when you're done."

"No, we don't. I have work to do." She walked away.

He stalked after her. "Damn it, Alex—"

She stopped so suddenly that he almost bowled her over. Each took a single step back from the other. Alex's mouth formed a tight, stubborn line beneath her nose.

"Exactly what else would you like me to do, Michael?" she demanded. "I've told you I'm not leaving Toronto, and I'm sure as Hell not sitting around my apartment while you brood and God knows who hunts me down. I'm working. You think I'm important enough to warrant protection, fine. Protect me. But you do it here, and you stop whining about it."

Anger welled in him, but even as he opened his mouth to remind her to whom she spoke, her blue eyes moved to stare over his shoulder and the corner of her mouth quivered. He hesitated. Cursed his insensitivity. Shook his head.

"You know, sometimes you do such a good job of pretending you're okay that even I believe you," he muttered.

Her startled gaze flew to his. "What?"

"Nothing." He sighed. "Nothing. And yes, I'll protect you here. For now. But we talk about it later, Alex."

"I don't want—"

"We talk about it later," he repeated. And he hoped by then he'd have come up with an argument she'd listen to.

HANDS RESTING on the table, Samael looked up from the charts spread before him. He raised an eyebrow at the recently liberated Fallen One he'd sent after the Naphil. Bethiel, he remembered.

"You're back already?" he asked. "Did you find her?"

The former Principality crossed his arms and leaned a shoulder against the doorframe of the war room. "Mittron," he said. "I want him."

A stocky former Virtue appeared at Samael's elbow, holding out a rolled-up paper. Samael took the roll and waved him off. He studied Bethiel, noting the subtle aggression in the other's posture. The determination underscored by a hint of the madness that haunted all of Limbo's former occupants.

"Why?" he asked, when the Virtue had departed again. He didn't bother denying knowledge of the former Highest. But he did wonder how Bethiel had found out about his connection to Mittron.

"Because I do."

Samael looked back down at the charts. "And why should I give him to you?"

Bethiel sat on a corner of the table, heedless of the chart he crushed beneath him. "We'll consider it a trade."

"So you did find her."

And apparently he and the Naphil had talked. An unsettling thought.

Bethiel shrugged. Samael returned to pretending he studied the chart before him. He had no compunction about giving up Mittron—he'd do so in a heartbeat at any other time. Just not now. Not until the Nephilim children had grown enough to be unleashed. Heaven's former executive administrator had more than proved his worth—at least temporarily—when it came to keeping Pripyat organized and defended. Without him in charge there, Samael would have to take over, a task he neither wanted nor had the time for right now. Not when he was already holding Hell itself together in the absence of Seth's desire to do so.

He raised his gaze to the Principality again. "We already had an agreement. The woman for evidence of your innocence."

"I changed the agreement. I want Mittron."

"Fine. He's yours. But not yet."

"Not good enough."

Impatience surged. He needed the Naphil to die. Now.

"Mittron is still useful to me," he growled. "You can have him when I'm done."

"And I have your word on that, have I?" Bethiel snorted. "Forgive my skepticism, but I'm not inclined to put a lot of stock in the promise of a Fallen One, Samael. You'll have your trade when Mittron becomes available."

"Or I can send others after her. If you found her, they can, too."

"If you had others to send after her, you'd have already done so. But you don't, do you? No one you can trust to do what you asked me to do, anyway. It's far more likely they'd turn the Naphil over to Seth, isn't it?" Bethiel swung one leg lazily, his arms crossed and expression bland. "Because that's what Seth wants. Perhaps if I—"

Samael's sword halted an inch from the Principality's throat. Fear pooled in Samael's belly. Weakness in his knees. If Seth knew—

"I don't respond well to threats," he snarled.

The Principality didn't flinch. "And I don't respond well to lies. You knew Mittron wasn't in Heaven. You know where he is now. You get the Naphil when I get the Seraph."

"Or I take the knowledge from you and then kill

you."

Bethiel laughed softly, without mirth. "Enter the mind of one who has known Limbo? You don't have the nerve."

The tip of the sword settled against the center of the Principality's chest. Oh, how Samael would have loved to prove him wrong...but he didn't dare. Limbo did awful things to an angel's mind. Unspeakable things. Mittron had warned him to guard against exactly that when he had opened the gates. To open himself now would be just plain foolish.

Tempting, but foolish.

Bethiel placed the flat of his hand against the blade and pushed it away. He stood up from the table.

"I'll leave you to consider my proposition," he said. "You can let me know when you're ready to make the trade."

He stopped at the door.

"Oh, and in the unlikely event you do happen to find someone you trust for the job, you might want to warn them that the Naphil is being protected."

Samael scowled. "You would fight for her?"

"I would if I had to, but fortunately for me, Mika'el has volunteered for the task. She's very popular, this Naphil of yours."

"Mika'el! What in bloody Heaven does he need with—" Samael broke off as realization dawned. "Fuck. He's using her to find Emmanuelle."

"And I'm using her to find Mittron." Bethiel chuckled. "It will be interesting to see which of her uses she fulfills first, don't you think? Care to reconsider my proposition now?"

For an instant, Samael wavered. Bethiel was right. Even if he could trust another Fallen to kill the Naphil and not take her to Seth in exchange for favor, it would be useless to send anyone up against Mika'el.

Almost anyone.

A chill slithered down his spine. Bloody Heaven, could he risk it? He met Bethiel's smug gaze.

How could he not?

Calmly, coldly, he returned the other's smile. "I think not," he said. "But thanks for the offer."

Bethiel's smile faltered. His lips pulled tight.

"Have it your way, Archangel. But don't say I didn't warn you."

Samael reached for a pen and dipped it into a nearby ink pot. Ignoring Bethiel, he put pen to chart and scratched a note along the edge, a question he needed to ask about troop movement along a less-protected stretch of Heaven's border.

The door opened. Closed. Silence fell.

He laid aside the pen and braced his hands against the table edge. He turned his plan over in his mind. Examined it from every possible angle. Saw its many, many flaws.

And knew he had no choice.

He'd just have to be careful.

Very careful.

TWENTY-THREE

"**Y**ou told me *you* would get her for me," Seth snarled.

Keeping one eye on the Appointed's bunched shoulders and curled fists, Samael retreated to a strategically safer place on the opposite side of the room. He injected a soothing note into his voice. He wanted—no, he *needed*—Seth to trust him.

"And I still can," he said. "I'm just not convinced I'm the best one to do so."

"I don't care who—"

"I think it should be you."

Seth put a fist through the paneled wall beside the fireplace, connecting with stone on the other side. The building trembled.

"Are you trying to be funny?" he asked.

"Not at—"

"It will be two weeks before I heal enough to cross the threshold. I told you I'm not waiting that long."

"And I understand your impatience," Samael

soothed. "But if we want to assure your long-term happiness with the Naphil—"

"*Alex.*"

"Apologies, Appointed, but I've been giving it great thought, and if we want to ensure your long-term happiness with *Alex*, you might want to re-consider your approach in getting her here. Sending someone to bring her to you by force would hardly be a good start to her life with you in Hell."

Seth's scowl remained, but he didn't respond. After a moment, Samael decided to interpret the silence as encouraging. He strolled the perimeter of the room, delivering his carefully prepared argument.

"Think about it," he encouraged. "You'll be spending eternity with this woman. Is it not better to exercise patience in acquiring her? To win her, rather than take her?"

"I tried that."

"I know, but what if she's had time to think about things since you left? Time to miss you, and to regret her actions? You're divinity itself, Seth. How can she not want to be with you?" Samael spread his hands wide to emphasize his words. "If you handle this right, it could be a fresh start for both of you. And if we focus every effort on healing you, I've been assured you'll be fit enough to cross between the realms within the week."

Samael saw no reason to add that Seth's nurse had given the assurance under threat of excruciating death. He smiled encouragement. Shored up his nerve. Readied himself to put his plan into action.

"One week, and you can have it all, Appointed," he said. "The woman, and a home to give her. A realm the two of you can rule over together. Perhaps even two realms, united by you, if the war goes according to plan."

Irritation flashed in Seth's eyes, and for an instant, Samael thought he might have pushed too hard. Too fast. He braced himself, but after a moment, the black gaze turned thoughtful.

"Maybe you're right." Seth rested an elbow on the fireplace mantel. Idly, he traced a finger across his lips. "But can we win the war in just one week? Heaven—"

"Is weak and growing weaker," Samael assured him. "Without the One to lead them, the angels are scattered at best. With a strong leader of our own..." He trailed off, willing Seth to finish the thought—to interpret the words the way he needed him to.

Hell had no chance of winning the entire war in a week, of course, but with the troops rallied behind Lucifer's son, answering his call to arms, it could certainly create a distraction. One that, with luck, would draw Mika'el's attention away from the Naphil for a moment or two. Long enough for Samael to finish what he'd sent Bethiel to do before Seth recovered and crossed the realms to fetch the love of his life—and Hell lost his interest forever.

Just as they'd lost his father's.

Seth grunted. For the first time since his arrival in Hell, it seemed he might actually be listening. Samael allowed himself a quiet exhalation of satisfaction.

"And Earth?" Seth asked. "What about that?"

"The Nephilim army grows strong under Mittron's care. They'll have their own leader soon, your father's final gift to you. They will ensure the destruction of humanity, you will be able to disavow responsibility, and Alex..." Samael paused for effect, and then delivered his lie. Blithely. Purposefully.

"Alex will have a new home," he said. "Here with you. With us. In time, she will learn to appreciate your consolation. And you'll have eternity to convince her to do so."

Long moments ticked. Seth drummed fingers against the mantel until Samael was ready to scream and rip them from his hand. At last, the black gaze met his again.

"You make a convincing argument, Archangel," Seth said. "Where do we start?"

And just like that, Samael had the time he needed to rid himself of their Naphil problem—and the power to do so.

TWENTY-FOUR

Raymond Joly was waiting for Alex when she emerged from the briefing. Her step faltered when she saw him, and she had to blink away their shared memory of the four dead cops before she could summon a semblance of a smile.

"You're back."

"Sitting by myself at home wasn't doing anybody any good." Joly shrugged. "Least of all me."

Alex nodded understanding. She searched for something to say but came up dry. Small talk seemed beyond her these days.

Michael had followed her from the conference room, and stood off to one side. As he'd promised, no one had taken notice of his presence among them.

Joly's handlebar mustache twitched from side to side as he pursed unseen lips. "Abrams told me about your sister," he said finally. "I'm sorry."

Again, Alex nodded but didn't speak. Again, there were no words.

"Do you know yet when the funeral is?"

"I haven't—I don't—" She shrugged. "No."

Her friend and coworker stared at her. Then he closed the space between them and wrapped her in a hug. "Goddamn, Alex. You don't deserve this. Not any of it."

Standing in the circle of her colleague's arms, Alex waited for the grief to wash over her, the loss to envelop her. There had been so much. Too much. But she felt nothing but hard. Empty. Jen had died in her arms last night, and already it felt like a lifetime ago. Nina was still out there somewhere, but the driving need to find her had been swallowed by the overwhelming needs of others.

So many others.

Her gaze fell on the board detailing the bombing in the church basement. She read the names of the seven women who had died. Thought about the families they had left behind.

So much pain.

She drew a shallow breath—her ribs no longer seemed to want to expand enough for a deep one—and returned Joly's hug. Then she stepped back.

"None of us deserves this," she said. Her gaze met Michael's over Joly's shoulder. "None of us," she repeated.

The Archangel's features might have been carved of marble for all the reaction he displayed. Resentment sitting like bitter dust on her tongue, Alex looked back to Joly.

"I'm okay," she told him. "Really. And we have bigger things to—"

A shout interrupted her, and she and Joly both turned to see Abrams waving everyone to silence.

Those who remained in the office gathered around the television screen mounted to the wall in the corner. Alex and Joly followed as Abrams pointed the remote control at the screen, and the volume rose.

"—in what the Russian government is calling a nuclear missile test gone horribly wrong," the grave newscaster said. "This footage from a Slavutych resident's cell phone shows the dramatic mushroom cloud over the town built to accommodate survivors from the city of Pripyat after the Chernobyl disaster in 1986. The immediate death toll from today's disaster is expected to be anywhere from fifteen to twenty thousand, virtually wiping out the town's population, with long-term numbers even higher. Ukrainian government officials..."

The newscaster's voice droned on, but her words were lost in the buzzing in Alex's ears, the heat spreading through her body. Her lungs screamed for air, but she couldn't expand them against the room crushing in on her. Hands settled on her shoulders, vise-like in their grip, warning against a struggle she couldn't have summoned if her life depended on it. She stumbled in the direction they steered, away from the others, to the back of the office, where her supervisor waited. The hands dropped away.

"Breathe," Roberts ordered.

Alex stared at him. At his haggard ace and shell-shocked eyes, at the determined rigidity of his shoulders. Tiny little lights swam across her vision. The hands settled on her shoulders again, softer this time. Gentler.

Michael.

Breathe, his touch urged, echoing Roberts's command.

She inhaled slowly, experimentally. Then, when she didn't shatter, deeply. Air filled her lungs. The lights across her vision disappeared. And then fury slammed into her gut. She shrugged off Michael's hands and met her supervisor's grim, raw horror.

"Lang," she bit out. "Boileau."

"We don't know that."

"Yes. We do. That was no accident, Staff, and you know it. The government—*every* government—has lost its fucking collective mind." She swallowed hard. Twenty thousand people. An entire city. Her entire being vibrated with horror.

"I warned Lang," she said hoarsely. "I *told* him they couldn't get at them."

"Get at whom?" Michael intervened.

When Alex didn't respond, Roberts sighed. "The—"

"Don't bother," she snarled. "He doesn't care."

"I never said I didn't care, Alex. I said—"

"If I told you the Fallen had engineered that"—she pointed at the television—"what would you do?"

Michael's expression turned stony. Despite the fact she'd expected the reaction, Alex's heart did likewise. She fought off the heaviness threatening to settle again in her chest.

"That's what I thought," she said, her voice flat. "Say what you like, Michael. In my book, refusing to help is the same thing as not caring."

She turned her back on him and glared at Roberts, furious at his passive acceptance, hating that his would be the attitude of so many. Too many.

Enough that the Langs and Boileaus of the world would continue pushing humanity to the brink of extinction.

"If that's everything, *sir*," she said. "I have a

demonstration to attend."

"Twenty-four hours, Jarvis," he called after her. "Twenty-four hours and then you're gone."

TWENTY-FIVE

"You're clear on what to do?" Samael asked the Cherub slouching against the wall. Razor-cut, bright blue hair made Zuriel's agate-colored eyes seem paler than they were. She'd stand out more than he would have liked, but she had a reputation for efficiency.

Despite the posture and attitude that suggested otherwise.

Zuriel raised an eyebrow dyed to match her hair. "Follow Bethiel, find the Naphil, report back to you. I think I can handle it."

"And?"

"Tell no one."

"*And?*"

She rolled her eyes. "And don't let Bethiel see me. Covert ops, Sam. I get it."

Samael's hand itched to reach out and slap the insolence from her demeanor. He'd seen a lot of that attitude from the troops in recent days. He knew how much dissatisfaction it masked, and it would quickly become outright insubordination if it wasn't handled.

Seth had damned well better make good on his agreement to step up as leader.

And Zuriel had damned well better follow through on finding the Naphil.

The blue-haired Cherub exaggeratedly cleared her throat. "Am I done here?" she asked. "Or did you want to go over the details a fourth time?"

Samael gritted his teeth. He waved a dismissal, and Zuriel tugged open the door beside her and disappeared into the corridor.

Now, he amended his thought. Seth had better step up *now.*

SETH WATCHED the blue-haired Cherub emerge from the war chamber and close the door behind her. He studied her. He didn't think he'd ever seen one with matching hair and wings. The effect was…interesting.

The Cherub strode down the corridor toward him, oblivious to his presence until he stepped from the shadows into her path. Her hand went swiftly to her sword. It was half-unsheathed before she stayed herself.

"Bloody Heaven," she grumbled. "Jumping out of dark corners is a good way to get yourself killed."

A corner of Seth's mouth tipped upward. "I doubt that," he said.

Pale, agate-colored eyes surveyed him from head to toe, then widened.

"Appointed." She resheathed her sword. "I didn't recognize you."

One cost of keeping to himself.

Another cost was the complete lack of intimidation he read in her bold gaze. Samael may have had a point about Seth needing to make his presence known and take up the reins.

Seth inclined his head. "And you are?"

"Zuriel."

He waited.

Zuriel looked away. "Your lordship," she added in a mutter.

"A pleasure to meet you," he said, his tone suggesting otherwise. Zuriel shot him another look, wariness entering her expression.

Better.

Seth folded his arms and leaned a shoulder against the stone pillar he'd stepped out from behind. "Tell me, Zuriel, why were you in visiting with Samael? Secret war plans?"

"You'd have to ask Sam—"

Seth's hand shot out and gripped her chin, just hard enough to cut off her words and make her draw a quick, surprised breath.

"I'm not asking Sam," he said. "I'm asking you. Because it doesn't seem right to keep secrets from the ruler of Hell, does it?"

She stared at him, then dropped her gaze. "Of course not. I wasn't thinking."

Seth released his grip and patted her cheek. "Why don't we start again? What were you talking with Samael about?"

The agate eyes flicked toward the massive oak door of the war chamber. "The angel who found the Naphil," she said. "Bethiel. I'm to track him to the woman and then report back to Samael."

The blood in Seth's veins slowed to a trickle. It

turned to ice. "Someone found the Naphil?"

Zuriel licked her lips and edged away. "One of those released from Limbo. Bethiel."

"And why didn't he bring her to me?"

"I don't—" Zuriel squeaked as his hand gripped her chin again, not quite so gently this time. Her pupils dilated. "I don't know! Samael didn't tell me! I swear. He just said to track Bethiel and report back when I found the Naphil."

Seth considered the possibility that the situation wasn't as underhanded as it seemed. That Samael had been going to tell him all this himself. That his so-called aide's intentions were good.

He wanted to believe that possibility.

But he didn't.

Not when the Archangel had failed-on multiple occasions-to tell him Alex had been found.

Zuriel's jawbone gave way beneath his grip. She squawked in pain. Seth closed his eyes for a long minute, then shoved her away. She sagged against the corridor wall, holding her face and glaring at him.

Seth stared back. "You'll continue," he said finally. "Do what Samael asks. But after you've reported to him, you come to me as well. And you tell me everything. What you found. What Samael does. Immediately. Understand?"

The Cherub hesitated. Seth narrowed his eyes. She nodded vigorously, wincing.

"Good. And Zuriel?"

A blue eyebrow twitched up.

"This secret you keep," he said.

She nodded again, once, and then scurried down the corridor. When she'd vanished, Seth took a deep breath, mustered his growing willpower, and completed his journey to the war chamber. Samael looked up from the table as he entered, and Seth forced a tight, grim smile.

"So," he said. "Why don't you show me where we're at?"

TWENTY-SIX

Mika'el watched Alex stamp her feet and tuck her gloved hands under her arms in an effort to warm them. Twice he'd offered to ease the discomfort of the cold for her; twice she'd refused. If he couldn't help them all, she'd told him, she wasn't interested. He hadn't decided yet whether he admired her stubbornness or found it irritating in the extreme.

Her hostile gaze met his, and his jaw flexed.

He was leaning toward irritating.

Even if she did have reason to feel the way she did.

He looked out at the crowd spilling over from the frozen, snow-covered lawn onto the street beyond. Despite the biting wind, a good three thousand had gathered in front of their government buildings to demand answers. Answers to the pregnancy threat they hadn't yet recognized as over, answers to the winged aliens caught on video, answers to eighty thousand missing babies.

Signs waved and bullhorn-equipped organizers

led varying chants, and a line of riot police stood three deep between the crowd and the buildings, faces impassive behind helmets and shields. Alex and several dozen other plainclothes officers stood behind them, each wearing a bulletproof vest and a heavy parka emblazoned with a bright yellow *Police* across the back, each carrying a baton.

The crowd's energy wavered somewhere between anger and outright hostility.

Damn it to Hell and back, what he wouldn't give to be able to wipe the slate clean and let these mortals start fresh. What might they have been if it hadn't been for Lucifer and the Grigori? Such potential. So much struggle. And now this.

Sadness washed over him. Humanity might not know of the One's absence, but it felt the effects nonetheless. Already they had begun to tear their own world apart. What would happen when they realized she was gone? Or when the Nephilim army reached its full potential? How many would survive? How many *could* survive? His gaze returned to Alex.

That she would live was certain. Physically, at least. But as strong as she might be, her psyche would never survive an eternity at Seth's side. It wouldn't survive an eternity, period. The human mind had never been intended for immortality; it simply wasn't strong enough.

Alex's blue gaze met his, flicked away again. The sheer rawness in the depths of her eyes made him blink, and then he remembered. She'd been injured in a gathering such as this not long ago, and Aramael had saved her. With so many other issues on his mind, Mika'el kept forgetting she still dealt with that aftermath, too. He stepped closer to her and cleared his throat. Alex pre-empted him.

"Don't," she said.

"You don't know what I was going to say."

"Yes, I do. And I don't want your sympathy."

"It might help to talk. The soulmate connection is—"

"Do you want my help finding Emmanuelle or not?"

He looked down at the blond head beside his shoulder. She glared out at the increasingly restless crowd.

"My way," she reminded him. "Or not at all."

Mika'el's mouth twisted. Perhaps he was wrong. If any human mind could withstand immortality, it would be Alex's. For her sake, however, he almost hoped it wouldn't, not when retaining her sanity meant eternal awareness. It would be better by far if she descended into the place her sister had gone. Either that or—

Something struck his cheek, startling him back to his surroundings. The crowd was pressing in on the police line, the shouts of many drowning out the bullhorns. A handful of projectiles clattered against the riot shields: bottles and rocks; bricks such as the one at Mika'el's feet. Mika'el put a hand out to Alex, his wings beginning to unfurl, but she shook him off and, grim-faced, moved to intercept a demonstrator doing an end run around the riot line.

Even as she and another officer brought the man to the ground, utter chaos erupted around them. In a matter of seconds, tear gas and cries of panic filled the air. Some of the protesters tried to run away, but the crush of others behind them pushed them into the police shields, bringing them within range of clubs wielded by those forced to defend themselves against sheer numbers. Mika'el watched as men and women alike went down beneath the trample of feet. The police line was forced back...one step, two...ten.

"Michael!"

He looked to Alex, met her fury, her plea. He hesitated. Mayhem surrounded him. For six thousand years, he had lived among mortals; had watched their civilizations rise and fall, borne witness to their failings and atrocities, their compassion and potential. Never once in all that time had he done anything to influence them or alter their course, because free will—the free will given to them by the One herself— had been sacrosanct. He had given up Heaven itself for it when the One had faltered in her own belief and stripped it from her angels.

Now that she was gone—especially with her gone— it was his job to continue believing in it, to uphold it. He had to, because it had never been Heaven's purpose to rescue humanity. Because mortals had to take responsibility for their own actions, their own future...

Never more so than now, when Heaven's own future had become uncertain.

"Damn it, Michael," Alex yelled over her shoulder as the police line broke entirely, "for once in your existence, *do* something!"

Verchiel would be livid.

Rightfully so.

But it would solve his Alex problem—and it might also be just what humanity needed.

Mika'el spread his massive wings wide, knocking those within their span to the ground. Drawing his sword, he launched himself upward. The gust from his wings cleared the noxious gases from the air and

flattened dozens of demonstrators. He stared down at
their confusion, and then, with a final, deep breath,
he took the last irreversible step of letting himself be
seen as he was—an Archangel of Heaven, fully clad in
the battle armor he summoned to him, revealed in all
his terrible glory.

"Enough!" he roared.

TWENTY-SEVEN

Holy Hell.

Alex gaped upward as Michael's powerful wings moved to keep him aloft. He was clad in armor as black as his feathers, and his sword flashed blue spears of light over the heads of the throng. As if someone had hit a switch, utter stillness dropped over all present. No one moved. No one made a sound. Sirens wailed in the distance, backup for the beleaguered police officers staring up in open-mouthed shock, some with clubs still raised, others straddling demonstrators they'd pinned to the snow-covered ground. Two dozen feet above the crowd, Michael's eyes met hers, his expression bleak. Inexpressibly sad.

Then his face went hard and he turned his attention to the gathering.

"Enough," he repeated, his voice ringing through the hush. "In the name of the Creator herself, stop. The war you need to fight is coming, but it's not here, it's not now, and it certainly isn't with one another."

Alex tore her gaze from the Archangel. Leaving the uniformed cop to manage the demonstrator they'd brought down, she clambered to her feet and looked around at the upturned faces. The doubt, the hope, the reverence...the deep, disbelieving suspicion. She caught her breath.

"Do something," she'd told Michael, but surely to Heaven she hadn't meant this. *Pitch in, give us a hand, hold that guy down—or that one—or that one.*

But reveal himself? Show the world who he was— *what* he was—against every tenet he was supposed to uphold? She watched cell phones appear in upstretched hands, snapping pictures, taking videos, recording the entire impossible event to share with the world. Her heart missed a beat and then plunged. In mere seconds, Michael would be seen by every government, every religious faction, every nutcase who had access to the Internet. The reactions playing out here would be magnified by a billion times, and Lang and Boileau and Roberts would be proved right.

She stared up at Michael again. *Stop. Don't say anything more. Just stop.*

As if he'd heard her, Michael shook his head, his expression turning weary.

"War is coming," he repeated. "In the name of the Creator herself, go home. Look to your families, your communities, your own souls. There is greater strength in your connection to one another than you know. Find it. Hold onto it. Have faith in it. For your own sakes, let that be your salvation rather than your ruin."

He lowered his sword, then slid it into its scabbard. A twitch of his wingtips took him to the air over Alex, another dropped him to the ground beside her. The stunned silence of the crowd gave way to whispers, then a murmur that grew in volume, punctuated by shouted questions.

"*Who the hell are you?*"

"*What are you?*"

Michael's emerald gaze met her own as the crowd pressed in on them, hands outstretched. "We have to leave," he said.

"What have you done?" she whispered.

She pushed away the hands grasping for Michael's wings. His armor. His hair. The questions grew louder. "*Will you save us?*"

"Now," Michael said. He gave her no time to protest, drawing her into his arms and folding his wings around her. Then, just as it had once before in a Vancouver alley, his body turned molten, flowed into hers, and tore her away from the world around them in a rush of heat and vibration.

TWENTY-EIGHT

Holding the tremble in her hand at bay through sheer willpower, Alex took the glass of Scotch from Michael and knocked it back in a single gulp. She slid the empty glass across the table toward him, fire coursing down her throat. He refilled it without comment, and she tried again to dial Roberts. Still no answer, most likely because he was just plain avoiding her. Shit. She could just imagine the chaos Michael's little stunt had created. How in hell would she be able to go back to work now? *Could* she go back?

Michael slid the glass back to her. She drained it a second time, then set it down with exaggerated care. Only then did she raise her gaze to his and break the silence that had sat between them since he had hauled her by angelic force from the riot.

"What the *fuck* were you thinking?" she snarled. "All those people...the exposure...how *could* you?"

"You wanted me to do something."

"But not that. Christ, not *that*." She stood up from

her kitchen table, toppling the chair to the floor with a crash. She raked a hand through her hair. Much as she hadn't wanted to admit it, she'd known all along that Boileau and Roberts were right. Humanity wasn't ready for things like angels and demons and war between a very real Heaven and Hell. Religious factions would be all over this. Worldwide, thanks to the goddamn Internet.

Humanity's troubles had just multiplied by a factor she didn't even want to contemplate.

"What did you expect?" Michael growled. "A wave of a magic wand to make everyone all loving and peaceful? The world doesn't work that way, Alex. *I* don't work that way. I'm an Archangel, not a bloody fairy godmother."

She rubbed both hands over her face, then crossed her arms. "I know what you are. Hell, the whole world knows what you are after that performance."

"Good."

"*Good?*" She gaped at him. "How can that be good?"

"Because what I said today will have reached at least some people. Resonated with them. If they spread the word, if they reach others like them, they might be able to effect change."

"Enough to save the world?" Alex snorted. "You're not that naive."

"Neither are you. I'm not trying to save the world. I'm trying to inspire a handful of mortals to save themselves, because that's the best we can hope for. I've told you all along that human survival hangs in the balance."

Alex sagged against the wall. His words buried themselves like a fist in her gut. Her mouth flapped. She made herself snap it shut, swallow, breathe.

Wished she'd bought two bottles of Scotch on their way back to the apartment instead of one.

"Yes," she said. "But I'm not sure I believed. There are so many of us. What you're suggesting—it doesn't seem possible."

Still seated, Michael rested his forearms on his knees and stared down at his linked fingers. "Did Aramael ever tell you how I abandoned Heaven?"

Alex blinked at the sudden change in topic and stared down at the bowed head. She waited, certain he neither sought nor needed an answer from her.

"The One and I didn't agree on the Cleanse," he continued. "I refused to give up my free will or...Well. That part doesn't matter. The bottom line is that I left Heaven for a period of time, and lived here on Earth, among humans."

"For how long?"

"Five thousand years, give or take. Long enough to see the rise and fall of civilizations that lasted a great deal longer than the current one has." Michael looked up again, his eyes tired, sad. "Sheer numbers don't give you immunity, Alex, they just give you a higher death count."

"*We can't save everyone*," Roberts's words echoed in her memory. "*There will be casualties*."

But Michael wasn't talking about casualties, was he? He was talking about more. Much more. About Armageddon in its truest, harshest, most biblical sense. Alex swallowed, and through sheer willpower, unlocked her throat enough for a single question. "So by survival, you mean...?"

"I mean, I'm hoping enough of you live to start over again."

"But that would only take..."

"A few thousand. Yes."

RETURNING TO THE OFFICE was like walking an endless gauntlet.

Tight-lipped, Alex strode along the hallway, booted heels on tile echoing in the silence that followed her, that spread before her, that surrounded her. Conversations stopped and people crowded into doorways, pressing against one another in an effort to catch a glimpse of her. And still not a single eye turned in Michael's direction. She scowled at him.

"You're the one who created this mess," she muttered. "The least you can do is take some of the flack for it."

"Let them see me for what I am again, you mean?" He looked grim. "You wouldn't want that to happen."

"If it meant they'd stop staring at me, I would."

She reached for the knob on the door leading into Homicide. Michael's hand on her arm stopped her.

"For creatures who are supposed to be self-sufficient, humans are remarkably needy," he said. "They're also lazy. If they could see me, if they knew the power I possess, how do you think they would respond?"

Alex glanced past his shoulder to the clusters of people lining the corridor. Saw in their eyes the hope, the fear, the distrust—and that was just what was directed at her.

She sighed. "Honestly? Half of them would want to destroy you."

"And the other half would expect me to rescue them."

"So that's it, then? You show yourself once and then disappear again?"

"We've had this discussion."

Yes, they had. And she still had the headache to prove it. Alex shoved open the door and stalked into Homicide. Utter stillness descended over the office, as if someone had hit the pause button on a recording. Her step hitched for an instant, and then, with Michael at her back, she walked past stone-faced colleagues and support staff, headed for Staff Inspector Roberts's door. No one spoke a word as she passed. No one moved.

She knocked at Roberts's door. Long seconds went by before he raised his head from his work. His gaze met hers through the window on the door. At last he lifted a hand and beckoned her inside. She shook her head at Michael when he would have followed. "No. I want to speak to him on my own."

She pushed into her supervisor's office, closed the door, and waited in silence for Roberts to look up again from his paperwork. He threw down his pen and spread his hands wide.

"I have no words," he said. "None."

Neither did she.

"You know the entire thing was caught on video."

She closed her eyes.

"A man with wings, hovering twenty feet in the air, holding a sword, delivering what can only be described as a warning. And then, when he's finished, he swoops down to where you're standing—you, a visibly identifiable police officer—wraps you in his wings, and the two of you disappear. How in the *hell* am I supposed to spin this, Alex?"

"You can't," she said. "I know you thought it best to keep the angel element quiet. For the record, I agreed with you after I thought it through. But—"

"But he"—Roberts waved at the television in the corner—"didn't."

Alex glanced at the screen, frozen on an image of Michael descending toward her, his black wings outstretched and expression fierce. She shivered and turned back to her supervisor. "No. He didn't."

Leaning back in his chair, he linked his fingers behind his head, stared at her, and muttered, "Fuck."

Alex indicated one of the visitors' chairs with a tilt of her head, and Roberts gave her a *whatever* shrug. She sat, leaning forward to balance elbows on knees, the sword ever-present against her spine. "What does the brass say?"

"You're on paid leave until they decide what to do with you."

She'd expected as much, but she still felt compelled to argue the decision. "I can be more help here than sitting on my ass at home."

"This video isn't like the one from the Parliament explosion, Detective. Your face is crystal clear and being shown worldwide. You cannot effectively do your job when you have that kind of recognition. We've already had thousands of calls asking about the police officer who was taken by the angel. If you're seen on the street, you'll be mobbed." Roberts scowled. "And if you're here in the office, Boileau will have you handcuffed and escorted to either Ottawa or jail, neither of which I want to see happen."

Alex contemplated her folded fingers. So that was it. Thirteen years on the job, and just like that, she was done. The emptiness inside her grew a little bigger. Roberts sighed.

"Look, I know this is hard. Keep a low profile for a couple of weeks, and then we'll see how things stand, all right? I'll try to get Boileau to climb down off his high horse in the meantime, and maybe...maybe you can still find Nina."

She lifted her gaze to his. Tightened her lips in a pretend smile. Pushed to her feet. "Sure," she said. "Maybe I'll do that."

Roberts stood up from his chair. "I'll work on him," he said. "Boileau, I mean. I'll do what I can."

She nodded. "Of course."

Silence fell, awkward and heavy with things left unsaid. Things like *goodbye* and *it's been nice knowing you*. Because they both knew how much could happen in two weeks. Alex roused herself to leave. She stopped halfway to the door.

"One thing, Staff. The two names I entered into the Interpol database. If anything comes through on either of them, particularly the female, I need to know. ASAP."

Interest flared in her supervisor's expression. A glimmer of hope.

"She can help?"

Alex hesitated. Michael wasn't looking for Emmanuelle on behalf of humankind, and he'd said nothing about her helping the mortal world if they did find her. But if she took over as Heaven's leader, if she could help the angels win the war against Hell—against Seth—then surely the world could only benefit.

Surely.

Before she could voice what she only half-believed, the cell phone at her waist vibrated. She unclipped it, saw Henderson's name on the display, and thumbed the answer button. "I'm fine," she told her Vancouver counterpart.

"Oh, I have no doubt of that," Henderson's voice drawled in her ear. "You look quite hale in all those videos I've been watching. Michael looks good, too. A little on the moody side, maybe, but otherwise fine."

Alex choked back a snort of laughter. Trust Henderson to make light of the situation. "I'm in a meeting right now," she said. "Can I call you back?"

"Having your butt suspended?"

"Put on paid leave. How did you know?"

"It makes sense from their perspective. Everyone will be scared shitless to work with you, and even if they weren't, with the kind of notoriety you just gained, you'd be more hindrance than help."

She glanced toward the windows overlooking the main office. The blinds were open, and Raymond Joly's grim gaze met and held hers. Then, with unmistakable deliberation, he turned his back on her. A new, small ache took up residence beneath Alex's breastbone.

"I suppose you're right."

"None of that matters, however, because I think we've found her, Alex. I think we've found Emmanuelle."

Alex sucked in a sharp breath, automatically seeking Michael. She found him leaning against the edge of her desk in the center of the office. Their gazes met. Locked. Then, reading something in her expression, he strode toward her.

"Did you hear me?" Henderson asked. "I said, I think we've found Emmanuelle."

Roberts's door crashed open, and Michael plucked the cell phone from her fingers. Alex surrendered it without argument, Henderson's words ringing in her ears, drowning out whatever Michael said to him now. *We've found her...we've found Emmanuelle.*

Words of satisfaction. Of hope.

For everyone but Alex.

She held onto the chair's armrests with aching fingers. If Hugh was right, if Emmanuelle had been found, it was over. Heaven would no longer need her. Michael would have no reason to continue protecting her. She would be on her own again, with no one to stop Seth from coming for her. Taking her. Binding her to him for all eternity...

In Hell itself.

She struggled for air, trying to remember how to breathe, as cold, quiet terror unfurled in her chest. She'd thought she could handle this. Thought she would be ready when the time came, that she had come to terms with the idea. She'd been wrong.

She'd been wrong, and there wasn't a damn thing she could do about it.

A hand settled on her shoulder and she jumped. Then, slowly, she turned her gaze up to meet the farewell waiting for her in Michael's emerald eyes.

TWENTY-NINE

"I don't understand." Alex stared at Michael, unable to process what he'd just told her. What did he mean, go with him? Go where?

Somewhere in the background, she was aware of Roberts watching in dumbfounded silence. Of other faces gathering on the other side of the window.

Michael gave her an impatient shake, fingers digging into her shoulders. "What's not to understand? I need you to come with me to Vancouver, Alex. To speak with Emmanuelle."

"But I thought—once we found her, I thought I was done. I thought—" *I thought you were going to leave me.* She couldn't make herself say the words.

Silence. Then Michael's fingers brushed back the hair from her face and tipped her chin up. Impatience gentled to compassion in his green gaze.

"It's not time yet," his voice was gruff. "I still need your help, so I get to protect you for a while longer."

Relief and gratitude collided in Alex's chest. *Get*

to protect you. Not just *I can*, but *I get to.* Her chin wobbled. Fiercely, she blinked back tears. She would *not* lose it. Not here, not in the office with everyone watching.

Hell, not at all, if she didn't want to go over the edge permanently. She sucked in a steadying breath.

"What do you need me to do?"

"Emmanuelle and I..." Michael trailed off, glancing at Staff Inspector Roberts. "How much does he know?"

"More than he thinks," Alex said. "And more than he'd like to."

Michael extended a hand to her. "May I?"

Frowning, she placed her hand in his. The office around her shifted, shimmered, and dissolved into an indistinct mass. A nothingness made of somethings she couldn't quite grasp, possibilities that moved further out of reach when she tried to see them. A tremor of disquiet slid down her spine. She pulled back instinctively, but Michael held fast.

"Don't let go," he warned.

Alex stared at the blur around them. The hairs along her arms stood on end. "Or?"

"You'll disintegrate."

Her fingers gave an involuntary twitch and his grip tightened.

"I'm serious, Alex. I've made your energy vibrate faster than that of the world around you. Not quite the level of my own, but close. If I lose physical contact with you, the results will be catastrophic."

She sucked in a quick breath. She wondered what the definition of *catastrophic* might be, but decided she'd rather not know. "Is this...?"

"Heaven? No. I can't increase your energy to that frequency. You wouldn't survive, even with your immortality. This is...between."

Between. The word fell into the stillness around them, swallowed. Alex shivered. No, this nothingness couldn't be Heaven. Hell, maybe, but not Heaven.

"Limbo, actually," Michael said, as if he'd heard her thoughts. "Or at least, near to where Limbo used to be."

Lovely.

Trying not to cling too hard to the hand holding hers, Alex straightened her shoulders and firmed her jaw. *Between*, near where Limbo used to be, wasn't somewhere she cared to remain for long.

"You wanted to tell me about Emmanuelle," she said.

Michael's face took on a granite-like quality above her. For several heartbeats, he said nothing, staring over her head. Then he sighed. "Emmanuelle was—is—my soulmate. We didn't part on good terms."

Her hand twitched in his again, and her mind twisted in on itself, trying to follow two disparate lines of thought at the same time. The Archangel Michael—Heaven's greatest warrior, fierce and focused and possibly the only thing holding together the angelic forces right now—had a soulmate? Had once loved someone?

And what the hell did he mean, they hadn't parted on good terms? How not good? Was this why Emmanuelle kept company with mortals who had turned their backs on Heaven?

Alex held up her free hand, as much to stop her runaway brain as to ward off anything Michael might say. She scowled at him. First things first.

"Define *not good*."

Michael's hard gaze met hers. "Emmanuelle saw

no end to the dispute between her parents. No end to the war. She foresaw their destruction of one another, and rather than stay to watch their decline, she left. I accused her of running away. She accused me of choosing my loyalty to the One over our connection. We haven't spoken since."

Alex's jaw went slack. A terrifying sense of déjà vu gripped her chest and made it hard to breathe. "You mean the woman...angel...being"—she waved her free hand impatiently—"whatever the hell`she is—"

"As the daughter of the One, she is a god in her own right."

"What*ever*," she snapped. "It doesn't change the fact she ran away from her responsibility just like Seth did, and now you're proposing she take over Heaven and lead the angels against him in war. How in bloody fucking *hell* is that supposed to work?"

"I don't know," Michael snarled back. He made a visible effort at control and the fingers crushing hers eased their grip. "I don't know. But when I say she's our only hope, I mean it. Without her, we're done. We have nothing else."

Alex dropped her gaze to the hand holding hers. That grip, the strength of his fingers, the warmth of his skin, was all she had in this place. The only concrete thing in the nothingness of *between*. The only thing holding her in existence. She would disintegrate if he lost his hold on her, he'd said. Her hand went limp in his. She would disintegrate, dissolve, disappear to where none of this would be her concern, none of it would matter...

To where Seth could never find her and she would never have to face an eternity of all the losses she had suffered.

You've done enough, her inner voice whispered. *Done enough, given enough, lost enough. If you stay, you can't win. You can't beat Seth. You can't trust Bethiel to kill you if you don't find Mittron. This might be—will be—your only chance.*

She began a slow pull away from Michael's touch. Then, with freedom a heartbeat away, when only their fingertips still touched, her feet settled back onto the carpeted floor of her staff inspector's office and Roberts's harsh voice intruded.

"Detective, I asked you a question. Who the hell is Emmanuelle?"

THIRTY

"I'm sorry."

Alex continued throwing clothes into the duffle bag on her bed. She didn't respond to the Archangel behind her. Couldn't, because her throat was too full of the pain of unshed tears to allow room for words. Wouldn't, because she was just too angry.

"I know what you wanted to do," Michael pressed. "And I'm sorry I couldn't allow it."

She should have moved faster. Then he wouldn't have guessed her intention. Wouldn't have been able to take her out of the place between in time to stop her. She blinked hard. Damn him to hell for not letting her go when she had the chance—probably her only chance—to escape.

"If I didn't need you—"

She whirled and threw a balled-up sweater at him. "Fuck you!" she snarled. "And *fuck* what you need. Do you realize what you've done to me? Do you have any idea what my life will be like for all of eternity?

Eternity, Michael. I will lose every single person I have ever loved or cared for, I will live forever with those losses, and Seth—*Seth*, Michael—will force me into Hell with him. He will force me to be at his side and in his bed, and I won't be able to do a goddamn thing to stop him. *Nothing.*"

Michael closed his eyes on an emotion she couldn't read. A muscle flickered in front of his ear. For a heartbeat—a single, tremulous, daring to hope heartbeat—Alex wondered if she might have made him understand. If he might reconsider. If he might—

Green eyes opened again, and then Michael strode to the bed, stuffed the sweater in with her other clothes, and zipped the bag shut. He held it out to her, his black wings unfurling with a thousand *snicks* of battle-ready feathers. "We need to go."

THEY LANDED in the Downtown Eastside alley where they'd met Henderson once before, back on the night Seth had gone missing and they'd found him in the company of Lucifer. Alex had wanted to go straight to the apartment, but Henderson had been so evasive about the idea that Michael had suggested the alley instead. Arriving after dark, in a neighborhood where most inhabitants were under the influence of one mind-altering substance or another, would be the best way to ensure no one noticed them, he'd said. And Henderson would know exactly where to find them.

Alex would have preferred just about anywhere else, given the memories attached to the location, but she'd known Michael was right, and so she'd swallowed her arguments. And Henderson, bless his heart, didn't give the memories much room when they did arrive.

Alex hadn't even cleared the cocoon of Michael's wings in the dank alley when strong arms enveloped her in a bear hug and lifted her from her feet, duffle bag and all.

"Damn, but it's good to see you," a voice rumbled beneath her cheek.

"I might say the same," Alex mumbled into his coat, "if I could see you."

Henderson chuckled and set her back on her feet. But he didn't release her, instead holding her at arms' length, hands clamped over her shoulders, studying her by the faint light coming into the alley from the lamp-lit street.

"Better?" he asked. Then he promptly pulled her in for a second hug. "You have no idea how many gray hairs you've given me these last few weeks, Jarvis. I swear to God, you're the worst person on the planet for returning phone calls."

"I've been a little busy."

"I know." Hugh gave her a final squeeze and then released her. She braced for the barrage of questions, but the Vancouver detective looked past her at the waiting Michael and shook his head. "Later. I'm in a no parking zone. We should go."

"To...?"

"My apartment, of course."

"I thought you said you didn't want us there."

"I didn't want you appearing out of thin air. I don't think Liz's nerves are quite up to that just yet." Henderson took the duffle bag from her and started toward the street. Alex fell into step beside him.

"Liz?"

"Didn't I tell you?" Henderson took a set of keys from his pocket and pressed a fob. A nearby sedan gave two chirps and flashed its headlights. "Elizabeth Riley and I are living together."

"YOU AND RILEY," Alex muttered for the tenth time, watching the ascension of numbers on the elevator panel. "How did I not see that one coming?"

Hugh gave her a sideways look of exasperation. "Maybe because you've been, I don't know...otherwise occupied? Christ, Jarvis, it's not like we were dating or anything. How could you see it coming? *We* didn't see it coming."

She grunted. "Still. I should have noticed something. There had to have been signs."

And it would have been so much better if she'd had advance warning. Time to wrap her head around the idea. Henderson and Riley. Laid-back but highly effective cop, and uptight, highly irritating shrink. Talk about oil and water. She shook her head. Henderson was right: She couldn't have seen it coming if she'd tried.

The elevator door slid open and Henderson put a hand out to hold it aside. "After you. Apartment—"

"I remember," she interrupted, stepping into the hallway she and Seth had so often traversed when Henderson had taken them in just short weeks ago. She stuffed her fists into her pockets. Seth had been caught in a tug of war between Heaven and Hell, with the fate of humanity resting on his choice, so it had hardly been a good time, but it had been...enough. Threaded through with a fragile hope, peppered with moments that drew them together and connected them. She'd seen his potential then. Believed in it.

Believed in herself.

A gentle hand in the small of her back nudged her forward. Michael, who hadn't said a word since their arrival, his green eyes slanting a question at her. *Are you all right?*

She tried not to be bitter about his sudden concern for her well-being.

She failed.

"I said I'd help you," she growled, "and I will. You can stop pretending I matter beyond that."

He scowled. "I didn't—"

The door to apartment 2016 opened, cutting him off. Elizabeth Riley stood in the doorway, wire-framed glasses framing a gaze even more knowing than Michael's. Alex's shoulders hunched. Hell. She should have known better than to come back here. Should have insisted on a hotel. She sucked in a hiss of air. Understanding flickered in Riley's sharp blue eyes and she stepped back.

"Come in," she said. "I've made coffee."

Alex lasted less than a minute inside the door before she snapped.

"Stop it!" she snarled at Henderson, who was taking her coat from her shoulders while Riley moved serenely from kitchen to dining room, carrying a tray.

Riley and Henderson both froze. Michael's gaze narrowed.

"Just stop it," Alex said again. She pulled the coat back over her shoulders and ran a shaking hand over her hair. "I can't do this."

"Do what?" Elizabeth asked.

Did her voice always have to sound so goddamn reasonable?

"This." Alex waved at the room. At Henderson, at the coffee tray, at the apartment transformed into a home by Riley's presence. "Any of it. I can't sit and make small talk. I can't drink coffee. I can't be here."

"Because of the memories?" Hugh's voice was gruff. "I wondered about that. We can go out instead, if you'd—"

"It's not the memories." Alex's gaze strayed to the door of the room she'd stayed in when she was here. The room where Lucifer had come to her as Seth. Where he'd—

"It's not *just* the memories," she amended. "It's the normal. I can't do normal, Hugh. I'm sorry, but I can't. Not anymore. It's best if you just tell me where I can find Emmanuelle so I can get this over with."

"I wish it was that easy, Alex, but it's not. We're going to have to wait until she turns up."

"What the hell do you mean, turns up? You said you'd found her."

"We have a confirmed sighting, but—" Hugh broke off with a frown directed at Michael. "Didn't he tell you any of this?"

Alex met Michael's flat gaze. Tempting as it might be to let him take the blame, it wouldn't be fair. She sighed. "I didn't give him the chance. I had...stuff to deal with."

At least this explained Michael's insistence that she bring extra clothing with her.

"How long?" she asked Hugh.

"A day. Two. Maybe a week. Her movements aren't predictable."

"Her movements? You mean you've been tracking her?"

It was Hugh's turn to sigh. "Come in," he said. "Take your coat off. Sit. I know nothing is normal, Alex, and I'm not pretending that it is. But if we have to talk anyway, it may as well be over a drink. Agreed?"

Across the apartment, Riley did an about-face and carried the tray back into the kitchen. Glass clinked against glass. She emerged again with four tumblers and a bottle of Scotch. Alex met the calm in her gaze, the understanding in Henderson's, the wary stubbornness in Michael's. She scowled, knowing she'd lost.

"Fine," she growled. "But just one."

THIRTY-ONE

Alex took the drink from Riley but declined an invitation to sit. Keeping her distance from Michael, who had taken up a post near the doors that led to the balcony, she paced the living room floor, waiting for Riley and Henderson to settle onto one of the sofas. Henderson draped an arm around Riley's shoulders; she rested a hand on his knee. Alex shook her head.

"I'm still trying to wrap my head around the two of you together," she muttered. "When did you decide?"

"When Liz came back from seeing you in Toronto."

"Any particular catalyst?"

"Apart from knowing the world could end at any given minute?" Hugh shrugged. "I've wasted too many years schlepping around my personal baggage. The threat of Armageddon kind of changed my outlook."

Alex watched the tender look her colleague slanted toward the woman tucked against his side. *The threat of Armageddon.* At some point, Henderson would figure out for himself that it wasn't just a threat anymore. She didn't need to tell him. Not yet. She took a swallow of Scotch.

"So. Emmanuelle," she said.

Hugh shook his head. "I know, right? What are the chances she'd turn up here in Vancouver?"

"It's not as much of a coincidence as you think," Michael said, and all heads turned to him. His gaze met Alex's. "In retrospect, I should have realized she was here."

"How could you have known?"

"Seth. His transition here instead of Toronto, where he wanted to be. Where you were." Michael slid his hands into his pockets. "There had to have been something to draw him here. A connection even stronger than the one he felt for you at the time. I just didn't put the events together."

Silence followed his words, thick with speculation that none of them wanted to voice. How much of the last two weeks wouldn't have happened if Heaven had found Emmanuelle sooner? How many would still be alive?

On the other hand, how many more might be dead?

Alex closed her eyes and knocked back the rest of her drink. She helped herself to more.

"None of that matters," she said. "I'm just interested in where we find her now. Hugh?"

"We're watching the bar she frequents," Henderson said. "As soon as she shows up, Criminal Intelligence will let me know."

"Criminal Intelligence?" Alex echoed.

"Didn't Michael tell you? That's who recognized her from the intelligence alert. She's been a CI for the last three years."

Alex choked on a mouthful of Scotch. Coughed. Caught her breath. Then blinked through watery eyes at Hugh. A confidential informant. "Seriously? For what, drugs?"

"And money laundering. And human trafficking. And just about any other organized crime activity you can think of."

Alex's gaze sought Michael's grim one. He'd known this, and he still wanted to find her?

"She runs with a gang of bikers," Henderson continued. "Former Hells Angels, most of them. A few Outlaws. A rumored Mongol or two."

"Rival gang members? They'd kill each other before they'd run together."

"I know." Henderson gave a shrug. "But they're running together anyway."

Another glance at Michael. The level of grimness hadn't changed. She scowled at him. "And you're okay with this?" she demanded. "Even though we've confirmed she's involved in criminal activity, you still think it's okay to put her in charge of Heaven?"

"But she's not really involved in criminal activity, is she?" Riley put in. "If she's an informant..."

Alex ignored her. She stayed focused on Michael, trying—and failing—to read the impassive face.

"You're really that desperate?" she asked.

"*We* are that desperate," he said quietly.

She turned back to Hugh. "How long to find her?"

"Like I said, we have eyes on a bar out near Delta. She hasn't been there for a few days, so she's due to turn up soon. We'll know as soon as she's spotted."

"That could take forever."

"It's the best I've got."

"And in the meantime?"

Riley spoke up again. "In the meantime, you can stay at my old condo. We haven't gotten around to fully combining households yet, so you'll be comfortable. Maybe you can try catching up on some sleep."

Alex shot her a look of annoyance. "Is that supposed to be some kind of comment?"

Riley arched a brow. "Should it be?"

Damn, but Alex hated that too-knowing blue gaze. Ignoring the question, she switched her attention to Michael. "I want to go back to Toronto. We can wait there as well as we can here, and you can bring us back when—*if*—Emmanuelle is found."

One shoulder resting against the glass door, Michael regarded her calmly. "Bethiel is already looking for your niece. There's nothing more you can do."

And she hated the too-knowing *green* gaze, too.

She lifted her chin. "Maybe not, but I can sure as hell do more there than I can here. And at least I'll be doing *some*thing."

Unlike other beings she knew.

Michael ignored the unspoken accusation. "You'll also be opening yourself up to attack. Seth will begin his search for you there."

"I have you to protect me."

"Part of protecting you is keeping you out of danger in the first place." Michael straightened up from the doorframe. Black wings unfurled ever so slightly behind his back, just enough to remind her of who he was and how useless it would be to argue with him. "We're staying here."

"THIS WILL BE FOR YOU," Michael said.

Alex looked up from her exploration of Riley's

condo kitchen. As unplanned as their arrival in Vancouver had been, Riley had still managed to stock a few essentials: eggs, bread, oranges, milk. Unfortunately, however, Alex had found none of the coffee she so desperately needed right now. She scowled at Michael's cryptic words.

"What will be for—"

A knock sounded at the door.

Michael returned to his study of the postage-stamp sized garden outside the French doors off the living room. She stared at his back, then went to the door. Riley greeted her with determined cheerfulness.

"I thought you might like this." The psychiatrist held up a small brown bag, its wire top folded down. "Freshly ground."

With a scant three hours of sleep under her belt, Alex wouldn't have cared if the coffee had been sitting on a shelf for a decade, as long as its caffeine content was still there. She reached for the bag, but Riley sidestepped her.

"Why don't I make us both a cup, and then we can get caught up?"

Do I have a choice? Alex held back the inhospitable words with an effort. She couldn't very well throw Riley out of her own home—even if the psychiatrist wasn't technically living here any longer. She followed her into the kitchen, glancing at the screen of the cell phone she'd left on the island counter. Still nothing from Henderson.

Raking both hands through her hair, Alex gathered it together and pulled it forward over one shoulder. She and Michael had been in Vancouver less than twelve hours and already she was ready to climb the walls. She had no idea how she'd survive sitting around doing nothing for, potentially, days on end.

She didn't *do* nothing.

At least, not gracefully. And not when she had so many reasons to want to stay busy. To keep her mind occupied.

"Does he drink coffee?" Riley murmured, jerking her out of her mini reverie.

Alex followed the shrink's gaze to Michael, still at the glass doors onto the garden.

"He has a name."

"I know what his name is," Riley said. "It just seems..."

"What?"

"Disrespectful, I suppose." Riley sighed. "He's an *angel*."

Alex snorted. "Let's try to remember it was Heaven that got us into this mess, shall we?"

Michael still didn't look her way, but an irritated ruffle of feathers told her he'd heard. Riley studied her narrowly.

"When exactly is the last time you slept?" she asked.

"Last night, of course."

"A full night. Without nightmares."

"I—" The lie died on Alex's lips as she met that damned blue gaze again. She looked away. "It's been a while."

"I can give you some—"

"No. Thank you. I'd rather not."

"You can't keep this up forever, Alex. All kinds of health issues arise from sleep deprivation."

"I'm fine."

"Alex—"

"I said I'm fine, Elizabeth."

In silence, Riley filled the coffee machine's water

reservoir, scooped coffee into the permanent filter, and pressed the start button. Then she turned and cleared her throat. "Michael, could you give us a few minutes?"

Alex shook her head at the Archangel. *Don't.* He tugged open the French doors.

"I'll be outside."

Traitor.

Riley pointed to one of the stools at the island's eating bar. "Sit."

"I—"

"I said *sit.*"

Maybe if she'd had more sleep or fewer nightmares, or if she hadn't been fighting too many battles for too long, Alex might have argued. Instead, as she met Elizabeth's clinical but oddly compassionate gaze, resistance whooshed out of her like the air from an overinflated balloon. She sat. Riley took the stool beside her.

"Talk."

"About what?"

"Your sister and your soulmate are dead, Alex. Your niece is missing and going to die. Your former lover— who just happens to be a divine being who's taken over Hell—is stalking you. How about you pick one and we'll go from there?"

Alex had thought it before, and she'd think it again: Riley would have made one hell of an interrogator. But the psychiatrist wouldn't wear her down that easily. Alex schooled herself to calmness. To detachment. She met the wire-framed gaze steadily.

"Fine. I'll pick," said Riley. "You saw Nina. How did she look?"

"Pregnant and sick and about to die. Probably

because that's how she is." The odor rising from the coffee mug made Alex's stomach churn. She slid it away from her and fixed Riley with a baleful glare. "I thought we weren't doing this anymore, Liz. The last time you saw me, you said you'd decided I was handling things. You said you'd back off."

Riley ignored her. "You must feel incredibly helpless."

Alex stared out the window at Michael's back, her jaw clenching until her head ached.

"You've lost so much already," Riley pressed. "Aramael, Seth, Jen. What happens if this Bethiel can't find Nina in time? What happens if she dies before you get to her? How will you survive?"

Alex curled her nails into her palms. She knew why Elizabeth pushed, knew what the psychiatrist tried to do. On some level, she might even have appreciated it, or at least the concern that motivated it. But on another level, in the dark and cavernous place growing inside her, she couldn't care. Couldn't let herself care. That's how mental compartments worked.

"I'll survive because breaking isn't an option, Elizabeth. It never was. Talking won't change that."

"Bullshit. You want to know why I changed my mind about talking? Because *you* changed. I thought I'd seen you strung as wire-taut as I've ever seen anyone before, but I haven't seen this. *You* haven't seen this." Riley paused. She reached out to cover Alex's hand with her own.

"How much longer do you think you can handle everything before you break, Alex?"

The compartment door in Alex's mind clanged shut. She slid from the stool and pulled her hand away from Riley's warmth. Her humanness.

"Wrong question," she said. She took her coat down from a hook by the door. "It's not how long I *can* handle everything, Liz, it's how long I have no choice but to handle it. And the answer is a fucking eternity."

THIRTY-TWO

Michael caught up with her before she'd reached the sidewalk, his hand descending onto her shoulder. She shrugged it off.

"Go away."

He caught hold of her again, his grip like iron this time, and pulled her to a stop. She turned to repeat herself in a more direct manner, but came up short against Aramael's sword, braced flat against her chest.

"Whether you care what happens to you or not," Michael informed her, "I do."

Bitter words found their way to her surface. "Until we speak with Emmanuelle, you mean."

Michael's mouth tightened and green fire flashed in his eyes. "I'm not as unfeeling as you'd like to think, Alexandra. If there was a way I could undo what Seth did to you, I would."

She pulled away a second time. "You had that chance. *I* had that chance, and you wouldn't let me take it."

He blocked her path, wings spread to keep her from going around him. "I *couldn't* let you take it, damn it. Everything hinges on Emmanuelle right now. If I screw this up, it's not just Heaven's survival at risk, it's that of the very universe."

She stared down the street, leafless trees lining it like sentries. A swirl of wind blew dust around her ankles. "I agreed to find her for you. Not to be your spokesperson."

"I know. But I'm asking you anyway. She won't listen to one of Heaven, not right away, and you're the only mort—human who knows enough to go to her.""

"You don't know she'll listen to me, either."

"I know you're our best chance."

"Why?" she snarled, throwing her hands wide. "What makes me so goddamned special that gods will listen to me and angels will fight for me, Michael? I never asked for this. I'm a goddamned mortal—or at least, I *was* until I landed in the middle of a fucking war between Heaven and Hell. So what is it about me? *What*?"

For a long moment, Michael looked down at her in silence, still holding the sheathed sword between them. Then he sighed. "I don't know. Not for certain."

"But you have a theory."

"This isn't the place to discuss it."

Alex followed his gaze to Riley, standing at the window of the condo, watching them. The psychiatrist held a cell phone to her ear. Henderson. She'd called Henderson. Alex swallowed a groan, regretting her parting shot about having to handle an eternity of loss. Of course Riley would tell Hugh about that, and he would demand the whole story, and then he'd want to take it on himself to try and fix it and then Alex would have to deal with his anger and his concern and—

An invisible knife blade slid between her ribs.

Hell. So much for not caring.

"Get me out of here," she said. "Please."

Michael held her gaze for a moment and then, without a word, swept her into the cocoon of his wings, his arms holding her tight as her essence melted into his.

They rematerialized on a rocky stretch of shoreline hemmed in by high tide on one side and the dense, towering rain forest on the other. Alex pushed free of Michael's hold the second she felt the ground beneath her. Scanning their surroundings, she found no other soul in sight. She put a dozen feet between her and the Archangel, crossing her arms against the chill wind.

"Well?" she said. "What's your theory?"

Michael settled the end of Aramael's sword scabbard on a flat rock at his feet. He rested his hands on the pommel. "I think your Naphil bloodline may have originated with an Archangel. Samael, to be exact."

So her great-great-great-great-great-etc. grandfather was trying to kill her? Lovely.

"What difference would that make?"

"Archangels are a great deal more powerful than any of the other choirs. It stands to reason the Naphil descendant of one might be somewhat beyond ordinary as well. You might carry a spark of divinity within you even after all these generations. If I'm right, it's why Mittron chose you to be Aramael's soulmate in the first place. It would have strengthened the soulmate bond, and it would explain why Aramael was able to hear you across two realms. Why I was able to hear you."

Alex waited for the catch in her throat to ease. "And Seth? How does it explain him?"

"It would have been the reason you attracted his attention to begin with."

"But not why he's become so obsessed with me."

"No."

She waited.

Michael gazed out over the water. "You know Seth saved your life."

She bit back the snarky response she would have liked to make about having been there, and said instead, "Twice. Yes."

"Both times you were so far gone that he had to take...extraordinary measures to bring you back."

The catch in her throat moved into her chest, squeezing her lungs. She forced her words past it. "How extraordinary?"

"Most extraordinary," Michael said. His voice was heavy. Rough with regret.

Or was that pity?

"I think Seth gave a little bit of his own soul to save you each of those times, Alex. To repair the damage to your own. I think it was the only way he *could* save you."

Funny how the world could suddenly seem so far away even when you remained standing in it. As if you were no longer a part of it. As if the ocean rolled past a stranger's feet rather than your own, and the cries of the seagulls fell on someone else's ears.

"You are quite literally a part of him now," Michael continued. "I don't think he even realizes it himself. He just knows he isn't complete without you."

Alex stared at Michael's hands, folded over the sword pommel. She waited for his words to sink in. To make sense. She shook her head.

"You're wrong," she whispered. "You have to be wrong."

But they both knew he wasn't.

Michael remained silent, and she waited some more, this time for the horror to envelop her. To paralyze her. It didn't come—or if it did, the nothingness inside her simply swallowed it whole. A nothingness that stretched out before her for all of the eternity to which Seth had condemned her. She thought again of the moment when she'd stood with Michael in the between place, when she'd begun to pull away, when she might have ended all of this. Wondered if maybe...

She raised her gaze to his, but found only bleakness there. He knew what she would ask, and already he shook his head.

"I can't," he said. "I wish I could, Alex, but I can't. I cannot willfully do anything to harm a mortal. None in Heaven can. Not without falling. To take you back there, to knowingly take part in ending your life—"

Alex turned away, cutting him off. She breathed in the tang of salt air. So that was it, then. Unless by some miracle she found Mittron and Bethiel upheld his end of their bargain, there really was no hope. No way to avoid the inevitability of eternity with Seth.

"I can, however, do this for you," Michael said.

She blinked as Aramael's sword appeared before her again. Unsheathed this time, glinting in the sunlight that had broken through the clouds. The ocean rolled over her boot.

"I don't understand."

"I can teach you to fight, Alex. To defend yourself."

"To what point? I still wouldn't stand a chance."

"Of winning, no."

She stared at the sword. Then at Michael. Then at the sword again. Understanding dawned. She stepped away from the water.

Her hand closed over the hilt of Aramael's sword, and the faint, residual energy of her soulmate crackled up her arm. She met Michael's glittering gaze.

No, she would never win.

But maybe, just maybe, she could die trying.

"Yes," she said.

THERE WASN'T MUCH finesse to swinging a broadsword to begin with, and Alex possessed even less than Mika'el had hoped for. He blocked her every swing without effort, watching pain spasm across her face each time metal clashed against metal, ripping a grunt from her as a shockwave traveled along her arms and down her spine. In soberingly few minutes, she was soaked with sweat and panting, and he felt certain the sword remained in her grip through its own energy and not hers. His jaw tightened grimly as she let the weapon droop to rest against the ground.

"Enough," she gasped. "I can't even lift it anymore."

He set the tip of his own sword in the sand and balanced his hands on its hilt. "Rest. We'll continue in a minute."

Blue eyes met his, anger and despair warring in their depths in equal measure. "Are you serious? This is useless. I can barely swing the damned thing, let alone land a blow."

"And yet you disabled Seth in that washroom even before I had the sword remade to fit your hand rather than Aramael's. You might have killed him if you'd known where to strike."

Alex tossed the blade onto the rocky beach. "That was different. He didn't expect me to—he wasn't fighting back."

"And no Fallen One who comes after you will expect it, either."

"So now you think I can kill one of them?" She held up a trembling hand and snorted her disbelief.

"If you get lucky, you might." Mika'el waved off the objection forming on her lips. "The way I see it, this can go one of three ways. Kill a Fallen One, and the next to come after you won't be as willing to follow instructions and bring you back alive. Wound a Fallen One, and you gain another day here. Engage a Fallen One in battle, and you might—*might*—get lucky and suffer a fatal blow. Especially if you know how to put yourself in the path of that blow."

Alex stared down at the shoreline between them. She nudged a broken oyster shell with the toe of her boot. Then she looked up again. "And what if it goes a fourth way?" she asked quietly. "What if it's not a Fallen One who comes for me, but Seth?"

"Then you will have one, and only one, very small chance to finish what you started."

She weighed his words, her expression alternating between fierce determination and the despair of self-doubt. Mika'el sheathed his sword and went to stand before her.

"I can make no promises to you, Alex. I don't know whether this will work or not. But I *can* give you the only chance you will have." He placed his hands on her shoulders and let a fraction of his energy course through her, healing the damage to her muscles, soothing her overwrought nerve endings. Surprised relief reflected back at him. He let his mouth curve into a half smile.

"And I can do that for you," he said, stepping back. "As often as you need me to. Ready to go again?"

He watched her flex her hands, testing the absence of pain.

"Why are you doing this?" she asked. "I'm one life among billions, and of Nephilim descent to boot. After we find Emmanuelle, what happens to me won't matter. Not to Heaven."

Mika'el held a hand out over the sword she had dropped to the ground, and it flew up into his grip. He extended it toward her, hilt first. "It will matter to me. You were right, Alex. You've lost enough. I may not be able to save you outright, but let me do what I can to help you save yourself."

She hesitated, then reached to take the sword from him. Her jawline flexing, she swung Aramael's blade in a wide arc toward him. Metal clashed against metal in a shower of sparks, and a handful of seagulls that had landed on the shore took flight, their protests loud and discordant. Alex stumbled. Michael put out a hand to steady her. She shrugged it off and spun away from him, returning with a grunt and another swing of the sword. Another clash. More sparks.

It was going to be a long day.

THIRTY-THREE

Emerging from the tub, Alex reached for the towel hanging on the bar. Air hissed between her teeth as her hand closed over the rough fabric. Michael might have been able to keep her on her feet for the day-long sword lesson, but his healing efforts had long since worn off, and the Epsom salts had barely taken the edge off the abuse through which she'd put her body. Right now, pain ranged from a dull, nagging ache in every joint to a fire-like sensitivity across both palms...and it covered just about every degree and body part between. But it had still been worth it. In more ways than one. Her lips pulled into a tight smile as she gingerly toweled her arms.

By the end of the day, Michael had pronounced himself satisfied with her progress—he might even have looked pleased in an unguarded moment. The faint praise he'd given her had somehow taken the edge off the emptiness that had invaded her center, made it seem less likely that it would take her over.

It had even made her less inclined to want it to do so.

Alex paused, studying her reflection in the mirror over the sink. Purpose stared back at her. For the first time since Seth had turned her immortal, she felt like she still had some control over her life. She might not be able to save the entire world—or even Nina—but as faint as the chance might be, she might yet manage to keep herself out of Seth's grasp, and that translated into a reason to keep going. A reason to hold onto that last, infinitesimal sliver of hope.

Hell, after all that activity, she might even sleep tonight. Without her usual liquid aid.

She dried between her toes and worked her way up each leg, leaving the contortions required for her back until last. Another hiss escaped her. Damn, that hurt, and it would only get worse by morning. She returned the towel to its bar and reached for the robe Riley had left for her on the back of the door.

Conscience twinged. She really needed to give that poor woman a break at some point. The psychiatrist had nothing but good intentions where she was concerned. She and Henderson both. They'd stood by Alex through crap that would have sent most people running. Would it really be so bad if she told them what she faced? What Seth had done to her? His plan to have her by his side for eternity?

Her brain shied sideways at the thought of the shock and sympathy that would follow. And the questions.

"*What will you do?*" she imagined Riley asking.

"*I'll try to pick a fight with a Fallen One,*" she heard herself answer, "*and then throw myself on his or her sword in exactly the right way, so that it pierces the immortality I never wanted in the first place. I'll try to die.*"

Suicide by Fallen One.

That would be a new one even to Henderson.

She traced fingertips over the center of her chest, where Michael said Seth's little gift to her resided, safely encased behind her breastbone. Remembered the phosphorescence that had leaked from Aramael's wound. The trickle of life-giving energy she hadn't been able to stem. Had it hurt? Had trying to protect her made it worse? If he'd remained still until the others had come to his aid, would they have been able to save him? If she'd tried harder—

Fuck.

Alex exhaled shakily. Reaching for the doorknob with one hand, she flicked off the light switch with the other. It was time to test her sleep theory.

Michael looked around from the French doors when she reached the living room. He hadn't turned on any of the lamps in the room, but enough light filtered from the hallway behind Alex that she saw his brows twitch together.

"You're in pain," he said.

She shrugged, then regretted doing so. "Nothing a couple of painkillers and a good night's sleep won't fix."

He straightened away from the door and Alex watched him approach. For the first time, it crossed her mind how hard it must be for him to be cooped up here, in a tiny apartment in a human city, babysitting a single Naphil when his own kind fought for the existence of the universe. And she thought *she* chafed at her impotence?

Michael stood in front of her. "You should have said something earlier."

"I thought the bath would help."

"And stubbornness didn't enter into it?"

She looked away.

Michael placed gentle hands on either side of her neck, just inside the robe's edge. His thumbs rested on her collarbones. A tingle spread outward from his touch, warm and electric. Her muscle fibers eased and joints unknotted in its wake. Alex closed her eyes and didn't even try to hold back a sigh.

"Better?" Michael asked. She heard the smile in his voice.

"You have no idea. Thank you."

"You're welcome."

His hands remained in place for a few seconds more, until she thought she might embarrass herself by folding into a heap at his feet. Then, with a final light squeeze, Michael withdrew his touch. Alex rolled her shoulders experimentally. She opened her eyes.

"Can all angels heal like that?"

"Not exactly like that, no. But to one degree or another."

"I see."

He raised a dark eyebrow. "And what do you see, exactly?"

"Disparity."

"You want to know why we don't help humanity with its illnesses. Its diseases."

"Because the One told you not to, would be my guess. The whole no interference bullshit."

Pain shadowed Michael's eyes, but he blinked and it disappeared. "Did Aramael ever tell you about Heaven? What it's like there?"

"We didn't have many opportunities for small talk."

"Of course. I'm sorry."

She lifted a shoulder. "It doesn't matter. But what does life in Heaven have to do with whether or not angels are allowed to heal?"

"It's beautiful," Michael said, as if she hadn't spoken. His face took on a faraway expression. "A place of gardens and forests, knowledge and learning. Our library contains a copy of every word humankind has ever inscribed on paper, our archives a record of every event in your history. Do you know how the One spent her days? Gardening. She loved to grow things. Her rose gardens are—were—stunning."

"I'm sure they were, but I still don't see—"

"You once had everything we do, Alex. Just as the One created mortals in her own image, she created your Earth in Heaven's image. The gardens and forests, the capacity for learning and knowledge and growth. The potential remains, but only if you choose it."

"You're saying our free will got us into this mess."

"And it can get you out of it again."

"But you could still help us. Guide us..." her voice trailed off. "The Guardians."

"Yes," he said again. "What the Grigori did, what they shared with you, was wrong. We knew that. The One knew it. That's why she gave you the Guardians. Little bits of her own energy, her own consciousness, there to guide humanity through its childhood. You have everything you need to become great, to become like Heaven, but the whole point of free will is that you must choose to do so."

"That's all well and good, but I'm not asking you to transform the planet, Michael. If you could just heal—"

Michael wheeled, his wings half-open, knocking

a stack of books from an end table to the floor. He threw his arms wide. "How many times?" he demanded. "How many times should we heal you, Alex? How many generations? Your world—the world *you* created—is toxic. Your very societies are toxic. We cannot save you from yourselves. Believe me, I've tried."

"You?"

"Me." He stooped to pick up the books he'd toppled. He set them back on the table, straightened them. Then he folded his wings behind him and looked up at Alex, his green eyes shadowed, his face without expression. "When I left Heaven—left the One—I came to Earth and lived among you as a physician. For five thousand years, I did all I could to heal those who crossed my path. Sometimes one at a time, sometimes an entire village. The knowledge the Grigori gave you didn't just contain harm, it contained good. As much as I could without violating the One's laws, I tried to show you that good, just as the Guardians try to do even now, every day, with billions of other souls."

Alex tugged the robe's lapels closer, folded her arms over it. "I didn't know."

"No one ever has."

"You had a whole universe to choose from. Why here?"

"At first, because of my love for the One. My entire existence had been for her until that point. It damn near killed me to leave her, and I thought I could remain close to her in some way by looking after the children she'd created. Then, as I got to know you, I began to see what she saw in you. Your potential for good, your capacity for love. I want to see humanity survive, Alex, but humanity needs to want it, too."

Alex padded across to the French doors, the hardwood floor cool beneath her bare feet. Outside, the tiny back yard had become a garden of shadows in the night, shades of dark and darker. Beyond it, a street lamp highlighted the bare, skeletal branches of the trees lining the road.

Beyond those, lights sparkled from the windows of houses and apartment buildings that made up a city.

And beyond that, an entire world filled with other cities and towns and villages. The billions of souls Michael had tried to serve. Tried to influence. She refocused on the reflection in the glass. Michael, standing in the middle of the room, tall and capable and oh, so powerful.

And still unable to change the course of humanity.

She turned, leaning back against the doors. "You have more faith in us than I do."

"I disagree. You wouldn't be a cop if you didn't believe in your fellow humans."

"I'm a cop so I can try to save—" She broke off with a grimace. "Touché. But even if I believe some people are worth saving, seeing how the world is reacting right now, I'm not sure it's possible."

"Anything is possible. You're living proof of that."

"Me?"

"Only one Archangel chose to follow Lucifer's fall from Heaven. You carry the blood of Samael within you, Alex. One of the most traitorous souls in the universe. And yet look at what you've become. What you've made of yourself without even the benefit of a Guardian's guidance. If you're not the epitome of the triumph of free will, I don't know what is."

She snorted. "Given the number of bad choices I've made?"

"None of us is perfect. The One herself made questionable decisions. What matters is that you've persisted. You've cared enough to keep trying, even now."

A little tingle of warmth formed in her belly at his words. She ignored it, shaking her head. "You're wrong. You've no idea how close I've come to just walking away from all of this."

From you.

"I do know," he said gruffly. "I also know you stayed."

The warmth spread outward. Alex straightened. "It's late. I should get to bed."

Michael stepped back to let her by, but his hand on her arm stopped her as she passed. A flutter followed in the wake of the warmth. She stared at the strong, tanned fingers against the white of her robe.

"You stayed," Michael repeated.

She raised her gaze to the steady green of his. "So did you."

His mouth twisted. "Staying to protect you for my own interests isn't quite the same thing."

"No, but doing what you did for me today is. Thank you for that."

"You're welcome. I only wish I could do more."

"It's more than I've had for a while," she assured him. "That makes it enough."

Michael looked as if he searched for words to say more, but Alex made herself pull away from his touch. Away from him. Away from a sudden *what the hell* flare of awareness she didn't want to feel. Had no business feeling. Refused to even consider. She stepped away from the silken brush of wings that had somehow moved to half-encircle her.

"It's enough," she said again, and then retreated to the bedroom for what would almost certainly be less sleep than she'd hoped for.

THIRTY-FOUR

Mika'el stared at his palm long after the *click* from the end of the hallway told him Alex's door had closed. What in bloody Hell had that been? And how in bloody, *bloody* Hell could he have let it happen? He slammed his open hand against the doorframe, just controlled enough not to shatter the wood. The unwelcome tingle remained, and a tightness in his chest moved up to grip his throat.

He closed his eyes. It wasn't what he thought, he assured himself. It had to be something else. Compassion, perhaps. After watching her go through so much, it was inevitable he feel something of the sort. He wouldn't be true to his nature if he didn't.

His hand tingled anew.

Bloody Hell.

He drew a steadying breath, forced his mind to calm, shook off the shock that clouded his thinking. He was the Archangel Mika'el. Whatever he thought he might have felt, he couldn't have. Wouldn't so much as consider the idea, because it went against everything he believed in, everything he fought for. Everything he was supposed to—

"Bad night?" a voice behind him inquired dryly.

Mika'el's sword was in his grasp before the thought of it had completed itself. Bethiel threw himself backward, out of reach of the swing.

"Easy, warrior!"

Mika'el caught short a second lunge. "Damn it, Bethiel—I might have killed you! You should know better than to sneak up—"

Jaw flexing, he stopped, glowering at the other angel. That anyone could sneak up on him at all should have been impossible, and they both knew it. But he was damned if he'd discuss it with one no longer even of Heaven. He shoved his sword back into its sheath.

"You're supposed to be looking for the girl."

"And *she*"—Bethiel inclined his head toward the hallway—"is supposed to be looking for Mittron."

"She's done what she can for the moment. If and when she learns anything, I will let you know."

The other angel's face turned stubborn. "I want to speak with her."

"She needs sleep. You can speak with me." Mika'el narrowed his gaze. "How did you even find us here?"

"She left me a note in her apartment, telling me you were bringing her here. Because it obviously hadn't occurred to *you* to do so."

Michael crossed his arms. Flexed his wings.

Bethiel sighed. "Fine. I may have something on Mittron and I want her to check it for me. There's a rumor among the Fallen that he's supervising the Nephilim army—and recruiting humans to help."

"Humans!"

"By way of something the Fallen are calling the Internet." Bethiel dropped onto the sofa and arranged his wings behind him. His expression turned brooding. "There can't be many places on Earth where you can hide eighty thousand Nephilim. If the Naphil can find where these human recruits are going, perhaps she will find Mittron as well."

Mika'el went still as he remembered Alex pointing at the devastation on the television. An entire city wiped out by a nuclear accident. He heard again her accusatory words. "*If I told you the Fallen had engineered that, what would you do?*"

She hadn't explained further, and Mika'el hadn't asked, because his answer, of course, would have been that he could do nothing. Because that's just how things were. Bethiel's revelation, however, complicated matters. Mika'el swung away from the Principality and walked to the glass doors overlooking the garden.

The destroyed city had been near Pripyat. The same Pripyat that had been abandoned after the Chernobyl disaster, where enough buildings still remained to house an army.

He heard Bethiel's weight shift against the leather. Felt the Principality's increased interest.

"You know something," Bethiel said.

Mika'el looked over his shoulder. "Perhaps."

Bethiel sat back again, one arm extended along the sofa back. His gaze narrowed. Turned watchful. "You don't want to tell me."

"No."

Watchful became cold. Ugly. Furious.

"The Seraph deserves to die for what he's done," Bethiel spat.

"I'm not arguing that," Mika'el said quietly. "Nor

am I disputing that it should be you who kills him. But it can't happen now. There's more at stake here than revenge, Bethiel. The Fallen can't know we've found the Nephilim. Not until I find—"

The Principality interrupted with a short, humorless bark of laughter. "You seriously think you can find a god who doesn't want to be found and talk her back into a place she doesn't want to be?"

"I seriously have to try," Mika'el retorted. "Because the universe seriously won't survive if I don't."

Bethiel's gaze flicked toward the hallway. "If you know, then the Naphil does, too."

Mika'el shook his head. "Don't. We both know I can stop you. I'd much rather not have to. You'll get Mittron. I promise. Just not now."

"Then when?" Bethiel shoved himself up from the couch. His snarl held the pent-up rage of three thousand years in Limbo. Three thousand years of silently, slowly going mad. "When *you* deem it time?"

Mika'el's right hand rested lightly on the hilt of the sword at his hip. "When the time is right. You still have it in you to be one of Heaven, Bethiel. You're still—"

"Bloody Hell. You haven't changed at all, have you? You're still trying to hold everyone else to your own standards."

Mika'el stalked across the room until he stood toe to toe with the other, their faces mere inches apart. "Be glad I do, Principality, because if I thought you couldn't be trusted—"

A door down the hall opened, and he froze. Great. They'd woken Alex. He glanced over his shoulder, but the hallway sat empty, the bedroom door at the end of it closed. He frowned. He'd been certain—he swiveled back to Bethiel.

"Were you followed?"

"Of course not."

"You took precautions?"

"Well—"

Another sound from down the hall. This time, the unmistakable hiss of a sword leaving its sheath.

THIRTY-FIVE

Alex came awake without moving, without breathing. Her back to the door, she stared at the vertical sliver of light on the wall. Watched it widen, fill with the shadow of someone entering the room, then narrow again. Her heartbeat thundered in her ears. Michael?

A faint pulse of blue pulled her gaze to the sword lying on the bed beside her. Inside its scabbard, Aramael's blade glowed, its light escaping where hilt met sheath. Her eyebrows twitched together. Had it always done that, or—?

The low rumble of two male voices reached her, one of them Michael's. The door clicked shut.

Ice gripped her belly. Splintered through her veins. If Michael was out there, then who the hell was in here?

She didn't wait for an announcement.

Throwing back the covers, she rolled away from the door, fingers closing over the sword's hilt as she gained her feet. Free of its scabbard, the blade glowed with a fierce blue light, pushing back the shadows in the room and highlighting the figure between the bed and the door. Between Alex and escape.

Without a word, the Fallen One—a female—flicked on the light switch and stalked toward her. Alex bit down on the terror that demanded she swing. She shifted her feet into the stance Michael had taught her. Adjusted her grip. Balanced the sword's weight...

The Fallen knocked the weapon aside as she might have done a twig. The fingers of one hand clamped over Alex's throat, all but cutting off her air. Her every nerve screaming at her to fight, Alex held herself rigid. She watched the vicious gleam in her attacker's eyes draw nearer.

"If I didn't know you were worth more to me alive than dead," the Fallen One whispered, her breath hot against Alex's ear, "I would slay you on the spot for daring to *think* about raising your hand to me."

"Let go of me and I'll try again," Alex croaked.

Disconcertingly colorless eyes went agate hard. "Try, Naphil bitch, and I'll beat you into the ground."

The Fallen's gaze moved to the sword in Alex's hand. It narrowed, then flashed back to pin Alex's again. "Is that an Archangel's sword?"

She didn't wait for Alex's response, instead turning greedy pale eyes back to the sword. Alex felt the blade shift in her grip as the other's hand closed over it. She tightened her hold, clinging to the hilt. Claw-like fingers prised at hers. Then sudden, sticky heat sprayed across her face, burning her cheek, her lips. The Fallen One shrieked and fell back, releasing both Alex and sword.

Sucking air through her bruised larynx, Alex

brought the sword up to striking height again. But her attacker had spun away, blood spurting from the stump at the end of her arm.

A severed hand lay twitching on the carpet.

Alex stared at it, then lifted her gaze to the grim countenance of Michael, towering over the huddled Fallen.

"Damn you, warrior!" Alex's attacker snarled, cradling the injured limb. "The female is Naphil— what do you care what happens to her?"

"My business with her is just that, Zuriel. *My* business."

The Fallen lifted her chin. "You remember my name."

"I remember all names. Including that of the one who sent you. I want you to deliver a message to him for me. To Samael."

"I'm not your messenger."

Michael raised the tip of his blade to rest against the center of Zuriel's chest. "Neither are you in a position to argue."

Zuriel growled something under her breath and flashed Alex a look of pure poison. She still cradled her arm stump, but the bleeding had slowed to a drip. She scowled at Michael again. "Fine. What's your message?"

"The Naphil woman is off limits. To anyone."

"Or...?"

Michael shot a pointed stare at the floor. Alex followed his gaze—and that of Zuriel—and horror uncoiled in her belly. The hand severed from Zuriel's wrist had become twisted, blackened, desiccated. A skeletal fraction of what it had been before.

"Leave it," Michael ordered.

Alex looked up to find that Zuriel had moved, as if to retrieve the monstrosity. Zuriel scowled at the Archangel, then dove toward the hand. White light flared. The appendage crumbled into black dust.

"I said leave it," Michael repeated, his voice flat.

Fury rolled off Zuriel in waves, pressing Alex back into the wall. For a second, she thought the Fallen One might go after Michael, consequences be damned, but instead she raised a hand, pushed aside the sword with which Michael threatened her, and disappeared.

"You should have killed her," another voice said. "She'll tell Samael where to find the Naphil. He'll send others."

For the first time since Michael's arrival, Alex looked beyond his shoulder to the figure in the doorway. Bethiel. The second voice she'd heard when Zuriel had come into the room. And he was right. There would be others. She sagged against the wall, staring at the sword to which she still clung. The blue light was gone, leaving only cold, dull steel in its wake. Others would come to retrieve her. And they would keep coming, until they succeeded. Because Michael couldn't stay to protect her forever, and all the training in the world couldn't equip her to protect herself.

She flinched, remembering how Zuriel had swiped aside the weapon, barely acknowledging its existence. Nausea slithered through her stomach. What a fool she'd been to think otherwise. To think she could stand up to any of the Fallen. To Seth.

She'd never stood a chance.

Never would.

Dropping the sword to the carpet, she bolted for the bathroom.

SAMAEL CLOSED HIS EYES, gripping the edge of the war table to keep from reaching out to throttle Zuriel. Teeth grinding together and nostrils flaring, he breathed in. Out. In. His eyes snapped open. Zuriel took a step back.

"So you let her get away," he said.

Temper flared in the former Cherub's pale eyes. "I didn't *let* her do anything. I was up against fucking Mika'el himself, damn it. You should have told me he was protecting her."

"My instructions were to locate her and then return to me. If you had done as you were told—"

"I wanted to bring her back for you. I thought—"

"No. No, you *didn't* think. You didn't think at all. You made a stupid, rash decision, and then compounded it by letting yourself be distracted by a sword!"

"But it wasn't just any sword," Zuriel objected. "It was that of an Archangel. Do you know what I could have done with a weapon like that? I would have been virtually undefeatable on the battlefield."

"And instead, you'll never fight again, Mika'el knows we're coming for the Naphil, and Bethiel knows I'm having him followed." Samael shoved against the table, sending it crashing against the far wall. He advanced on the Cherub, his steps as measured as they were furious. "In short, Cherub, you've failed me and rendered yourself useless in the process."

Zuriel tucked the stump of her arm behind her and skittered backward until her spine met the wall. Two more strides carried Samael to her. His fist smashed into her face, shattering bone and teeth, slamming her head against the stone. She slid to the floor, her screech pressing in on his ears and bringing two other Fallen at a run into the war room. They looked from

Samael to the Principality curled into a ball and then, without reacting, withdrew. Samael reached down to drag Zuriel to her feet, shaking her until her head flopped back and forth and bloody spittle flew from her mouth.

"Do you have any idea what you've done?" he demanded. "You stupid, useless *bitch*. I've been working toward this for millennia. I had to depose fucking Lucifer himself to get this far! Then I give you one task—one simple, tiny task, to find the Naphil— and you...screw...it...up." He punctuated the words with a shake between each. "Everything rides on her death, and you *fail*."

Zuriel scrabbled with her remaining hand at his, trying to escape his grasp. His loathing for her at war with sheer fury, Samael threw her from him, and she scuttled into a corner.

Apologies and promises ran together in a babble. "I'm sorry I'm so sorry I don't know what I was thinking forgive me I didn't mean it I'm sorry!"

He stared at her, remembering his own pain and terror at the hands of Lucifer. He'd thought the Light-bearer too harsh at the time, but he understood now. Knew why Lucifer had demanded absolute obedience, even if he'd had to beat it out of him. He was certain he could extract the same obedience from Zuriel, and he might have done so but for one thing. His gaze settled on the stump of her arm, seeping fresh blood through its bandage, rendering her useless to him, to Seth, to Hell.

Samael crossed to the wall where his armor hung and lifted the sword from its place. He unsheathed it, laid the scabbard aside on the table, and then turned. Zuriel's pain-glazed eyes shone with tears.

With pleading. Her head moved from side to side. He pressed the blade's tip against the center of her chest. She grasped frantically at the blade, slicing her hand, powerless to move it against his strength. His resolve. Steel began a slow, unrelenting slide through flesh and bone, and her eyes went wide. Samael felt the faint resistance of her immortality. He took a deep breath.

Useless, he reminded himself. *Except as an example to others.*

He tightened his grip and shoved.

THIRTY-SIX

Alex emerged from the bathroom to find Michael waiting for her in the hallway, back against the wall, arms crossed. She held up a hand. "Don't," she said. "Just...don't."

She brushed past him and made her way to the kitchen, any hope of sleep long gone. Perhaps for good.

Michael followed her. "We need to talk, Alex."

"No. We don't." She took the coffee pot from the machine and filled it with cold water. Poured it into the reservoir. Replaced the pot on its element. Scooped coffee into the filter.

"You can't just give up like this."

Her hand jerked, dumping coffee grounds across the counter. She rested fists on either side of the mess and closed her eyes. "I'm not giving up. I'm facing reality. That Fallen One didn't even hesitate. She pushed aside that sword as if it didn't exist. As if *I* didn't exist. I don't care how much practice I get, I can't fight that, Michael. I could never fight that."

"Alex—"

"Stop it. Please." Alex set the scoop on the counter and turned to him, folding her arms over her belly. "I've promised to help you with Emmanuelle, and as long as you're able to keep me here, I will. But beyond that, we're done. You don't have to pretend you want to help me anymore."

"I wasn't pretending. I thought—I wanted—" Michael's brilliant green gaze met hers, equal parts ferocity, pity, and guilt glittering there. His jaw flexed as he compressed his lips. "You're right, I do need you to help me with Emmanuelle, but I wanted to give you something in return. You almost killed Seth with that sword once. That should have been impossible. No human hand should be able to wield an Archangel's sword at all, let alone with enough force to wound one of Heaven or Hell. I honestly thought..."

"What? That I was special? Well, I'm not. I'm nothing more than what Caim said I was at the beginning of all this—a pawn in some fucking cosmic game I have no control over. As for the sword, Aramael was still alive when I used it against Seth. Did it ever cross your mind that *that* was why I could do what I did?"

Michael braced his hands against the island counter. "Even if that's true, it doesn't explain how you summoned me across—"

"Don't you get it?" Alex snarled. "Whatever you think, it doesn't matter. It doesn't change anything. I get that you're trying to give me some kind of hope I can escape this"— she waved a vague hand—"but we both know there's no point. There never was. Unless you're willing to end my life when this is done, there's nothing you can do, Michael."

There. She'd said it. She'd asked.

And now she waited for his answer.

"You know I can't," he said.

Self-righteous fury boiled over in her chest. The one thing she asked for in all this, the one thing she needed, and—

Pain tugged at the corners of Michael's mouth. The fury in Alex hesitated. She took in the shadows in his eyes, the rigid line of the wings he kept tightly furled behind him, the bleak, hard planes of his face...

Something inside her folded. Crumpled. She blinked back the sting of tears. What the hell was she doing? This magnificent being—aggravating though he might be on occasion—was doing his level best to hold the universe together, and she accused him of not caring? Dared to ask him to go against everything he stood for, everything he was? The slap of clarity made her inhale sharply. Was this what she had become? What Seth had made her into? She slumped into the corner where pantry met countertop.

"I'm sorry," she muttered. "I shouldn't have said that."

Shoulders that carried the weight of two realms still managed a shrug. "You have every right to be angry. None of this should ever have happened."

None of it. Not Aramael or Seth or Lucifer...

Not Jen and Nina.

She swallowed. "But it did."

"Yes."

Silence drifted between them, a vast ocean filled with the knowledge that she would spend eternity with a divine being she both pitied and despised. The certainty that neither her soulmate's sword nor Heaven's greatest warrior himself could stop it from happening. The realization that it no longer mattered.

Not in the grand scheme of things. Not when it was one life measured against billions; her life against the world's very survival.

Eternity.

She couldn't even fathom the concept.

She refocused on Michael, on the self-recrimination scrawled across his face. He had enough to deal with. She wouldn't make it more difficult for him. Not anymore. With a sigh, she crossed to the island and reached to cover one of his hands with hers, trying not to think about the incongruity of offering comfort to an Archangel.

"I'm not angry, Michael. Not really. Terrified, yes, but not angry. And despite what I may have said in past, I don't blame you for what's happened. You've done everything you can."

A muscle in Michael's jaw flexed, and he stared over her head. "I'm not accustomed to feeling helpless," he said. "Or to not knowing what to do."

"Then do what you set out to do. Find Emmanuelle. Convince her to return to Heaven."

Michael's mouth thinned. "And you? What about you?"

"I'll help. I said I would."

"That's not what I meant."

"I know."

For long heartbeats, they stood in silence, Alex coming to terms with the inevitable, and Michael— no. It didn't matter what Michael thought. He had a job to do. A war to win, a god to find, a Heaven to save. Alex had a job, too, if the world was to stand a chance of survival for those who remained behind. Those such as Henderson, and Elizabeth, and—

Michael's hand moved beneath hers, turning until

their fingers linked. She looked up at him, jolted from her dark reverie.

"When did you decide?" he asked.

"About ten seconds ago," she admitted. "The entire world is falling apart, Michael. If I stay here, it won't matter very much in the long run, but maybe I can make a difference there, with—in Hell. Maybe I can influence him."

"And maybe you overestimate your powers of persuasion."

"Most likely. But either way, he's not going to stop until he has me."

Michael pulled his hand from hers and walked to the French doors on the far side of the living room, an entire world away. Bracing his hands against the frame, he stared out into the night. His glossy black wings were half-unfurled behind him, their quiver mirroring the tension Alex read across his shoulders, in the set of his head.

"I wish I could argue with you," he said. "You know that, right?"

Turning from his reflection's gaze, she went back to bed.

"IN," SETH ORDERED the unknown Fallen who'd knocked at his door. He frowned at the charts spread across his desk—a battle plan Samael had sent over for his approval. Whatever issues he might have with his aide, he had to admit the Archangel was a brilliant strategist. Not to mention a formidable adversary.

He scrawled his signature across the bottom of the top chart and then looked up, expecting delivery of his tea tray. Instead, he found a Cherub staring at the floor, hands gripping one another so hard that his knuckles had turned white. Seth straightened.

"You are—?"

"S-Sintiel, lordship."

Seth waited. The Cherub stayed quiet but for shallow, labored breathing interspersed by audible swallows.

"And?" Seth asked.

The Cherub jumped. Ruby eyes flicked up to Seth's, then down again. Sintiel swallowed again. Seth sighed.

"Why are you here?"

"Zuriel, lordship. You left orders that you wanted to know when she returned."

Oh, for the love of—Seth broke off the thought. He set his pen on the desk, refraining from the impulse to bounce it off the Cherub's skull.

"Am I to understand she has?"

Sintiel nodded. Shook his head. Nodded. Then ducked the stylus pitched in his direction.

"She returned," he said hastily, "but Samael... Zuriel...Samael..."

Seth's blood ran cold. A buzzing sound began deep in his brain. "Samael what?"

"He killed her."

Seth's heart began a slow folding-in on itself, each beat labored, shuddering, excruciating. *Alex.* Buzzing filled his skull, and the world receded to a pinpoint of light. He clawed his way toward it, fighting the agony that tried to pull him under.

"Samael killed Alex?"

"Who is Alex?"

The Cherub's question penetrated as nothing else could have, snapping Samael back into himself. He stared at Sintiel.

"What?"

"You said Samael killed Alex. Who is Alex?"

"He didn't kill her?"

Sintiel shrugged both shoulders and spread his hands. "I have no idea. I just know he killed Zuriel. Do you wish me to—"

"Get out," muttered Seth.

"Pardon?"

"Get *out!*" A roar this time.

The Cherub scrambled for the door, tripping in his haste, colliding with the frame, falling over the sill. At last the heavy oaken door closed behind him with a thud. Stillness filled the room. Seth sank slowly to his knees, his head and shoulders bowed, fists resting on his thighs. Great shudders shook his frame. He gulped for air, squeezing his eyes shut until he saw starbursts of light.

Alex lived, but in the moment he'd thought otherwise—that one instant—his world had ended. Become an eternity of emptiness that had taken away his breath, his heart, his soul. A void that had reflected back to him what he was without her.

Nothing.

His heart threatened to shatter all over again at the very thought. Seth let out a long, shaky breath. He opened his eyes and stared at the desk with its battle charts in front of him.

Fuck Samael and his *be patient.*

Fuck the war with Heaven.

And fuck his injury.

He would cross over into the human realm and find Alex himself. Not a week from now. Not tomorrow. Today.

Now.

THIRTY-SEVEN

"You need to eat."

Alex gave a little start at Michael's gruff words, then looked down at the pile of crumbs—formerly an uneaten slice of toast—on her plate. She pushed away the plate and her cold coffee, then drew the newspaper toward her.

Death toll climbs, its headline blared. More news about Slavutych and the man-made disaster engineered by Lang and his cronies, all because they wouldn't listen to her. Didn't want to hear.

Michael cleared his throat.

"I'll have something later," she said.

"Alex—"

"I forgot to ask why Bethiel was here last night." She pushed the newspaper away again. "Does he have a lead on Nina?"

Michael regarded her in tight-lipped silence from his post in the living room. Then he shook his head. "Not your niece. Mittron. He's heard rumors in Hell that the former Highest might be overseeing the care of the Nephilim children."

The Fallen...and Mittron? Her gaze strayed back to the newspaper headline. Of course. She should have thought of that herself. It made sense, him aligning with Seth, because where else would he go? It also made sense that his would be the mind behind the New Children of God, and the hundreds of people flocking to help raise Lucifer's Nephilim army. After engineering the Apocalypse and plunging the world into Armageddon, he'd more than proved his capacity for such machinations.

And Bethiel could stop him from doing further damage.

But if she told Bethiel, he would stop looking for Nina.

The coffee machine gurgled. Alex flexed cramped fingers, then leaned her elbows on the counter and cradled her head in her hands. Christ, she was tired of making impossible decisions. Her life vs. the world's continued existence; Nina vs. the hundreds stupid enough to answer the call to Pripyat. Was there anything she *wouldn't* have to sacrifice?

"I know about Pripyat." Michael's voice at her elbow made her jump again.

A headache born from lack of sleep pressed against the back of her eyes. Her fingertips traced an endless circle on the cool, granite countertop as she struggled to separate herself from the words she had to speak. From their impact.

"You'll have to tell Bethiel," she said.

How much would she have to sacrifice?

Everything.

"Not yet," said Michael.

Her gaze flashed back to him. "But—"

"Your niece has only a few days left. Let him continue looking for her."

She swallowed a lump in her throat. "Thank you, but no. Not if it means more people will die."

"More *will* die," Michael said, "but we can't let the Fallen know we've found the Nephilim. Not until we have Emmanuelle."

Relief swamped Alex. Guilt rushed in after it. Bethiel would continue looking for Nina. Countless others would die because of that. And her only consolation in any of it was that, for once, the decision wasn't hers.

It was Michael's.

She tried to find words to thank him, but they eluded her. She nodded and reached again for the newspaper. At that instant, the condo's front door burst open, and her hand slammed against the plate instead, sending it flying in a spray of toast crumbs as Henderson strode in, Riley hot on his heels.

The plate hit the floor and shattered.

"We've found her," Henderson said. "We've found Emmanuelle."

IT TOOK EVERY FIBER of willpower Seth possessed to remain where he was. To watch. Wait. Not go to the woman emerging from the door down the street. The woman whose very existence consumed him.

Alex lifted her hair free of her coat collar and let it fall in a blond cascade over her shoulders. Seth caught his breath. His heart hammered in his chest.

She was so beautiful.

So alive.

So vibrant with the gift he had given her.

His entire soul swelled with pure, unadulterated joy...

And then another figure emerged behind her, tall and powerful, with a commanding presence as unmistakable as the huge black wings rising behind him. Mika'el.

Fucking Hell.

Swiftly, Seth pulled back, further down the street. He tamped down his powers, smoothed over his aura, stilled his vibration. Held his breath. Mika'el paused on the doorstep, scanning their surroundings. He nodded, and Alex descended the stairs and crossed the sidewalk to get into a car waiting curbside. Mika'el waited until her door closed and then stepped back into the building.

Seth hesitated. His injury tugged at his side. The crossover into this realm had taken more effort than he would have liked. While he had no doubt he could still take on Heaven's greatest warrior, it would be wiser not to seek battle if he could avoid it.

The car with Alex in it pulled away from the curb.

Panic licked at Seth. He couldn't lose her. Not again. Not when he was so close. But any use of power to follow her would only reveal his presence to—

His gaze settled on a bright yellow car parked across the street, with *Yellow Cab* emblazoned in black on its side, a matching sign capping its roof, and a bearded man napping in the driver's seat. A half-dozen strides took him to the vehicle. He pulled open the passenger door and slid in beside the driver, who startled awake and stared at him, bleary-eyed.

"Hey, you can't be in the front sea—"

Seth turned to him, and the cab driver's objection died mid-word. The man swallowed and raised both his hands.

"I'm not looking for trouble, man."

"Good. Neither am I. I am, however, looking for a driver." Seth pointed down the street. "The blue car. Follow it. Carefully."

The cabbie hesitated. Seth turned to him again.

"Now," he said, and in the space of seconds, they were in motion.

THIRTY-EIGHT

"This is it," said Henderson. He pulled over to the side of the road and slipped the sedan's gearshift into park. "Formerly the most notorious biker bar in the Lower Mainland, owned and operated by the Hells Angels themselves."

"Formerly?" Alex looked out the windshield at the only building visible for miles along the flats.

Squat, wooden, and ugly, the Blackwater Bar & Grill wasn't exactly the kind of place that invited a casual passerby to come in and sit awhile. The stain had worn off most of the cedar siding, leaving it weathered in an unattractive patchy way; the covered porch that ran the width of the building had pulled free of the wall at one corner; and the 'l' in the first word on the electric sign had burned out, resulting in an unfortunate—but most likely apt—name change.

And if all of that wasn't enough to discourage most people from stopping, there were the motorcycles lined up along the front of the building. Fifty of them—Alex had counted—all Harleys.

It was no wonder Heaven hadn't been able to locate Emmanuelle here.

"Ownership changed ten years ago," Henderson answered. "A numbered company. We were never able to find out who was behind it, but I suspect we know now."

Alex reached for the door handle. Henderson's hand closed over her wrist.

"I don't care how reformed the organized crime guys say these shitheads are—you are *not* going in there alone."

"I'll be fine."

"Right up until they identify you as a cop."

"Hugh—"

"At least take this," he interrupted. He held out a small pistol. "It's my spare."

She patted the sword across her lap. She'd balked at continuing to carry it, but Michael had pointed out that Emmanuelle—if she was at the bar—would recognize it for what it was.

"It might tip the scale in your favor," he'd told her. *"At least make her listen to what you have to say."*

Alex had raised both eyebrows at that, but she'd kept her questions to herself about just how much hostility she should expect from his soulmate, because it really hadn't mattered. Emmanuelle *had* to listen, and if the sword could help make that happen, then she would carry it.

She gave Henderson a lopsided smile. "I have this, remember?"

"Against fifty-odd bikers, reformed or otherwise?" Henderson snorted. "I don't think so. Take the gun, Jarvis."

Alex sighed. "Fine." She stuffed the pistol into her pocket. "Satisfied?"

"No, but it will have to do."

Alex climbed out of the vehicle. Under Henderson's watchful eye, she removed her borrowed leather jacket and shrugged into the harness that held the sword's scabbard in place across her back. She slid the jacket back on. Then, catching Henderson's scowl, she said again, "I'll be fine."

"I still don't like not having Michael here. If one of the Fallen comes after you..."

"He's watching for them. They won't get within a fifty-mile radius. Besides, I'll be with Emmanuelle. If I ask nicely, maybe she'll save me."

If she doesn't strike me down on the spot.

"Funny," Henderson growled.

She closed the car door.

"Alex."

Leaning down to the open window, she met Henderson's sober brown gaze.

"Be careful."

She straightened up, gave the sword hilt a final tug of adjustment, and shifted her attention to the Blackwater. The deep bass of music thumped across the parking lot. This was it. Their time of reckoning. Time to see if Emmanuelle was in there, to see if Alex could persuade her to talk to Michael, to find out if Heaven stood a chance against Hell.

To learn whether the world stood a chance of survival.

No pressure, Jarvis.

"Ten minutes," Henderson called after her. "If you don't call me in ten minutes, I'm coming in after you, understand?"

Alex flapped a hand at him in response and started down the road toward the bar. She really should tell him about the immortality thing one of these days, if only to put his mind at rest. Except knowing about it would raise a whole lot of other concerns she had a hard enough time dealing with on her own. She wasn't sure she could handle fielding them from Henderson, too. Or Riley.

She walked along the narrow parking strip in front of the porch, past the row of gleaming chrome and black that was punctuated with an occasional bright blue or shiny red. She paused beside the bike nearest the door.

Painted matte black from front to back, with raised handlebars and studded leather saddlebags, it had an understated look that distinguished it from the others. As did the image engraved on the gas tank: a warrior angel, down on one knee, head bowed, both hands gripping the upright sword resting on the ground before him.

Alex raised her head and stared at the bar's front door. If she had to guess, she'd venture to say Henderson's intelligence was good. Emmanuelle was here, all right.

She climbed the steps, crossed the porch, and stepped into the Blackwater's dim, shuttered interior. The door swung shut behind her. Almost instantly, the music dropped into oblivion, and she sensed every head in the place swiveling in her direction.

She paused to get her bearings and let her eyes adjust to the murky lighting. Her gaze swept the room, spotting two pool tables, one on either side of the door. A row of booths ran the length of the wall on the left, disappearing into the shadows at the back.

Mismatched wooden stools sat along the bar to the right. Motorcycle parts and pictures of buxom women dressed—or half-dressed—in Harley gear passed as I.

And dozens of requisite beefy, bearded, heavily tattooed men and equally tattooed women all surveyed her with varying degrees of suspicion.

She zeroed in on the barkeeper. He was in his fifties, with his hair pulled back in a ponytail and a winged skull tattooed on his massive bicep—the trademark sign of a Hells Angel. He was also one of the largest men in the place, and his hands were out of sight beneath the counter. Baseball bat? Shotgun? Either way, she'd rather be facing him than have him at her back. She'd start there.

She walked into the silent room, her booted heels thudding against the wooden floor. At the counter, she took the sketch of Emmanuelle from the pocket where it nestled beside the lonely and completely inadequate pistol Henderson had given her.

"I'm looking for someone." She unfolded the paper and set it before the bartender.

His unblinking gaze held hers. "You got the wrong place."

"You haven't looked at the picture."

"Don't matter. You still got the wrong place."

Behind her, chair legs scraped over floorboards. Footsteps approached. At least four sets. Alex tensed, her reflexes on high alert. Reformed or not, these people were still hostile and highly dangerous. For a second, Alex wondered whether—even if she couldn't die—she would still feel pain when she had the crap beaten out of her. Then, tension strumming across her shoulders, she lifted the sketch and held it in front of the bartender's face, high enough to put it in his line of sight, low enough to see the flicker of recognition in his eyes.

"I'm not out to cause trouble," she said. "I just want to talk to her."

The bartender shook his head. "Never seen her." But even as he uttered the denial, his gaze darted right, toward the back of the bar, so briefly that she would have missed it if she hadn't been staring at him, waiting for the tell.

Three minutes, her internal clock warned. *You've been here three minutes. Seven more and Henderson comes after you.*

And then they'd both get themselves killed. One of them permanently.

Alex folded the paper again and slid it into her pocket. "All right," she said. "Thanks anyway."

She stepped back from the counter and turned, as if to leave. Then she glanced over her shoulder. "Mind if I use the facilities before I go? It's a long way back to town."

Eyes narrowed, the bartender considered the idea, then grunted and shrugged. "Make it fast."

SETH WATCHED ALEX disappear alone into the ramshackle building. Beside him, the cab driver clung to the steering wheel, sneaking wary sideways looks at him. Seth could hear the rapid thud of his heart. Smell the stink of his sweat. Feel his fragility.

Seth ignored him, waiting.

The car that had brought Alex here sat at the roadside, a hundred yards away, its driver still inside. There was no sign of Mika'el. No hint of his presence.

Cautiously, Seth expanded his awareness. Still

nothing.

Alex was here alone. Unprotected.

His to take.

He reached out to the cab driver, gripped the sweat-slick neck, and twisted his fingers. Bone snapped. The man's feet jerked. Seth climbed out of the cab and strolled down the road toward the other car.

THIRTY-NINE

Alex spotted her three tables from the back of the bar. A slender, leather-clad woman, sitting with her back to the room, dark hair pulled back in a ponytail, one leg drawn up with a heavily booted foot resting on the chair, arm slung across her knee. Alex couldn't see her face, but the tattoo beneath her left ear left no room for doubt.

It was a sword, its blade wrapped in blue flames, seeming to glow with a surreal light of its own making. Not just any sword, but that of an Archangel. Alex would have recognized it anywhere. She stopped a few feet away. The three men seated at the table with the woman rose as one, a formidable wall of muscled, colorfully tattooed flesh amply displayed around t-shirts and vests. Alex met the cold, pale gray gaze of the nearest.

"Ladies' room is that way." He inclined his bearded head to the right. He was sixty years old if he was a day, but he had a solid self-assurance about him that said he could take on most men half his age—and win.

Alex held up her hands, palms out. "I just want to talk to her."

"She doesn't want to talk to you. Ladies' room"—he repeated his nod—"is that way."

She hesitated. What if she was wrong and it wasn't Emmanuelle? Or worse, what if it was, and these thugs weren't as reformed as Criminal Intelligence wanted to think? The wall of flesh parted and came around to flank the woman on either side.

Christ.

"Michael," she said. "Michael sent me."

The arm resting across the woman's knee gave an almost imperceptible twitch. Tattooed muscles stopped in their tracks. Was it just Alex, or did the entire bar hold its collective breath?

The woman's booted foot settled onto the floor with a controlled thud. She stood, unfolding her length from the chair, steely tension written in every line of her back and shoulders. One second ticked past. Two. Three. The woman turned.

Alex took an involuntary step back from the iridescent gaze, a swirl of color that couldn't decide between the silver of the One's eyes or the purple of Lucifer's. If the sword tattoo hadn't been enough to identify Emmanuelle to her, those eyes—the undeniable eyes of a divine being—would have done it. She took a deep breath. No point in retreating now.

"Michael sent me," she repeated.

The iridescent gaze swept over her, head to toes and back again. "You're not—"

Emmanuelle stopped, glancing at the men around her. Alex finished the phrase in her mind: *like me.* She shook her head.

"No. I'm not."

"Then you can't be his messenger. He wouldn't use a—one like you."

A human.

"And yet he did." Alex drew her hair to one side and craned her neck to expose the hilt of Aramael's sword at her back. Swirling eyes widened, then narrowed, flashing with suspicion.

"Why didn't he come himself?"

"He was afraid you'd know he was coming and run. That you wouldn't talk to him."

"He was right," Emmanuelle retorted. "This conversation is over."

"Wait," Alex said to her departing back. "Things have happened. Things you don't know about."

Emmanuelle kept walking. A rose-and-thorn-tattooed bicep kept Alex from following.

"You're right. I'm not like you," she called. "But I'm not like the others, either. Seth changed me, Emmanuelle. He changed everything."

The daughter of the One and Lucifer reached the front door. Michael's caution not to say too much rang in Alex's ears. "*Leave it to me to tell her what's happened. All you have to do is get her to agree to see me. I'll do the rest.*"

Hell.

"Your mother is dead, damn it!" she shouted past the bicep. "They—the others—the ones like you—"

The weight of a dozen gazes pressed in on her, stalling her explanation. What the hell could she say that wouldn't make it onto the Internet in a matter of seconds and compound the world's problems even further?

Fuck.

She realized Emmanuelle remained at the door, one hand upraised to push, waiting. Listening. She stepped aside from the arm blocking her way. *Tread carefully*, her inner voice warned. *Push, and you'll lose her.*

"Things have happened," she said again. "You need to know about them."

A dozen heartbeats passed before Emmanuelle turned and silver eyes met Alex's once more.

"You have three minutes."

"I need to call someone first, just to—"

"Two minutes, fifty-seven seconds."

Alex raked a hand through her hair, hoping to hell Henderson's time-keeping skills were on the fluid side. She glanced around the room. "Is there somewhere private we can talk?"

"Two minutes, forty-nine seconds." Emmanuelle's gaze glinted a challenge at her.

Everything in Alex began a slow, downward spiral, much like water circling a drain. Or a toilet. She clenched her fists. Unclenched them. Physically bit down on her tongue as she glared at the woman facing her down. She tried to reason with herself, to tell herself it would serve no purpose to come unhinged now.

But it was no good. She'd had it with the lot of them. Their machinations, their arrogance, their high-handed presence. She...was...done.

"Fine," she snarled. She pushed the bicep aside and stalked to the front of the bar, stopping a few feet short of the god she'd been sent to recruit. "Here's the condensed version. The One and Lucifer are both dead and your brother has taken over Hell. The angels are losing the war because they have no one to lead them, and eighty thousand Nephilim are about to be unleashed on the world. Is there anything else you need to know, or will that do?"

Silence descended in the wake of her words. Absolute. Tomb-like. Unbroken by so much as a wheeze of breath. Alex's gaze locked with Emmanuelle's, and she flinched from the fury there. Would she ever learn not to inflame those who could destroy her on a whim?

"I'm sorry," she muttered, "but—"

The door behind Emmanuelle swung open and a man stood in the doorway, silhouetted against the bright afternoon light. Alex's heart pitched down to her toes. Henderson. Damn.

"I'm okay," she called out, willing him to take the hint. A few more minutes, that's all she needed. "Everything's under control."

A low chuckle rumbled, and a voice—male, but not Hugh—responded, "I'm very glad to hear that."

Ice splintered down Alex's spine and shot through her core. Oh, god, no...it couldn't be. She stepped back hastily, involuntarily, stumbling into one of Emmanuelle's protectors, falling against him. Meaty hands gripped her arms and set her back on her feet. The man in the doorway stepped inside, brushing Emmanuelle aside. The bottomless black eyes Alex had hoped never to see again pinned her in place, threatening to suck her into their void.

How in Hell had he found her? And Michael. Where was Michael?

"Alex," said Seth. "Are you ready to go home?"

Bile rose in Alex's throat. Michael wouldn't come. Not for her. Not now they'd found—

From the corner of her eye, she saw Emmanuelle

regain her balance. Iridescent eyes darkened with irritation, and her mouth—so like Seth's—pulled tight. Alex reached instinctively for the sword at her back, a warning shout forming on her lips even as Emmanuelle stalked toward her brother.

"Emmanuelle, no!"

Emmanuelle ignored her, focused wholly on Seth. "I don't know who you think you are, but this is—"

Seth flung out an arm in her direction. He didn't make contact, but still sent Emmanuelle spinning through the air. She crashed into the mirrored wall behind the counter, glass and alcohol showering over her as she slid to the floor. In an instant, baseball bat in hand, the bartender cleared the counter and charged forward. The brawn in the bar followed, the floor shaking beneath their feet as they stampeded toward Seth, shoving Alex and her sword out of their way.

Before she could recover her footing a second time, all were sent crashing backward amid splintered tables and shattered chairs—not by Seth this time, but by a massive gust of wind.

The wind of a black-armored warrior who arrived amid a whirl of hardened feathers and leveled the flashing metal of his sword at Seth. Alex's heart leapt.

"Michael," she whispered.

EMMANUELLE PUSHED UP onto hands and knees amid the shards of glass on the floor behind the bar. She shook her head, dazed not by her impact, but by the turn of events. Or more specifically, the speed with which they'd turned. The woman's arrival had been shock enough, but this? What the Hell was—?

"Michael."

The woman's whisper reached through the stunned silence that followed in the wake of the mini hurricane. Emmanuelle froze at the sound. Michael. Mika'el. He was here?

But she wasn't ready...

"You!" her attacker spat. "Always interfering!"

Another voice, deep, achingly familiar. "Are you all right? Where is she?"

She. Did he mean...?

Energy crackled through the air. Blue sparks snapped over Emmanuelle's head, and her heart lunged into her throat. Shit. Only four beings in the universe were capable of that kind of power, and two of them—if she were to believe the woman—no longer existed.

Her attacker snarled again. "I'm talking to you, warrior."

"And I'm ignoring you," Mika'el retorted. "Alex. Where is Emmanuelle?"

Bloody Hell.

For an instant, Emmanuelle considered simply disappearing. This wasn't her fight, and she had no intention of letting it become so. There was no reason to—

At the end of the bar, Wookie stirred, groaning.

Emmanuelle closed her eyes. No reason except Wookie, and Spider, and Cosmo, and—ah, Hell. She pushed up to her knees and then stood.

"Here," she said. Brushing shards of glass from her hair, she took in the wreckage strewn across room. Over by the pool tables, Scorpion made to rise from the splintered remains of the chair beneath him. She shook her head at him, and scowling, he subsided.

Emmanuelle took a deep breath, straightened her

shoulders, and looked upon the soulmate she'd left behind almost five thousand years ago. "I'm here."

Emerald eyes turned on her, and time itself stood still under their gaze. Ferocity, pain, regret—all this and more flared in Mika'el's eyes, spearing Emmanuelle to her core and waking a long-forgotten ache of what should never have been. What still could not be. Then Mika'el's expression turned grim and the mask of a warrior slipped back into place.

"Get everyone out of here," he ordered. "Take Alex somewhere safe."

"No," the woman objected. "Michael—"

"Forget it," said Emmanuelle at the same time. She strode around the bar, her boots crunching over the glass littering the floor. She jerked her head toward her attacker and the blue crackles surrounding him. "If that's who I think it is, you'll need help."

"Just do it," Mika'el said. "I'll find you later."

"Why don't I save everyone the argument?" Seth snarled. "I'll just take her off your hands, because she's *mine*."

The crackles of energy formed a wall and pushed toward Michael. The Archangel's sword flared white in response, so brilliant that Emmanuelle had to turn away. The glare faded. A quick look at Michael found him two strides back from where he'd been. Near his feet, a biker rolled out of the way and scrambled upright. A second wall of blue slammed into the biker, enveloped him, moved through him. Emmanuelle stretched out a hand, but before she could summon more than shock, he crumbled into dust, his shriek of agony hanging in the room's stunned silence. Emmanuelle stared at the emptiness that had been her friend.

"She's mine," Seth repeated.

Mika'el's face had turned to granite. "Not a chance in Hell."

"Then we will fight, and all those present will die, and I will still have her."

Fury uncoiled in Emmanuelle's belly. Her hands itched to gather her power and launch an attack at the smug arrogance that had taken over her brother. Then she glanced again around the room. Seth was right. If she fought him here, now, everyone in this room—and probably many beyond—would die. She caught Mika'el's eye and gave a terse nod. She would do as he said.

Mika'el's attention flicked back to Seth. A smile curved his lips. Humorless, ice cold, distinctly unpleasant. "I don't think so."

Seth launched another blast of energy, but Mika'el's wings blocked it, and this time he held firm—despite blue flames eating a hole through outstretched bone and feathers alike.

"Emmanuelle, now!" he roared.

Emmanuelle grabbed the woman's arm with one hand and tossed a fireball with the other. The bar's front wall exploded outward in a hail of splintered wood. Emmanuelle shoved her charge through the opening and across the remains of the porch, then steered her to the row of motorcycles. She stopped beside a low-slung Harley, all matte black and chrome and indisputable business.

Flames erupted from the bar behind them, making the silver etching of the angel on the tank flicker and glow, weirdly life-like. Without pause, Emmanuelle swung a leg over the bike.

"Get on," she ordered. She turned the key, and the

bike throbbed to life beneath her.

The woman looked back at the bar. "The others—"

Tattooed men and women bailed out of the flames, falling over themselves, limping, dragging one another. A wall of blue swept out behind them, engulfing and destroying a second life without pause, without hesitation...without time for even a scream. Spider. Emmanuelle's heart bled quietly in her chest.

Her hand closed over the woman's wrist.

"They'll be fine," she yelled over the Harley's deep, throaty rumble. "Now get on the goddamned bike!"

The woman stared at her. Looked down at the sword still gripped in her other hand. At the men and women desperately mounting their own bikes and making their escapes. At the building engulfed in blue and gold flames before them.

"Michael," she whispered.

Emmanuelle's heart twisted. Her grip on frail human bones tightened.

Then meaty hands clamped around the woman's arms, lifted her, and jammed her into the bike seat behind Emmanuelle. Wookie's unsmiling eyes met Emmanuelle's, then the gray-bearded man limped away, mounted his own bike, and gunned out of the parking lot in a spray of gravel.

Emmanuelle followed.

FORTY

For the first forty minutes after getting back to the beach house, Emmanuelle worked in silence alongside Black Widow to patch up the wounded. The thirty-year member of the Hells Angels had three dead husbands and more than her fair share of triage behind her, and her embroidery hobby lent itself well to stitching together skin and muscle. She worked quickly and efficiently, passing the lesser injured off to Emmanuelle for cleaning and bandaging. In turn, the bandaged helped tend the others, two dozen in all. Two dozen out of more than twice that number present in the bar.

Emmanuelle slammed a door on the thought. She cut a length of first-aid tape, crouched at Wookie's side, and secured the gauze around his forearm. He cleared his throat, and she lifted her gaze to meet his. Clear, steady gray eyes looked back at her from the overgrowth of hair that had earned him his name.

"A place goes up in flames like that, there's going to

be questions," he said.

"And if I had answers, I'd give them to you."

"I meant cop questions. Especially if one of theirs"—he jerked his head toward the living room to which Emmanuelle had exiled the woman—"is missing. Your handler is going to want to talk to you."

Surprise rocked her back on her heels. "You know about that?"

"That you're an informant? We all do."

"You never said anything."

Wookie shrugged. "It was none of our business. It's not like any of us has anything to hide anymore."

Not if they wanted to be within ten miles of her, no. It was her one ironclad rule: *Keep your noses clean.* She surveyed her friend and self-appointed bodyguard through narrowed eyes. "But you've never tried to keep anything from me. News. Rumors. You've always spoken openly when I'm around."

Another shrug. "Some of us may be jaded sons of bitches, but who are we to stand in your way of trying to make this a better world?"

Emmanuelle cut a second strip of tape. She pressed it in place, half on gauze, half on skin. "And the rest of it?"

"Rest of what?"

"What happened at the bar. The...warrior and the other one. You must have questions about them."

"Are you going to answer them if we do?"

Her gaze flicked up to his again. "I don't know."

"Well, when you decide, you let me know. Then I'll ask."

She swallowed, her throat suddenly tight. But before she could formulate an answer, the back door swung open. The kitchen occupants collectively held their breath, and then relaxed as Wookie's older brother stepped inside. From the threshold, the man they'd dubbed Preacher surveyed the damage. His gaze skimmed over Emmanuelle and settled on Wookie.

"Has an ambulance been called?" he asked.

"No need, big brother. Everything's under control."

Wookie delivered the words in a casual, comfortable tone, but a fine tension hummed through the forearm beneath Emmanuelle's hands. His brother had only been with them for a few weeks. So far, he'd accepted without comment the colorful backgrounds and personalities, but his loyalty was untested. Emmanuelle watched Preacher scan the room a second time. Then, his face settling into a calm determination, he rolled up the sleeves of his black clergy shirt.

"How can I help?" he asked.

Wookie relaxed under Emmanuelle's hands, then he pulled his arm away from her and stood. "I'm good now. I'll give Preacher a hand with the others."

Emmanuelle pushed to her feet. They were better than three-quarters done. Widow was on her last stitching job, and only the more minor scrapes and bruises remained. After that—Emmanuelle stooped to pick up the bowl of bloody water from the floor. After that, she would have to decide what she would say. If she would say anything at all. If she would *do* anything.

Or if she would just leave.

"Here," said a voice. "I'll trade you."

She looked down at the mug of coffee held out to her by the stocky Jezebel. She shook her head. "Thanks, but I'm fine."

"It has a little something in it." Jezebel reached for her free hand and curled its fingers around the mug handle. "For fortitude."

Emmanuelle traded her for the bowl of red water. She might not derive the same fortitude humans would, but a little something still sounded good. "Thank you."

"You're welcome. The others have been checking in, by the way."

The ones who hadn't come back here.

Emmanuelle paused with the coffee halfway to her mouth. "How many?"

"All but six. They've gone to Scorpion's safe house."

She closed her eyes. Six friends gone. It wasn't as bad as it could have been, but still...six gone. Her heart twisted. A soft hand gripped her chin and gave her a gentle shake. Jezebel's brown eyes glistened equally with tears and ferocity when she looked into them.

"It's not your fault, Manny."

But it was. She'd known for weeks now that it was time to move on. She'd felt the universe's imbalance, sensed its shifting, *known* that something was happening. Just as she'd known someone would come looking for her. But she'd refused to tap into the energies in order to be certain. Refused to open herself up to discovery, and in her denial, she'd put every one of these people—

"Hey."

She blinked and focused again on Jezebel.

The unnaturally platinum blond scowled fiercely. "It is *not* your fault."

"You don't know that, Jez. And you don't know me as well as you think." Emmanuelle gazed sadly around the room. "None of you do."

"Maybe not. But I suspect we know you better than *you* think." Jezebel chuckled. "Honey, why do you think none of us is freaking about the winged guy? Or the blue sparkles? I'll admit I was a little taken aback when you threw that fireball yourself—didn't expect you could do that—but I've been waiting for a whole choir of angels to appear ever since I met you. We all have."

"You—I—" Emmanuelle snapped her mouth shut. Stared. "You can't know. It's impossible."

"Yet here we are." Jezebel reached up again to pat her cheek. "Drink up. You still have work to do. And then you need to check on the poor girl you shoved into the living room. After what I overheard in the bar, I'd say the two of you have some talking to do."

FORTY-ONE

Alex thumbed the *end call* button, tucked the cell phone into her back pocket, and wrapped her arms around herself again. She'd quit counting the attempts to reach Henderson after thirty. Now she just redialed every minute or so, hoping—praying—that this would be the time he picked up. That he was all right and her next call wouldn't have to be to Riley.

That he would be able to tell her what had happened to Michael.

She stared out the window at the gray stretch of beach, the darker gray water beyond, the sullen sky that dipped down to meet it. A bellow of pain came from beyond the closed kitchen door, followed by Emmanuelle's voice, threaded with both compassion and impatience. It had been almost an hour since she'd refused Alex's offer to help patch up the bikers who had trickled into the beach house in their wake. An hour since she'd ordered her from the kitchen with a look of such venom that Alex half-expected to be turfed out of the house altogether.

Alex sighed and fished the phone from her pocket again.

One ring. Two rings. Three...and voice mail. She ended the call.

Christ, Henderson...where the hell are you?

The faint crunch of tires on gravel heralded the arrival of a vehicle at the rear of the house, too heavy and quiet to be a Harley. Alex turned toward the sound as the door between the kitchen and living room opened, and a frowning Emmanuelle strode into the room. Her hair was back in its ponytail again, and she'd shed her leather jacket. Blood streaked the plain white t-shirt she wore. Her shimmering gaze zoomed in on Alex.

"That's a car, not a bike."

Alex stuck her right hand into her jacket pocket. She curled her fingers around the handgrip of the pistol Henderson had given her. "I heard."

"Not your doing?"

"No."

Glancing over her shoulder past the door she still held open, Emmanuelle jerked her head at someone Alex couldn't see. Booted feet clumped across the kitchen floor and the back door creaked open.

"Stay here," she ordered Alex.

"Wait. Have you heard what happened to Michael yet?"

The other woman's scowl deepened. "*Mika'el,*" she emphasized, "can look after himself. Right now I'm busy cleaning up the mess you and he brought with you."

She turned to go back into the kitchen but stopped short. The hand she'd wrapped around the doorknob went white at the knuckles, and her quick inhale was audible clear across the room. Alex crossed the room in two strides.

Without so much as an *excuse me*, she shoved Emmanuelle aside and barged into the kitchen. Her gaze swept the company there. Half a dozen bikers with varying injuries sat along benches flanking a worn wooden table, another half dozen sat on the countertops, several more stood in clusters around the big room's perimeter. All of them stared in silence at the newcomers to the party: Hugh, sporting a baseball-sized purple lump on one temple; and Michael, swaying on his feet and looking stunningly, sickeningly bedraggled.

For a moment, she couldn't move. Could do no more than take in the exhaustion and pain etched into his face, the blood-matted feathers of his left wing, the battered armor clinging to him by unseen threads. She'd seen his power. Seen him stand against a dozen Fallen and emerge without a scratch. For this to happen, for him to have been hurt to this degree...

Training took over. She rushed forward to take Michael's arm, her heart dropping when he let her drape it over her shoulders. Christ, how injured was he to accept this kind of help? She shot a look at Hugh, who tightened his lips and shook his head.

"I scraped him off the parking lot when the flames died down enough to get to him," he said. "He hasn't said a word beyond ordering me to find you."

Alex hobbled toward the table, straining under Michael's weight. Emmanuelle's biker friends cleared the way for her without being asked, sidling to the farthest reaches of the kitchen but not leaving—and not once taking their eyes from the fully exposed angel in their midst.

Maneuvering Michael around, Alex backed him up against the wood, and he collapsed onto the edge of the table. Pain-filled emerald eyes met hers, then drifted closed. Alex turned her mind away from the panic that desperately wanted to set in. She set about figuring out his armor.

"How *did* you find me?" she asked Hugh, running her fingers along the edges of the shattered breastplate, probing for some kind of release.

"GPS. In your phone."

Of course. "Is anyone else coming?"

Hugh shook his head and winced. "No. They're pretty busy with the scene, and I've been granted certain...latitude where you're concerned."

"Good." She jerked her chin to indicate the lump on his forehead. "What happened?"

Mouth twisting, he touched the bruise. "Seth. It's my own fault. I saw a cab following us, but it never occurred to me it could be him." He dropped his voice. "I mean, the son of freaking Lucifer. In a cab. Really?"

"It would have been his only way of following me. He would have wanted me away from Michael."

Hugh snorted. "That worked out well."

Alex shot him a look, and he touched fingertips to the lump on his temple.

"I didn't realize he'd even gotten out of the cab until he was beside the car. He smashed my phone, then whacked my head against the steering wheel. I didn't wake up until the whole place was in flames and everyone was gone. Well, everyone who could move, anyway."

"You're lucky you're alive."

Henderson scowled. "I'm aware of that, thanks."

Alex realized she'd made zero progress with the armor. She took a step back and glowered at it. "For chrissakes! Is this stuff *glued* on?"

"Here," said Emmanuelle. "Let me do it."

Alex glanced back to find the other woman's closed, unreadable gaze fixed on Michael. She moved aside, and Emmanuelle stepped forward. With the nimble fingers of someone who had done the task many, many times before, she stripped the armor from the Archangel's body, leaving the most damaged—the breastplate—for last. Her gaze flicked to Alex's as she took hold of its edges.

"It's fused to him," she said quietly. "He may pass out when I remove it."

Alex's heart shriveled. Her breathing stopped. *Fused...?* She stared at Emmanuelle, horror and disbelief vying for top billing in her brain. Then, grimly, she stepped in to brace Michael's right side with her body so he wouldn't pitch forward.

She looked around the room for help. With that lump on his head, she didn't trust Henderson not to pass out in Michael's wake. She singled out the least damaged of the bikers, a bald man with a flaming red beard and tattooed sleeves covering both arms.

"You. On his other side. Don't let him fall."

For all the bulk he possessed, the man moved fast. All the way to the door and out to the living room in the blink of an eye. Alex opened her mouth to bellow after him, but another voice interjected before she could.

"I'll do it."

A man she hadn't noticed stepped out from a corner, clad entirely in black but for the rectangle of white at his throat. Her jaw dropped further. A priest? What the hell was a priest—

"*Marcus?*" Hugh demanded.

Alex narrowed her eyes at the name, unable to place it despite the familiar ring. "Who?"

"Marcus," Hugh repeated, disbelief chasing confusion across his face. "Father Marcus. With the scrolls. You remember."

Michael swayed against her and she shifted her stance. She remembered, all right. Especially the part about the scrolls having gone missing at the same time Marcus had, but now wasn't the time.

"Fine," she said. "Get over here."

The priest—no small man himself—settled against Michael's side, braced against the table. Faded blue eyes met hers over Michael's head. He nodded.

"Ready," he said.

Emmanuelle took a deep breath. Alex watched her fingers flex, then curve around the edges of the breastplate. Her hands and forearms went taut with strain. A look of intense concentration settled over her features. Sweat beaded at her temple. Her eyes glazed over, closed for a second, then flashed open again. The breastplate tore free.

Michael's roar of pain filled the room, landing like a sledgehammer against Alex's skull. He lunged forward, and she gritted her teeth, straining to keep him from falling to the floor, Father Marcus doing likewise on his other side. The agonized bellow went on and on, until big, tough bikers tumbled over themselves in their haste to escape the kitchen. Until Hugh followed, and Father Marcus, eyes streaming, released his hold and stumbled after them, hands pressed over his ears. Until only Alex remained to hold Michael upright while Emmanuelle looked on, hands still gripping the armored breastplate, a thousand agonies at war in her face.

At last Michael's voice, hoarse by now, trailed off into silence. Battered, bloodied wings hung limp from his back, shedding feathers in their wake. His head rested against Alex's chest, shuddering breath warming her arm beneath her sweater. She stifled the urge to stroke the dark hair back from his forehead and glanced up to find Emmanuelle watching them, her gaze hard.

"Are you all right?" Alex asked.

Emmanuelle looked startled by the question. Then annoyed.

"I'm fine," she snapped. She set the breastplate aside and reached for Michael, easing him back until his chest was visible.

Or what had once been his chest.

Alex bit down and swallowed hard against the roll in her belly. Holy hell, how was he still alive? She cringed at the morass of raw, bloodied flesh, at the splinters of bone remaining from a ribcage torn away, at the rhythmic, steady pulse of the exposed heart, still purple with the lifeblood pumping through it. Her gaze flicked to the breastplate and the missing pieces of an Archangel forever fused to it. Then she looked to a grim Emmanuelle and swallowed again.

"Will he—?"

"His immortality is intact, but he's badly damaged. I'm going to—"

"Don't you dare," Michael whispered. Emerald eyes, dulled by pain and shock, glared at Emmanuelle. "If you heal me, you expose everyone here."

"Everyone? Or just her?" She jutted her chin at Alex.

Alex gave a start. Whoa. She thought—?

"It's not like that," she began.

"Everyone," Michael's voice overrode hers. "Seth lives, Emmanuelle. Any display of power on your part will tip him off, and I'm in no shape to fight right now. Especially if he returns with reinforcements."

"Which is why I need to heal you."

"No. I'll return to Heaven. I'll heal faster there. I'll be gone a few hours—a day at most. If you lie low, you should be safe."

"*I* should be safe?" Emmanuelle arched a brow.

She and Michael locked gazes for an uncomfortable few seconds, and then Michael reached up to cover Alex's hand, still resting on his shoulder, with his own.

"Give us a minute."

Alex stared at him, the events of the afternoon filtering out from the chaos and falling into place. She'd found Emmanuelle, brought her and Michael together. He didn't need to protect her anymore. And if this was what Seth was capable of—her gaze skimmed the battered flesh and broken bone of his chest again, and she shook her head. "Michael—"

"No."

"But—"

"I said no. It's not an option, Alex. Not right now."

"You don't even know—"

"I do know what you're thinking, and the answer is no. You're still needed."

"Bullshit," she said. "I knew going into this—"

"No."

"Will you please shut up and let me finish a goddamn sentence?"

He squeezed her hand lightly, and his grip trembled. "We'll talk later. Please."

Alex looked at the lines of fatigue and pain carved

into his face. She bit back the arguments piling up in her throat, and blinked away the tears prickling behind her eyes. Then she scowled her capitulation and tugged her hand from his, heading for the living room.

Goddamn stubborn Archangel.

Emmanuelle's voice followed her. "The bathroom is down the hall, first door to the left. You can find a clean t-shirt in the bedroom across from it. Middle drawer."

Alex pushed open the door without pausing.

"Five minutes," she told Michael. "Then I'm coming back."

FORTY-TWO

In the silence that followed Alex's departure from the kitchen, Mika'el closed his eyes against a pain so intense that, for a moment, it became his entire existence. He ground his teeth together, riding it out, waiting for it to recede, his breathing ragged in his own ears. Seth's final blow had very nearly been a killing one—would have been, if the Appointed hadn't still been weakened by the injury inflicted by Alex.

Mika'el had been lucky to escape with only his chest ripped out.

A throat cleared. He took another cautious breath around the agony that had replaced his breastbone and half his ribcage. He'd have to make this fast, before he passed out and had to do his healing here. The process would take far longer on Earth than in Heaven, and it would leave all of them vulnerable for the duration.

He looked up to find his soulmate stationed a few feet away, arms crossed. Guarded eyes, so like her mother's in expression, watched him.

"Is it true?" she asked. "The One is gone?"

"How did you know?"

"I felt—thought I felt—" Emmanuelle pressed her lips together. Her eyes hardened. "The woman confirmed it for me."

He nodded, tightening his grip on the table's edge against another wave of pain.

"And the rest of it is true, too? About Seth turning to Hell, and the Nephilim army? About the angels losing the war?"

Annoyance tugged at Mika'el. How in bloody hell had Alex managed to say so much in so little time? "There's a great deal more to it than—"

"Yes or no, Mika'el."

"Yes."

Emmanuelle closed her eyes. "Fuck it to Hell and back," she muttered. "I *told* her it would come to this. She was so blind, so damned shortsighted—"

"She was incomplete."

"What is that supposed to mean?"

"She gave up too much of herself in creating your father. She wasn't strong enough to destroy him."

"She—" Emmanuelle gaped at him. "You're serious. But wait. The woman said Lucifer was gone, too. If the One didn't kill him, then how—?"

"He went to her on his own. Helped her to bind the two of them together again, to become what she was before she created all of this." Mika'el contented himself with a feeble nod at their surroundings, not daring to take a hand from the table.

"But not until after he'd created a Nephilim army to do his dirty work. A Nephilim army the One did nothing to prevent." Anger made Emmanuelle's voice a growl. She stalked to the back door and stared out the window. "Conflicted until the end, the two of them."

"You're right." Mika'el's consciousness began to unravel around the edges. He held on to it stubbornly. "But that doesn't change anything. We still need you, Emmanuelle. Heaven and Earth still need you."

Silence.

"And you, Mika'el?" she asked. "Do you need me?"

Light sparked behind his eyes and his fingers ached from holding him upright. Damn, he was losing ground fast. Too fast. "Can we discuss this later? I need..."

"What? You need what? To keep on being the hero? The mart—" Emmanuelle broke off as she glanced over her shoulder. She scowled. "Ah, Hell. Do you have the strength to get back?"

He nodded. Or rather, let his head droop in imitation of a nod.

"Then go."

"The woman. You'll look after her until I get back? Protect her from your brother?"

Emmanuelle's face went tight. He wanted to tell her it wasn't like that, but he didn't have enough words to spare. He needed to leave. Now. But not before he'd secured her promise. He held her gaze, pushing back the shadows that threatened. At last she nodded.

"Fine."

"Promise me."

Silver fire flashed in her eyes.

"Promise me," he repeated. *Because it's the only way I can be sure you'll still be here when I return.*

He swayed, overbalanced, began a forward plunge. Strong, capable hands caught him and lifted him upright. Emmanuelle's lips pressed against his cheek.

"I promise, damn it," she whispered. "Now go."

HENDERSON WAS WAITING in the hallway when Alex emerged from the bathroom. She brushed past his concern and opened the door on the opposite side of the hallway. He followed, watching in silence when she stooped to take a t-shirt from the middle drawer of the long, low dresser, turning his back when she moved to strip off the blood-soaked one. She balled up the soiled shirt and dropped it on top of a hamper. Catching a glimpse of her reflection in the mirror, she grimaced. Michael's blood had soaked all the way through the material, leaving her looking like something out of a bad horror movie. Briefly, she toyed with the idea of returning to the bathroom for a more thorough scrub. Then she pulled the clean t-shirt over her head and slid her arms through the holes. No one cared what she looked like, least of all her.

She tugged the shirt over her belly and turned to Henderson. "Done."

Without speaking, he covered the distance between them and wrapped her in a bear hug. Alex didn't have the energy to return the gesture. A low rumble of voices filtered through the door from down the hall. Michael's wasn't among them.

"The others told me how close he came to getting you." Henderson said, his voice rough. "You must have been—"

"I'm going to go to him."

He went still. Then he thrust her away. His hands remained on her shoulders, and his mouth hung open. "To—you can't mean—what the hell, Jarvis!"

He released her with an abruptness that made her stagger. He paced the spartan room. Dresser to bed, bed to closet. Back again. He rounded on her.

"No," he said. "No fucking way in Hell am I letting him get you."

Alex leaned back against the dresser—the only piece of furniture in the room apart from the single bed, a nightstand, and a wooden chair near the window. The room was devoid of art or photos, or any object that might hint at the life of its occupant. She scooped the hair back from her forehead.

"You don't have a choice, Hugh. And neither do I. Seth is..."

"A class-A fucking prick? Yeah. Got that."

"His obsession with me isn't his fault."

Hugh's head snapped back as if she'd slapped him. He stared at her. "Tell me you didn't just excuse your stalker because it's not his fault."

"That's not what I—"

"For the love of God, Alex, you're a *cop*. You know better than this. You've dealt with these goddamn mother—" Hugh bit off the last word and scrubbed both hands over his face. "Liz is right, isn't she? You're beginning to crack."

An automatic bristle crawled up Alex's spine at Riley's name. Then she laughed. A half snort, half chuckle of wry amusement. "Honestly? Liz doesn't know half of what's going on in my head."

"And me? Do I know half of it?"

She held her friend's gaze. Saw his pain. Felt his confusion. Knew she couldn't avoid it anymore. She closed her eyes. It was time to tell him what Seth had done. She gripped the dresser top on either side of her and took a deep breath. "Hugh—"

"Am I interrupting?" a new voice came from the doorway. The priest.

Hell and damnation. Alex winced. Not the best turn of phrase under the circumstances. She watched impatience cross Henderson's face, soon chased away by a forced smile.

"Marcus. Of course not. Come in."

Father Marcus instead leaned a shoulder against the doorpost, his hands tucked into the pockets of his black pants. Guarded, pale blue eyes glanced at Alex, then settled on Hugh. "Have you told her?"

"Not yet. We had—other matters."

"Told me what?"

"Marcus..." Hugh trailed off.

"I have the scrolls, Detective Jarvis. I took them from the Vatican."

Alex blinked at the priest, then looked to Hugh for confirmation. He nodded.

"They're here. In this house. He's been staying with Emmanuelle. Well, with his brother, who lives with Emmanuelle."

Another blink. And a jaw-drop. Her gaze darted to the single bed beside Hugh.

"Not that kind of living with," Hugh added. "Several of the bikers share the house."

Heir to the throne of Heaven, living with a bunch of former Hells Angels.

Alex wondered whether anyone kept headache medication in the house. She held up both hands against further words from Hugh, then pointed at Father Marcus. "You. Start at the beginning. You were recalled to the Vatican. Why?"

"Because of my work translating the scrolls when they were first uncovered. There were three of us who worked on them together. Father Paul has since passed away, and Father James has advanced Alzheimer's. I was the only one remaining outside the Vatican who knew what the scrolls contained."

"They recalled you because they didn't trust you?" She frowned.

"It was more of a control issue. They didn't want word leaking before they were ready to take the scrolls public."

"They wanted to *release* them? Why?"

"It was to be a strategic move."

"Inflammatory is more like it. The religious nuts are already crawling out of the woodwork." From the corner of her eye, Alex saw Hugh wince. She ignored him. "The information in those scrolls would be like putting a match to a refinery. What could the Vatican possibly hope to gain?"

The priest looked down at the painted floorboards. After a few seconds, Hugh answered instead.

"Control," he said quietly. "By producing the only information on the Nephilim at just the right time, the Vatican would become the expert. The scrolls would stand as proof that the Church is the one true religion. People would flock to it."

Alex stared at him. Then at Father Marcus, who still hadn't looked up from the floor. Her fingers cramped in their hold on the dresser. She let go her grip and flexed her hands.

"Is that true?" she demanded.

Marcus sighed. "Unfortunately, yes. I love my Church, detective, but the truth is, the men who run it are still only men. Some of them don't always make the wisest of decisions."

"And others?"

"Others aided my efforts to remove the scrolls."

"Well, thank bloody common sense for that," she muttered. "So how in the world did you end up here?"

"My brother ran with the Hells Angels in California for almost twenty years. Three years ago, he suddenly turned up in Vancouver, a reformed man. Clean, sober, working as an accountant, and volunteering with a youth shelter in the East End. He'd found faith, he told me. Not in a church, but in his own soul. Him, and a group of others like him."

Alex couldn't help but raise an eyebrow. Marcus nodded. "Yes, it sounded like a cult to me, too, but despite my questions, I found no evidence of any such thing, and I couldn't deny the change. Anyway, when I took the scrolls, this was the safest place I could think of. I'd never met this Emmanuelle until she and Timothy met me at the airport."

"Emmanuelle met you? She knows about the scrolls?"

"Of course not. No one does. That was the point of my taking them. I told Timothy I was taking a sabbatical and needed a quiet place where I could be anonymous."

"Anonymous. A priest living among bikers."

"Play nice, Jarvis." Hugh muttered.

Father Marcus's lips curved. "It's all right, Hugh, I'm a big boy. And yes, Detective Jarvis, I know it seems improbable, but"—he shrugged—"it worked. I kept a low profile, Timothy's friends respected my privacy, and Emmanuelle didn't ask questions."

"Then you being here—with her—is just pure coincidence."

"Or the divine hand of—"

"Spare me," she growled. She pushed away from the

desk and prowled the room, muttering as she passed Hugh, "Of all the gin joints in all the world."

"Maybe he's right," Hugh responded. "Maybe it's not a coincidence."

"Oh, please. We both know the One is—"

"Still influencing events," Emmanuelle's voice interrupted from the doorway. "More than you can imagine."

Alex stopped pacing to face her. Emmanuelle held her gaze, then swept an encompassing glance over Hugh and Father Marcus.

"If you gentlemen wouldn't mind leaving us for a few minutes?"

To their credit, both men looked to Alex for confirmation. She nodded.

"I'm fine," she said.

Without speaking, Father Marcus inclined his head and stepped past Emmanuelle into the hallway. Hugh stopped beside Alex on his way to follow suit.

"Marcus has questions," he murmured. "How much do I tell him?"

Alex looked at the god waiting beside the door. "As much as he wants to know," she said, pitching her voice to reach Emmanuelle. "There are no more secrets."

FORTY-THREE

"Bloody Heaven!" Seth snarled. "If you keep picking at me like that, I'll be here for eternity." He shoved aside the Virtue's hands and ripped the tattered shirt from the wounds that had already begun to heal over the fabric. The Virtue compressed her lips but said nothing. Her flat, garnet-red eyes looked past him, to where Samael stood in silence. Her gaze flickered, and she dipped her head in acknowledgement. Then, leaving the tray of supplies she'd brought on the corner of Seth's desk, she turned and departed, closing the office door behind her.

Seth shot a venomous glare over his shoulder. "Giving orders for me again, Samael?"

The former Archangel's mouth compressed. Seth took up the washcloth from beside the bandages and sponged roughly at his side. The wound that had plagued him for so long, the one inflicted by Alex, seeped fresh blood.

"You seem to have things well in hand," Samael

responded with a careful lack of inflection. "But I'm happy to call her back if you'd prefer."

Seth hurled the bloodied rag at Samael's head. It missed, landing against the window with a wet splat and leaving a crimson smear behind.

"Fuck you!" he growled. "And fuck this whole godforsaken place. I had her, Samael. No thanks to you, I found her and I *had* her. She was close enough to touch. I could smell her. *Taste* her. And then fucking Mika'el shows up, and some random female throws a fireball at the wall, and *what the fuck happened?*"

Samael looked away.

Seth's jaw clenched. "First Alex's whereabouts, then Zuriel's death"—he watched Samael's eyes flicker— "yes, I know about Zuriel. And now this. You're keeping an awful lot of secrets from me, Archangel."

"I'm your aide, Appointed. It's my job—"

"What are you hiding from me, Samael?"

"I didn't think it necessary—"

Seth's fingers closed around Sam's throat, lifting him from the ground and applying just enough pressure to ensure the other knew he was unimpeded by his latest injuries.

"I asked," he said, "what you're hiding."

Sam swallowed. Seth held tight for a count of three, then loosened his grip a fraction. But only a fraction. He wanted his aide conveniently in hand in case Samael decided not to cooperate as much as Seth thought he should.

"Your sister," Samael said. "The female is your sister."

Seth dropped him out of sheer shock.

THERE WAS NOTHING graceful about Mika'el's arrival in Verchiel's office. Uncontrolled, definitely. Borderline catastrophic, perhaps. But not graceful. He sprawled amid scattered books and broken shelves, clinging desperately to the remnants of consciousness, hoping against hope that Verchiel was in residence.

Robes rustled near his head. A cool, soft hand brushed back his hair. "Dear Heaven, Mika'el!" Verchiel gasped. "What happened?"

Even if he could have found words to explain, he couldn't have uttered them.

"Never mind. I'll get help." More rustling. A door opening. And then a bellow for assistance that shook the venerable old building to its very foundation and startled Mika'el's eyes wide.

That had been the soft-spoken Highest Seraph?

A dozen pairs of feet came running into the room.

"Don't move him," Verchiel barked. "Not until we assess the injuries."

Her voice drew nearer as she gave more orders. "Galadriel and Arkiel, clear away the rubble. Nariel, we need water and bandages. Tsekiel, send for Gabriel."

Mika'el raised his head to protest. Verchiel's hand, still cool but not so soft this time, pushed it back down and held him in place.

"Go quickly, Tsekiel," she added, "and tell no one else of this."

Irritation sparked at the Seraph's high-handedness, then it gave way to a soul-deep gratitude for her calm presence. Her sureness. The simple fact that, for once, a decision was not his to make.

Gentle hands lifted him from the floor, carried him, deposited him carefully on a hard surface. With a sigh,

Mika'el gave himself over to his kin and let himself slip—finally, blessedly—into the unconsciousness that would allow him to heal. To return to Emmanuelle.

And to Alex.

FORTY-FOUR

I n the wake of Hugh's departure, Alex carefully put the full width of the room between her and Emmanuelle. It wouldn't do her any good, but she found comfort in the space. Especially in view of her first question.

"Michael?" she asked.

Emmanuelle's expression darkened. She stepped into the room and closed the door. "Gone. His injuries will heal faster in Heaven."

"But he'll be all right? He won't..."

"Die? No. His immortality is intact." Emmanuelle leaned against the wall, tucking fingertips into the front pockets of her black jeans and crossing one booted foot over the other. "You care for him."

The hairs on the back of Alex's neck prickled at the phrasing. *For*, not *about*.

"We've been through a lot together, so yes, I care what happens to him."

Emmanuelle studied her. "He cares for you."

Alex shoved away the memory of a spark. An unbidden awareness. She snorted. "Only as far as my usefulness to the cause is concerned."

"Recruiting me to step into my mother's shoes, you mean?" The dark head shook. "Not going to happen. I'd already be out of here if he hadn't made me promise to watch over you until he returns."

"You're still needed." Michael's words echoed in Alex's head. He'd known Emmanuelle would flee. Had used Alex to tie her here until he could talk to her. Convince her.

So much for *he cares for you.*

Alex swallowed a pang of disappointment she had no right to feel.

"This isn't my fight," Emmanuelle added. "It never was. I'll keep my promise, but when Mika'el gets back, I'm leaving."

She straightened away from the wall and reached for the doorknob.

"Is that what you'll tell your friends?" Alex asked. "When they're facing the Nephilim or the Fallen—or both—will that be your response?"

Emmanuelle's hand tightened perceptibly on the knob. "You might want to remember who you're talking to."

Alex snorted. "Or what? You'll strike me down? Be my guest, because you'd be doing me a greater favor than you can imagine."

Iridescent eyes narrowed. Long seconds passed. "You actually mean that."

"You've no idea."

More seconds, and then Emmanuelle released the knob again. "I'm listening."

Alex walked to the window. Like the one in the living

room, it overlooked the beach, gray and deserted in the sullen, late afternoon. Michael wouldn't want her to tell Emmanuelle the whole sordid tale. He would probably be pissed at how much she had already let slip. She stared out at the white-capped water. But what if Emmanuelle was wrong? What if he didn't return? Who would tell her then? Hell.

She took a deep breath, centering herself. Readying for the memories. Trying to decide where to begin, how much to tell. A line from *Alice in Wonderland* surfaced in her mind—a line that had so tickled Nina's fancy that the little girl had quoted it for days after Alex read her the story: *"Begin at the beginning,"* *the King said, very gravely, "and go on till you come to* *the end: then stop."*

She pushed away the pain tangled up in the memory of her niece. "Did you know a Power by the name of Aramael?" she asked.

"One of seventeen tasked with capturing the Fallen who interfere with mortals. I don't know him personally, but I know—wait. You used the past tense. He's—?"

"Two weeks ago, trying to protect me from Seth."

"You again." Irritation laced Emmanuelle's voice. "What the Hell is so special about you?"

"I was his soulmate."

Shock rippled through the room. Outside, in the hallway, another door opened, then closed.

"That's impossible," Emmanuelle said. "An angel and a mortal? It could never happen."

"An angel and a Naphil," Alex corrected. "And thanks to Mittron, it did happen."

"Mittron! The Highest Seraph...*that* Mittron?"

"I sincerely hope there's only one of him, so yes.

That Mittron. Only he's not the Highest Seraph anymore. He was exiled to Earth—" Alex realized she was jumping ahead. *Begin at the beginning*, she reminded herself. She took another breath. "Aramael's brother, Caim, was one of the imprisoned Fallen. He escaped Limbo—" She broke off at a noise of dissent behind her. Flashing a dark look over her shoulder, she repeated, "He escaped Limbo with Mittron's help and started killing people in Toronto, looking for a Naphil soul. He thought one might be able to carry him back to Heaven."

Emmanuelle raised an eyebrow. "The serial killer a couple of months back—that was Mittron's doing?"

"It was. And it was my case. Aramael was assigned to be my partner—"

"Your *police* partner?"

Alex glowered at her. "If you keep interrupting, we're going to be here all bloody night."

Emmanuelle's chin lifted, but she waved at Alex to continue.

"Aramael was to hunt Caim, and to act as my guardian at the same time." Alex turned to the window again. This was where the story became difficult...and stayed that way. She stared into the fading light that marked the end of day.

"Right from the start, there was something between us. I saw his wings, he had trouble focusing on Caim's presence when I was near. When Caim eventually came for me, Aramael lost control and killed him, ending the pact between your—between Heaven and Hell. I was injured in the fight and would have died if Seth hadn't brought me back."

"Wait. How does Seth factor into this?"

"He was the one who found out about Mittron's

involvement. He told Aramael about the soulmate connection and stayed to help."

"Go on."

"Aramael was exiled, and Seth returned to Heaven to fulfill his role as Appointed in the secondary agreement your parents made. You know about that?"

"About my brother being the ultimate pawn in my parents' game intended to decide humanity's fate through his own choices?" Emmanuelle's mouth twisted. "I'm aware."

"He enlisted Mittron's help instead. To become mortal."

"That's what he was supposed to do."

"*Adult* mortal," Alex clarified. "So he could be with me."

Emmanuelle expelled a long, slow breath. "I see."

"Something went wrong with the transition," Alex continued when the other woman said nothing more. "He retained his powers and his immortality, but lost all language and knowledge of who he was. Your mother's solution was to send an assassin after him."

"Aramael."

Alex shot her a guarded look of surprise.

Emmanuelle shrugged. "He was the obvious choice. With no connection to Heaven, he wouldn't trigger the failsafe clause my father insisted on. What happened next?"

"I found Seth first. I helped him regain language, but he still remembered nothing. Then Lucifer got to him, Michael intervened, and the two of them decided that Seth's role as Appointed would continue, with all parties involved keeping their distance from him."

"Except you."

"Except me. And I was succeeding, damn it. He

wanted to choose humanity's survival." Alex leaned her forehead against the cool window. She closed her eyes under the weight of the memories.

"And then?" Emmanuelle prompted.

"And then your father—Lucifer—came to me. I thought he was Seth."

"Came to—" Emmanuelle's jaw dropped. "Bloody Hell. You mean he *raped* you?"

It took three swallows before Alex could support her nod with actual words. "And impregnated me and made Seth think I'd been with Aramael. He"— she drew a shuddering breath—"Seth stormed out. He was on the verge choosing your father's side—he was going to kill a man...a homeless man. We were all there. Me, Aramael, Lucifer, Michael, and all the Archangels. The Fallen had already bred an army of Nephilim—eighty thousand of them—and Lucifer intended his child, the one I carried, to lead them. I had to stop them, Lucifer and Seth both, so I did the only thing I could. I took the knife from Seth and killed Lucifer's child."

"You—"

Alex heard booted feet approach, then fingers grasped her shoulder and pulled her around. An astounded Emmanuelle stared at her.

"You stabbed yourself? And you didn't die?"

"I did die."

Emmanuelle's eyes widened a tiny fraction. "Seth brought you back a second time."

"Yes. And then he made his choice."

"I don't understand. If he chose—"

"Me." The word emerged as a croak, forced from a throat rigid with remembered pain. And there was still so much to tell. Alex clenched jaw and fists, and made herself repeat, "He chose me."

Emmanuelle's mouth flapped soundlessly as understanding settled in. She groped behind her for the wooden chair and slumped into it, legs akimbo, elbows resting on knees.

"The idiot gave up everything for you. Heaven, his power, responsibility...everything. No wonder it felt as if the world was going to rip itself apart."

She'd felt that? Then why hadn't she returned to Heaven? Why...? Alex stifled the questions. Her own story first, and then Emmanuelle's. If the other would tell her story.

"The One couldn't control it," she said. "The harder she tried, the weaker she became. She needed Seth to take back his powers, but he wouldn't. He wouldn't give me up, not even to save the world."

"You asked him to?"

"I didn't want to hurt him, but to allow him to choose his own happiness over the entire world? I could never have lived with that. But he didn't understand, and the more I pressed, the angrier he became. The more controlling. Then one of the Fallen got to him and convinced him there was a way he could have it all— his power, control over Hell...me."

Arms folded over her belly, Alex glanced at Emmanuelle and found her watching with an unreadable expression that reminded Alex all too much of Seth. She shivered.

"So he took the power back and came after me. He and Aramael fought." Alex heard Emmanuelle's indrawn hiss of disbelief, but she pressed on. Doggedly, hoarsely, knowing if she stopped now, she might not continue. "Aramael was injured. He—his immortality—"

Christ almighty, this was hard. She swallowed. Hardened her voice. "His immortality was pierced. I called for Michael, but before he could get there, Seth got to me. He turned me immortal."

Emmanuelle catapulted from the chair so fast that Alex flinched.

"Stop," the god—goddess?—ordered. "Just stop. You called Michael—and he *came*? From where?"

"Heaven."

Emmanuelle stared at her, then paced the floor in short, heavy strides, her boots thudding against the painted wood surface, both hands holding the hair back from her face. "It's impossible," she muttered.

"Which part?" Alex asked wearily.

"All of it. No one can call an angel across two realms. Not even another angel. And *immortality?*"

Alex shrugged at her disbelief. "Do you want me to finish?"

"What more can there be?" Emmanuelle growled.

"Samael breaking all the Fallen out of Limbo and turning them loose on Toronto, one at a time, until Michael agreed to let him have Seth. Me wounding Seth with Aramael's sword. Aramael dying in my arms." A tear slid down Alex's cheek, its trail first hot, then cool on her skin. She blinked back the others that would have followed. "And now all of this. Seth has stepped into his father's place in Hell and wants me to join him there. Mittron is overseeing the raising of the Nephilim children—in Pripyat, we think—and the angels are losing the war against Hell because they have no will of their own to drive them."

On the other side of the room, now, Emmanuelle clenched and unclenched her fists, her entire body rigid, nostrils flaring.

"You don't know what you're asking."

"I know we have nowhere else to turn."

A harsh laugh ripped from Emmanuelle. "How rich is that?"

"I don't understand."

"You don't need to." Emmanuelle reached for the doorknob. "I'm going for a walk."

Alex gaped at her. One moment she'd thought she was getting through to their potential savior, and then it was like someone had flicked a switch. What the hell had she said? "But—"

"Stay in the house. You'll be safe here. Not even my own mother could find the place." Emmanuelle stepped into the hallway and sent a last, cold glare over her shoulder. "If she'd ever bothered to try."

FORTY-FIVE

" *S ister?*" Seth snarled, spittle flying from between his teeth. "I have a sister and you didn't think you should inform me? What the *fuck*, Samael!"

Samael scowled back at him, wiping away the blood dripping into his eye from a split eyebrow—an injury sustained from connecting with the desk rather than Seth's hand...for a change. He tried to muster his thoughts.

He'd expected Seth to be surprised by Emmanuelle's presence, but not by her existence.

"No one ever told you?" he asked.

Seth wheeled away and stalked the perimeter of the room. "No! Yes. I don't know." He raked a hand over his hair. "I think Mittron hinted at it once, but no. No one told me. Bloody Heaven!"

Samael would second that. He wiped his fingers against his sleeve. "It doesn't change anything. We can still—"

"Are you out of your mind? It changes everything."

Seth gestured at his oozing, bloody wound. "I barely managed to stand against a single Archangel today, Samael. There's no way in all of Creation I can stand against my own sibling."

He paced away, shaking his head. "No. No, we're done. The war is over. We negotiate another treaty. They give me Alex, and we leave the mortals alone."

Samael gaped at him. "You can't be serious. What about your father's legacy?"

"My father is dead," Seth snapped. "I owe him no loyalty. His Nephilim army is legacy enough."

Samael bit back an oath, trying for calm. Reason. "The rest of Hell, then. You can't expect the Fallen to remain tied to this—this—"

"Hellhole?" Seth suggested, a flicker of dark amusement in darker eyes. "Fine. We'll redecorate. You can choose the curtain fabric. Happy?"

Samael's hand itched to draw the sword from his scabbard. Seth's stillness dared him to try. Samael curled the hand into a fist instead, squeezing until the blood left his fingers.

"This is not what we agreed."

"And you haven't delivered Alex as we agreed, either. Let's do you a favor and call it even, shall we?" Seth sank into the chair behind his desk with a grimace of pain, but the tension across his shoulders and the watchful expression told Samael he was far from incapacitated.

Samael swallowed his response.

Seth smiled. "Much better," he said. "Now go to my sister. Tell her I want to talk. You have twenty-four hours. And, Samael..."

Samael was already at the door, shaking with a gut-wrenching rage unlike anything he'd ever felt before.

He stopped. He didn't turn.

"I suggest you do a better job of this task than you did of finding Alex," came the drawl, so arrogant and so like Lucifer's that it made Samael's skin crawl, "or I'll begin to think you're not really on my side."

Without answering, Samael stepped into the corridor and closed the door behind him. Then he put his fist through the stone wall opposite. Seth's faint chuckle floated through the wood between them.

"Twenty-four hours, Samael," he called. "I'm counting on you."

Samael swallowed a roar of pure frustration, refusing to give the Appointed the satisfaction. Just as he wouldn't give him a treaty, either.

"Like fucking Heaven, I'll negotiate," he hissed at the oaken door between him and the mewling infant in whom he'd placed such high hope. He'd been so damned shortsighted—so sure of himself...

He gritted his teeth.

And he still was.

As long as he could get to the Naphil woman before Seth did, as long as he could make it look as though she'd died at Heaven's hands, he could still pull this off. Still make that pansy-ass into a fucking leader.

Or die trying.

FORTY-SIX

Bethiel staggered as he landed and nearly pitched headfirst into the wooden gate marking the entrance to Heaven. His wings trembled with the effort of traveling between the realms. He'd never been to Earth when he was still a part of Heaven, so he didn't know whether it was supposed to be this difficult—but he suspected not. Proof that Heaven itself knew he no longer belonged.

He shook out his feathers and folded his wings behind him, gazing across the sweep of lawn on the other side of the low, wood-rail fence. The forest he had once wandered stood just beyond, and on the other side of that would be the One's beloved gardens, meticulously maintained. A shiver rippled down Bethiel's spine at the thought of seeing them again—them, but not her.

Mittron had much to answer for.

The very thought of the former Highest Seraph brought Bethiel up short, but before the familiar hatred could follow, he recalled why he had come here. Remembered the unexpected compassion that had overwhelmed him when he'd found her. The girl with the pale face and matted hair. The hollow eyes. The bulging belly.

The girl who was running out of time.

He reached for the gate. The instant his fingers brushed wood, a shock of energy jolted through him, slamming him to the ground. Damnation. He'd forgotten about that layer of protection. He would need someone to let him in. He regained his feet and shook the grass from his wings. Studied again the lawn, peered into the trees beyond, scanned the skies above.

Nothing. No one coming to investigate his attempted breach—or to defend against it. Bethiel scowled.

Was Heaven really that far gone?

He stepped up to the gate again, careful this time not to touch it. Then, drawing a deep breath, he shouted, "Mika'el!"

His voice rolled across the expanse of lawn and was swallowed by the forest.

He bellowed again.

More silence followed.

What if Mika'el wasn't even here? Just because he'd been gone from the condo didn't mean he'd returned to Heaven. On the other hand—Bethiel sighed. On the other hand, he didn't know where else to look, and Heaven was at least a place to start.

He shouted until he was hoarse, and then until his voice cracked and failed altogether. Then he retrieved anything he could find on his side of the fence— stones, sticks, and finally handfuls of grass—and pitched them against the energy protecting Heaven's borders.

It was hardest to throw the grass, because for it to make contact with the fence, he had to stand near enough that the jolts still reached him, singeing his wings and hair. At last, exhausted, he sprawled on his back, parallel to the fence, plucking single blades from the lawn beside his head. He aimed them one at a time at the lowest rail, the odor of burnt feathers acrid in his nose.

"What in bloody Hell do you think you're doing?"

Eyes closed, Bethiel froze in mid-toss. A voice. Real or—

"I asked," came a growl, "what in bloody Hell you think you're doing."

Real. Definitely real.

Bethiel squinted up at the figure looming over him. Black armor glinted dully in the setting sun, sparking caution in his belly. An Archangel. His gaze sharpened, sweeping over the dents and the dried, crusted spots of phosphorescence mingled with blood. Massive wings extended to their fullest. The metallic whisper of battle-ready feathers. He stopped breathing.

Not just any Archangel, but one just back from the front, ill-tempered and with the heat of battle still running through his veins.

"I won't ask again." Metal scraped against hardened leather as a broadsword left its sheath.

"Mika'el," Bethiel croaked. "I seek Mika'el."

An ebony face, almost as dark as the armor its owner wore, scowled at him. "One: How did you know he was here? Two: How did a Fallen One manage to get here? Three: Why should I believe anything you tell me? And four: You have thirty seconds to answer before I kill you."

Any inclination Bethiel might have had toward meekness disappeared with the *Fallen* accusation.

"I'm not Fallen," he snarled back. "I was falsely imprisoned by Mittron—that would probably be the reason I got as far as I did. And I don't know Mika'el is here, but I sure as Hell hope so, because he's the only way I have of finding the Naphil woman before her niece dies giving birth to Lucifer's child."

Golden eyes studied him narrowly. "You know I'll kill you if you lie."

"I also know no one could make up a story like that if they tried. Not without at least some truth behind it."

A grunt. The Archangel slid the sword back into its sheath and then reached down to grasp Bethiel's shirtfront and haul him to his feet.

"Name?" he asked.

"Bethiel. Formerly of the Principalities."

"Raphael. Still of the Archangels." The Archangel's gaze swept over Bethiel's scorched wings. "Can you fly with those things, or do I need to carry you?"

Bethiel pulled away. Suffer himself to be carried on his one and only return to Heaven? Not.

"I'll fly."

They landed amid the One's rose garden—or what had once been the rose garden but was now a riot of overgrowth. Raphael led the way, striding along equally overgrown paths, past a fountain that no longer functioned, greenhouses standing open and untended, and the One's former residence, its windows shattered. Bethiel's jaw tightened. He might no longer be a part of Heaven—nor would he ever be again—but he still felt the loss. The emptiness.

And Raphael's watchful gaze.

Bethiel looked to the Archangel. "Things go that badly?"

"*Things*," Raphael retorted, "are none of your bloody business."

Arriving at a simple stone building, the Archangel raised his hand and knocked on the door. "In," a muffled voice responded.

A haggard Mika'el stood in the middle of the room as they entered, his back to them and his arms spread wide as a Virtue unwound the bandage from around his chest. He looked over his shoulder, and his gaze settled at once on Bethiel.

"Alex?" he demanded. In almost the same breath he shook his head at his own question. "Of course not. You don't even know where she is."

"That's why I'm here. I've found the niece. She has a matter of hours left. The Naphil should be with her."

Mika'el's gaze narrowed. "Compassion, Bethiel? There may be more hope for you than I thought."

"I don't want your hope. I want you to hold up your end of the bargain."

"She's with Emmanuelle. Raphael will take you and the girl to her."

The Archangel at Bethiel's side stiffened. "What? But—"

"The girl will be guarded." Mika'el looked to Bethiel for confirmation, and Bethiel nodded.

"Qemuel," he said. "Big. Nasty."

"I'm not ready for a fight," Mika'el told Raphael. "In a few hours, maybe, but not yet. The girl doesn't have that long."

"And this is important enough to pull me away

from the battlefront?"

Over the Virtue's head, Mika'el's emerald eyes turned bleak. Infinite sadness paired with a commander's determination in their depths, and his mouth pulled tight. He nodded. "It is that important, Raphael, yes."

Raphael muttered something under his breath, and Bethiel glanced his way. He took in the temper etched on the Archangel's face, then the gauntlet resting atop the sword hilt. He inched away. He considered requesting someone less hulkingly volatile, then decided against the idea. If he was heading into a fight with Qemuel, a bad-tempered Archangel on his side would be a benefit, not a detriment.

Mika'el lowered his arms as the Virtue attending him stepped back and stooped to collect the soiled gauze she'd dropped to the floor. Bethiel frowned. Hold on. Mika'el. Bandages...?

He lifted his gaze as the Archangel turned. He sucked in a quick breath.

"Bloody Hell," he whispered. "What happened to you?"

"Seth happened." Mika'el reached for a shirt draped over a chair and slid his arms into the sleeves. "He found Alex."

The Virtue stepped past the Archangel to deposit her armload of bandages on a cloth-covered table. She gathered the cloth's corners and expertly tied everything into a tidy bundle.

Alex. Bethiel's eyes narrowed as the Archangel buttoned up the shirt over the massive scarring that encompassed his entire ribcage. Again, Mika'el referred to the Naphil woman by name. What was it about this woman that inspired such loyalty from angels? Aramael he could understand, given the soulmate connection, but Seth? And now Mika'el? He shook his head. A puzzle, yes, but not one he cared to solve. He had other matters to attend to. He cleared his throat, but Raphael beat him to speech.

"What do I do with the girl when I have her?"

"Take her to Alex. I'll be there as soon as I can."

"And the child? What do I do with that?"

Mika'el murmured his thanks to the Virtue as she carried her bundle past him. She slipped between Raphael and Bethiel, then disappeared out the door they'd left open. When Bethiel looked back to Mika'el, the other's mouth had drawn into a hard line.

"Ask Emmanuelle," he said. "It can be her first decision as ruler."

"Then she has agreed to return."

"Let's just say she hasn't refused."

Looking just as grim as Mika'el, Raphael pushed Bethiel out of the Archangel's residence ahead of him. He closed the door behind him with a thud that echoed across the empty lawns. Neither of them gave voice to the word that hung in the air between them. Emmanuelle hadn't refused to return...

Yet.

FORTY-SEVEN

A large hand slapped against the sliding glass door at eye level, holding it shut. Nostrils flaring, Emmanuelle inhaled deeply, fighting back the turmoil that wanted to swallow her. The savagery that edged it. She met Wookie's scowl with one of her own.

"I need air," she said.

"Alone?" He shook his hairy head. "I don't think so. Not after today."

Emmanuelle bit back a snarl. Tried to make herself sound reasonable. "Nothing will happen. We've been here three years and they—no one has found this place."

"They found you at the bar."

The others in the room had fallen silent, and Emmanuelle felt them listening. The vortex at her center churned faster. She clenched her teeth against it. "I got careless. It won't happen again."

"Good to hear." He folded his arms across his chest and leaned against the door. "If it does, however, I'm going to be there."

"To do what, Wookie? You saw what happened at the bar. If they do find me again, there's nothing you can do to stop them. Besides, I'm not the one in danger. The woman is."

"Fine. Then if I'm going to die protecting one of you, I choose you."

She glared at him, loving and hating him at the same time for the loyalty she had never asked for, never wanted. Had come to depend on.

"I could stop you," she said.

"But you won't."

"Oh, for—" She sighed. "Fine. If it means that much, you can come with me. But you stay back. A hundred feet."

"Fifty."

"Seventy-five."

"Done." Wookie looked around and barked, "Scorpion! Let's go for a walk."

"Damn it, Wookie—" She bit off the rest of her complaint. There was no point. Wookie would be true to his word and give her the space she needed, and having one more body along wouldn't make a difference. Hell, having everyone in the house follow her wouldn't make a difference. She still faced the same demons. Still needed to make the most difficult decision of her existence. Run, or—

Wookie pulled open the door and Emmanuelle shoved past him onto the porch, sucking in the clean salt air, fighting down the panic. *Not here. Not yet.* Her two bodyguards followed, both reaching to zip up their jackets in the same instant. Scorpion shook his head at her short-sleeved t-shirt.

"At least now I get why you never feel the cold," he

said.

She had no response. The equanimity with which her friends had accepted the events of the day was a whole other issue she would have to deal with at some point. *But not here. Not yet.*

She headed down the stairs and across the strip of lawn. Beyond, the beach stretched for miles to either side, utterly deserted at this hour. She hesitated, feeling the pull of its emptiness, then walked instead to meet the incoming tide, counting off her steps. She'd meant what she said to Wookie about the house remaining undetected, but she wouldn't take chances. She wouldn't leave them without her protection.

The power that, until today, she hadn't used for five thousand years.

Bloody Hell.

Wookie and Scorpion stopped at the edge of the sand, letting her continue alone. Ten feet separated her from them. Then twenty. Then thirty. She halted at the seventy-foot mark. Another few dozen feet of sand sat between her and the water, but it wouldn't do so for long. In just a few minutes, the surf would force her to begin retracing her steps, push her to return to the others.

Emmanuelle closed her eyes and looked into her vortex. Thoughts battered at her, but as soon as she tried to grasp one, another surfaced and took its place, and then another. Mika'el. Heaven. The One and Lucifer. The war. A Nephilim army. The woman. So much. Too much.

The weight of the universe itself pressed in on her, forcing her into a crouch. She locked her hands together over the back of her neck, huddling against the memories.

A thousand years of knowing that her conception had been a mistake, that she had fallen short of every expectation. Lucifer's. The One's. Mika'el's. Her own.

A thousand years of watching her parents tear themselves apart while her soulmate steadfastly stood by her mother's side, supporting every flawed decision the One made.

And five thousand years alone, here on Earth, after she'd turned her back on the conflict that grew darker by the day—refusing to watch her soulmate pulled into the downward spiral her parents had become.

Emmanuelle turned her face to the sky and the emerging pinpoints of light that marked the stars in the vastness her mother had created.

Mika'el had remained with the One, his loyalty to her outweighing his connection to Emmanuelle. And now...now he asked her to return. Not for his sake, but for that of the Heaven that hadn't even noticed her departure.

He needed her not to be his soulmate, but to lead a war against her own brother, to continue the endless, unwinnable conflict that had driven her from her home in the first place.

Emmanuelle stared out across the ocean. The foam rolling onto the shore, the ceaseless rise and fall of the waves, the seemingly endless expanse of water. Tears blurred her vision. She couldn't do it. She couldn't go back and pretend she cared about the realm that had let her slip away so easily. Couldn't pretend she wanted to be its leader.

And wouldn't be her mother.

"Is that what you'll tell your friends?" the woman's voice whispered through her mind. *"When they're facing the Nephilim or the Fallen—or both—will that*

be your response?"

Her heart twisted, and she looked back over her shoulder. A sudden gleam of moonlight highlighted Wookie's profile. The fierce loyalty stamped across his face. The solemn trust in his eyes. Hot tears spilled over onto her cheeks.

The scent of roses filled her nostrils.

Fuck.

FORTY-EIGHT

"Well?" Henderson strolled into the room, hands in pockets, and took up Alex's former position against the dresser. "What did she say?"

Alex returned to staring out the window, arms folded the chest-high sill. "She won't help."

She had reached the edge of the surf now and stood facing the ocean beneath the full moon's light, long dark hair whipping in the wind.

Hugh cleared his throat. "That's it? All she said was no? Did you tell her—"

"I told her everything, Hugh. Aramael, Seth, the Nephilim. Everything. Her answer was no."

"Jesus."

The two figures who had followed Emmanuelle from the house hung back at the edge of the sand. The graying beard of one flapped over his shoulder. Wookie, she recalled. Standing watch?

Fat lot of good that would do him.

"That's it, then. If she doesn't help, there's nothing

more we can do." A note of awe crept into Hugh's voice. "It all ends. The world, Heaven...everything."

Everything except Alex.

She caught her breath. Waited for the knife in her chest to withdraw. It stayed. Hugh's footsteps approached, and his hands settled onto her shoulders. He turned her to face him. His gentle brown gaze searched hers.

"Liz told me what you said about having to deal with this for eternity."

She started. He knew?

"What did he do to you, Alex?"

She shook her head. "It doesn't matter. Talking won't change it."

"God damn, Alex." Her friend drew her into a hug, resting his chin on top of her head, swaying from side to side with her. "Armageddon. How in all that is holy did we get here?"

She had no reply. Knew he didn't expect one. Closing her eyes, she let herself be held, let herself draw on someone else's strength, just for a moment. Then, when a clatter of dishes from the kitchen intruded on the silence, she pulled away.

"Go home, Hugh," she said. "Go home to Liz. Hold her. Be with her. Take what you can for the two of you."

"Does that mean we're giving up, then?"

"Have you ever known me to give up?" She forced a lightness into her voice. A smile of reassurance intended to distract him. "Think of it as regrouping."

It would be more of a redeployment of forces—but she couldn't tell him that part. Couldn't tell him about her conversation with Michael.

"*...maybe I can make a difference...maybe I can*

influence him..."

She wouldn't tell him about her realization that ultimately, she would have no choice.

Or rather, she would choose the world's survival over her own sanity.

"*He's not going to stop until he has me.*"

"Are you sure you're okay?" Hugh's hands gripped her arms. "I can stay if you need me. Liz will understand."

And she dared not tell him about Michael's implicit agreement.

"*I wish I could argue with you.*"

She stepped back until Hugh's hands dropped to his sides. "Go home," she said again. "Tell Liz I said hi."

"And you'll call if you need me? For anything."

"Of course."

Her friend and colleague ruffled her hair in acceptance of her lie, then turned and left.

"WHAT THE HELL are you doing?"

Mika'el settled the newly crafted breastplate over still-tender scars before looking around at Gabriel. "Given your familiarity with armor, I'm guessing that's a rhetorical question."

Gabriel scowled at him, arms crossed over her own armor and sapphire eyes flashing. "You know what I mean. You haven't healed enough for battle."

"Then I'll have to do my best to avoid getting into one." Mika'el reached for a pauldron and slipped it over his shoulder.

"That's not even slightly amusing. You damn near died, Mika'el. You need at least another day here."

"You've seen what's happening on Earth, Gabriel.

Humanity is tearing itself apart as we speak. We don't have another day. We're down to counting hours. I need to get back to Emmanuelle. If she disappears again, we're lost."

"And if you die? What do you think will happen to us then?"

"If you have Emmanuelle on your side? Heaven will prevail as it always has." He settled the second pauldron into place. "You're a better commander than you think you are, Gabriel. I can think of no one better to lead the host."

"I know exactly how good I am." Gabriel tossed flaming red hair over a black-armored shoulder. "That's not the point. I don't want to *be* the commander. This is *your* army, Mika'el. We need you here, with us."

"And you'll have me here, as soon as I convince Emmanuelle to return."

"Then let me send someone with you."

"Raphael is already away, and—"

"On a fool's errand," Gabriel growled.

Mika'el ignored her as if she hadn't spoken. "And we cannot spare anyone else. I'll be fine. Once Emmanuelle agrees—"

"*If* she bloody agrees."

Setting his jaw, Mika'el put down the couter he'd been about to slip into place over his elbow. He faced Gabriel and met her glare with the cold stare of a commander. Her commander.

"I'm going to Earth to speak with Emmanuelle," he said. "I would like to leave you in charge of the host's forces in my absence. If you have a problem with the latter, I will assign someone else. The former, however, is none of your business. Am I clear?"

Gabriel's lips thinned. "Crystal," she snapped.

Wheeling, she stomped out of the room, nearly bowling over Verchiel as she pushed past her in the doorway. The Highest Seraph raised an eyebrow in the departing Archangel's direction.

"Trouble?" she murmured.

Mika'el sighed and picked up the couter again. "Isn't there always?"

Verchiel strolled into the room, her hands hidden in the folds of her scarlet robe. "You're leaving. Do you think you're—"

"Don't you start."

"I see."

He reached for a pauldron. "I'm sorry. I shouldn't take my frustrations with Gabriel out on you."

"She's doing her best, Mika'el. You ask a lot of her."

"I ask what I must, Verchiel. Of her, of the others...I know it's a lot, but what would you have me do? You're the one who insisted we need Emmanuelle in the first place."

Verchiel pursed her lips at the blatant unfairness of his accusation, but she let it pass without comment. "Then you think she'll wait for you?" she asked instead.

"I think the promise I elicited from her to protect Alex is tenuous at best. Emmanuelle has been away a long time. Her loyalties to Heaven, to us—they'll be muddied."

"If they ever existed at all."

Mika'el continued securing armor in place. Verchiel didn't leave.

"You have a question?" he prompted.

"The woman. Alex."

"What about her?"

"You said you didn't let her go to Seth because

you needed her to keep Emmanuelle there until you healed and returned."

"Correct."

"But that doesn't explain why you saved her from Seth in the first place. You'd already found Emmanuelle. You could have let Seth have the Naphil, and there would have been no battle. No one would have died, and you wouldn't have been injured. You didn't just risk yourself, Mika'el, you risked all of us. Heaven, Earth, everything. Why?"

Mika'el didn't answer right away. Instead, he stared down at the breastplate he wore, studying the artistry etched into its surface. Vines, leaf-laden and graceful. The face of a woman—the One—not quite hidden amid the foliage. It was the first new armor he had needed in six thousand years, and its craftsmanship had stunned him. Appalled him.

He would have sent it back if he'd had the time, but he didn't, and so he would wear it. He would wear the One's likeness and it would remind him of all that was wrong with what they had become. Because the armory didn't just produce armor and weapons anymore, it crafted works of art. Art meant to wound, maim, kill. An effort too parallel by far to the one humanity put into its own methods of destruction.

Verchiel cleared her throat.

"I saved her because we're supposed to be better, Verchiel."

"Better than what, the Fallen? But we are."

"Are we?"

The Highest recoiled from the question. "You can't seriously be comparing us to the ones who abandoned Heaven..."

Mika'el threaded fingers through hair badly in

need of a trim. In his spare time. His voice curt, he said, "At least the Fallen are honest about who they are, Verchiel. Can we say the same about ourselves? We've been at war or on the edge of it for so long, we've forgotten the very reason for our creation. We're supposed to celebrate life, to protect it, not decide who is entitled to it and who is not."

Verchiel was silent for a long moment. Then she cleared her throat. "We didn't start the war, Mika'el."

He closed his eyes. "I know."

"Nor can we save everyone. Thousands have already died, and millions more will be lost. We cannot stop that."

"I know that, too. But sometimes, when you hold a single life in your hands, it's different. In that moment, in that decision, you define yourself. You define who you will become. If I had let Seth take Alex when it was in my power to stop him—" Mika'el broke off. He opened his eyes again to meet the Highest Seraph's pale blue gaze, trying to find the words to tell her of the guilt that threatened to consume him from the inside. Guilt for deeds he had not yet committed...but knew he would.

"I need to be more than that, Verchiel," he said quietly. "If I am to do what I must, I need to know we are all more than that."

FORTY-NINE

"I thought you could use this."

Alex looked around from the sliding door to find Father Marcus holding out a steaming cup to her.

"Tea," he said. "With a little extra something."

She would have preferred the something without the tea, but she took the cup from him anyway. A single sip made her eyes water. She coughed.

"A little?"

He shrugged. "I wasn't really measuring."

Alex sipped again, grateful for the heat of the whiskey sliding into her belly. Wishing it could fill the hollowness residing there. She shifted to make room for the priest beside her. Hands behind his back, he looked out into the night, to where Emmanuelle's friends stood guard at the edge of the lawn, and Emmanuelle herself still sat at the edge of the water.

"So Hugh told me quite a tale," he said.

"He told you the truth."

Silence. A sigh. "I'm sure you believe it to be so,

Alex, but—"

"Look," Alex interrupted. "I don't mean to be rude, Father Marcus, but I'm not up for a theological debate right now, and I really don't give a rat's ass whether you believe what Hugh told you or not. It doesn't change anything either way. The One is still dead, and we're still in the middle of Armageddon with no one but *her*" —she jabbed a thumb in Emmanuelle's direction— "who can do a goddamn thing about it."

Father Marcus rocked back and forth on his heels. "I was eighteen when I entered the seminary," he said, "but I was certain of my calling even before then. The Lord has been my father and the Church my family for my entire life. Together, they form the very basis of my existence."

Alex suppressed a surge of impatience. Christ, couldn't he take a hint? He hadn't given her nearly enough whiskey to take the edge off this kind of conver—

"Hugh told me about your sister," the priest continued. "And your niece."

She blinked at the sudden change in direction.

Marcus turned his head to look at her. Pale blue eyes swam with an intense sadness he made no effort to hide. "I'm sorry for your loss. I'm not sure I could endure such pain."

Alex stared out the door again, swallowing the knife in her throat. She gritted her teeth. Forced back the memories. Heard, in her traitorous mind, Jen's quick, warm laugh. For a moment, every fiber of her being ached to feel her sister's hug again, and every atom cried out at knowing she never would.

"That is why I must question Hugh's story," he said softly. "Do you see? Because if he's right—and if I believe him—I lose the only thing that makes it possible for me to survive. I lose everything I ever lived for. Everything that defines me. I lose my faith."

"It's no wonder we're in such a mess," Alex muttered, only just refraining from rolling her eyes.

Marcus's expression turned offended. "I beg your pardon?"

"Every religion on the face of the planet is run by people who think their faith defines them, Marcus. People who think their way is the only way. The true way. Why? Because it makes them feel safe. Like someone's in control. But you want to know the truth?"

She pointed out the window to the figure crouched on the beach. "*That* is the truth. That's our reality. A god who doesn't want to be a god, and who's no more in control of this mess than anyone else in the universe. You don't want to accept that? Fine. I can't say I blame you. But let's be honest about why. It's not that you can't accept it. You just choose not to."

Marcus drew himself tall, visibly bristling, his lips pressed together in denial. But before he could refute her words, a bellow from outside filtered through the partly open door. Alex jerked her head around. Her gaze swept the beach, and in an instant—a heart-stopping, world-altering instant—she took in the scene unfolding there. Emmanuelle, on her feet and racing across the sand, her two bodyguards on an intercept—

No. They weren't intercepting Emmanuelle, they were running toward two angels who had appeared. One, an Archangel, armored and armed. The other— the other was Bethiel, with a bundle in his grasp. A limp, unmoving bundle.

Nina.

"Holy Mother of God," Father Marcus whispered beside her.

Alex dropped the whiskey-laced tea and wrenched open the door.

THE ANGELS ARRIVED on the beach without warning. Two of them, in a rush of wind and sand and feathers that brought Emmanuelle to her feet in a single, fluid movement. Instinctively, without conscious thought, she brought her energies to bear and ran toward them, zeroing in on the one with the sword. He deflected the first surge of power, but not before it knocked him to one knee.

"Hold!" he roared. "I am Raphael of the Archangels, sent by Mika'el!"

With more effort than she would have liked, Emmanuelle caught back a second, more deadly blast. Damn, but she was out of practice. She waved off Wookie and Scorpion, both halfway to the angels already, and leaned forward, hands on thighs, drawing air into lungs that felt like they trembled as much or more than the rest of her. She glowered at the angel she'd fired at.

"Bloody Hell," she spat. "I could have killed you! What in Creation were you thinking, dropping in out of nowhere like that?"

Raphael regained his feet. "No time. The Naphil—where is she?"

"Why? What do you want with her?" Emmanuelle tensed again. She had nothing but his word that Mika'el had—

The clouds parted overhead. Bright moonlight

lit the intruders, glistening off wet smears on the Archangel's black armor, the slash that laid open his cheek. Her gaze flicked to the other angel. No armor on this one, but his clothing, too, bore evidence of battle. She straightened. What in Hell was going on?

Before she could ask, the sliding glass door from the living room crashed open and the woman bolted across the porch and down the stairs. Half a dozen of the house's occupants followed, taking up positions along the deck rail. The woman ran full at the angels, dodging Scorpion's outstretched hand.

Emmanuelle gathered herself for battle, cursing again the promise she'd made to her soulmate, knowing Mika'el would never forgive her if anything happened to the woman. But instead of attacking, the Archangel Raphael stepped to one side and allowed the woman to stagger past him. She stopped before the other, swayed on her feet, dropped to her knees. Despair rolled off her in waves.

The woman lifted her hands, and the angel deposited his bundle in her arms with the utmost tenderness. The blankets fell away to reveal the pale, form of a young girl, barely alive, too far gone even for Emmanuelle to save A moan broke from the woman, deep and guttural. Primal in its agony.

The sound slammed into Emmanuelle, burying itself in her gut. Her hands fell to her sides. She stepped forward, driven to offer solace by a force she hadn't known existed, a need she hadn't known she possessed. A hand on her arm stopped her. She looked over her shoulder and met Mika'el's gaze.

He'd returned.

"It's her niece," he said quietly, his own voice raw with grief. "She was taken by Lucifer, and now she has died in childbirth."

Taken. Emmanuelle's stomach rolled at the horror behind the word. Behind her father's actions.

"But she's so young," she whispered.

"She was seventeen."

Bile rose into her throat. "Bloody Hell, Mika'el, what have my parents done to this world?"

Immense sadness met her in his gaze. "What you said they would, Emmanuelle. They've put it at great risk. Perhaps beyond salvage."

She swallowed. He had been blind to the One's faults for so long, it must kill him to admit her mother might have been less than perfect; that she might have played a role in the events unfolding now. She looked back to the woman.

"Let me help her," she said. "I can ease the pain..."

He shook his head. "She wouldn't want that."

Emmanuelle shored her defenses against the continued onslaught of agony radiating from the woman. "Her mind—it might not survive."

Mika'el's jaw flexed. "I know. And for her sake, I hope it doesn't. Not with what she faces."

"Seth, you mean? But she loved him once. Surely that will ease things for her."

"She tried to love him because I told her to."

Emmanuelle caught her breath. "You interfered with a mortal?"

"I was trying to save a world."

"You were trying to save the One."

He stared over her head, toward the woman and her niece. "Yes."

She felt it then, the guilt he had so carefully shielded from her. His own pain at knowing what he had caused.

"Oh, Mika'el..." She put a hand out to him, but found only the cold steel of his armor, a physical barrier that mirrored the invisible one between them. Her mouth twisted. Then she remembered, and her heart rate shot up.

"Hell. *Hell.* You have to get her out of here. Now."

In typical Mika'el fashion, he grasped her meaning without question. His hand went to the hilt of his sword. "You used power."

"When the Archangel and the other arrived." Emmanuelle's gaze skated over their surroundings: beach, sky, water, road beyond the house. Nothing moved, but it didn't mean nothing would. "I thought the Fallen were attacking. If they were watching for signs—you have to go."

"I can't leave if they might be coming here."

"Are you willing to hand over the woman without a fight?" Even through the armor, she felt him tense. "I didn't think so. Leave. If she's not here, they may simply retreat and continue their search for her."

"And if they don't?" he growled. "If Seth is the one that comes for her again?"

"I'll deal with it."

"Emmanuelle—"

"If she remains, a fight is inevitable, Mika'el. These people are my friends. I won't put them at risk. Take her and go. Give my people a chance."

His gaze fastened on hers. "You'll stay to protect them?"

You won't run? You won't disappear again?

"I'll stay."

"And we'll talk."

She scowled. "We'll see."

He opened his mouth to argue, but a bellow of

rage cut between them. Emmanuelle jerked her head around in time to see Raphael launch himself at a third Archangel who had appeared nearby. The new arrival, dressed in armor unfamiliar to her, twisted aside, and Raphael's lunge passed by without touching him. Raphael pulled up short and swung to face him, dropping into a fighting stance, his sword in his right hand, his gauntleted left shielding the immortality in the center of his chest.

"Samael," he snarled.

Emmanuelle's heart kicked against her breastbone. The Fallen had found them.

"Little brother," the other responded, his tone threaded with amusement. "As hot-headed as ever, I see."

A rush of wind pressed against Emmanuelle's back as Mika'el's wings unfolded with a crack that resounded across the water.

"Raphael!" he roared. "Stand down!"

For a long moment, Raphael held his pose without moving, sword trembling under the strain of holding back. Then, his expression dark with fury, he stepped back and lowered his weapon. He didn't sheath it.

"And still a well-trained puppy, too," Samael drawled. His gaze, as golden in the moonlight as that of Raphael, turned to Mika'el. His head dipped once. "Warrior."

"You're not taking her." Mika'el's voice was as inflexible as his gaze.

Samael shrugged. "We all know he'll have her eventually. Whether we fight over her or not is up to you."

Emmanuelle heard the slide of metal against hardened leather as Mika'el's sword left its sheath. Her gaze went to the others who watched, her friends and companions, mortals who had never seemed so fragile as they did now, with Heaven and Hell themselves standing before them. She put a hand out to grasp the cold gauntlet of her soulmate.

"Mika'el, no," she said.

Samael grinned, teeth flashing white against his skin. "I'd listen to her, if I were you. Do you really want to risk all these fine specimens of mortality?"

He strolled toward the woman, but Raphael's sword brought him up short, leveled at his chest. Annoyance flashed across Samael's face. He looked over his shoulder at Mika'el and Emmanuelle.

"You're wasting time, warrior. I will take the woman from you just as I took Seth."

"Except you're alone this time."

"Am I? Others are out looking for her. All I have to do is hold two of you off until they are drawn to our fight, and then it will be you and my brother against me and a small army. Mortal lives will be forfeit. Many of them."

Mika'el's frustration battered at Emmanuelle's back. Then his murmur reached her ears. "How fast can you clear everyone out of here?"

She sent him a startled glance. "What are you thinking?"

"How fast?"

"Five minutes."

"Do you have somewhere safe to go?"

She nodded. "But what about him? Samael?"

"Rafael will take care of his brother," Mika'el's voice was grim, "and I will take care of the woman. We'll follow—"

Emmanuelle cut him off. "No. I won't have her near

the others. I won't put them at risk."

"We need to talk, Emmanuelle."

She wanted to deny him, but her gaze traveled over their little gathering, and she knew he was right. It was time to stop running and make some decisions. Many of them.

"Take the woman to safety," she said. "I'll come to you there."

FIFTY

Samael scowled as the woman with Mika'el circled her hand in the air above her head. She pointed toward the house, and as one, the mortals on the beach near him turned in that direction. Now what? He reached for the bearded one passing near him, but the man was torn from his grip like a leaf ripped from a tree in a hurricane. Samael blinked. That hadn't been either Raphael's or Mika'el's doing. Not against one of equal power. What the—?

He scanned the beach, his gaze flicking over his brother, the angel standing over the Naphil and her bloodied armful, the cluster of mortals heading for the house. The woman and Mika'el, striding toward him.

Clear, iridescent eyes met Samael's.

Shock jolted through him.

Her eyes. Bloody Heaven, how could he not have noticed?

He took a step back as Mika'el and the One's

daughter neared. They wouldn't—

His lip curled as Emmanuelle parted company with the warrior and broke into a jog, following the mortals. Of course. True to her mother's influence, she *would* want to safeguard her precious mortals. Which left just five of them on the beach. Him, Raphael, Mika'el, the Naphil, and the traitor Bethi—

A thin, mewling wail pierced the night.

For a moment, time itself froze. Then Samael's head whipped around, and he stared at Bethiel, silent until now. The former Principality grimaced at Mika'el and drew back the corner of a dirty bundle of rags held in the crook of one arm. A tiny, red-faced infant thrust out an angry fist and wailed again, stronger this time. Louder.

"The child," he said. "Born of the girl and taken from Qemuel."

"Bloody Hell," Mika'el growled. "I forgot about it."

Samael found little comfort in knowing the Archangel was as startled as he was by the presence of the infant. So that was where Qemuel had been all this time: still following Lucifer's orders. Despite himself, he hesitated, torn now between targets. While he hated to admit it, his chances of getting through two Archangels to the woman were slim in the extreme. The child, however...they might not fight as hard for the child.

And if Seth followed through on that ludicrous idea of a new pact, the Nephilim army would be all that remained to Samael. His only hope of continuing hostilities. Of fighting his way back into the Heaven he so desperately wanted.

Mika'el made the decision for him.

"Take the infant," the Archangel directed Bethiel.

"Go with Emmanuelle."

From beyond the house came the guttural throb of multiple, powerful engines. Bethiel gave a single nod and launched into the air, and Samael turned his head from the sting of wind-driven sand. Well. That narrowed the options.

Without looking in her direction, he shifted his focus to the woman in the sand. The Naphil it would have to be. His hand went to his sword and he straightened his shoulders. He would have to move fast, because contrary to his claims, no reinforcements would come no matter how long he fought. He'd been so sure of himself, so certain Mika'el would still be recovering from his battle with Seth, so desperate to keep his treason a secret...

A bead of sweat trickled down his neck. He could have taken the Naphil from a wounded Archangel, but finding Raphael here had changed matters significantly. His only chance at getting her and getting out alive lay in the element of surprise.

His gaze went again to the woman. He gauged the distance to her. Shifted his stance in the sand. Tensed.

"Not this night, Samael," Mika'el said. "In fact, not any night. Raphael?"

Samael's brother stepped forward. The earlier fire in his eyes had banked to a cold, slow burn, and his jawline had taken on a grim set. His gaze never leaving Samael's, Raphael again raised his left hand to protect his immortality, his right to rotate his sword in silent challenge.

Samael went still. The Naphil woman's presence tugged at him. But six thousand years of deep, vicious hatred tugged harder. Mika'el skirted around him, and he heard the Naphil's whimper as the Archangel picked her up from the sand. He stared into his brother's golden eyes. He drew his sword.

"You're certain?" he asked, wondering what it would be like to strike down his own flesh and blood. Anticipating it.

Raphael twirled his sword again.

"To the death," he agreed—and lunged.

HANDS CLOSED OVER Alex's shoulders and pulled her up, away from the limp fragility that had once been her niece. For a moment, she considered fighting to remain, but what was the point? Nina—sweet, loving, gentle Nina—was gone. Alex had felt the last whisper of breath against her cheek as she held her. She knew she could do nothing more for her niece. Could offer her no comfort, no solace, no apology.

The hands turned her.

That it was Michael's eyes she looked up into, and not those of one who had come to take her, meant nothing. That more sadness resided in the green gaze than she had ever imagined could exist...that meant nothing, either.

"We have to go," Michael said.

Alex studied him. Should she agree? Disagree?

Would either make a difference?

Would anything she ever did make a difference?

She twisted her head around and looked down at the soiled, blood-soaked blanket wrapped around her dead niece's body. At the thin, bruised arm that had come free of its folds, skin paper-white and parchment-thin. At the long matted hair Nina had once taken such pride in. So many pains with.

Oh, the battles that hair had caused in the mornings

when mother and daughter had shared a single bathroom.

Those didn't matter anymore, either.

"Alex."

A firm hand beneath her chin turned her head away from her niece. Made her look into the sad green eyes again.

"We have to go," Michael repeated. The clang of metal against metal sounded from the beach behind him. A shower of sparks outlined his head and shoulders.

"Nina?" she asked.

"I can't take her," he said. "Her energy is gone. There's nothing left for me to—she's just a—"

Michael broke off and looked past her, his jaw flexing and his mouth pulling tight. Flint underscored the sadness when his gaze met hers again.

"I'm sorry," he said. "But we have to leave. Now."

Alex sidestepped, evading his arms. Her chest tightened. She waited for the grief to envelop her at the thought of leaving her beloved niece here, alone on a beach, uncared for. Anger licked through her instead.

Her gaze went past him to the angels fighting knee-deep in the encroaching ocean. Settled on the one with the black wings of an Archangel, but not the armor. Anger became fury. White-hot, all-consuming, absolute fury.

Her hand went to the hilt of Aramael's sword at her back. Blade drawn, she lunged past her protector, driven by the sheer, primal need for revenge. A strong arm encircled her mid-step and pulled her back. Feathers, still sharp with the edge of battle, sliced her skin. Alex struggled, not against the physical pain, but against the embrace itself.

"Let me go!" she snarled. "I can do this, Michael. I can kill him! For Nina and Jen and—"

"I'm sorry," Michael's voice rumbled above her head. "But this isn't your battle."

Alex shoved harder, trying to free the sword. Kicking, flailing, beyond wanting to listen. Beyond being able to hear. Michael's grip tightened. Fingertips settled against her temple. Warmth pulsated through her, beginning at the touch against her skin and spreading along her every nerve, smothering the rage. Changing the fury. And then...

Nothing.

Blissful, blessed nothing.

So. This was his answer, then. Seth stared down at the body rolling gently in the incoming waves. Sodden feathers swayed with the ocean's rhythm. Faint phosphorescence clung to the broken breastplate. Seth had sent an emissary to Emmanuelle in good faith, and this—Samael dead and bobbing along the shore—was her response.

This, and the taking of Alex from him yet again.

A wave lifted Samael's body onto the shore and then dragged it back again. Seth raised his head. Sand stretched as far as he could see, as deserted as the house through which he'd already passed. No sign of god, angel, or Naphil, though traces of all three presences remained.

He closed his eyes and inhaled Alex's faint scent, still carried on the breeze. Emptiness gnawed at his core. Emptiness and a cold, dark seethe of anger. He'd tried to be reasonable. Tried to bring peace back to

Heaven and Hell. Tried to do what was right. All he'd asked in return was the woman he loved. The woman he needed as he needed breath itself.

And all he'd received was insult.

A veritable slap in the face from his own sister.

The bitch.

He looked down again at the dead Archangel by his feet.

The fucking bitch.

How dared she think she could take Alex from him? Did she really think he wouldn't pursue her? That he wouldn't know where to start?

The fucking, *arrogant* bitch.

"She belongs to *me*, Emmanuelle!" he bellowed at the wind. His voice echoed down the empty sand, and the night swallowed it. Loss slit him from belly to throat, and he staggered, caught himself, fought past the panic gripping his throat.

"I'll find her," he whispered viciously. "I'll find her, and I'll take her from you, and then I will take away everything *you've* ever loved."

But how? How could he find her? Was she still here, in the city, or had they taken her further from him? Where did he even begin looking?

The ocean rolled onto the shore.

And then he remembered.

He gave a sharp inhale, and with a last, brief glance at his former aide, turned his focus inward. He thought back to what seemed another lifetime altogether, pulling up details from his memory. Watching television, watching Alex, long conversations as she tried to help him relate to the human race. A low-slung leather sofa, a glass coffee table, the sweep of windows looking out onto a balcony and the city beyond.

A time of falling in love, when potential had still existed.

A place that was a mere thought away.

With someone who would know where he could start looking.

He closed his eyes. Felt again the carpet beneath his feet, the cool solidity of the sliding glass door against his shoulder where he leaned. Saw in his mind's eye the city spread before him. Waited for the whisper of Alex's footsteps to cross the room as she joined him.

A muffled gasp broke his thoughts.

Seth's eyes opened. He stared at the woman in the kitchen doorway of Hugh Henderson's condo, dishtowel clutched in one hand. Slight of build, gray hair pulled back at the nape of her neck, bright blue eyes behind wire-framed glasses, undeniably familiar. Seth's gaze narrowed, then he relaxed. Of course. She was the one who had found him when his mortal transition had gone so wrong. The psychiatrist who had locked him in the hospital room until Alex had come to his rescue.

He glanced around the apartment, noting the small, subtle changes. Cushions on the couch, a blanket folded over the back of a chair, plants arrayed in front of the expanse of windows. A photo of the woman and a man on the table beside him.

Her...and Henderson?

"Dr. Riley," he said. "What a pleasant surprise to find you here."

Panic fluttered in the pulse at the base of Elizabeth Riley's throat, and her gaze flicked to the dining room table between them. The cell phone sitting there flew off the table and smashed into the wall by her head. She flinched. Paled. Then straightened her shoulders.

"It's good to see you again, Seth," she said. Her voice wavered but, to her credit, didn't break.

Yet.

He shook his head. "Don't," he said. "I have neither the time nor the patience. I want to know where Alex is, and I want you to tell me."

"I—I don't know. I haven't spoken to her since—"

Elizabeth Riley broke off as a key scraped in the lock of the apartment's door. Her head snapped around, and her mouth opened wide.

Seth lifted a single finger, cutting off the warning before it left her throat. Across the room to his left, the door opened. Elizabeth Riley turned back to him, struggling for air, her mouth flapping soundlessly. Her eyes widened, then went dark with a terror that reached up from her very soul.

Hugh Henderson stepped into the apartment.

"WE'LL NEED formula for her."

Emmanuelle jerked out of her reverie at the sound of Jezebel's voice behind her. No, not a reverie, because she hadn't actually been thinking about anything. Hadn't been feeling. Hadn't been doing anything more than taking up space and air, too shocked by events to function. Lucifer and that poor girl...

The memory of Alexandra Jarvis's agony still resided in her chest, a hollowness that refused to subside.

She pushed it away. Pushed her hair back from her face. Focused on Jezebel.

"What?"

"Formula. We need formula for the baby."

Emmanuelle followed her pointing finger to the tattered-looking angel from the beach and the filthy bundle of rags he held in one arm, both standing under the security floodlight their arrival had triggered. Disgust rolled off him, turning his zircon eyes cold and hard. Disgust for her father's Naphil bastard. She shuddered as something slimy slithered across her soul, overshadowing the other's distaste. Bloody Hell. Her father's child, born of a human mother. Her half sibling. A Naphil. With eighty thousand more like it out there in the world.

Humanity was toast.

Unless—

Jezebel cleared her throat. "There's a pharmacy about twenty minutes back. I'm sending—"

"No. We need to stay together so I—" Emmanuelle clamped her lips together. *So I can protect you.*

"We need to stay together," she repeated, looking over Jez's head to where the others stood, half in shadow, helmets in hand, looking as lost and unnerved as Emmanuelle felt. Except they were unnerved by Emmanuelle herself, their collective fear pushing against her. Despite their earlier acceptance of events, the beach had taken its toll.

She tightened her lips and then raised her voice. "No one leaves."

Jez crossed her arms. "She's hungry."

Emmanuelle's gaze went back to the rag bundle. A thin arm poked out, fist clenched, and the child wailed a demand. Her stomach rolling, she turned her gaze from it.

"No one leaves," she repeated, shooting a hard look at Jezebel.

"You can't be serious." Jez stared at her. "Emmanuelle, she'll die if we don't feed her."

Emmanuelle's lips compressed. *I wish.*

"Unfortunately not," she responded. Jez's eyes widened and Emmanuelle sighed. "It's not what you think it is, Jez. It's not a baby."

"What the hell—of course she's a baby! A hungry one at that, and I'm damned if I'll stand here doing nothing while the poor thing wastes away."

In a huff, Jez pushed past, heading for Bethiel and the child, but Emmanuelle caught her arm and swung her around to face her.

"It's not a baby," she repeated, unleashing the finest hint of her otherness. Her command. Jez paled. She swallowed hard. Emmanuelle reined herself in, guilt twisting inside her. Jez was a friend. She deserved better than to have the living daylights scared out of her by someone she trusted. All these people deserved better.

But she didn't have the patience to coddle them. Didn't have the energy.

She released her hold on Jez and stalked toward the house. Bethiel's wings opened to block her path. She stopped in her tracks and paused before turning her gaze to meet his. She let another moment tick by.

"You would do well to remember who I am, Principality," she said finally, her voice soft but edged with warning.

He met her stare for stare. "So would you."

Her hands formed fists at her sides. Another pause. Then she reached up, seized the offending wing, and applied just enough pressure to fold it against Bethiel's back. A film of sweat broke out on the angel's forehead as he resisted. The infant in his arms squawked a protest when his hold became too tight.

Emmanuelle stepped past him, headed for the door. She halted with one hand on the knob. "They stay here," she told Bethiel, jerking her head toward her friends. "No one leaves this house, and no one goes near *that*. And, Principality..."

Bethiel's chin lifted a fraction.

"Just so we understand one another," she said heavily. "I may not like who I am, but I've never forgotten."

FIFTY-ONE

S eth stared down at the bodies on the floor. Elizabeth Riley lay on her back, sightless eyes turned toward the leather sofa, her body shattered in more places than Seth had thought she would survive, her features grotesquely twisted by the pain she had endured before her heart had given up. Beside her, Hugh Henderson curled into a fetal position, breath rattling in his throat. One hand clutched Riley's lifeless fingers, the other was pressed against his own gaping belly wound that seeped blood into the already saturated carpet.

The wound that had finally given Seth the information he needed.

He scowled at the memory of his own incompetence. As the son of Lucifer and the One, he'd expected more of himself. Expected to be able to crack open their minds and take what he wanted from them. He sure as Hell hadn't anticipated a level of resistance that had required a...messier approach.

He grimaced at the gore covering his hand and shirtfront. Not that it much mattered how he'd achieved his end. It mattered only that he knew where to find Alex. That he would have what belonged to him—as soon as he'd dealt with those who would keep her from him.

Hugh Henderson gurgled at his feet, and Seth looked down again. For a brief moment, he considered putting the mortal out of his misery. Then he dismissed the notion. After the way Henderson and Riley had defied him, they'd deserved every bit of pain he'd meted out—and more. In retrospect, he was rather glad his mind-breaking idea hadn't worked, because this approach had been infinitely more satisfying. He squatted beside Henderson and tilted his head to one side, regarding him thoughtfully.

"To be honest," he said, "I've half a mind to heal you so you can watch me take Alex and then live out the rest of your days knowing how you failed her."

Brown eyes, glazed with pain, didn't react. Seth sighed.

"On the other hand, why bother? Those days would be so limited. Between me bringing the war here to Earth and turning the Nephilim loose, you'd have a few months at most. It hardly seems worth the effort, does it? So there you have it. You get to die in peace." He patted Henderson's pale, stubbled cheek, and rose to his feet.

With a lingering smile, he stepped across the dying man and strolled toward the bank of windows overlooking the city.

"I'll tell Alex you said hello," he added over his shoulder, and then he stepped out of the human realm and into Hell.

"You!" he snarled at a passing Virtue. "Bring me Samael's second-in-command. We take the war to Earth!"

VERCHIEL DROPPED INTO the chair behind her desk with an audible thump. She stared at the red-haired Archangel across from her.

"All of them?" she whispered. "They've *all* gone to Earth?"

Gabriel rubbed the back of one hand over an oozing gash on her cheek and then wiped the blood off on her black-armored thigh. "All of them," she agreed grimly. "I've sent the host after them, but the damage—"

Her voice cracked. She swallowed, set her jaw, and continued, "Even though we outnumber them almost three to one, it will take time. There will be collateral damage, Verchiel. A great deal of collateral damage."

A tidy way of saying that all of humanity would likely be destroyed. Or at least enough of it that the Nephilim who followed would have no difficulty wiping out the remainder. Verchiel rested an elbow on the arm of the chair and put a trembling hand to her temple. Heaven's worst nightmare had come to pass: They had failed the One. Failed her mortal children.

The war had gone to Earth.

"We need to tell Mika'el."

Gabriel's voice penetrated Verchiel's fog. She nodded.

"Of course. Yes. We must."

"You know where he is?"

Now her head shook. "No. Raphael caught an image of where Emmanuelle was taking the humans, but Mika'el's thoughts stayed hidden from him."

"Then I'll go to Emmanuelle. She'll know where to find him."

"We don't know that she—"

"We have to take the chance."

"Of course." Verchiel described the house Raphael had seen in the minds of the humans who had left the beach with Emmanuelle, finishing with, "One of them thought of the city of Victoria, another of a town known as Colwood. Raphael didn't have time to delve for details, but I looked into both places. Colwood is less populated and more remote."

"Fewer Guardians. Easier to hide." Gabriel nodded agreement. "Good. I'll start there."

"How is he, by the way? Raphael."

"Battered, but still able to fight. I put him in charge of the angels defending the Earth's United Kingdom." Gabriel reached for the doorknob, adding over her shoulder, "Pull in the Guardians and make sure they're armed. As soon as I've spoken to Mika'el, I'll be back to deploy them."

"And me."

Halfway out the door, Gabriel stopped. She turned and swept her gaze over Verchiel. "You're certain? You're the executive administrator. Heaven needs—"

"Heaven won't exist if we don't win this, Gabriel."

The Archangel inclined her head. "Very well. Be ready to go when I return."

FIFTY-TWO

Emmanuelle took refuge on the deck that stretched the length of one side of Scorpion's safe house. She stared out over treetops that dropped away down the hillside on the forest's way to the ocean, a shimmer of light below in the slow approach of dawn. Her breath fogged the air in long puffs. The chill of reality seeped into her core, and the harshness of loss into her heart.

Spider, Scissors, Wizard, Hog, Tiny, Queenie...gone.

Her independence and anonymity...gone.

And the One...gone.

That loss was the one that surprised her most. Not because it had happened—though she had to admit that a part of her couldn't quite fathom the death of the Creator herself—but because of how keenly she felt it. Like a razor had been drawn over her heart again and again, its blade so fine, she hadn't felt its presence until it was too late. Until her heart was laid open in a thousand quivering slivers, bleeding into her soul.

They had never talked again after Emmanuelle

had left Heaven. Never reconciled. Never forgiven one another. They'd had neither chance nor reason. Emmanuelle had never intended to return to Heaven, and her mother was supposed to go on forever there, to prove Emmanuelle wrong, to finally come into her own and wrest control of the universe back from Lucifer.

Because despite what Mika'el and the One had thought, the Light-bearer had been very much in control. From the moment the Creator had sought—and failed—to distract him from his jealousies over her mortal children by giving him a child of his own, she had been lost. The One hadn't been able to see that, and Mika'el had refused to, but a tiny part of Emmanuelle had never given up hope that they might.

And now they had come to this, with Heaven on the brink of destruction, dependent on the choice of the one being who wanted no part of it. Who had long ago severed her connection to it and had no reason to care whether it—or its inhabitants—survived.

Emmanuelle rested her elbows on the railing. No reason except knowing humanity's own survival hinged on the outcome—and she *did* care about them.

One of the French doors behind her swung open on hinges that needed oiling. Booted footsteps approached, vibrating through the deck. A mug appeared under her nose.

"Coffee," Scorpion said. "Jez made a pot."

She took it from him, raising an eyebrow as she caught a whiff of alcohol. "A little early for that, don't you think?"

"It was a rough night." Scorpion shrugged. "You looked like you could use it."

She didn't have the heart to tell him it would have

no effect on her. That it never had and never would, because she wasn't—

"Thank you," she said. She sipped at the whiskey-laced coffee. She thought about asking how the others fared, but she didn't need to. Now that she had opened herself to her power again, she could feel them in the house behind her. Their presence. Their shock. Their fear. Some had taken refuge in sleep. Others hunkered around the kitchen table, talking in low murmurs that Emmanuelle chose not to listen in on. It had only been a couple of hours since they'd left the beach for the dark, winding ride up to Scorpion's mountain house, a handful of hours since their friends had died at the bar, and already it seemed an eternity. So many changes had been wrought.

"So." Scorpion cleared his throat. "You want to talk?"

The invitation was calm and non-accusatory, reminding her of Jezebel's earlier, easy acceptance of blue sparkles and fireballs, and Wookie's casual observation about understanding why she never felt the cold. Did they still feel the same way about her now, after the beach and Mika'el, after her own high-handed behavior?

Jaw flexing, Emmanuelle blinked back a prickle of tears and tightened her grip on the mug. If by some miracle they did, talking to Scorpion would end that. Expectations would change. The friendships she treasured would come to an end. The family she'd built would be no more.

Beefy fingers plucked the mug from her hands and set it on the rail, then settled on her shoulder. Scorpion turned her to face him, his expression earnest. Determined.

"What Jez told you yesterday was right, you know. We've always known you were special. Tonight didn't change anything, and neither will anything you tell me now."

Oh, how she wished that could be true. She shook her head. "People died yesterday, Scorpion. Your friends died. Because of me."

"*Our* friends died, Manny. And they would do it again. Willingly. As would any of the rest of us."

"Don't." She tried to pull away, but his grip held firm. She stared at the hollow at the base of his throat. "Don't say that."

"Why not? It's the truth. Some things are worth dying for. Like it or not, we consider you one of them."

She shuddered at the words, thinking of the millions in Earth's history who had died in the name of her mother.

One more reason she didn't want what Mika'el asked her to take. Couldn't step into her mother's shoes.

She shook her head. "That's easy for you to say, but you don't know—"

"Then don't tell me."

She blinked. "What?"

"I mean it. If it's that hard for you, don't say anything. We forget the whole thing. Put it behind us. We rest up here today, get on the bikes tomorrow, and hit the road. Simple as that. It wouldn't be the first time any of us have pulled up roots and started over."

"You would do that for me?" She stared up at the wall of a man towering over her. "Even after the way I behaved—after what I said about the baby?"

"You're the only thing that matters to any of us, Manny." Massive tattooed shoulders shrugged beneath the tank top Scorpion wore. He reached out to cradle her cheek with a gentleness that belied his sheer brute strength. "You're family. We trust you. If you say we don't feed that squalling little scrap, we don't feed it. And if you want to leave, we leave."

For a moment, she considered the idea.

No, she embraced it. Heart, mind, and soul, she wrapped herself around the possibility, imagined the feel of the bike beneath her and the wind in her hair, and made it her choice. With ever fiber of her—

She put her hand over Scorpion's against her cheek. "I can't," she whispered. "I'm not what you think, Scorpion."

"You're like them. The ones with the wings. We know that." He shrugged again. "We don't need to know more."

She shook her head. "No. I'm..."

More? Less? Different? How in Hell did she explain what she was when she didn't know herself?

"Hey."

Scorpion's gruff voice drew her attention back to him again.

"You're what you choose to be," he said. "Remember? We all are. That's what you told each of us when we found you. You don't want to be an angel, then don't. We have your back no matter what you decide. The power of choice, Emmanuelle. It was the gift you gave us, and now you need to remember it's your gift, too."

She opened her mouth to respond, to tell him she knew that, but then she stopped.

"*Choices have consequences, Emmanuelle,*" Mika'el's voice came back to her from five thousand years before. "*Are you sure this one is how you wish to define yourself?*"

She hadn't understood then. Not like she did now.

If she'd stayed, she might have seen Mittron's machinations.

Might have stopped him.

Might have influenced her brother or been the strength her mother needed to stop Lucifer.

Might have prevented a mortal woman from suffering the agonies Alexandra Jarvis had been through.

She might have done so, so much.

She turned her head to gaze out across the treetops and the ocean and the sky that grew lighter with each passing moment. She pushed her sight outward, to the slumbering town nearby, the city beyond that. There was a whole realm sprawling beneath the sky. A realm of intricate, finely balanced glory, filled with the children of her mother's creation. Children like Wookie and Jez and Scorpion and all the others Emmanuelle had known and cared for over her years among them.

Children who hovered on the brink of extinction because of choices. Hers. Her parents'. Mika'el's. Their own.

Choices.

Consequences.

Crushing responsibility.

This was what Mika'el had understood.

What her mother had lived with.

The faint scent of roses filtered in on the breeze. Then the French door banged open and Bethiel stood framed in the opening.

"The human news," he said. "You need to see it."

Before Emmanuelle could react, another presence appeared, this one in a whirl of black wings and a gust of wind that knocked the mountain-like Scorpion clean off his feet and rattled the windows in their frames. Emmanuelle stared at the armor-clad female Archangel.

"Gabriel?"

The red-headed warrior turned. A fierce, sapphire-blue gaze raked over Emmanuelle, then rose to meet hers, becoming bleak, cold, barren.

"The Fallen have brought the war to Earth," Gabriel said. "We're out of time."

FIFTY-THREE

M ika'el stared out the French doors at the tiny yard beyond. The flowers were gone at this time of year, but the streetlight just beyond the fence still showed the beds to be tidy and well tended. The One would have liked this Elizabeth Riley who gardened here. She'd had a special place in her heart for all those who had shared her love of growing things, of caring for life.

Of preserving it rather than plotting to destroy it.

His mouth tightened and he swung away from the doors. The television in the corner beckoned. It was a poor way to get the information he wanted, but short of leaving Alex to go back to Heaven—or sending out a beacon to nearby Guardians that might be traced by others—it was all he had. With a grimace, he waved a hand, and the television flickered to life. Tanks and armored vehicles rumbled across the screen.

"...as overwhelmed U.N. troops left the country, marking the fifth retreat in the last week," said the voice of the female newscaster. "The U.N. has already abandoned similar peacekeeping efforts in South Sudan, Mali, Darfur, and the Democratic Republic of Congo, and officials announced today that it will pull out of its remaining eleven operations by the end of next week. With unrest continuing to mount across the world, troops will return to their own countries to aid in efforts to minimize the escalating chaos."

The video disappeared, replaced by the somber newscaster. "The death toll continues to mount in the wake of the retreat, with an estimated thirteen thousand civilians killed in missile attacks by Hezbollah."

The camera angle changed. The newscaster's gaze followed it. "In other news, there are reports from Moscow, the U.K., and South Korea today of more winged aliens. Governments continue to claim these so-called appearances are little more than a well-executed hoax, but a number of home videos have surfaced of the aliens seeming to destroy entire buildings as they fight among themselves. We'll be back with that story—and the video footage—in a moment."

An advertisement took over the television screen, its music and pitch for some kind of alcoholic beverage blasting into the living room. Mika'el felt Alex stir in the bed down the hall. He waved his hand, and the television went blank and silent.

Winged aliens. Angels. Here, visible, with buildings falling in the wake of their battles. He waited, expecting shock to settle in, but he could summon nothing more than fatigue. Resignation.

So the war had come to Earth at last. Even if Emmanuelle decided to side with Heaven, it might very well be too late for humani—

A guttural wail echoed through the condo, filled with despair, and Michael's heart stopped.

Alex.

ALEX WOKE in a bed, the sheets cool against her naked skin, the darkened room speaking to night. The lights of a passing vehicle slid across the ceiling, illuminating enough for her to recognize Elizabeth Riley's bedroom. She was back in the condo, but how—? And what and where and when—?

Something had happened. She knew that. Felt it in the hollowness of her heart, the clench of her belly. Something had happened, but the harder she tried to recall what, the more ephemeral became the memories. The shadows of memories. She squeezed her eyes closed and pushed against the barrier she sensed in her mind. It stayed solid, unmoved by her increasing desperation to remember.

She scowled. It was no use. Something might have happened, but some*one* didn't want her to remember it. And she knew only one someone capable of that kind of interference. Someone who should damned well know better than to screw with her brain. She pushed aside the covers to slip from the bed, then paused.

Outside, a motorcycle slowed for the stop sign at the corner, its distinctive, throaty rumble marking it as a Harley-Davidson. A memory struggled to the surface of Alex's brain but sank again before she could grasp it. The Harley's motor revved. An image flared in her mind.

Bikes lined up outside a bar.

The motor gunned. More images flashed.

A woman—Emmanuelle—flying backward into a mirror behind a bar. Shattered glass. Splintered tables. Seth. Michael.

The Harley roared away, shattering the neighborhood's quiet—and with it, whatever barrier had been placed between Alex and what had come before. In one tumbling, tumultuous, devastating rush, she remembered. Remembered it all.

Emmanuelle pulling her from the wreckage of the bar. The injured bikers. Michael's armor fused to his body. Emmanuelle tearing it away from him. His roar of agony. The arrival of Bethiel on the beach.

Nina.

Oh God. Nina.

Alex sucked for air. It slid down her throat like razor blades, slicing her open from the inside. Agony swept in its wake, and she whimpered. Nina was gone. Dead before she'd been found. Dead alone in childbirth, beyond Alex's reach.

Alex had failed her. Failed the last person she'd loved. The last of her family. She curled into a ball, her knees drawn up to protect her chest, her heart. Fingers threaded themselves into her hair. Tangled. Tightened. Pulled. Physical pain warred with mental agony. Carefully built compartment walls cracked. Crumbled. Alex's whimper became a moan.

Nina. Jen. Aramael. All gone—because of her.

Seth loosed on the world—because of her.

The existence of humanity itself hanging in the balance—because of her.

Immortality.

The last thought slammed into her brain with the force of a locomotive, stopping the flood of thoughts and images in their tracks. For an instant, a heartbeat, her mind ceased to function at all.

Then—finally, blessedly—she felt the threads of sanity begin to unravel. Stood on the edge of a precipice, staring into the abyss she instinctively knew had swallowed Jen, and before her, their mother. Stood, stared, and willed her mind to plunge over the edge, into the darkness that waited. The nothingness.

The madness that would be so much less mad than her reality could ever be.

From a long way away came a low, keening wail, filling her ears, pushing her closer and closer to oblivion.

And then the strong arms that had lifted her from Nina's side at the beach picked her up from the bed, sheet and all, and cradled her with a tenderness and compassion she didn't want, didn't deserve...couldn't bear.

The wail became one of protest and loss and anguish. She fought the arms, but they held tighter, refusing to let go. Refusing to let her splinter into the fragments she wanted to become. Refusing to give her up to the grief that raged at her core and tried to swallow her from the inside out.

Until only the grief and the arms existed at all, locked in a battle for her very soul, and a warrior's compassion became her entire world.

FIFTY-FOUR

"Where is Mika'el?"

Emmanuelle pulled Scorpion to his feet, ignoring his look of surprise at the ease with which she tugged his two hundred and thirty-plus pounds upright. Still reeling from Gabriel's news, she didn't immediately turn back to answer the Archangel's question. Gabriel's gauntleted hand dropped onto her shoulder.

"I asked where Mika'el—"

Emmanuelle swung around, grasping Gabriel's wrist and holding it away from her. "You forget to whom you speak, Archangel."

"I know exactly to whom I speak," Gabriel corrected. "You left, Emmanuelle, and you didn't come back. Your mother—"

"My mother"—Emmanuelle's hand tightened, bending the gauntlet's metal beneath her fingers—"is not the issue here."

Gabriel's sapphire eyes flashed, and for a moment,

Emmanuelle didn't think the Archangel would back down. What would Emmanuelle do then? Fight her? Jaw aching with the effort, Emmanuelle made herself release the other's wrist. She turned away, trying to pull her thoughts together, ignoring the pulse of fury directed between her shoulder blades as she might an annoying mosquito. Gabriel's anger faltered.

As it should.

Emmanuelle gave an inward wince. Damn. Her escalation to godlike expectations hadn't taken long, had it?

She pointed at Bethiel, still standing in the open doorway. "You. Can you find Mika'el?"

"I should be the one—" Gabriel began.

Emmanuelle cut her off without so much as glancing at her. "Forget it. You're staying to tell me what's going on." She raised an eyebrow at Bethiel. "Well?"

The former Principality looked like he might raise an objection of his own, then he shrugged. "I think I know where he might be."

"Good. Find him, and bring him back here. The woman, too," she added as an afterthought.

Bethiel hesitated. Then, sketching what could only be termed a sardonic salute, he disappeared. Emmanuelle turned her attention to Scorpion. He had remained stoutly at her side, but the convulsive movement of his Adam's apple belied the belligerent look he leveled at Gabriel.

"Wait inside with the others," she told him. "I'll be there in a few minutes."

Scorpion's scowl deepened, and Emmanuelle touched his arm.

"Go," she said. "I'll be fine."

Like Bethiel, he hesitated an instant more, then

stomped across the deck to the house, his heavy footsteps echoing through the otherwise quiet dawn. Emmanuelle waited until the door closed behind him, then she drew a deep breath and faced Gabriel. The Archangel stood with feet planted wide and gauntleted hands resting on armored hips.

"You left us," she snarled. "And you didn't come back. Not even when your mother—when the One—" She broke off and spread her arms wide, the metal of her gloves glinting in the early morning light. "You had to have felt it happen, Emmanuelle. You had to have known."

"I felt a shift," Emmanuelle admitted. "But that was all."

"And you couldn't open yourself up for thirty seconds to at least see what was going on?"

"I was done with Heaven, Gabriel. Done with my parents and their endless battles. I didn't *want* to know what had happened."

"You selfish, pretentious—" The Archangel bit off whatever she'd been about to say, her teeth snapping closed. She stalked to the other end of the deck, as far from Emmanuelle as the railing would allow. There, she braced her hands against the wood and let her head sag. So many emotions churned from her that Emmanuelle couldn't even begin to sort through them.

She was too out of practice.

She'd been gone too long.

She'd forgotten too much.

Panic licked at her. What was she thinking? She couldn't step into the void left by her mother. She knew nothing about overseeing the likes of Heaven, nothing about leading a fight against Hell, and nothing about caring for two entire realms. There was no way she could do this.

Scorpion's offer sidled into her mind. *"We forget the whole thing. Put it behind us. We rest up here today, get on the bikes tomorrow, and hit the road. Simple as that."*

Scorpion.

Jezebel.

Wookie.

All the others.

All of humanity.

"Choices have consequences."

The deck bucked beneath her feet as a rumble rolled through the Earth. Gabriel straightened and spun around. Emmanuelle met her alarm, her resignation, her weariness.

Her own heart plummeted.

"Seth," she said.

The red-haired Archangel lifted her chin, her sapphire eyes flashing a challenge.

"Seth," she agreed. "So what's it going to be, Emmanuelle? Are you in or out?"

Bloody Hell.

ALEX TOOK THE MUG Michael held out to her, curling both hands around its warmth. Michael retreated to stand by the French doors, one shoulder resting against the frame, arms crossed. Silence sat heavy between them. The same silence that had prevailed since she had pulled away from him in the bedroom—raw and beaten and emptier than she'd ever been in her life. Emptier than should have been possible if one was still able to function.

The mug in her hands trembled, and she tightened her grip. Closed her eyes.

"Alex—" Michael began.

She cut him off, her voice harsh even in its whisper. "You shouldn't have pulled me back. I've done enough for you. You should have let me go."

"You have done enough," he said quietly. "And I didn't pull you back."

Her eyelids snapped open. She scowled at him. "Don't. Don't lie to me. I felt you."

"I only held you, nothing more. I knew you were going mad, and I didn't try to stop it." Michael sighed and rubbed a hand across his forehead. "I just didn't want you to be alone when it happened."

She held the emerald gaze, blinking back the sharp prickle of unwanted tears. "So if you didn't stop it, what did? Is it because of what Seth did to me?"

"No." He shook his head. "Immortality doesn't guarantee sanity."

"Then why, damn it? Why am I still here?"

"I suspect only you can answer that."

Her fingers tightened on the mug, and she fought the urge to pitch it at his head. Fuck, but she was sick of obscure answers. She turned her gaze to the window and the darkened garden beyond.

"Why didn't you want me to be alone?" she asked wearily. "Why did it matter?"

Long seconds ticked past without answer. So many that she finally looked back to him. Self-loathing filled his expression. She frowned.

"Michael?"

A muscle in the corner of his jaw worked. His eyes closed. Pain etched itself into the lines around his mouth. The heart she hadn't thought capable of further feeling gave a flutter of unexpected compassion. Alex hesitated, then leaned forward and touched the corded muscle of his forearm. He flinched but didn't pull away. A ragged exhale escaped him.

"Because so very much of this is my fault," he said, his voice as rough as it was quiet. "Because my faith in the One blinded me to Emmanuelle's warnings. Because I've asked you to do things no angel should ever ask of one who is only..."

He trailed off, and she finished bitterly, "Only human? But I'm not, am I? I'm..."

She couldn't finish, either, because she didn't know what she was any more than Michael did. Not anymore. Hell, she'd been broken and cobbled back together so many times, she didn't think the One herself would have known what she was.

But it sure as Hell wasn't *only human*.

Michael's voice gentled. "It doesn't matter," he said. "It matters only that you were mortal, and in my arrogance, my certainty that I was right, I interfered with your choices. I'm the reason you are where you are right now, Alexandra Jarvis. I'm the reason you've lost so much. *Will* lose so much. And for that, for all of that, I am profoundly sorry."

She waited for the expected anger to stir in her. The refusal of his apology to spill from her lips. The familiar accusations to follow. None of those things happened. Instead, through her own despair, she saw the slump of powerful shoulders, the droop of magnificent wings, and her breath caught.

Compassion fluttered again in her breast. What must it be like to carry the weight that he did? The responsibility for not just one, but two, entire races—two worlds? Her gaze traced the hopelessness around

Michael's mouth, the worry etched into his brow.

Her fingers slid down his forearm and linked with his.

"Don't," she said. "You forget I could have said no. At any one of a thousand times, I could have made a different choice, a different decision. We both made mistakes, Michael. We all did."

He stared down at their hands.

"I did it for myself," he said.

"Pardon?"

His emerald gaze lifted to hers. Held it without flinching, without hiding. "I held you for myself. Because I needed to remember that I'm more than the war between Heaven and Hell. More than the sum of bad decisions and poor choices. For once, just for a moment, I needed to be an angel, and not a destroyer."

Down the hall in the bedroom, Alex's cell phone rang.

FIFTY-FIVE

Alex picked up the cell phone on its seventh ring. She'd counted as she stood up from the couch beside Michael and walked the short distance to the bedroom. Counting had kept her feet moving. Kept her from going back to Michael and—

And what? Wrapping her arms around him? Cradling his head against her shoulder? Telling him everything would be all right? Even if that were true—and they both knew it wasn't—he was an Archangel. Heaven's greatest warrior. Soulmate to Emmanuelle, daughter of Lucifer and the One.

She thumbed the answer icon.

No, Michael didn't need the paltry comfort of a screwed-up Naphil, immortal or otherwise. And she most definitely did not need to be feeling—

"Jarvis," she said into the phone.

Silence responded. Then labored breathing.

Alex took the phone from her ear and glanced at the display. She frowned. "Hugh?"

A gasp. A groan.

The skin over Alex's entire body went tight. Cold. The first lashings of panic whipped through her belly.

"Hugh? What's wrong? Where are you?"

"Alex..."

A bare croak of sound.

Alex fought back a terror that threatened to devolve into hysteria. She struggled for calm. Authority. Air. "Tell me where you are. I'm on my way. I'll call for backup."

She stumbled for the door and pulled it open. Michael met her on the other side. The labored breathing in her ear continued.

"Hugh, for God's sake—"

"Alex...Seth...*run*."

The line went dead. Alex's knees buckled. Strong hands caught and held her upright.

"Hugh," she whispered.

Oh, God...Hugh.

"ALEX? ALEX!"

Michael's voice came from a long way off, hollow and harsh.

Alex inhaled. Clamped her teeth together. Hard, until they ached. Darkness beckoned at the edges of her mind. She shook it off. She wouldn't lose it again. Couldn't. Not while Hugh needed—

Hugh.

Elizabeth.

"Alexandra Jarvis!"

This time Michael's voice was accompanied by a shake of her shoulders. Alex's head snapped back, jolting her into the immediate. She stared at the phone still gripped in fingers white with strain. Hugh and Elizabeth. She lifted her gaze to Michael's, to the fierceness there, the sadness that underlined it. Her stomach rolled again.

"We have to go to them," she whispered. "We have to..."

Her voice trailed off even before Michael's head shook.

"It's too late," he said. "Seth—"

Hugh's last words to her echoed in her mind, drowning out Michael's voice.

"Alex...Seth...run."

Seth.

Alex sucked in another breath. "Seth is coming. Here. For me."

"Not just Seth," Michael responded grimly. "Him and a small army. The angels are holding them off, but we need to leave. Now."

"No." She shook her head. Reached past the grief tangled around her heart for the calm she needed. Calm to speak the only words she could. The only words left. "No," she whispered. "You go. Leave me here."

Michael's hands tightened on her shoulders. He shook his head. "You going to him won't stop him. Not anymore."

Alex flinched from what she knew to be the truth and, for a moment, quailed from her decision. But the calm she sought grew out of the grief she couldn't escape, and together they became the only decision she could make. The only choice that remained.

"I know." Alex put a hand on Michael's arm as he made to step back. "But it might buy you some time."

Michael went still, staring down at her fingers.

Silent seconds slipped by, broken only by the sound of their breathing. Hers rapid and shallow in her ears, his ragged. She steeled herself, waiting for his agreement to seal her fate. Then the emerald eyes closed.

"I won't leave you to him, Alex," he said. "I can't."

Her hand trembled. She dropped it to her side and curled it into a fist. *You're not helping,* she wanted to tell him. *Please don't make this any harder,* she tried to say. Instead she stared at the powerful warrior before her, seeing, for the second time that night, the lines of defeat etched in his posture. A ripple of misgiving slid through her.

Michael's shoulders straightened, and his gaze met hers, bleak with despair, hard with resolve.

"I'm going to have to do something unforgivable soon," he continued quietly. "Something I won't be able to come back from. It will likely destroy me."

Alex's breath hissed out, and he held up a hand to ward off her objection.

"Before I do," he said, "I need to know I'm capable of more, that I've been able to do something good. I need to know you're safe, Alex. I need to know I've saved you from Seth."

Mouth flapping soundlessly, she stared at him. Tiny electric shocks of alarm traveled over her skin, raising the hairs along her arms and the back of her neck. What in hell—?

Before she could muddle through the confusion of her thoughts to form an actual question, wind gusted from the bedroom behind her, slamming into her back and throwing her against Michael. Glass shattered behind her, signaling the demise of Elizabeth's windows and the arrival of—

"Bethiel!" Michael snarled above her head.

Alex blinked against his chest, acutely aware of three things: blood trickling from wounds inflicted on her arms by the battle-ready wings sweeping forward to protect her; the sheer relief coursing through her veins at hearing Bethiel's name and not Seth's; and the strong, steady beat of the heart beneath her cheek.

Alex pushed away from Michael and fought her way out of the feathered cocoon, turning to face the new arrival and the dawn filtering through the missing window. Down the street, a dog barked, a note of hysteria lacing its voice.

"You were supposed to stay with Emmanuelle," Michael said.

"She sent me to get you. And the Naphil." Bethiel jerked his chin at Alex. "Gabriel is with her. The war has come to Earth."

FIFTY-SIX

M ika'el strode down the length of the deck to where Emmanuelle and Gabriel waited. The two could not have been more different—or more alike. One petite, dark-haired, and clad in leather, the other tall, with brilliantly red hair, sheathed in armor. Both impossibly strong and hard-headed.

The next few thousand years would be interesting.

He met Gabriel's sapphire gaze. "Give us a minute?"

"Seth—" She stopped, her eyes traveling between him and Emmanuelle. She nodded. "I'll be inside."

Mika'el waited until the door closed with a thump. Then, wordlessly, he stepped forward and gathered his soulmate into his arms. Emmanuelle resisted for a moment, then, with a long, quaking sigh, she buried her face against his chest. Her heat reached through the armor to wrap him close.

So long.

It had been so very long.

And now...

Now.

"I'm sorry," he whispered. Closing his eyes, he buried his lips against her hair, inhaled her scent. He wondered if she knew she smelled like the roses of her mother's garden. She'd always smelled that way. Like roses and sunshine.

Like Heaven.

Like a promise.

He drew back and looked down into the swirl of her iridescent eyes. "I knew you were right about them," he said. "I knew they would destroy one another, but I thought if I tried hard enough, if I believed—"

Emmanuelle placed gentle fingers over his lips.

"And maybe if I'd chosen to stay instead of running away," she said, "maybe then things would have been different as well. Or maybe none of this was ours to control, Mika'el. Maybe it needed to play out as it has, mistakes and all. Maybe..."

She took a breath and reached up to cup his face in both her hands.

"Maybe we accept the consequences of all the choices that have been made by everyone, and we try to save this world. And ours. Together."

Mika'el looked over her head. She went still.

"Mika'el?"

Slowly, he shook his head. He brushed the hair away from her forehead. Looked into the iridescent, purple-silver eyes.

"We can't," he said. "Not together. Not like you mean."

Emmanuelle stepped back. Her face had gone stiff. Wary. "I don't understand."

"Even if we win, even if we push back the Fallen and you fight your brother and triumph, the damage to this realm will be enormous," he said quietly. "It will take every strength humanity possesses just to recover."

He willed his soulmate to grasp his meaning the way she once would have without making him speak the words. But too much time had passed, or perhaps too much of everything else, and Emmanuelle's eyes held no understanding, only questions.

The call of an eagle overhead pierced the morning, echoing over the trees. Mika'el closed his eyes and steeled himself.

"The Nephilim," he said. "Humanity will never survive the Nephilim."

Emmanuelle caught her breath. "You want me to—"

"No." The word came out sharper than he intended. He laid his forehead against hers in apology. "No," he said. "Not you."

Utter silence came between them. Long seconds slipped by. Then Emmanuelle went rigid beneath his touch. She pulled back, away from him, taking her warmth with her. Her heartbeat.

"I can't ask you do that," she said, "and I—"

"You're not asking."

"And I won't let you," she finished, her eyes flashing. "You'd never survive the fall, Mika'el. They may be Nephilim, but they're children, too. No matter what they're destined to be, you won't be able to separate yourself from the innocence they are *now*."

His soul shuddered at the truth of her words, but he steadfastly held to the truth of his own. "There's no other way, Emmanuelle. It must be done."

He put his hands on her shoulders, but she shrugged him off. Anger and denial warred in her expression. Fear underlined both.

She shook her head. "No. No way. I'm not doing this without you, Mika'el. I can't. I know nothing about ruling the realms!"

"You'll have help. Verchiel will guide you, and Gabriel will see that the others—"

"That the others what...don't turf me out on my ass?" Emmanuelle's chin quivered.

Despite himself, Mika'el smiled at the idea. "You know that won't happen. It just might take a bit of time for them to warm to you, that's all. Gabriel will help pave the way."

"And us? What about us? I'm just supposed to stand by and watch my soulmate throw himself on the pyre for me? I'm supposed to give my blessing? Are you fucking kidding me?" Emmanuelle planted hands on hips and swung away. Her heels thudded as she stomped along the short width of the deck.

Mika'el didn't have an answer for her. Not one that she would like.

"Hell," she muttered. And then again, "*Hell.*"

She flicked a look over her shoulder. "Can't someone else...?"

"No one else has the power. It has to be me, Emmanuelle." Mika'el took a deep breath. "It should have been me when all this began. I could have stopped your father then, but your mother wouldn't let me because she couldn't bear to lose me, and instead we lost you. You need to be stronger than that. You need to let me stop this."

His soulmate leaned back against the deck railing, her fists bunched at her sides, her hair blowing across her face. She stared at him, looking small and lost and infinitely sad.

"I don't think I can," she whispered. "Not when I've

just found you again."

"Don't." He shook his head. "Don't make this more than it needs to be. Even if I stayed, too much has come between us. Too many years. Too many lessons."

"Even though we're soulmates?"

"Especially because of that. The ruler of Heaven should be connected to all souls, not just one. Don't make the same mistakes as your mother, Emmanuelle. Don't need anyone. Don't need me. Let me go. Let me do what needs to be done. Please."

She held his gaze for a long, silent minute. Then she gave a tremulous sigh and straightened away from the rail. Standing tall, she lifted her chin and blinked back her tears.

"You know I'll miss you every day of my life, Mika'el of the Archangels."

"I know."

"But I'll make you proud. I may not be what Heaven or Earth is used to, but I'll be the best damned ruler they've ever seen. And I'll defeat my brother. You have my word."

I know hovered a second time on Mika'el's lips, but he couldn't bring himself to say it, because they both knew the outcome of this battle was far from certain.

Emmanuelle raised a new topic, saving them from his lie.

"What of the woman?" she asked.

"She made a pact with Bethiel—Mittron's life for hers. At first, I wanted to prevent it, but now—" Michael broke off with a sigh, then finished quietly, "I want her safe from Seth."

A tiny frown pulled at Emmanuelle's forehead. "You care for her."

"She has earned my respect," he said, "and my

gratitude for all she has done. All she has sacrificed."

"Mika'el."

Though Emmanuelle spoke only his name, it was a command all the same. An insistence that he be honest with her—and with himself.

Mika'el looked out over the treetops. He thought back on the unwavering strength of the woman he had come to know better than any other human in all his time on Earth. The sheer, dogged refusal to give up, even when she wanted to. The pain she had endured, the trust she had placed in him, the honor and integrity that drove her every step.

And the spark that had flared between them, catching them both by surprise.

Did he care about Alex? Yes. More than he wanted to, and far, far more than he should. But none of that mattered. None of it held meaning. Not anymore.

Meeting Emmanuelle's waiting gaze, he knew he didn't have to tell his soulmate any of that. She knew. All of it. And she struggled with it, the shadows in her eyes reminding him briefly—chillingly—of Seth. Of Lucifer.

Too much. Too many years. Too many lessons.

Emmanuelle shook her head and tightened her lips. "Damn, but we've made a mess of things, haven't we?"

She didn't refer to war.

He didn't know how to answer.

Emmanuelle sighed. "I can remove her immortality," she said. "Give her back her life."

"And if Seth comes after her again? If—" Mika'el broke off, unwilling—unable—to voice the unthinkable.

If you don't defeat him?

Emmanuelle's chin lifted, but she didn't object.

Didn't deny the unspoken possibility. Couldn't deny it, Mika'el thought. None of them could.

The door opened at the other end of the deck, and Gabriel's voice intruded on their silence.

"We might want to hurry it up," she said. "Seth is in the city of Vancouver. It isn't faring well."

Mika'el's gaze met and held Emmanuelle's. "Are we ready?"

The leather-clad god laughed, a short, sharp bark of sound that held more sadness than it did mirth. "We'll never be ready, Mika'el. Not for this. Never for this."

Before Mika'el could respond, one of Emmanuelle's biker friends shoved past Gabriel onto the deck.

"She's gone," said the man. "Jezebel is gone. And she took the baby."

Silence met the announcement.

Then Emmanuelle sighed. "Bloody fucking Hell," she muttered. "It doesn't matter whether I'm ready or not, does it? Things are just going to happen regardless."

She scowled at the bearded man and the Archangel in the doorway. "Gabriel, you stay. Wookie, wait inside for me."

"What about Jez? Shouldn't I go after her?"

"No. You're safer here." Iridescent eyes flicked back to Mika'el's, understanding in their depths. "I need to know the ones I care about are safe."

A tiny fraction of the weight across Mika'el's shoulders lifted. Emmanuelle looked back to the others.

"Wait inside," she said again to Wookie. "And send Bethiel to me."

FIFTY-SEVEN

Alex stood in the back corner of the kitchen, apart from the others, ignoring their curious looks, uninterested in their murmur of conversation. She stared at the baby monitor on the counter. Soft noises filtered through it: snuffles, whimpers, the movement of a tiny body.

"Do you want to see her?"

Alex jumped. She turned to the harshly bleached blond who had appeared by her elbow. "What?"

"The baby." The woman nodded at the monitor. "She was your niece's, so that makes her yours now. You should meet her."

Bile surged up into Alex's chest. Her throat. She gagged. Swallowed. Curled fingernails into palms.

"*That,*" she grated, "is a monster, not a baby. You should have done us all a favor and left it on the beach."

Startled brown eyes, eyeliner tattooed along their lids, blinked at her. The woman's mouth opened to object, but Alex turned her back on her. She had no interest in argument. No interest in the woman. And didn't even want to think about the creature that had taken Nina's life. The monitor wailed again, and the woman hurried from the kitchen in response. Alex's stomach rolled. A Naphil in the purest sense. Lucifer's bastard, born to lead an army. She shivered.

"Here. This will help."

Another voice intruded on her thoughts, this one belonging to Father Marcus. He held out a cup of tea to her.

She regarded it, remembering the last cup of tea he'd offered her, heavily laced with whiskey, just before Bethiel had arrived with—

Father Marcus lifted her hand and wrapped it around the cup handle.

"There's nothing in it this time, I'm afraid," he said, his voice brusque. "The only thing I could find in the house was a bottle of cherry liqueur, and that didn't seem like such a good idea."

Alex took the cup without comment.

"Do you want to talk?" he asked.

The others had vacated the room, leaving the two of them alone. The woman's voice drifted from the plastic box on the counter, singing *Rockabye, Baby*.

Nina's baby.

Nina's and Lucifer's.

Alex put the cup in the sink.

"Alex—" Father Marcus began.

"He's dead," she said.

Marcus frowned.

"Hugh," she said. "He's dead. So is Elizabeth."

The priest sagged against the counter. His face turned grey, aging before her eyes.

"He can't be," he whispered. "He's too strong. He's

made it through so much...survived so much..."

A tear trickled down Marcus's lined cheek and dropped onto the black clerical shirt. A second followed in its wake. He swiped at his eyes and made a visible effort to gather himself.

"I'm sorry," he said, his voice wobbling. "You've lost so much already, and now this. I know how close you were to him. To both of them. I'm so sorry, Alex."

She looked away as breathing became an act of willpower. Tears fogged her vision. Pain clawed at her throat. And then Marcus was reaching through his own loss to envelop her in his arms. Cradling her. Rocking her.

There was no struggle with madness this time, only a sharing of grief. For their friends, for Alex's family, for their world. Alex cried until she could cry no more. Until her tears ran dry and Marcus's shirtfront was soaked against her cheek, and her breath came in huge, shuddering hiccups.

And still Marcus quietly rocked her.

When she pulled away at last, only emptiness remained. Not the dark, terrifying emptiness of before, but the quiet kind. The sad kind. The kind that simply was.

And would be for eternity.

The kitchen door opened, and Gabriel stood framed in the doorway. Her sapphire gaze met Alex's.

"You're needed," she said.

ALEX STARED AT MICHAEL, her mouth dry, shock sitting like lead in her belly. His gruff, infinitely compassionate words reverberated in her skull. "*I won't stand in Bethiel's way.*"

The unspoken message behind them reverberated just as loudly in her soul.

I'll let him kill you. I'll let you die.

She inhaled a shallow, cautious breath into lungs that felt as if they might shatter. It was what she'd wanted all along. But now that it was here...her gaze flicked to Emmanuelle, daughter of the One, wondering if there might not be an alternative. If someone equal to Seth might be able to—

"She can," Michael answered her unspoken question. "But even if you're mortal again, you'll still carry a piece of Seth in you. He'll still be connected to you. Still be drawn to you."

And there's no guarantee that Emmanuelle will defeat him. That he won't come after you again and again and again. That he won't find you. Take you. Own you forever.

More unspoken words—possibilities too horrifying to voice. Alex swallowed. She tried to make herself nod but seemed to have lost communication with her body.

She was going to die.

Bethiel would take her out into the woods and kill her.

She would be done fighting and running, but she would never know if Heaven won, or if humanity survived, or if everything—everyone—she'd lost had been in vain, because she would be gone.

"Alex?" Michael's voice prompted. Still gruff, still gentle.

"I didn't think it would be like this," she said. "I thought I was ready—I *am* ready—but it's..."

"It's the human spirit." Gabriel spoke up from the corner. "You don't want to die."

Alex's gaze moved to her. The Archangel's sapphire eyes were suspiciously bright.

Tears? For her?

Gabriel scowled as if she'd heard Alex's thoughts. She crossed her arms. But she continued speaking.

"When the One made you in her image, it wasn't just physical. The life spark that exists within each of you is an echo of hers. It drives your species' very survival." She shrugged, the top curve of her black wings brushing the ceiling. "It's stronger in some of you than in others."

Perhaps. But was it strong enough to endure forever?

"You're the only one who can decide," Michael said.

She scowled at him. Did he read all her thoughts these days?

Emmanuelle cleared her throat. "He's escalating," she said. "We need to move."

Michael's gaze didn't leave Alex's. "You need to choose."

Alex closed her eyes. It wasn't supposed to be like this. None of it was supposed to be like this. Not Aramael, not Jen or Nina, not Hugh and Elizabeth, not Michael...

And sure as fucking Hell not Seth.

Seth, whom she'd once saved and tried to love, because she'd seen something in him. Seen a spark of his mother. A spark of promise. A whisper of good.

But all that was gone now, and if she chose to live, she would have nothing but memories. Regrets. Loss.

Eternity.

She took another breath, savoring it as one of her last, and looked across the room to meet Bethiel's gaze.

She nodded her decision.

He nodded his understanding.

Michael broke the silence.

"I can wait no more than half an hour," he told Bethiel. "After that..."

"I'll be there," Bethiel said. "Thank you."

Michael looked to Gabriel. "Look after her," he said, nodding at Emmanuelle. "Be more than just her warrior."

There was no mistaking the sheen in Gabriel's eyes this time. Or the quiver that ran through the wings tightly folded against the Archangel's back as she squared her jaw and stood tall, meeting Michael's gaze without flinching.

"You know I will," she said.

Alex scowled. Preoccupied though she might be by her own impending death, the undercurrents running through the room were hard to miss. Something was up. Something more than—

She shut her thoughts down cold. The war between Heaven and Hell was none of her concern anymore. It belonged to the angels now. To Michael and Gabriel and the others who followed them, and to Emmanuelle and Seth. Whatever Alex might sense beneath the surface here, it was out of her control.

It was none of her business.

She watched Michael take Emmanuelle's hands in his. Volumes seemed to pass between them, though neither spoke a word. Unutterable sadness settled over Emmanuelle's expression. But even as Alex crushed a spark of curiosity, a niggle of doubt, the One's daughter took a deep breath and stretched up on tiptoe to press her lips to Michael's cheek. Briefly. Fleetingly.

"Heaven is with you, my warrior," she said. "Always."

Then, turning, she was gone, Gabriel in her wake.

Michael's eyes closed for a moment before his attention returned to Alex. His gaze burned into her with the intensity of the sun itself, leaving no room for shadows, no thoughts unseen. Sorrow crept out from a hidden place deep within her, fragile and lost and achingly empty.

"Alex," he said.

Her breath caught. This was it. This was the last time she would marvel at the strength and sheer beauty of the powerful wings rising behind him, the last time she would hear the rumble of his voice.

"Michael..." She trailed off, the rest of her words tangling in her throat. Her heart.

I don't want to die. I don't want to lose any more. I'm afraid.

I'm so afraid.

Michael wrapped her in the cocoon of his wings and held her against his chest. His heart thudded beneath her ear, strong and steady.

"I wish I could do it myself," he said. "I owe you that much. But I—"

"No." She shook her head against him. "I would never ask that of you, Michael. Bethiel...we had a deal. Bethiel is enough. Thank you."

His hands cupped her face, and one thumb wiped away a tear that rolled down her cheek. Emerald eyes looked into hers one last time. Warm lips brushed against her forehead.

"I'm glad you'll be safe," he whispered.

And then he, too, was gone.

FIFTY-EIGHT

Seth stared at the remains of Elizabeth Riley's home. The empty remains, for Alex hadn't been here after all.

Behind him, sword clashed against sword in a cacophony of sound that nearly drowned out the wail of sirens that came from every corner of the city. Around him, the wind of a hundred wings snapped trees off at their bases and hurled cars down the street.

Seth ignored it all.

None of it mattered, because Alex *had* been here. The residual energy of her presence whispered to him from every ruined nook and cranny. Her presence... and Mika'el's. Intertwined. Linked. Inseparable.

Bile rose in Seth's throat.

Something had happened here. Something wrong and intimate and terrifying. Something that made breathing almost impossible.

A touching of souls.

A connection.

And because of Heaven's interference, because of those fucking angels, Seth had been too late to stop it, and now she was gone again. Taken from him. Again.

He clenched his fists.

Alex.

A Fallen One dropped from the sky in a tangle of feathers and clatter of armor. He landed at Seth's feet, gauntleted hand outstretched for help, phosphorescence oozing from his chest. Seth closed his eyes.

He stilled his center, shut out the chaos around him, and focused. Calm spread through him. Cold followed in its wake. Cold, then dark, then—

Seth threw his arms wide, hands and fingers outstretched. Energy poured from him, catastrophic in its power. Under his feet, the earth trembled. It rolled and bucked, spreading outward in an ever-widening circle around him. Wind slammed like an unseen fist into buildings. Windows imploded. Roofs collapsed. Walls crumbled. Angels and Fallen alike were tossed about the sky.

A building at a time, the entire block fell before his fury. Then a dozen more. Then a hundred.

Thousands of souls shrieked in terror, then fell silent.

Seth dropped his arms to his sides. The wind died abruptly, and the earth stood still once more. Utter silence reigned.

And still no Alex had surfaced.

He surveyed the devastation he'd wreaked, watching angels and Fallen alike pick themselves out of the wreckage, searching for swords and bits of armor, straightening bent and broken wings. Then he turned toward the greater part of the city, outlined

against a backdrop of snow-capped mountains. She
was out there somewhere. If not in this city, then in
another. He would find her if he had to take the world
apart piece by—

Another energy loomed, sudden and powerful, and
Seth stumbled. Catching his balance, he stopped in his
tracks. His breath quieted. He searched for the source.
Found it in a presence miles away, calm, calculating,
watchful.

Waiting.

For him.

So. It began.

"WE SHOULD GO," Bethiel said.

With an effort, Alex brought her vision back into
focus. She looked up into the zircon eyes, seeing the
same conflict there that roiled in her. She tried to take
comfort in knowing this wasn't any easier for Bethiel
than it was for her, but that knowledge actually made
it worse.

"You're sure you want to...do this?" she asked.

"You gave me Mittron. I gave you my word."

She nodded. Her gaze traveled the silent room,
passing over Wookie and Scorpion and the others.
It rested briefly on Father Marcus. Settled back on
Bethiel.

"What did Michael mean, he can only wait half an
hour?" she asked. "Half an hour for what?"

Bethiel's expression became shuttered. His gaze
skidded away from hers. "It's nothing."

The knot of uneasiness residing in Alex's gut doubled
in size, pressing against her diaphragm, turning her
breath shallow. She glowered at the angel. "Bethiel, tell

me what's going on. Half an hour for what?"

Bethiel sighed. "Half an hour to kill Mittron."

"But why the time limit?" she pressed. "What happens after that?"

"After that—" The angel's gaze met hers, unutterable sadness in its depths. "After that, Mika'el destroys the Nephilim army."

Air whooshed from Alex. Blindly, she reached a hand out in search of something solid. Something that would keep her upright as all capacity to stand fled. A strong hand grasped her elbow, and Father Marcus became her support. She stared at him blankly, then shook her head at Bethiel.

"He can't," she whispered. "He's an Archangel, and the Nephilim are mortal. They're still just..."

She trailed off. But spoken or not, her words hung heavy in the air. Filled the room. Made everyone present look anywhere but at her.

Children.

The Nephilim were just children.

Eighty thousand of them.

"No," said Bethiel. "They're not. Every despot in the world, every serial killer, every sociopath—they all descended from the Nephilim. Hitler, Genghis Khan, Mugabe, Hussein, all of them. There were just one hundred original Nephilim, Alex, and yet their murderous descendants continue today, too many to even list. And now there are eighty thousand of them. Humanity will never survive that. It can't."

He looked around the room, addressing them all. "They're not just children," he said. "They were never just children."

"And Michael?" Alex asked. "Will he see it that way when he kills them?"

Bethiel's silence was her answer. She sucked in a ragged breath.

"*I'm going to have to do something unforgivable soon*," Michael's voice echoed in her memory. "*Something I won't be able to come back from. It will likely destroy me.*"

"What happens?" she demanded. "What happens to an Archangel if he kills eighty thousand children, Bethiel?"

Clear zircon eyes met hers.

"He falls," Bethiel said simply.

The world rocked beneath Alex's feet, and she clutched harder at Father Marcus's support. The Archangel Michael, Heaven's greatest warrior, the One's most trusted advisor...*fall?*

"He'll never survive." Her voice was hoarse with horror.

"He is immortal," Bethiel hedged.

"You know what I mean, Bethiel. He told me himself this would destroy him. His mind—Hell, his *soul*—will never survive this." Alex pulled away from Marcus. She wheeled and stalked the room, raking fingers through her hair. "You have to take me to him."

"You can't save him, Alex."

"I know." She made herself stop in front of the angel. Made herself breathe. Made herself meet his gaze with all the steadiness she could muster. She remembered the arms of a warrior that had held her when the darkness had tried to swallow her. Remembered the compassion that had become her anchor, her salvation.

Michael hadn't tried to save her, he'd said. "*I just didn't want you to be alone when it happened.*"

"I know I can't save him," she told Bethiel. "But I *can* be with him. No one should have to be alone in the dark, Bethiel. Not even an Archangel.""

Bethiel held her gaze for a moment, then his dropped away.

"I can't," he said miserably. "I don't have the power to transport a mortal with me, and flying would take too long. We wouldn't get there in time."

"But you brought Nina and the baby with you to the beach."

"That was Raphael, not—" Bethiel broke off. His expression cleared. "Of course. Raphael."

"What?"

"I can't take you to Mika'el, but Raphael can. Wait here. I'll be back."

Alex put a hand on his arm. "What about Mittron? Will you have enough time...?"

The angel raised an eyebrow. "What about Seth?" he countered. "If I don't end your life now..."

He, too, trailed off. They stared at one another in mutual understanding, knowing that each might be giving up the one thing they wanted most. Bethiel, the dream of revenge against Mittron; Alex, the only certainty that Seth wouldn't be able to claim her.

Alex dropped her hand and stepped back. She lifted her chin. "He deserves better than this, Bethiel."

The Principality's mouth pulled tight. He nodded. Then he disappeared.

FIFTY-NINE

Emmanuelle swiped with the back of her hand at the blood trickling from her bottom lip. From her ignominious position against the base of a high-rise building, she looked up and sideways at her brother, hiding the first tremors of uncertainty behind a glower.

This was not going well.

Seth waved the fingertips of one hand, leveling another blast at her. Emmanuelle shielded herself. The building behind her exploded into dust and rubble.

Not well at all.

Concrete and glass showered over her as she pushed herself up from the ground. She brushed off the seat of her leather pants, using the time to test again the availability of Heaven's strength. She and her brother were more evenly matched than she'd hoped. They'd already destroyed Vancouver's west end and were halfway through the downtown core. At this rate, the entire city would be in ruins before she was able to put a stop to it.

If she could stop it at all.

She fielded another bolt of energy from Seth and watched an apartment tower shudder, crumble, and fall. Tried and failed to shut out the terror of the occupants cowering within. Felt in her core the deaths of every single one.

Impotent fury coursed through her, and she curled her hands into fists at her sides.

Bloody Hell, what if she couldn't tap into Heaven's power after all? What if she and Seth ended up slugging it out until they were all that was left? Just the two of them. Brother and sister, locked in endless battle the way their parents had been.

The way she'd sworn she would never be.

"You could just give up," Seth suggested, as if he knew her thoughts. "Give me Alex, and I'll let you keep Heaven."

Emmanuelle struggled not to throw a fireball in response. She hadn't yet been directly responsible for the mayhem around them, and she wouldn't start now. No matter how much she wanted to wipe that smug haughtiness from his face.

Because the indirect mayhem she'd caused was bad enough.

"Damn it, Seth, it doesn't have to be this way," she gritted. "I told you, I—"

She took the full brunt of an invisible blow that slammed her into a parked car and rattled her teeth. She reacted without thinking, lobbing an orb of blue fire at Seth that would have hurt like Hell if he hadn't ducked. The storefront behind him exploded. Seth raised an eyebrow and brushed glass from his shoulder.

"Well," he said. "So you *can* fight back. I was beginning to think you favored our mother's side too much for your own good. It's nice to see some of daddy's spirit, too. Do it again."

Fucking Hell.

"Damn it, Seth, I don't want to fight you. I just want—"

"I *know* what you want!" he bellowed, and the entire street shook beneath her feet.

Emmanuelle's skin tightened at the raw, unbridled fury. Furtively, she scanned their surroundings. A dozen buildings collapsed already; hundreds more sitting like tin cans lined up for target practice. She needed to draw him away from here, out to where their fight would do less damage.

"You want to talk," Seth snarled. "To *negotiate*. You want me to go back to Hell and leave your precious mortals alone, but don't you see I *can't*? As long as there's a single, solitary human still alive in this forsaken realm, it will come between me and Alex. She'll want to save it, just like you do. She'll love it and feel responsible for it and—"

He broke off and ran both his hands over his head, tangling his fingers in his hair.

"And I can't share her like that," he finished raggedly. "She is my *life*. My entire reason for being. Once she understands that, once she sees how much I—"

"She doesn't love you," Emmanuelle said.

Her brother's head snapped sideways as if she'd slapped him. Pain—pure, white-hot, searing pain—meshed with the fury in his eyes and radiated outward to slice into Emmanuelle's own soul.

The sheer magnitude of it took away her breath and brought her up short. That was no ordinary pain of rejection. It was more. So much more. And it was utterly unbearable.

She stared at her brother in shock.

Holy Hell. No wonder—

A blue wall hurtled her way.

RAPHAEL'S BLADE STOPPED just short of removing Bethiel's head. In one swift motion, the Archangel replaced sword with gauntleted hand, holding Bethiel off the ground and shaking him until Bethiel's brain rattled.

"Are you out of your fucking mind, sneaking up on me like that?" Raphael shook again. "Do you have any idea how close I came to killing you?"

Unable to breathe, let alone speak, Bethiel clawed at the metal fingers clamped around his throat. With a sound of disgust, Raphael tossed him away, then turned to meet the blade of an incoming Fallen. Sword met sword, gauntleted fist met skull, blade pierced immortality, and in less than a heartbeat, the Fallen One lay unmoving.

Bethiel massaged his intact throat. Raphael took hold of his arm and dragged him to the shelter of a wall.

"Talk," he ordered.

In clipped words and holding back nothing, Bethiel told him about the Nephilim army and Mika'el's plan, and about the sacrifice Alex wanted to make. Golden eyes turned bleak, and Raphael's mouth went tight. He looked out at the battle raging over the city of London, the skies dark with smoke and dust. Precious seconds ticked by as Raphael processed what Bethiel had told him, each one eroding Bethiel's chances of confronting Mittron. How long had it been since Mika'el gave him the time limit? Ten minutes? Fifteen?

He pushed away his impatience. Alex was right. Mika'el was more important now.

"I should have expected as much," Raphael muttered. "If humanity is to have a chance, we have no choice but to destroy the Nephilim."

His gaze returned to Bethiel. "The Naphil woman knows she can't save him, and she would do this for him? Give up her only chance to escape Seth?"

"She would."

More seconds.

Raphael straightened his shoulders. His jawline hardened. Massive black wings folded behind his back, and he sheathed his sword.

"Take me to her."

SIXTY

Bethiel landed amid a sea of children. A teeming, seething, knee-deep ocean of flesh. Eighty thousand tiny bodies surged around him, weeping and wailing, crying out in hunger and need. Not a single adult was present.

He fought to block the voices hammering at him. To get his bearings amid the din of their demands. The pull of their needs.

Nephilim, he reminded himself, gritting his teeth. *Not children. Not to be saved.*

He waded through the tear-streaked faces, the grasping, grubby fingers that clutched at his clothing. Focused his thoughts, focused his reach. Searched for the one presence, the one anomaly—

He stopped in the middle of the street. The Nephilim crushed in on him. Ignoring them, he stared up at a squat, broken building. At first glance, it was identical to a dozen others along the street: chunks of concrete missing, graffiti scrawled across its walls, all its windows shattered or missing.

All its windows but one, high above on the top floor, catching the rays of the setting sun, reflecting them back in a dazzling square of pink light.

One intact window in all of Pripyat.

And behind that window, the presence he sought.

The angel he'd dreamed of finding for three thousand years.

Mittron.

Bethiel shoved his way through the Nephilim, knocking them to the ground, oblivious to their outrage. He pushed into the building and closed the door against them. Scanning the dilapidated entrance, he found the stairs against the left wall. He walked across to them and stood at their base, staring up at where they disappeared into shadow. Placing one foot on the first step, he began the long climb, the wails of the Nephilim becoming fainter with each floor he passed.

He ran out of stairs after the sixth flight.

A corridor stretched before him, lit only by the bits of fading daylight brought into it by the doors open along its length. The door at the end stood closed.

Bethiel withdrew his sword from its scabbard. The hilt snugged into his hand, comfortable and familiar. He took a deep breath, exhaled, and walked down the hallway. He stopped before the door and stared at the stained, worn surface.

So this was it. He'd found Mittron. Found the angel who had framed him, betrayed him, sentenced him to an eternity in a place of empty madness.

Bethiel waited for the surge of triumph. A tingle of anticipation. A thread of caring. He found instead only a flat, sad weariness and a bitter irony.

Three thousand very long years he'd dreamed of this revenge—lived for it—and now he wanted only to be done.

Wasn't sure he wanted it at all.

Impatiently, he shook off the unexpected melancholy and shored up his resolve. Too many had suffered for him to give up now. If he couldn't kill Mittron for himself, he would do so for the two realms the Seraph had brought to their knees. For the girl who had died in his arms after giving birth to Lucifer's spawn. For the warrior who would sacrifice himself for the sake of the world.

And for the woman named Alex who would suffer eternity for the sake of that warrior.

Bethiel inhaled. Gritted his teeth. Reached for the knob.

His hand had barely closed over the metal when the door was flung wide and Mittron loomed before him, amber eyes glowing with a wild light, face split by a wide, maniacal grin.

"Bethiel! I've been waiting for you," he said happily.

And then, before Bethiel could recover, the Seraph plunged a sharpened stick deep into his belly.

Bethiel's sword flew from his hand.

MITTRON PLUNGED his makeshift spear into Bethiel's body over and over, targeting his shoulders, arms, thighs—anywhere but his chest. Anywhere but the globe of immortality contained in him. He wanted the Principality to suffer as he had suffered.

A wound for each hour since his release from Limbo.

Stab.

For each hour Mittron had lived in fear of his reprisal.

Stab.

Through the window came the wails of the neglected Nephilim, like fingernails over the chalkboard of his brain, already scraped raw from the return of the voices.

Stab.

He'd run out of Samael's drug two days ago, and the fucking Archangel had yet to deliver more.

Stab.

And now the Fallen had all taken off, and the mortals had shut down his supply line of caregivers, and he was alone—stab—with eighty thousand screaming, putrid—stab—Nephilim with no respite in sight—and Bethiel had come for him, and—

With a howl of rage, Mittron scooped the limp Principality from the floor and hurled him through the window in a spray of glass shards and crimson droplets. He leapt out after him and landed in the midst of a crowd of children shocked into silence. Spittle running down his chin and blue eyes dark with hatred, Bethiel struggled to rise. Mittron stabbed again, hitting him in the neck. Then he seized a filthy, blood-spattered grey wing and dragged him down the street.

More and more children fell silent at their approach, then trailed them. They reached the faded, overgrown remains of a small park, and Mittron dumped Bethiel onto the sparse, winter-brown grass. He scowled at the Nephilim, gathering around him in a silent circle, waiting. He kicked the downed Principality. A giggle rippled through the horde, ever so much easier to listen to than the howls that had plagued him since yesterday.

He stuck his spear into Bethiel's wing. The angel writhed in agony. More laughter spread through the children, and an answering smile tugged at the corner of Mittron's mouth.

Fucking hell, if he'd known it was this easy to achieve peace, he would have stabbed someone sooner.

He raised his spear, widened his stance, and set about entertaining his charges.

SIXTY-ONE

Raphael dumped Alex unceremoniously in the center of a deserted street. "I can take you no further," he said. "I must return to battle."

Alex nodded, her attention only half on him. She scanned the stretch of concrete and pavement, broken by nature's slow, relentless reclamation of the city. Plants and trees had grown up through the street and sidewalks and out of walls and windows, pushing aside what could be pushed, incorporating what could not. Most were leafless and dormant in the face of the coming winter. Many of the low-lying ones had been trampled flat by thousands of feet.

And yet there was no sign of a living soul anywhere in sight.

Alex's breath caught. Was she too late? Had Michael already—

A touch on her arm brought her up short. She met the gaze of the Archangel who had brought her here.

"No," he answered her thoughts. "If he had—when

he does-"

He broke off and stared into the distance.

"There won't be anything left," he said.

She swallowed. "Then where...?"

Raphael cocked his head. "Listen. Can you hear them?"

She held her breath. Strained to hear what he could.

Voices. Children's voices. Happy. Laughing. Bizarrely, obscenely normal.

Alex shuddered and wrapped her arms around herself against a chill that had nothing to do with Ukraine in November.

"That way," Raphael pointed down a street to their left. In the distance, the skeletal hulk of a Ferris wheel loomed, unmoving.

Alex nodded. Shivered again. "Thank you," she whispered.

She started walking, skirting the debris littering the buckled pavement. Raphael's voice stopped her.

"Naphil." He cleared his throat. "Alexandra."

She looked back over her shoulder. The Archangel's warm golden gaze held hers for a moment.

"What you do for Mika'el," he said. "Thank you."

And with that, he lifted away and disappeared in a great sweep of black wings and a gust of wind that swirled down the street to dance around Alex's ankles.

She closed her eyes and listed to the silence around her, the voices in the distance, the utter stillness between. Would Michael be with the Nephilim or watching from somewhere? Would he have seen Raphael arrive with her? Would he know she was here?

Would she find him in time?

Again, alone, she started toward the voices. Squeals

and giggles punctuated the overall babble, and she frowned as she drew nearer to the source. It almost sounded as if something entertained them. Something repetitive. Regu—

She stepped past the rusted remains of a car, its tires long gone, rounded the corner of a building, and stopped in her tracks. Coherent thought disintegrated in the face of stunned disbelief. Horror.

Ahead of her, stretched as far as she could see, across every street and sidewalk and surface in view, stretched a sea of children. Not babies, but children. Toddlers, interspersed by the occasional older one, standing, walking, dancing. A writhing, incessantly moving body of...bodies. Every skin color. Every hair color. Every—

"Have you come to watch the angels play?" a voice asked.

Alex looked down at the little girl who had come to stand beside her. Eight years old, she would have guessed in normal times. These weren't normal times.

Or normal children.

A frisson of unease tracked down her spine.

"Angels?" she asked.

Bright brown eyes smiled up at her. A child's finger pointed over the heads of the moving masses. "Over there!"

Alex followed the direction of the point. Far out in the center of the horde, two figures towered. One with gray wings, the other with none.

"You can't tell that Mittron is an angel," the little girl said, "because he doesn't have his wings anymore. A lady god took them away from him. But he told us he's still an angel anyway."

The wingless figure raised something in one hand

and brought it down on the other. A muffled shriek rolled over the heads of the gathered children. Giggles and squeals swallowed it.

Bethiel.

Alex's knees buckled under the realization. Blindly, she reached out a hand for support. Small fingers grasped it, warm and soft against hers. She pulled back from their touch. Staggered sideways. The girl cocked her head to one side.

"Don't you like watching them play?" she asked.

For a moment, Alex couldn't speak. Couldn't respond. Couldn't move. And then, from a place of abhorrence so deep in her that she hadn't known it existed, she pulled a cold, crystalline fury, perfect in its towering strength.

Its absoluteness.

Her head snapped around and her gaze zeroed in on the display at the center of the Nephilim throng. The time Michael had given Bethiel would be up soon. Whatever power he planned to unleash on the Nephilim might kill Mittron, too, but it didn't matter, because it wasn't enough.

Bethiel deserved better.

Alex waded forward through the ocean of children. Pudgy toddler hands reached for her, tugging at her clothing, pulling at her arms. She brushed them off, not looking down, focusing only on the bloodied gray wings that tried to extend. Tried to lift their owner from the ground. Tried to save an angel that had already suffered enough at the hands of his tormentor.

Three thousand years in Limbo.

Bethiel deserved so much better.

Ahead of her, in a circle clear of children, Mittron pulled a crimson-slick spear from Bethiel's shoulder.

It left with a wet, sucking sound, and the Nephilim sea cackled with glee. Bethiel staggered and went down on one knee.

Alex lifted her right hand and reached up over her shoulder. Her fingers brushed the hilt of her soulmate's sword. Closed over it.

Aramael deserved better, too.

And so did Jen and Nina and Hugh and Elizabeth and the cops and all the women who had died in childbirth.

Mittron drew back the spear for another attack.

Only a dozen feet away now, and free at last of the grasping hands, Alex pulled the sword free of its scabbard. The focus of the Nephilim surrounding Mittron and Bethiel turned to her. Their quiet grew, spreading outward in a hush that reached the farthest corners of their kin.

Mittron stilled. He tipped his head to the left, a minute, barely there movement. Just enough to tell her he listened. Sensed her approach. Readied for attack.

Alex balanced herself on the balls of her feet, the way Michael had taught her to an eon ago on the beach.

Bethiel deserved to see his enemy die.

And Mittron...Mittron deserved to see his death coming.

The former executive administrator of Heaven spun. Locked gazes with her. Lunged. Alex stepped to the side and grabbed the spear in her left hand. Her fingers slipped on the bloody shaft, then found purchase. She braced herself. Pulled. Mittron's forward momentum became impossible to escape. He staggered and released his weapon, but too late.

He wore no armor.

Alex's sword penetrated his chest without effort on her part, sliding through breastbone, sinking deep, finding its target. She felt an instant's resistance in the blade, and then the give. Mittron's eyes widened.

Crimson welled around the sword still buried in him, flecked with specks of phosphorescence. He looked down, his expression a study in disbelief. Shock. Then his gaze lifted to meet Alex's.

Coldly, deliberately, she twisted the sword a quarter turn to the right, then pulled it out. Blood and phosphors gushed from the wound. Mittron's head jerked back, and a howl erupted from him. A sound of agony, fury, loss.

Alex watched him crumple to the ground. He twitched twice, then lay still. A Naphil child near her whimpered. Another followed suit, then another and another. The whimpers grew to howls of disappointment. Children deprived of their entertainment. Alex's legs quaked beneath her, but she locked her knees and forced herself forward.

Michael would know Mittron had died. They had minutes at most.

She knelt beside the broken Bethiel, laying her sword on the ground. He lifted his head, and zircon eyes met hers, their blaze fierce.

"Thank you," he rasped.

Alex smoothed the hair back from the battered forehead of the angel who had been willing to forfeit his soul for her. She swallowed a lump at the base of her throat.

"You should get out of here," she said. "Can you walk?"

He shook his head. "No."

Alex slipped a hand beneath his arm. Bethiel took it

in his and held it.

"No," he said again.

"But—" Alex broke off. She stared into his blue, blue eyes and then nodded. She glanced at the sword on the ground at her side and steeled herself to make an offer she would never have dreamed possible. "Do you want me to...?"

Bethiel looked first shocked, then grateful. He shook his head again. "Thank you, but no," he said. "Just give me Mittron's spear, and I'll be fine."

Alex turned her gaze to where Mittron sprawled face first in the dirt, the spear on the ground beside him, crimson with Bethiel's blood. Then she lifted Aramael's sword and pressed it into Bethiel's hand. The angel-forged steel sat quietly there, giving none of its usual blue sparks of disapproval. Bethiel tried to resist, but she curled his fingers around the hilt and held them there.

"I'm not going to need it anymore," she said. "And Aramael would approve."

Bethiel stared at the weapon. Then up at her.

"I get it now," he said. "I understand what the others see in you. Your honor would do any angel proud, Alexandra Jarvis. It has been a privilege to know you."

Tears sprang to Alex's eyes, and she blinked back their sting. Swallowed the burn in her throat. She opened her mouth, but whatever words she might have spoken died unuttered as the ground vibrated beneath them. Rumbled. Slowly began to undulate.

Silence, sudden and absolute, dropped over the Nephilim.

The air itself stilled.

Michael.

Alex shot to her feet. Her eyes searched as far as she

could see, scanning over the heads of the Nephilim, flicking up to the rooftops and back down again. She had to find him. Had to know where he was before—

Her gaze fell on a lone figure in the distance, at the base of the Ferris wheel that towered over the remnants of an amusement park.

Michael stood in profile to her, his magnificent black wings folded behind his back, his sword held aloft in both hands, pointing at the sky. Clouds gathered above him, dark and swirling, flashes of pale blue in their depths.

Alex caught her breath.

"Alex, you need to get out of here!" Bethiel tugged at her pant leg.

She barely registered voice or touch.

The blue flickers increased. Spread. Began to snap above the heads of the Nephilim. The children cowered. Whimpered. One, somewhere to the left and far behind Alex, began to cry, a single voice rising above the others. A small hand stole into hers, and she looked down, into wide brown eyes in milk-chocolate skin. Her heart faltered.

Children.

"*No,*" the memory of Bethiel's voice whispered. "*They're not. Every despot in the world, every serial killer, every sociopath—they all descended from the Nephilim. They're not just children. They were never just children.*"

Alex lifted her gaze back to Michael. The clouds above him churned black, pulsated blue, spread out over the park, the street, the city. Their roil became organized, rotating over them in a slow, boiling circle. The outer sweep grew darker as the blue flickers gravitated to the center, and the snaps and sparks above the crowd of children raced to join their light there.

"Alex!" Bethiel shouted.

The very air went still. Waited.

The hand holding Alex's squeezed tighter, and a small body pressed against her leg. She struggled not to pull the child closer, to try to protect him from—

Michael's wings opened with a crack of sound that ricocheted across the ruined city. The vortex above him narrowed, and its blue light became white, nearly blinding, then shot from the sky to join with his sword. The instant the two touched, Michael turned the sword, fell to one knee, and drove the blade into the ground.

The power of Heaven itself rolled out from him in a great wave of white fire.

"Alex!"

Bethiel lunged up from the ground, his strong arms encircling her. He tore her away from the Naphil child's grasp and bore her to the ground. Feathers brushed her cheek. Softness encased her.

"A privilege," Bethiel whispered in her ear, and then he and the world disappeared in a rush of heat that burned all the way to Alex's soul.

SIXTY-TWO

Emmanuelle pushed away the concrete slab that covered her and spat out the grit filling her mouth. She wiped more grit from her eyes. One hand came away warm and sticky, and she peered at it through the dim light that filtered through the wreckage into her tomb. Faint shock registered at the sight of blood.

She'd never bled before.

It was sobering as Hell to find out she *could* bleed.

As far as wakeup calls went, this was a doozy.

She pushed to her feet and dusted off the front and shoulders of her leather jacket, the thighs and butt of her leather pants. It was time to put a stop to this. Time to stop holding back her own power in an effort to protect what Seth would only destroy anyway. Time to—

A wave of nausea rolled through her, and she sagged to her knees. An invisible force crushed down on her. She struggled not to let it push her into the floor. Not to panic. Seth? But how? Where had he found that kind of power? There was no way in Hell he should be able to—

And then it hit her.

It wasn't Seth, and it had nothing to do with Hell.

It was Mika'el.

He'd done it. Tapped into the power of Heaven itself and loosed it upon the world. Upon the Nephilim. But the flow wasn't stopping. It was going on and on, draining Heaven. Flooding the Earth. Something had gone wrong. Terribly, horribly wrong.

Mika'el.

Gritting her teeth, Emmanuelle summoned every atom of her power and thrust herself upright and through the wreckage. She landed with a grunt at her brother's feet. Black eyes stared down at her in astonishment. A frown furrowed Seth's brow. Then the unseen force slammed into him as well, knocking him to the ground beside her.

All around them, angels and Fallen rained from the sky.

The universe shuddered.

THE WEIGHT of Bethiel's body pressed down on Alex as she fought off the nightmare memories and tried desperately to shut down the voice in her head that wouldn't quit shrieking.

Not again not again not again.

She squeezed her eyes shut. Sucked in a breath. Feathers filled her nose.

Not again not again oh sweet Jesus not again.

She gritted her teeth against the scream clawing at her throat. Bit down on her lip until she tasted blood.

For fuck's sake, Jarvis, get a grip.

This wasn't Aramael. Seth wasn't waiting for her outside the shelter of Bethiel's wings. And she didn't have time for hysterics. Michael needed her.

Now.

She shoved aside the wing weighing her down and rolled out from under it—into the body of the child whose hand she'd held. Vacant eyes stared into hers for a split second, and then, before she could fully register the horror, the body disintegrated into dust.

"Fucking Hell!" she growled, scrambling to her feet. She stared at the street around her, its surface covered in bodies draped over and across one another, piled knee-high.

Her stomach clenched. Heaved.

One by one, the bodies crumbled. Children one second, dust the next. A wind swirled through, picking up bits and flinging them into Alex's eyes, her nose, her mouth. She sheltered behind a hand, clamped her lips closed against the rising bile, and tore her gaze from the macabre scene.

Michael. She needed to find—

Her heart contracted as her gaze settled on the place where he'd last been. The place he still was...but not really.

Michael.

Crumpled on the ground, his powerful wings splayed about him, his eyes closed. Defeated. Broken.

Fallen.

And beside him, the sword he'd plunged into the earth, glowing brilliant blue with the light that poured into it from the heavens above.

The wind gained momentum, shoving Alex one way and then the other, tearing at her clothes. She cast a last glance at Bethiel's body and the phosphorescence pooled around a shard of steel protruding from his back. Then, bracing herself against the onslaught, she staggered toward the Ferris wheel and the Archangel lying beneath it.

Step by step, she fought her way through the stinging sand that pelted her, focused only on the being who had given himself to save the world. Twice she stumbled and fell to her hands and knees, buried up to her elbows in the dust of children. Twice she swallowed the nausea and struggled again to her feet, tears turning to mud as they streamed down her face.

At last she stood over him, swaying as she stared down at the angel slowly being swallowed by the remains of the army he had destroyed. He lay unmoving on his side, one knee drawn up, a hand outstretched toward the sword he'd released. His powerful shoulders slumped, limp and lifeless, and his wings sagged along the ground, their black feathers riffling in the wind.

Alex lifted her gaze to the sword beyond him. To the light that poured into it from above. The power.

A tremble vibrated through the ground beneath her feet. The air surrounding her crackled with pent-up electricity.

Too much power.

Ice crept through her veins. It wasn't supposed to be like this. Whatever Michael had started, it hadn't stopped. And it needed to. Dear Heaven, it needed to.

Alex looked to the unmoving Archangel, willing him to wake, knowing he wouldn't. She stared again at the sword. Could she? Did she dare?

Just how immortal was she?

She closed her eyes against the brilliance that grew more blinding by the second. Against the choice that faced her. So much had already been sacrificed for this world, and now—now, if she didn't survive, Michael would have no one to hold him as he had held her. He would be forever alone in the darkness.

Choices.

Alex turned and knelt at the Archangel's side. Her tears dropped onto his face, leaving dark stains in the dust that covered him. She tugged a corner of her t-shirt free and, with shaking fingers, wiped the dirt from his eyelids, his nose, his mouth. Then she leaned down until her lips were beside his ear.

"I don't know if you can hear me, Mika'el of the Archangels," she said, "or if my words will make a difference, but know that you did the right thing. You made the right choice. The only choice. And I—"

Her voice broke, and fresh tears spilled from her eyes. She cupped Michael's face in her hands and pressed her forehead to his.

"I'm sorry," she whispered. "I'm sorry I can't be here for you like you were for me. I'm sorry I didn't say thank you. I'm sorry I wasn't good enough or strong enough or brave enough to do more for you, Michael. I'm so, so sorry."

Then, before she could reconsider, she shoved to her feet, turned, and threw herself into the inferno that had swallowed the sword.

MIKA'EL SCREAMED until he was hoarse and could scream no more. Until his throat bled, and he choked on the liquid warmth of his own blood. Until his ears shrieked in protest at the sound of his voice.

And then he screamed some more.

But no one heard.

Because no one was there.

No one to hear him, no one to witness the agony of his splintered, shattered soul. No one to break his fall.

Thou shalt not interfere.

It was the Cardinal Rule, the one law that could not be broken. Could never be broken, not without a price.

Those in Hell had paid one price; Mika'el would pay another. They had fallen only so far before coming to terms with their penance. But he—he who had been Heaven's greatest warrior and protector of all life, he who had become destroyer—he would never come to terms with what he had done. Could never come to terms with it.

Eighty thousand lives.

Eighty thousand *children*.

He screamed again.

Continued to fall.

Would never stop falling.

That was *his* price.

Then, in the breath he drew between screams, came a voice.

"...the only choice," it whispered.

Mika'el's breath hitched. His descent slowed for an instant, then resumed.

"I'm sorry," the voice said.

He turned, frantic, peering through the dark, stretching out his hands, trying to catch hold of something—anything—to stop his fall. He knew that voice. Knew it, cared about it, clung to it.

"...wasn't good enough or strong enough or brave enough," it whispered. "I'm so, so sorry."

Realization surged through him, and his fall ended with an abruptness that rattled his teeth, jarred his spine, shocked through his entire being.

He hung, suspended in the dark, grappling with the impossibility.

Alex.

But she was supposed to be dead. Safe from Seth. Mika'el had made sure it would happen, counted on it as his only salvation in the face of what he would become. If she was here, if she was holding him...

New agony ripped through him.

If she was holding him, she was still alive. Seth would come for her. And Mika'el would have failed at the only thing that might have saved a tiny part of his soul.

Bloody Hell, Alex, what have you done?

Her presence withdrew.

SIXTY-THREE

The outpouring of Heaven's power into the human realm stopped abruptly. Emmanuelle reacted a scant microsecond before Seth did, but it was enough. Enough to have her on her feet before he was, enough that she could strike the first blow. And the second. And the third.

It was not, however, enough to stop him.

Blue heat swallowed her, setting fire to her form, her mind, her consciousness. She shrieked, beating at the flames, reeling from the onslaught. Panic set in, and for an instant, she lost her bearings. Her resolve faltered.

It's not your fight, a voice inside her whispered. *It was never your fight. Never your war. You walked away once...*

No. Emmanuelle snuffed out the last flame licking at the edges of her consciousness. No. She might have walked away once, but not now. Not this time. And sure as Heaven not from this fight, because Mika'el had had given his soul for her today, and in return, she had made him a promise she intended to keep.

"I'll make you proud. I may not be what Heaven or Earth is used to, but I'll be the best damned ruler they've ever seen. And I'll defeat my brother. You have my word."

She lifted herself from the pool of blue fire she'd sunk into on the street. She'd lost her mother, she'd lost friends, and she'd lost her soulmate. She had no intention of losing the war.

And she was done fighting by Seth's rules.

"Enough!" she roared. In a dozen strides, she stood before her brother, hands wrapped around his throat, face so close to his that she could feel his breath. "Damn it to Hell and back, Seth, enough! Don't you understand? You can't win. Not against me."

Seth drove his arms up between hers, breaking her grip. He wheeled out of reach, his face as dark with rage as his eyes.

"Then we will destroy one another," he spat, "along with your precious mortal realm, because you can't win against me, either."

"You forget I'm the daughter of the One Creator."

"And you forget I'm her son," Seth snarled. "Same mother, same father, equal in every respect."

"You're wrong." Emmanuelle held a hand over her head, arm straight, palm open to the skies above. She stretched her thoughts toward Heaven. Followed with her heart. Her mind. Her entire being.

Then she chose.

And in choosing, she tapped into the awesome power that was Creation itself. The power Mika'el had used to destroy the Nephilim, that had very nearly destroyed the entire Earth instead. It flooded her with light. Dark. Heat. Cold. Compassion. Indifference. Love. Hatred. Pure bliss. Absolute despair.

It was everything.

It was nothing.

It was All.

She was All.

As if in slow motion, she watched understanding dawn across Seth's face. Rejection followed. He lifted both hands to gather the blue, then pushed it at her, a massive, towering inferno of everything he could muster.

It enveloped Emmanuelle with a fury fired by Seth's own wrath, but this time it didn't touch her. It didn't come near her. Instead, it raged at a distance, held at bay by something greater than Seth would ever be. Could ever be. And when at last it fizzled out, when it was just Seth and Emmanuelle again, she went to him and held him as he wept with a pain he'd held inside him for too long.

Wept with him for all they had lost and would never find again.

THE CLIMB BACK from where he'd fallen took everything Mika'el possessed. All his will, all his strength, all his determination. And it took forever.

By the time he opened his eyes, the world around him had stilled. Utterly. Not so much as a puff of wind stirred the air. No sound whispered across the city whose ruin he had completed. Nothing moved.

Nothing.

He bolted upright, wiping grit from his eyes. As if drawn by a magnet, his gaze settled on the smoldering pile of rags no more than a dozen feet away. And then on the sword clutched in charred, skeletal fingers.

The sword of an Archangel.

His sword.

Slowly, he pushed up from the ground and walked over. A distant part of him noted that he left no footprints. The ground was bare again, with no trace of the eighty thousand children he had turned to dust.

"*You did the right thing,*" Alex's voice whispered. "*You made the right choice. The only choice.*"

He stopped at her side. A haze covered the sightless, lake-blue eyes. White bone gleamed through the charred flesh of face and arms. Her entire ribcage had been laid bare—along with the shriveled, desiccated organs beneath. Mika'el's breath caught, and for a moment, everything in him quailed from what he might find. But he made himself crouch beside the woman who had stopped his fall, the woman who had saved the world. He blew out a gentle puff of air, just enough to clear the ash covering her chest.

And there, in its cage of bone, nestled between blackened lungs, he saw it. A sphere of phosphorescence. Intact.

Michael inhaled a shaking breath, then lowered himself to the ground, took the blackened fingers from his sword, cradled them in his hand, and settled in to wait.

Alex's heart trembled. Quivered. Began to beat.

SIXTY-FOUR

Alex surfaced slowly, in stages of awareness. Sensation came first: the cold, hard ground beneath her; a rock digging into her spine; warm fingers curled around her hand. Smell was next, bringing with it the acrid scent of burnt flesh. Then taste, closely resembling smell and making her stomach heave. Sound followed, with the thud of a heartbeat beneath her ear.

Her eyelids shot open at the last awareness, and she added sight to her list of accomplishments, staring into a shadowed emerald gaze.

"You're back," Michael said.

Alex frowned. "Was I gone?"

"In a manner of speaking."

"Where are we?" She tried to look past him, but couldn't see past the black wings or bare chest. She blinked. Bare...?

"Still in Pripyat," Michael answered. "Though there's not much of Pripyat left."

She tried to focus again on his face. "Your sword...it was...I thought something was wrong. I tried to pull it out of the ground."

The hand around hers gripped a little tighter. "Something was very wrong. And you did pull it out. Thank you."

Nope. It was no use.

"Um...why are you half-naked?" she asked.

"You needed my shirt."

Alex looked down at herself. A whisper of memory flitted across the edge of her mind. She flinched from the pain it contained. Smelled again the odor of charred flesh. Wondered how much *not much of Pripyat* Michael had meant. She closed her eyes on a wave of nausea.

Well, at least her question about how immortal she was had been answered. Which brought up a whole other issue.

"Is it over? The war? Did Emmanuelle—" She broke off, unable to finish.

"The fighting is over," Michael agreed. "But damage is...extensive."

Alex went quiet. Then, deciding this was a conversation best held upright, she pulled back from the heartbeat beneath her cheek. Michael slid an arm beneath her shoulders and eased her into a sitting position. His free hand swept back the hair from her face.

"Okay?" he asked.

Alex nodded. A wave of vertigo swept over her. She bit her lip.

"It will ease soon," said Michael. He released his hold on her and shifted back to rest his arms across his knees.

Alex suppressed a shiver at the loss of his warmth. She wrapped her arms around her own knees, hugging them close. "How bad is it?" she asked. "The damage."

Michael's mouth pulled tight, and pain flashed across his eyes. "Tens of millions," he said quietly. "Perhaps hundreds."

Shock flooded her. She turned her head away to stare at the barren, burnt landscape before her, so empty that the setting sun cast no shadows but her own and Michael's. She wanted to cry, but no tears came. Just...disbelief. Hundreds of millions of people...dead? How did one even begin to wrap one's head around numbers like that? How was such a thing even possible?

She swallowed, and pain lanced through her throat.

"We won't know for certain until we go through the cities," Michael continued, his voice matter-of-fact. "But it's enough that the world will be profoundly changed."

"Yes," she said, her own voice carrying so little inflection, they might as well have been discussing the weather. "I suppose it will."

Cloudy today with a chance of angels. Watch out for dead bodies.

She shuddered, and then something Michael had said snagged her attention. "You said *we*. Does that mean you're staying?"

It was his turn to look away.

"Some of the angels are, just for a week or two, to help with the rebuilding. And with the dead. Infrastructure has been damaged beyond the capacity to cope with the numbers."

Alex raised an eyebrow. "What happened to not interfering?"

Michael almost smiled. "You—and the rest of Heaven, I suspect—will find that Emmanuelle isn't her mother. She won't rescue mortals from themselves, but she believes in cleaning up her own mess. And perhaps setting humanity straight on a few key points."

"You've talked with her...recently."

"I called on her to help heal you."

"And she answered? Even though you—" Alex broke off. Hell. That was not how she'd planned to bring up this particular topic. She looked sideways at the Archangel. He'd gone as still as marble, his shoulders gleaming golden in the rays of the setting sun, his wings blacker than the approaching night.

"Michael—" she began.

He cut her off. "Seth won't be bothering you anymore," he said. He gazed into the distance. "What I said about him giving up parts of his soul to heal you—I was right about that, but there was more. The pieces were still connected to him. He was quite literally incomplete without you, and the pain drove him mad. Emmanuelle severed the connection, and they've agreed he will remain in Hell. With Samael gone, things should be less volatile there, and Emmanuelle is hoping they can maintain some kind of peace between the realms."

Alex had instinctively caught her breath at the sound of Seth's name. She still held it, not quite knowing what to do with it. Or with Michael's news. She should be angry, she thought. No, she should be furious. Beyond furious. She had every right to be.

Seth had done so much. Was responsible for so much more. Aramael. Jen. Nina. Hugh and Elizabeth. Michael's fall. Her own immortality.

Hundreds of millions of lives.

And now he would live peacefully in Hell.

She *should* be angry, but she wasn't. She was just... she didn't know what she was. Didn't really care.

"So that's it, then," she said. "We rebuild and everyone lives happily ever after?"

A shadow crossed Michael's face. "I wouldn't put it quite like that."

She stared down the path into her future. Into an eternity of living with the losses she'd already suffered. Those still to come. She gave a tremulous sigh.

"No, I don't suppose I'd put it like that, either."

Michael fell silent. Then he cleared his throat. "She can take it away, you know."

"Who can take what?"

He nodded toward the setting sun, and for the first time, Alex noticed a figure walking toward them, silhouetted by the last rays of the day. Michael stood up from the ground and held out his hand. Alex hesitated, then reached to accept it. Warm, strong fingers closed around hers, and he pulled her to her feet.

"Emmanuelle," Michael said. "She can take away the immortality Seth gave you."

He turned and walked away.

SIXTY-FIVE

Emmanuelle stopped a few feet from Alex, hands shoved into the pockets of her leather jacket. Her gaze traveled Alex's length, resting a moment on the inadequate hem of Michael's shirt, then flicking to where Michael himself stood framed against the emptiness.

Alex's gaze followed, and her hand crept up to massage the tight spot that had taken root in her chest following his bombshell.

"So," said Heaven's new ruler.

Alex turned to face her.

"The world owes you a great debt, Alexandra Jarvis." Pressing her lips together, Emmanuelle shook her head. "*I* owe you. If you hadn't come after Mika'el..."

A breeze stirred between them, lifting Michael's shirt against Alex's legs, and whirling the dust at their feet into an eddy. Alex shivered, and Emmanuelle stripped off her leather jacket and handed it across the space separating them.

"Why did you?" asked the One's daughter as Alex slid her arms into leather warmed by a god's heat. "You knew there was a chance I wouldn't defeat Seth. A chance he would come after you again. You would have had to live an eternity with him—in Hell. And yet you took that risk to be here with Mika'el. Why?"

"I owed him," Alex said simply. She crossed her arms over the jacket, holding it shut. It smelled like roses.

"Your life?"

"My sanity. Quite possibly my soul."

Emmanuelle regarded her in silence, iridescent eyes inscrutable. She tipped her head toward Michael. "He told you I can undo what Seth did to you? Take away the immortality?"

Alex's gaze drifted back to the Archangel standing alone. He'd extended his wings and tipped back his head, his every line speaking to a torment she could never begin to understand. A fall she could barely comprehend.

The tightness in her chest returned.

Instead of answering Emmanuelle's question, she asked one of her own. "What will happen to him?"

"He's asked to remain here," the One's daughter said. Quiet grief had settled over her face. "I've agreed."

"What will he do?"

"Help where he can. Wrestle his demons. Survive."

"Will he ever be allowed to return to Heaven? You can't...?"

"Make an exception? You'd think I could, wouldn't you? Being the new Almighty and all." Emmanuelle shook her head. "But sadly, there are some laws that not even I can change."

The knot in Alex's chest became a soul-deep ache

at the thought. The Archangel Michael, Heaven's greatest warrior, living in exile, cut off from everyone he cared about. Alone for eternity, as she once thought she would be.

She shook her head. "No," she said.

Emmanuelle frowned. "No, what?"

"No, I don't want you to take my immortality. I want to stay with—" Too late, Alex remembered she spoke not only to the ruler of the universe, but also Michael's own soulmate. Shit. She flushed hot, then cold, bracing for the fallout.

But no divine retribution rained down on her head. Instead, Emmanuelle regarded her with...hope?

"You're certain?" she asked. "Forever is a very long time, Alex. You'll still have your memories, you'll still face losses. And Mika'el...Mika'el will have demons of his own to deal with. It won't be easy for either of you."

"Wait." Alex shook her head in confusion. "You don't mind? But you—he—"

"I rule Heaven and Earth," Emmanuelle said. "Even if Mika'el hadn't fallen, he was right. We've seen how badly partnerships end in my line of work."

Alex couldn't argue that.

"But that doesn't mean he shouldn't have someone," Emmanuelle continued. "He cares for you, Alexandra Jarvis. And you've made it clear you care for him. It won't be easy for either of you, but together, I'm hoping you both might find more than just survival."

Alex looked at Michael again. They'd both survived so much. Lost so much. Given so much. Was it really enough on which to build an eternity together?

"Well?" Emmanuelle asked. "The choice is yours."

Alex slid her arms out of the jacket and handed it back to Emmanuelle, then she turned and walked toward the waiting Archangel. She had no illusions about this. As she had once been connected to Aramael, so would Michael remain connected to Emmanuelle for as long as the two of them existed. But Michael himself had once told her that the soulmate system was imperfect—as flawed as the soulmates themselves were.

As flawed as the Heaven that had created it.

Michael watched her approach, his emerald gaze dark and haunted.

"You've made your choice, then," he said when she reached him.

Alex nodded, and the shadows in his eyes deepened. Powerful wings quivered at his back. He looked past her to where she'd left Emmanuelle. Even before he frowned and his gaze flicked back to her, Alex knew the god was gone.

"I don't understand," he said.

Alex held her hand out to him, palm up. "I chose you," she said simply.

Raw longing shone from Michael's eyes, but it warred with something darker, and he shook his head. "I'm not what I was, Alex. What I did today—it changed me."

"I know." Her hand remained steady between them.

"Why?" he asked.

The words *because I love you* hovered on Alex's lips, but true as they might be, she held them back. After all she and Michael had been through, all they had done, a declaration of love seemed too easy. Too trite. Each of them had lost a soulmate, a part of themselves, and the place that should have been theirs in life. Their coming together was more than just love. It was all that remained. It was inevitable. It was—

"Right," Alex told her Archangel. "Because it's right."

The emerald gaze held hers for a long, silent moment, and then, at last, Michael lifted his hand and placed it in hers.

Choices.

EPILOGUE

Alex watched the plume of dust growing closer. Sensing a presence at her shoulder, she looked around to see that Father Marcus had joined her at the top of the stairs. He, too, gazed into the distance as the motorcycle brigade drew nearer.

Alex nodded at the building behind them. "Everyone here?"

Marcus rolled his eyes. "Here, yes. Happy about it, no. Did we really have to haul the Archbishop of Canterbury out of bed and transport him here in his pajamas? And having all those imams in the same room..."

"The Archbishop was issued the same invitation as everyone else," Alex pointed out. "And the same warning about what would happen if he chose not to attend under his own steam. As for the imams, I think Emmanuelle can handle them."

"It's my nerves I'm more concerned about at the moment," muttered Marcus. He shook his head. "So many different factions, so many opposing views... things aren't what one would call amicable in there."

"And they're even less amicable out here," she reminded him. "Marcus, the entire world very nearly came to a premature end, and not just because of the war. You saw how humanity reacted. And now that everyone knows angels and Heaven are real, those idiots"—she jerked her head toward the building and its occupants—"are in a pissing contest over who owns the rights to them. Seriously?"

Marcus took a deep breath and let it out on a sigh. "Religion is a funny thing," he began.

"Religion," Alex interrupted, "has no place in the face of truth."

"Is that what Emmanuelle will tell them?"

Alex watched the long line of bikers come into view. They rode in two lines, side by side, except for the woman alone at the front.

"Among other things, yes."

"It won't solve all the world's problems," Marcus said. "Especially once she leaves."

"It's not supposed to solve all the problems. Humanity is supposed to do that for itself. Choices, remember?"

"But informed ones."

"Now you're getting it."

The line of bikes pulled up in front of the sweep of stairs. Kickstands settled into place. Helmets came off. The woman on the lead bike, a plain, matte-black Harley with a warrior angel engraved on its tank, swung her leg over the leather seat and, eyes hidden behind sunglasses, stood looking up at Alex and Marcus.

At the building her angels had erected for the

express purpose of this meeting.

The site had been chosen with care. Kept secret from all but a handful of media invited to record the session. Too isolated for the masses to flock to it. Accessible enough for the participants to reach by car—and for the bikers accompanying Emmanuelle on her final ride.

It would be the one and only time Emmanuelle would expose herself to humanity as the ruler of Heaven. Afterward, the building would come down to ensure it didn't become another place of pilgrimage the world didn't need, Emmanuelle would return to Heaven, and the angels who had remained to help restore the cities most damaged by the war would follow her.

Life, in short, would return to normal.

Or at least, its new version of normal.

Alex excused herself to Marcus and walked down to meet Emmanuelle.

"Nice ride in?"

"You have no idea." Leaning back against the bike, Emmanuelle stripped off her gloves and tucked them into a pocket of her leather jacket. She ran a hand over the seat beside her. "I think I've missed riding the most out of everything here."

"You could always take it with you. There must be places in Heaven you can ride."

"One day, maybe. I don't think poor Verchiel could handle it just now, though." Emmanuelle grimaced. She slid her sunglasses up to rest on top of her head. "She's having enough trouble with me refusing to wear robes or answer to 'Eminence'."

Alex smiled. "She'll come around."

"I suppose. In the meantime, don't be surprised if I

drop in for tea now and then when I come back here for a ride." Emmanuelle's iridescent eyes turned to her. "If that would be all right with you and Mika'el, of course."

Alex met her gaze steadily. "You're always welcome, Emmanuelle."

Heaven's ruler gave a tiny nod of acceptance. Appreciation. Shared respect. Then she cleared her throat. "Speaking of Mika'el, how is he?"

"Currently putting Mumbai back together, I believe."

"I didn't ask where, Alex. *How* is he?"

Alex hesitated, thinking of the hollowness that continued to haunt Michael's emerald eyes. The torment he still carried in his soul—and probably always would. She weighed the responses she might make. *Darker than he was before. Lost. Alone even when we're together. Broken but trying.*

The truth was that falling had nearly destroyed Michael, but he had survived, and he was strong. Stronger than any of them. She shrugged one shoulder.

"He's getting there," she said.

Emmanuelle's mouth tightened, and she looked away, nodding understanding. Alex changed the subject.

"Any word on Jezebel and the...child?"

"Nothing so far. I'm not sure we'll find them, to be honest."

Alex shuddered at the idea of Lucifer's spawn remaining at large in the world. Emmanuelle put a hand on her arm.

"Jez is a good person," she said. "And you've more than proved that a Naphil doesn't have to make bad choices. So there's always hope."

"Sure," Alex said. "We'll go with that."

Emmanuelle snorted at the skeptical tone, then with a sigh, straightened up from her leaning post against her Harley. "Well, I suppose I've kept them waiting long enough. Time to go lay down some new laws."

"You know they won't be very receptive."

"Are you kidding? I'm counting on it." Emmanuelle removed the elastic from her ponytail and shook out her long, dark hair. "God isn't just a woman, but a biker chick? This will be the most fun I've ever had."

Grinning, she slid her sunglasses back into place and started up the stairs.

"They'll make demands," Alex warned. "They'll want things from you—you know what they're like."

They. Humans. Would it ever not be unnerving that she didn't identify with her own race anymore?

The new normal.

Emmanuelle stopped halfway up the stairs and turned back to her. A ray of sunlight broke through the clouds, highlighting her and the path she took. She smiled.

"I'm leaving them my finest angel and his immortal consort, Alexandra Jarvis," she said. "I can give them no greater gift than that."

She went up a few more stairs, then stopped again, looking back over her shoulder.

"You will look after him for me, won't you?"

Alex smiled up at Heaven's ruler, thinking of the Michael she was coming to know so well. His strength. His compassion. His fragility. Thinking how easy it was to make the promise to be with him.

"Forever," she said.

LINDA POITEVIN is a writer possessed of both a light side and a dark one. On the dark side, she's the author of the Grigori Legacy, an urban fantasy series featuring a hard-as-nails cop caught up in the war between Heaven and Hell. In her lighter moments, she writes the sweet and funny Ever After contemporary romance series. And when she's not plotting the world's downfall or next great love story, she's a wife, mom, friend, coffee snob, gardener, walker of a Giant Dog, minion to the Itty Bitty Kitty, and avid food preserver (you know, just in case that whole Zombie Apocalypse thing really happens). She loves to hear from readers and can be reached through her website at www.lindapoitevin.com.

CPSIA information can be obtained
at www.ICGtesting.com
Printed in the USA
LVOW03s1500080218
565809LV00001B/1/P